Patricia Burns was born in Essex. After a variety of jobs, she decided to train as a teacher, which she now combines with writing novels.

She is now very happily single and still lives in Essex with her three children. *Cinnamon Alley* is Patricia Burns's second novel. Her previous one, *Trinidad Street* is also available in Arrow paperbacks.

By the same author

Trinidad Street

CINNAMON ALLEY

Patricia Burns

ARROW

This edition published by Arrow Books Limited in 1995

1 3 5 7 9 10 8 6 4 2

First published in the United Kingdom in 1993
by Century, Random House UK Limited

Arrow Books Limited
Random House UK, 20 Vauxhall Bridge Road, London SW1V 2SA

Random House Australia (Pty) Limited
20 Alfred Street, Milsons Point, Sydney,
New South Wales 2061, Australia

Random House New Zealand Limited
18 Poland Road, Glenfield
Auckland 10, New Zealand

Random House South Africa (Pty) Limited
PO Box 337, Bergvlei, South Africa

Random House UK Limited Reg. No. 954009

Papers used by Random House UK Limited
are natural, recyclable products made from wood grown in
sustainable forests. The manufacturing processes conform
to the environmental regulations of the country of origin.

A CIP catalogue record for this book
is available from the British Library

ISBN 0 09 916251 2

Printed and bound in Germany by
Elsnerdruck, Berlin

To the memory of Ivy Benson, queen of bandleaders

PART ONE

1

1910

Poppy Powers gazed at the shiny brass trumpet. Her best friend, Elsie Booth, held it up, her face glowing with the pride of possession.

'There – ain't it a cracker?'

Poppy's fingers reached out, longing to touch, to feel the weight of it, stroke the cool metal, finger the keys.

'Yeah,' she agreed, choking with envy. 'Yeah, it is an' all.'

'Want to hear me play it?'

She did not want to do anything of the sort. She wanted to play it herself. It was not fair that Elsie should have such a thing when she did not. In the ten years of her short life, she had come to learn that things were very rarely fair, but this was just sickening.

'If you want,' she said.

Elsie took a deep breath, put the instrument to her lips and blew. Her cheeks puffed out, her face grew red, her eyes bulged. Eventually, a rather rude noise came out.

Poppy crowed with laughter. 'Lovely! That's real musical, that is. Sound a treat in the band.'

Elsie stamped her foot. 'It ain't easy, you know. Bet you couldn't do it no better.'

'Bet you I could.'

She knew she could, knew it in her heart.

'Come on,' she coaxed, 'let us. Let us have a try.'

Elsie hesitated, letting Poppy plead. When a satisfying amount of wheedling had been extracted from her friend, she relented. Poppy grinned. She always got her way in the end.

The trumpet felt right in her hands. She ran her fingers over it, savouring the pleasure of holding an instrument again. She

3

had never tried playing a trumpet before, but instinct coupled with the lessons her father had given her on his saxophone guided her. She drew in a lungful of air and blew.

At first nothing came out, then a blast like a cow in labour. Elsie collapsed into howls of laughter.

'Oh yeah, much better than me – I don't think!'

Poppy ignored her. This was far too important for a game of point-scoring. She tossed her copper-coloured plaits back over her shoulders and frowned at the trumpet, considering. Lips. It must be a question of lips, and breath control like it was on the sax. She tried again, releasing her breath in a steady stream. A raucous blare came out. She altered the shape of her mouth and the note changed, into something clear, bold, challenging.

Crimson-faced and pulsing with excitement, she had a third go, this time pressing the keys. An embryonic tune emerged, filling the tiny room, and floated out over the grey streets of North Millwall.

'I done it! I done it! I made it play!'

Sitting on the lumpy double bed that took up almost all the room, Elsie had taken on a sulky look.

'You must of cheated. You must of done it before.'

'I never. My Dad learnt me his sax, but I never played a trumpet,' Poppy assured her. She plumped down beside her best friend, the trumpet still held lovingly in her hands. 'You are lucky, Elsie. Your mum and dad let you have this.'

'It ain't mine. It belongs to the Sally Army.'

'I know, but they let you learn. My gran won't. Won't even let me speak to her about it. "Not having no more musicians in the family," that's what she says.'

'She let you join the Army and play the tambourine,' Elsie pointed out.

'Yeah, but only because it gets me out of the house of a Sunday. She don't like having me hanging about getting under her feet. Mean old cow. I hate my gran.'

Elsie looked shocked. 'Poppy! She's your family. You didn't ought to say that sort of thing. It's wicked.'

4

'It's wicked to lie and all, and it'd be a lie to say I didn't hate her. She's horrible to me and even worse to Mum. Just because she married Dad. I'll tell you something, my dad's a thousand time's better than what she is. He's lovely, my dad is.'

'Yeah,' Elsie agreed. 'He's nice, you dad.'

They were both silent for a few moments, wrapped in their own thoughts. Through the open window came the sounds of the streets, children playing, street sellers shouting their wares, the clop of horses' hooves. Mixed up with them was continual background rumble of the industries of the Isle of Dogs, the clank and roar and stench of factories and foundaries, repair yards and processing plants, of the count-less ships and steam engines and drays that serviced them. The two girls hardly heard it. It was part of their lives, as normal as the stink of summer, or the chill fogs of winter.

Poppy sighed and stood up.

'I better get home. She'll be wanting me to do my jobs.'

Elsie came downstairs with her.

'You can come and have a go of my trumpet any time you want,' she offered.

'Thanks, Elsie. You're a real pal.'

But as Poppy set off along the street, she knew it was not enough. She wanted an instrument of her own. A saxophone, like her father's. Most children here in Dog Island would have known that a dream like that was beyond imagining. You were lucky if you had a coat to wear in winter, lucky to have food in your belly each day. To want a musical instrument was plain foolish.

Poppy did not see it like that. A skinny girl with long thin legs ending in clumpy boots, she marched along, her small face set. It was not fair that Elsie was allowed to learn the trumpet. It was not fair that she was going to join in with the band. Poppy adored the band. She thrilled to the stirring rhythms, the blend of the notes, the way the voices of the instruments could be heard singly and as a whole. To be part of that would be the nearest thing to heaven. And the only thing standing between her and that bliss was Gran.

Poppy stopped at the end of the row of mean terraced houses while a brewer's dray loaded with barrels and pulled by two great Shire horses rumbled past, heading for the Rum Puncheon pub at the other end of the road. There on the opposite corner of Trinidad Street was Cinnamon Alley and her home. A three-storey building in the same drab brick as all the other houses, but standing out because of its added height. Poppy crossed the road reluctantly and paused by the house, delaying the moment of going in. Like all the houses, it let straight out onto a stretch of swept pavement, with a step which had been white that morning from its daily scrubbing. The clue to what made her home different was in the front window. It was covered with a net curtain, and two yellowing cards were displayed in one corner. The smaller one read 'J. Powers, Dressmaker. Alterations taken in'. The larger simply stated 'Clean Lodgings'. Poppy made a face at it. They were clean all right. She should know. It was she who did most of the scrubbing. She pushed open the door and went in.

The smell of onions hit her as she entered. Poppy's stomach rumbled. With a bit of luck onions meant tripe for tea. She cheered up a little and went along the dark narrow hallway, past the front parlour that was kept for important visitors and, as a special concession, as a fitting room for her mother's customers. She walked softly, hoping that her gran would not hear her. Carefully up the stairs, up into the twilight of the landing. She had made it. She pushed open the door to the back bedroom which she shared with her mother.

'Hello, Mum.'

'Poppy, love –'

Her mother was sitting by the open window, stitching buttonholes. She put down her work and held out her arms, her flushed face breaking into a smile of welcome.

'How's my little girl? Had a good day? Teacher not been nasty to you?'

'Oh, Mum – Elsie's got this trumpet –'

It all poured out, the envy, the longing. Her mother sighed, and patted her shoulder.

'You know I would if I could, lovely –'

The rest did not need to be said. Gran would not like it. Gran had hated musicians since the day Poppy's dad came along to sweep her mum off her feet and leave her pregnant with Poppy. It had been Gran who had run him to ground and forced him to marry her.

Gran had had other plans for her daughter. She had saved for years to apprentice Jane to a court dressmaker so that she would not have to go into one of the great food processing plants like most of the other girls on the Island. And then Owen Powers came along asking for lodgings and ruined everything with his charm and his patter and his devil-may-care attitude.

'When Dad comes back, I'll get him to teach me his sax again. I'll learn to play it real well, better than what Elsie can,' Poppy vowed.

'Hush, lovely –' Jane looked nervously over her shoulder at the door, as if expecting to see Gran hovering there. 'Don't say things like that.'

And as though summoned by thought, a voice came shrilling up the stairs. 'That you, girl?'

Poppy stuck her lip out and said nothing.

'Poppy, answer her!' her mother hissed.

'You there or not?' the voice demanded.

'Please, Poppy – for me?'

Poppy kicked at the curly cast iron of the sewing machine stand.

'Yes, Gran.'

'You come down here at once, you hear me? You're late.'

'Old cow,' Poppy muttered, making her mother gasp with apprehension. She made her way slowly out of the crowded little room, negotiating the double bed they shared, the work table cluttered with threads and pins and tape measures, the dummy on its stand.

Her grandmother was waiting for her at the foot of the stairs, a diminutive figure dressed entirely in black, her grey hair scraped back from a pudding-like face. There was no softening of her expression as Poppy approached.

'What you doing up there?' There was still a trace of a Cambridgeshire accent beneath the familiar tones of the East End.

Poppy looked her straight in the eyes, the only member of the household who dared do it.

'Talking to me mum.'

'Gossip. We got no time for gossip in this house, girl. Not like them lot down the street, standing out on their steps wasting their lives away. You got boots on your feet, roof over your head, decent clothes on your back, and how? Because I put 'em there. So don't think you can be a waster, gossiping with your mother. You got to earn your keep. You hear me?'

They stood glaring at each other like a couple of cats disputing the rights to an alleyway. Poppy refused to drop her eyes.

'You hear me, girl?'

The rebellion that was never far away surfaced. 'I got a name,' Poppy stated. She knew as she said it that she had gone too far.

A hard hand lashed out and fetched her a clip round the ear. It made her head ring. She clamped her mouth shut so as not to cry out.

'Insolence! That's your name. Now get to cleaning the first-floor front and do it proper or there's no tea for you tonight.'

The smell of onions was stronger than ever, overcoming the urge to resistance. If Gran made a threat, she carried it out. Stiff with resentment, Poppy went out to the scullery to fetch the bucket and scrubbing brush.

Gran was still standing in the hall, hands on hips, when she came back lugging the water. She held her tongue as she toiled up the stairs. Of all the jobs she had to do in the house, she most hated cleaning the lodgers' rooms. Her mother just said that everyone had to do cleaning. Poppy knew this. All her friends had to help in the house. Many of their mothers had to go out scrubbing steps, or worse still, the cabins of the great ships that came into the docks. But none of them seemed to

8

understand how she felt about clearing up after the lodgers. Three men shared the first-floor front. All Gran's lodgers were men. She automatically suspected single girls looking for lodgings. A respectable girl stayed with her parents until she was married, or if overcrowding or some other circumstances forced her out, then she lodged with a relative. She did not, if she was decent, go seeking rooms on her own.

Some of the men stopped only for a week or so, moving on with their work or to something better, or cheaper. Others stayed for months, even years and graduated to the best rooms. Such were the ones in the room Poppy now scrubbed with an effort born of fury.

If only her father would come home again. Things were so different when he was around. There was laughter and teasing and music in the dour house. Her mother became a new woman, glowing with adoration of her handsome musician. Poppy did not even mind having to sleep in Gran's room when it meant there would be outings all over London and stories of life on the road to liven up the dull tea table. When her dad came home, usually before the summer season started and in the gap between summer and the pantos, then brightness filled her life. Gran tried to put a stop to it, sitting there like a black cloud casting gloom all around her, but Dad just laughed.

'Come on, my special girls, let's escape from the Gorgon and have a night out on the Town,' he would cry. And off they would go, all done up in their best clothes, to the music hall. Dad could always get them in somewhere for free. After the show it would be off to someone's dressing-room, then out to a pub or a chophouse, with Poppy listening open-mouthed to all the talk and banter and taking in every gesture. It was a wonderful world, the one her father inhabited. The trouble was, it always ended too soon. The money slipped through his fingers, and the days would become full of anxious trips to acts, to managements, and then would come the call from the agent and off he would go, to Scotland, or the Midlands, or the North, and Poppy and her mother would be left once more to Gran.

She could hear her now, stomping up the stairs. Poppy banged the brush around extra hard, so that she would know she was getting on with it. But Gran went instead into the back bedroom. Poppy could hear her haranguing her mother.

'. . . I got twelve mouths to feed this evening. I can't do it single-handed. How much longer you going to be?'

Her mother was muttering something about a job having to be finished for tomorrow.

'You can sit up this evening and do it. It's summer. It's light till late.'

That seemed to be the end of the discussion. If Gran wanted help in the kitchen, Mum would not even think of holding out against her. But Gran was in the mood for a confrontation. Poppy was guiltily aware that it was her fault. Whenever she tried to stand up to the grandmother, she took it out on Mum.

'And another thing. Where's that waster of a husband of yours, eh?' she was demanding, for what seemed like the thousandth time. 'When's he coming back to help pay for that child? It's his part to provide for her upkeep, not mine.'

Poppy could not hear what her mother said. Whatever it was, it did nothing to appease Gran.

'And how long has he been gone this time? Six months? Seven? He ain't never been that long before. And when did you last hear from him, eh? Months ago. And never a penny. I tell you what I think, my girl, I think he's gone for good this time. You won't be seeing him no more. Now you got old and thin working to look after his child, he's gone and scarpered with another woman.'

Poppy's knuckles whitened round the brush. Anger boiled in her heart. She could hear her mother sobbing.

'– And you can stop that row. You're better off without him, I can tell you. Never was no good. I saw that from the moment I clapped eyes on him. If it wasn't for him, you could of made something of yourself. But you had to go and disgrace yourself with a saxophone player –'

Poppy could stand it no longer. She threw the brush at the wall and jumped to her feet.

10

'Stop it!' she screamed. She ran along the landing to where her grandmother stood in the doorway of the back bedroom. She stamped her foot.

'You horrible old witch! It's all lies. He is coming home, he *is*! My dad would never leave us. He loves us.'

'Love!'

Two stinging blows landed on her head, one on each ear.

'Love, is it? It's easy to see whose daughter you are.' Gran's face was scarlet with rage. Her pale eyes bulged. 'I'll teach you to speak like that to your elders. You'll clean all the upstairs, then it's straight to bed without no tea. And there'll be no going down that church on Sunday neither. You'll stay in till you learnt the meaning of respect.'

Tears started in Poppy's eyes. She knew it was no use fighting, it only made things worse. Her mother was looking at her, her expression clearly pleading with her not to say anything else. But she could not help it.

'When my dad comes home, I'll tell him how horrible you are to us. And he'll take us away with him. We'll have our own home and you won't make us work for you ever again.'

'Ha!' Her head snapped sideways under the force of her grandmother's hand. 'Take you away, is it? I wish he would. Now go upstairs and do as you're told and don't come down till you're ready to say you're sorry.'

'Never!' Poppy cried. 'I'll never say I'm sorry.'

She turned and ran up to the second floor, flinging herself down on the landing and bursting into tears.

'I'll show her, I'll show her,' she repeated to herself, and she thumped the unyielding floor with her fists. It seemed an empty threat, for her grandmother held the power in the house. There was nothing she could do except wait for the wonderful day when her father came home again.

And then it came to her. She still had that pawn ticket. The one her father had given her for safekeeping.

2

When everyone had gone down for tea, Poppy left her cleaning things, went into her room and crept underneath her mother's work table. There, in a small cardboard box, she kept her treasures. She sat cross-legged on the floor, the box in her lap, listening. Reassuring noises came to her ears. The clatter of knives and forks on plates, gruff voices. Yes, everyone was busy for a while. Most importantly, her gran was busy. The tea was the culmination of Gran's day. For now, Poppy was safe from interference.

She opened the box lid. On top was the handkerchief with the lace corner that her dad had given her last Christmas. Then came some half a dozen postcards from various seaside resorts where he had been working the summer seasons. Poppy was distracted by them, gazing at the brown and white scenes of piers and beaches and bandstands. She had been to the sea twice, once with the Sunday School to Southend and once, for two whole days, to Brighton with her parents. They had been the happiest two days of her life. For a few moments she sat remembering that magical time, until a noise downstairs brought her purpose sharply to mind. She scrabbled beneath the pressed flowers and the newspaper cuttings, shuffled amongst the heap of pennies and ha'pennies, and there it was, tucked in a corner at the very bottom. A pawn ticket.

'Now then, my little flower,' her dad had said to her, 'I want you to do something for me. It's a secret, mind.' He had looked very solemn and mysterious. 'You mustn't tell anyone, not even your mum, see?'

'Cross my heart and hope to die.' She made the binding signs with her finger, a cross on her chest and a slitting motion across her throat.

Her dad laughed and hugged her.

'No need to die over it, Pops.'

And he handed her the little piece of paper with "Body's" printed on it, together with the number 697 and the date, 20 December 1909.

'Keep that safe for me, Popsy. It's very important. Think you can do that all right, eh?'

She nodded. "Course. Be safe as houses with me, it will. But what's special about it, Dad?'

'Ah –' he tapped the side of his nose. 'You'll see, all in good time. Just look after it, all right? It's between you and me.'

She had felt so important and trusted and special at that moment. The next day, he had gone off for a Christmas date. Up in Geordieland, he had said. Poppy had looked for Geordieland on the map of the British Isles hanging on the classroom wall, but she had not been able to find it. Christmas came and went. The lace handkerchief joined the teasures in her box. The panto season passed, but her father did not return.

'He's got variety work up there,' her mum said, but Poppy never saw the letter that announced this piece of news. Summer came, but no postcards arrived. Her mother looked so upset when Poppy asked where Dad was that she stopped asking.

Now, sitting under the table with the little buff-coloured ticket in her hand, Gran's words came unbidden back to her: *He's gone for good this time. You won't be seeing him no more.*

It was not true. He would be back. Perhaps next week, perhaps – and this was more likely – in the autumn, when the summer season ended. In the meantime, to bring him just a little closer, she would go and find out what this ticket was for.

The next day after school, she resisted the temptation to go and have another play on Elsie's trumpet and hurried off down the West Ferry Road, with its rows of small shops and its never-ending flow of traffic to and from the docks and the factories. Fumes from the chimneys hung heavy in the July air.

On the pavement outside Body's, she stopped. She looked

up at the three golden balls hanging above her head. Nobody in her family had ever been in here. Gran did not hold with credit, let alone hocking the household goods.

Many of her schoolfriends' mums were in here every week. The Sunday clothes went in on Monday or Tuesday and came out again on payday, Saturday evening, regular as clockwork. If their dads failed to find work, then more items would be 'put away'. It was a way of life.

But if Gran found out that Poppy had been in Body's, there would be the devil to pay. Poppy took a quick glance up and down the street. There didn't seem to be anyone she knew around. She slipped into the shop.

The bell jangled, stirring the dusty atmosphere. Inside, it was twilight. Poppy stood in the cramped space in front of the tall oak counter and gazed about. All around were shelves and cupboards stacked with shadowy goods, each with a little label like the ticket in her hand. There was a suffocating smell about the place, of must and mothballs and old human sweat. The smell of poverty.

'Well?'

Poppy jumped. There behind the counter an old man was staring down at her. He had a red-veined nose and grey stubbled chin and his head was completely bald. But his small colourless eyes were as sharp as a bird's.

'I – er –' Poppy held out the precious ticket. 'I come for this.'

The man looked at the ticket as if it might bite him. He grunted.

'You got the money?'

'Money?'

'You ain't got no money, you don't get nothing.'

'Oh –' She had not thought of this. She should have realized it. 'It – it don't say how much,' she said.

With ill-contained impatience, the man opened the fat ledger that lay on the counter in front of him. Slowly, as if it were a great labour, he turned over the pages, running his knotted finger down columns of numbers. It came to rest at 697.

'Two pounds seventeen and six,' he said.

'Two pounds seventeen and six?'

'Plus interest.'

'Interest? What's that when it's at home?'

He explained. Poppy was appalled.

'That's daylight blooming robbery, that is.'

'Listen, girl,' the old man fixed her with his piercing eyes. 'I got a business to run. This ain't no charity. Now do you want this here instrument, or not?'

'Instrument?'

'Yes, instrument. What's the matter with you, you deaf or something? Some sort of horn thing, if I remember rightly. If you want it back you better bring in the money, or I'll be selling it. Six months is well up.'

'But you can't – it's my dad's – that's how he earns his living, he plays the saxophone.'

This was dreadful. She had to do something, and do it fast.

'Look – you wait here. I'll be back,' she said, and raced out of the shop.

Fear thudded in her heart as she ran home. That horrible old man must not sell her dad's sax. He mustn't, he mustn't. She reached the house and stopped, breathless, then eased open the door. On tiptoes, she crept along the hall and up the stairs. Her boots creaked against the lino. She winced, expecting every moment for her grandmother to appear. She reached the safety of her room.

'Poppy, love!'

Poppy rolled her eyes in expressive agony and put a finger to her lips.

'What – ?' her mother did not understand.

'Hush, Mum,' she hissed. 'Please!'

She dived beneath the table and grabbed the box. Out came all her savings, rolling and clinking on the floorboards. She knew to the last coin how much there was. She had earned it, in pennies, from running errands for the lodgers. If they needed tobacco or a jug of beer or a bet placing, Poppy was quick and willing, never forgetting the exact instructions.

Usually, she was told to keep the change. Once or twice, when a horse had come in first, she had got a cut of the winnings. And all of it she had put away here, never quite knowing what it was that she was saving for, but sure that it was something very important. Now she knew. She swept it all into the lace-cornered handkerchief and crawled out from under the table.

'Poppy, what are – ?'

Poppy sped across the room and kissed her mother on the cheek.

'I ain't been home, right?' she said. 'You ain't seen hide nor hair of me since breakfast.'

She slipped out again, scarcely daring to breathe until the front door was closed behind her, than raced back to Body's.

'There – ' She placed the bulging handkerchief on the counter in front of the man and let the corners go, so that the coppers spilled out. 'Eleven and fivepence, and the handkerchief. That's new, ain't never been used.'

The man looked at her as if she was an imbecile.

'I said two pounds seventeen and six plus interest, not eleven and fivepence.'

'I know, but this is just to be going on with. There'll be more.' Poppy leaned forward and gazed at him earnestly. The counter was high, so that she could only just get her arms on it if her elbows were out sideways. She rested her chin on her hands and regarded him with the wide-eyed look that never failed to wheedle whatever she wanted out of her father. 'You won't go and sell that sax, will you? You'll hold on to it until I get the rest?'

The man looked back at her, unmoved.

'Depends how long it takes. I got a business to run.'

'Not long at all, honest.' It had taken her all her life until now to earn that much. But she truly believed she could do it.

The man mumbled and grumbled, but in the end he agreed, since there was not much call for saxophones on Dog Island and he did not want the bother of the journey to sell it on elsewhere. Poppy's pennies and ha'pennies and farthings were counted out and entered in the book, and the precious ticket handed back. Triumphant, she emerged into the brassy summer sunlight.

Two pounds, six shillings and a penny to find, plus interest. Hollow and dizzy with the excitement of it all, she wandered back home. She went about her jobs in a daze. She was going to rescue her dad's sax for him. It did not matter that the amount she had to earn was a fortune. She was going to get it if it killed her.

She started that very evening, running out for a paper for one of the lodgers and getting a pair of boots from the cobbler's for another. It was not until bedtime that another aspect of the whole business hit her: if her dad's sax was lying on a shelf in the pawnbroker's, what was he playing? The question gnawed at her half the night as she tossed and turned in the sagging bed beside her sleeping mother. At one point, she even considered consulting her mum about it, but decided Mum had enough to worry about. But try as she might, she could not think of an answer, and it added to the cold voice of reason that said that her grandmother was right, and that her father was never coming back. The thought of life without him was unspeakably grey. But with the coming of the day, she managed to push it to the back of her mind. He would come back. He must.

Jane Powers kept very much the same thought in her head. He was coming back, her Owen, her love. He was just having a bit of difficulty, that was all. They had happened in the past, these unexplained absences, and he had always turned up again in the end. But as the summer ended and autumn drew in, it became more and more difficult to hold on to her faith. This was the dead time, the space between the summer season and Christmas. This was when he should be home.

She sat at the window in the little back bedroom, hour after hour, sewing. If she moved her head a little, she could see out, but she did not often bother, for the view was less than inspiring. In the foreground, backyards marched between Cinnamon Alley and Trinidad Street and the backs of the

17

houses in the next road, and in the distance rose the new grain elevator at the Millwall docks, the factories and warehouses and in between them, the masts and funnels of the ships. It was not a sight to help the days along as her feet rocked the treadle of the black Singer sewing machine and her hands guided the fabric under the needle. Often it was black, for mourning clothes, not that there was much call for new clothes on Dog Island. The women in the street, her friends, never had a new dress from one year's end to the next. They went up the Chrisp Street market and bought them from a second-hand stall. If they came to Jane for altering them, she always obliged, never charging. It was her little rebellion against her mother and her obsession with laying by for a rainy day. She could have made lots of odd pennies from jobs down Trinidad Street, but she didn't. Helping her friends was a small area over which she had control, a source of pride.

Her Owen never thought about rainy days. He never even thought about tomorrow. 'Eat, drink and be merry, for tomorrow we may be in Eastbourne,' that was what he always said.

If only he would come back. If only she just knew where he was. But he never did do what you expected. Except that she thought he might at least have sent a postcard to Poppy. Which brought her wandering thoughts on to her daughter. Poppy had been behaving very strangely lately. Ever since the summer, in fact. She was always pestering the lodgers for jobs, and when she wasn't out earning, she was under the table counting out her money. When Jane asked her what she was doing, she was always told that it was a secret. Jane had inspected the hoard from time to time. The amount in it varied, so the child must be spending it on something, and yet no sweets or toys came into the house. There was a lot she couldn't make out about her daughter. Poppy looked a lot like she herself used to, except that she had her father's colouring, but in character, Poppy was quite different. Where Jane just let herself be pushed by every tide of chance, Poppy was a rebel, a fighter. It frightened Jane, the way she stood up to her grandmother. If she went through life like that, she was sure to get hurt. But then – Jane considered this as her neat fingers guided the fabric – the one time she herself had defied her mother was over Owen. She had ended up with a saxophone player who turned her life upside down, and she did not regret it.

As Christmas approached, so her hard-tried faith in him began to trickle away. A year, a whole year, since he went away, and not a word, not a message, nothing to let her know where he was or when he was coming back. An oppressive grey cloud lay about her, weighing her down like a cloak of lead. What was the point of anything, if her Owen had gone away?

Poppy and her little friend Elsie were sitting on the bedroom floor, playing shops with snippets of fabric.

'What're you doing for Christmas? We're having a big do. My Mum's made a huge meat pudding. You should see it! Big as a football, it is, all done up in a cloth. She's going to start boiling it tonight. And my Uncle George is bringing some oranges from up the market and my cousin Joe's nicked a tin of ham from off of the lighter and my Aunty Vi and the cousins are all coming. We're going to have a real blow-out and a sing-song.'

Guilt gnawed at Jane. She had not thought about Christmas at all. If Owen were here, there would be presents hidden under the bed. Often he had to leave on Christmas Eve in order to open somewhere for a panto on Boxing Day, which meant that they had their celebrations early. He would go out and spend the last of his money on wonderful, foolish presents before they went to see him off on the last train from Euston or King's Cross. But not this year. Trembling, she listened for Poppy's reply.

'Oh, we'll be putting up the decorations tomorrow, won't we, Mum? We'll have a lovely time. We always do. Lots of presents and things to eat and that. Lots. And singing and that. Everything. Last year I got a lovely lace hanky. My Dad give it me, a real lace hanky. It was so beautiful I never used it.

19

You couldn't never blow your nose on it, just have it in your pocket, like what a lady does. It was lovely, wasn't it, Mum?'

'Yeah, lovely,' Jane echoed obediently. The poor child. All she had was memories. That was all they both had. But somehow she could not rouse herself to do anything about this year, however much she knew she should for Poppy's sake.

She might have known that her daughter was not going to let things slide. On the morning of Christmas Eve, just as she had said to Elsie, she pulled the box of decorations out from the back of the wardrobe.

'We got to put these up,' she insisted.

Her small face was set. There was to be no getting out of it. Times like this, she frightened Jane a little. There was no denying it, when she got that look on her face, Poppy was just like her grandmother.

'Oh – yeah – if you like, dear.'

Poppy dumped the box on the bed. Faded and crumpled paperchains from happier Christmasses spilled out onto the cover. The rest of the house was never decorated, since Gran did not hold with it, but in their own room, they always went to town. Poppy fished down inside the box and found a tin of rusting drawing pins. She began clambering about on chairs and tables and the sewing machine, trailing paperchains.

'Here, you take an end, Mum. Where we going to put it? How about all loopy around the edge, then across the middle. That'd look pretty, wouldn't it?'

Another scrabble in the box, a sharp exclamation. Poppy sucked her finger, then carefully drew out a sprig of holly. The leaves were hard and leathery, the berries shrivelled.

'Oh look, Mum, do you remember this? Dad said it reminded him of when he was a boy. They used to take the tram as far as it went, then walk out in the country and pick holly and ivy. Do you remember?'

Jane remembered all right. One of Owen's tales. He always made everything sound exciting.

In spite of herself, Jane found she was caught up in the preparations. She pretended for Poppy's sake, and she knew that Poppy was pretending as well, pretending that everything was all right. The only difference was Poppy could still live in a make-believe world, while Jane came face to face with the truth at last. Owen was not going to come home, not this Christmas or any other Christmas. From now on, it was just her, her mother and Poppy. She had her daughter. She was worth living for, worth going on for.

3

Gran stood in the kitchen and listened to the noises of the house. She knew every creaking board, every hinge. This was her kingdom, the house and Cinnamon Alley. There were no other dwellings in the little turning, only storage buildings, so she looked on it all as hers.

It was unusually quiet for the time of day. Normally, the men would be getting up for work at this hour, but the strike had changed all that. Those who were dockers or rivermen of any kind were actually on strike, nearly all the others were strikebound. When she heard about it, Gran took action.

'Now then,' she said, sitting at the head of the table at teatime, 'about this nonsense at the docks.'

Eight faces turned to look at her, eight pairs of wary eyes. The jaws carried on chewing. She was reminded of a field of cows.

'I suppose this means there'll be no money coming in. Now, you all know what the rules of this house have always been: no credit. I've never owed a penny in my life, and I don't see why anyone else should. Never a borrower nor a lender be.'

The jaws had stopped now. They were beginning to catch her drift. She knew them. They had nothing laid by for a rainy day. If they had anything left over at the end of the week, they went out and drank it away on Saturday night, each and every one of them.

'I'm not a hard woman,' she went on. There was no reply to this. 'I'm not going to turn you out into the street if you can't pay me.'

She paused. The words sunk in. Smiles of relief dawned on their faces. They were not going to lose the roof over their heads. With things as they were at the moment, they wouldn't get anything else. There were mutterings of gratitude.

'No, I'm not a hard woman,' she repeated. 'But I'm not a rich woman neither. I can't afford to feed you. Not with no money coming in. For just this once, I'll let you stay on here on credit, but you'll have to find your own food. I think that's fair enough.'

They didn't like that, of course. But they didn't have much choice.

'So that's agreed, then,' she said.

The discussion, such as it was, ended there. Gran had had her say.

That was two weeks ago. The strike was still on and the men went out each day and joined the others sitting about in Trinidad Street. A poor spirited lot, Margaret considered them. Didn't know the meaning of hard work. If they had put by for a rainy day, like she had, they would not be going hungry now.

Margaret knew the meaning of hard work. She had never stopped. Back in her home village, in Cambridgeshire, she had worked from three or four years old. The eldest of an ever-growing family, she had to care for the younger ones. It had been a relief to go into service at the age of twelve, even when it meant working from six in the morning till late at night. At the Big House she had a bed that she only had to share with one other girl, decent clothes, three solid meals a day and all the tea she could drink. During her rare time off, she tried to catch up with the education she had missed, setting herself pages of sums, and reading improving books. Somehow or other, she was going to Get On.

When she met Arthur Todd, the new under carpenter, she recognized a kindred spirit. He did not tease and backchat like the other men. He was careful with his words, thinking before he spoke, not making a joke of everything.

'A right boring old stick,' was what the other maid said of him.

But Margaret respected him. They were drawn to each other by a mutual lack of frivolity. After a long courtship and much saving, they were married in borrowed finery at the village church and set off that very day to London.

'London's the place to be,' Arthur said. 'The amount of building that's going on there, you'd not believe your eyes. Work aplenty for a good chippy. Two years, three years, and I'll be a sub-contractor. My own boss.'

Margaret did not allow herself to remember past this. The footsteps scampered down the stairs. Margaret's face lost the slackness brought on by memory and tightened into its usual severe lines. Of one thing she was quite certain, that Poppy was not going to go the way of her stupid mother. Oh, no. One member of the family had to make a success of life and Poppy was the only one left to do it.

'Morning, Gran.'

Never a natural expression on the girl's face. Never a proper look of submission to her elders. With Margaret she was always either defiant, like today, or sullen, or downright insolent. She was flighty, too. Margaret had seen her, making up to the lodgers, smiling and wheedling. She got that from her father, of course. Margaret knew just where that sort of behaviour got a girl – in the sort of trouble her daughter had found herself.

'What's that you're wearing?' she demanded.

It was a cotton dress with frills over the shoulders and a full gathered skirt. The print was faded, but you could still see the blue flowers on the green ground.

'Mum give it me. She found it down the market and altered it.' The defiant look again, a challenging lift of the chin. 'She ain't got much work on now, not with this strike and all. So she done it for me. Pretty, ain't it?'

She pulled the skirt out to one side like a dancer, showing its fullness. For a moment, Margaret thought she was actually going to prance around, showing her legs. She was going to have to be watched closely, this one. Margaret had always known it. If she was not kept in check, she would be off on the stage somewhere, like that wicked Irish madam down the street. She was not going to have that sort of thing in the family. A musician for a son-in-law was bad enough.

'Stop that,' she ordered. 'Sit down and have your breakfast. What are you doing today?'

'I'm helping Elsie look after the little ones.'

Margaret could not understand this. She had been *made* to look after her younger brothers and sisters. That Poppy should do it voluntarily was beyond her comprehension.

'Well, before you go off helping those as won't help themselves, you can do something for me. I got enough to do here. The lodgers' rooms need sweeping out.'

Poppy's spoon stopped halfway to her mouth.

'Why?' she demanded.

Immediately, Margaret's fighting instincts were roused. Young people should obey, not question.

'Because I say so, and I'll have none of your cheek, miss.'

Her granddaughter was looking back at her with just the same aggressive light in her eyes.

'That's not right. They're not paying, so why should they have their rooms cleaned? Why can't they do it for themselves?'

The neat logic of this appealed to Margaret. Why indeed? They were living here on her charity, she was not their slave. For a moment she saw Poppy in a new light, saw herself in the child, clear and bright beneath the sloppiness inherited from her father. It was a meeting point, an opportunity to get closer to the granddaughter on whom she pinned her hopes and expectations. But long habits could not be broken. The moment passed. Young people should not get to think that they knew better than their elders. If she gave in now, the girl would start getting above herself, and she was bad enough already.

'Because they wouldn't do it the way I want it done. They're only ignorant working men. They don't know how

25

things ought to be. I do. This is my house and I have it cleaned proper. So you'll do as you're told, miss, and go and give them all a good sweep out before you go off enjoying yourself.'

Poppy opened her mouth to argue, then shut it again. The defiant expression subsided into sullenness. She finished her breakfast in silence. Margaret stood watching her for a while before turning away to tidy the scullery. Despite herself, her triumph was tinged with doubt. A niggling idea remained, that agreeing with the child might just have been more pleasurable than riding roughshod over her. She gave herself a mental shake. It was nonsense. Nobody had ever asked her what she wanted in life, or agreed with her ideas. All the time, life dealt out hard blows. It was best that the girl was toughened up now. She banged the saucepans about, re-arranging them on the shelves. She was right, she knew she was right. Right for the child and right for herself. Nothing remained of all those plans she and Arthur had made. All she had was a disappointing daughter, a rebellious grand-daughter and this house. Of the three, the house was the only thing she was really sure of. Here, she was mistress, and that she could never relinquish, not even to see a smile of pleasure on her granddaughter's face.

Poppy's moneymaking schemes had come to a full stop. Everything had gone quite well up till now. Every couple of weeks she went into the pawnbroker's with another sixpence or even shilling to take off the total. She became familiar with Mr Body's problems.

'How's your chest today, Mr Body? Cough not troubling you this foggy weather?'

At first he would glare at her with unconcealed suspicion.

'No good thinking you're going to get round me that way, girl.'

But as time went on he began to unbend a little, and accept her solicitous remarks with grudging pleasure. He even put her in the way of earning a little more, recommending her to the shop next door for a delivery job.

The dockers were on strike, and the whole island had ground to a halt. Without raw materials, the industries could not operate. Those who were not actually on strike were laid off. Mr Body was inundated with pledges, so that he had to turn custom away.

Out in the street, tension was running high. The one or two families with men still in work had to eat behind closed doors. Usually in bad times, those with helped those without, but when practically everyone was going hungry, the minority could not perform the miracle of the loaves and fishes. Angry men hung about all day, mothers worried about how to feed wailing children.

Poppy's income dried up with all the rest. With the men precariously staying on by way of Gran's grudging credit, there was no money about for errands. So it was with even greater resentment than usual that she lugged the broom, dustpan and brush upstairs to sweep the rooms.

'Oi, Poppy – ' the one lodger still working hissed at her from behind his door.

'What?'

He beckoned her into his room.

'Want you to put one on a horse for me. But keep it quiet like, see?'

Poppy saw. He did not want to flash his spare cash around in front of the others.

She nodded. 'Right.'

'Good girl. It's a bob to win on the three o'clock at York. Look – ' He held his paper out to her, with its list of runners, pointing with a grimy finger. 'See – Traffino, two to one on. Dead cert.'

But Poppy's eyes focused on the name above. The Music Man.

'What about that one?' she asked, trying to keep her voice level.

'The Music Man? Yeah, nice little colt, likes hard going. But he's seven to one. I'm going for Traffino. He's come in for me before.'

27

'Oh. I just thought – ' It wasn't so much a thought as a feeling. If she had known the word intuition, she would have called it that.

'So you pop out and put it on for me, eh?'

'What? Oh – right you are, Mr Webb.' She repeated the details. A shilling piece was pressed into her hand.

Outside her own room she paused, racked with indecision. She had a shilling in the cardboard box from before the strike. If she put that on The Music Man, and it won, she would be there. But if it didn't, that would be one less shilling, months and months more of errands, and maybe Mr Body would finally give up on her and sell. Only the other day he had told her that it had been nothing but pay out for the last few weeks and he was taking stuff south of the river to get rid of it. If someone should just happen to say to him that they wanted a saxophone . . .

She knew what a risky business racing was. She had placed bets for the men many a time, and nearly always the money had been lost. And yet – and yet – The Music Man. It had to be lucky. She chewed her lip, hopped from one foot to the other, held her breath. Downstairs, she heard Gran stumping around, and her anger at her lost battle over the cleaning came simmering to the boil again. Gran did not hold with gambling. That decided her – she would do it. She went into the room, where her mother was turning sheets sides to middle, and took the precious money out of the box.

'Just going out. Won't be long,' she said, and went before any questions could be asked.

On the corner of Trinidad Street, opposite the pub, a little man in a flat cap and patched clothes was hanging about. Poppy looked swiftly around for policemen, and as she did so, another idea hit her. If she put Mr Webb's money on The Music Man as well, he would stand to win much more. He would probably split the difference with her, and then she would have enough to redeem the saxophone. Before she had time to think of all the consequences, she passed the bookie's runner the money.

'A bob and another bob on The Music Man, three o'clock at York.'

Two slips were scribbled out and handed to her. She hurried back, weak at the knees. The deed was done.

The next few hours were the longest she had ever lived. She was extra glad that it was the school holidays. If she had been forced to sit through a day's boring lessons, she would have been in real trouble for not concentrating. As it was, when she had finished her chores in the house, she went round to Elsie's, and the pair of them were charged with looking after the three youngest, two little boys and a baby girl. Elsie's mum, at her wits' end with a house full of children and a husband on strike, gave them a hunk of bread each and a bottle of water and told them to go out for the day. They trailed along to the Torrington Stairs, where the boys played around in the mud and paddled in the filthy water at the river's edge. It was a boiling hot day and the Thames was unnaturally still. All along the banks and in lines in the waterway, ships and barges were moored up, strikebound. Across the glassy water came the whiff of food rotting in the holds.

'It ain't half getting nasty in the street,' Elsie told her. 'That Siobhan O'Donoghue, her what sings on the halls, we can smell her dinners all down the street, and there's little kids with nothing but bread, and that's if they're lucky. My mum says there's going to be trouble. Perhaps there'll be a fight. That'd be good.'

But Poppy could think of nothing but her bet. If only that horse would win, if only . . . But if it didn't, what was she going to say to Mr Webb? Worse still, if Traffino came in, she was going to have to pay him back his money. And what if he told her gran? It didn't bear thinking about.

In the end, she had to admit to Elsie what she had done. Her friend looked at her, wide-eyed with horror.

'Oh, Poppy – you gone and done it now. You won't half get a hiding.'

'I might not. It might win. The Music Man. It will win. I know it will.'

'That's what they all say,' Elsie told her, with the voice of long experience. 'My dad always says that, but they hardly ever do.'

Poppy felt sick. She divided her piece of bread between the others, who stuffed it down ravenously. By the time three o'clock came she could hardly bear the tension. She sat on the rough stone steps, her hands clenched and her eyes tight shut, willing the horse on. Elsie, caught up in the drama, added her wishes. 'Come on, Music Man, come on Music, Man,' they chanted together, while the baby grizzled and wriggled between them.

It was even worse once she got home. She did not know how she got through the time until Mr Webb got in. She heard his heavy step in the hall and her stomach churned, tying itself into knots. Whatever the consequences, she had to find out. She met him on the landing. He had an evening newspaper under his arm. She scanned his tired face, trying to gain a clue.

'Wotcher, girl.'

She opened her mouth, and a strange strangled squeak came out.

'E-evening, Mr Webb.'

'You got that slip of mine still?'

The world swayed around her. She was finished. Traffino had won.

'Er – er – ' Supposing she said she had lost it? It might be better than admitting she had put it on the wrong horse.

'Not that it matters. Reckon I ought to listen to you next time.'

'What?'

'That one you fancied – The Music Man. Come in first. Next time –'

He never did finish his remark. With a cry of joy, Poppy launched herself at him, hugging him with arms and legs.

'I done it! I done it! It won – I knew it would – I just knew! The Music Man!'

Half an hour later, she stood outside Body's, dazed,

30

elated, overcome. In her arms she cradled her father's saxophone.

4

They were lucky in the boys' part of the school. They had Mr
Hetherington for singing. You could hear the voices echoing
down the brown tiled corridors, enthusiastically belting out
'Hearts Of Oak' or droning through 'The Ash Grove', with
Mr Hetherington calling out instructions in his peculiar high
voice. Poppy could see that he loved music. In the girls' school
they only had Miss Yates, with her boiled gooseberry stare
and her way of thumping the piano as if she meant it harm.

Poppy was thinking about Mr Hetherington as she slid out of
her hiding place behind the coke bunkers at the back of the
playground. It was half past four of an October afternoon and all
the children had gone home. Carrying her saxophone, she put
an arm carefully through the broken window and eased up the
catch, then climbed into the twilit school. Along the corridors
and up the stairs she went, her boots ringing loud in the silence,
until she reached the hall. There in the corner the piano stood,
and in front of it the stool with its store of sheet music.

Poppy knew just what she was looking for. The boys might
not think much of 'The Ash Grove', but she thought it was a
lovely tune. She propped it up on the stand on the piano and
studied the notes, trying to remember all that her dad had
taught her about it. Then she put her lips to the sax and ran up
and down some scales to warm up before again turning her
attention to the music. Slowly, tentatively, the ballad emerged
– halting at first, with wrong notes here and there, but
gradually gaining in accuracy and style as she went over it
successive times. The liquid notes of the saxophone took the
lilting melody flowing round the stark hall, turning its
darkening shadows into a place of magic. Poppy was totally
engrossed. She did not hear the handle turn on the door, nor
the soft footfalls across the floor.

'Where did you learn to play like that?'

Poppy yelped and nearly dropped the saxophone. Mr Hetherington was standing right by her shoulder.

'D'you have to creep up on people like that?' she said, then blushed, for she was in double trouble now, being at school after hours and cheeking a teacher.

He ignored her question, holding out a hand for the saxophone. Reluctantly, Poppy gave it to him. He was a small man, only a head taller than she was, but there was something strangely compelling about him, something in his odd eyes that appeared to be almost colourless. He examined the instrument, then tried it out. A fluid series of notes rippled out.

'Nice. Nice tone. Curious hybrid of an instrument, the saxophone. Pity it's not been taken up by serious composers. It deserves better than the popular rubbish it's used for. Where did you get this from?'

'It's my dad's. He's a musician.'

'I see. And he taught you to play?'

'He started to, but I'm learning by myself now. He's – he's away a lot.'

'Ah.' He handed back the saxophone. 'Play me some more.'

Poppy played. It was the first time she had performed for anyone other than Elsie. It was wonderful, almost like having her dad back again.

'Right. Stop. Tell me, how long have you been playing?'

'Oh – not long. My dad started teaching me before he went away. Then I've been practising every day since August.'

'By yourself?'

'Yeah.' Poppy sighed. 'But there's so much I don't know – I remember things Dad done, the sounds he made, but I don't know how to do it.'

'Do you want to know how to do it?'

'Oh, yes!'

Mr Hetherington was looking at her closely. In the half light, it was difficult to make out his expression.

'A good musician needs talent, discipline and good tuition.

33

You have talent and you seem to have the discipline. I could give you the tuition.'

'Oh – ' Poppy could not have been more surprised or delighted if she had been handed the crown jewels on a plate. 'Do you really mean it? You'd teach me to do it properly?'

He reached out and flicked one of her plaits back over her shoulder.

'As long as you prove you're worth the teaching – yes.'

She was so delighted, she almost launched herself at him, but something stopped her.

'That's – that's very kind of you,' she said lamely. 'Where – I mean, here? At school?'

He stepped back and studied her as she stood silhouetted against the grey light coming from the tall windows.

'No, not here. You can come to my rooms.'

It was almost too marvellous to believe. At last, someone to stand in for her dad until he came back.

It took a number of different stories to get away on Saturday afternoon. For some reason she could not explain to herself, Poppy did not want to tell even Elsie where she was going. Just getting out of the house was difficult, with the bulky saxophone case. She had to go the back way between the smelly privies.

Mr Hetherington lived on the other side of the island, in Cubitt Town. She found herself at last walking down a street of three-storied terraced houses with heavy bay windows, each with a little front garden bordered by walls and a privet hedge. Down the edge of the pavement on either side of the road were a line of pollarded plane trees. After the unrelieved brick of North Millwall, it seemed almost suburban. She stopped and looked up at the house. There was a coloured tile path up to the front door, a brass knocker, net curtains at all the windows. The only time she had ever been inside a place as grand as this was when she stayed in the boarding house at Brighton. She clutched the saxophone case with both arms, holding it in front of her like a shield, then marched up to the door.

A faded woman in an apron answered her knock. She looked her up and down, then said, 'Not today, thank you.'

She started to shut the door, but Poppy got her foot in.

'I've come to see him. He's going to give me music lessons.'

'Oh.' The woman still looked doubtful, but she opened the door just wide enough for Poppy to squeeze in. 'He's up the stairs, on the top floor. And don't touch nothing on the way,' she added, as Poppy went past her.

It was dark on the stairs and landings, with a lingering smell of cabbage and polish, mixed with something Poppy could not identify that grew stronger as she climbed higher.

'Ah, Poppy –'

Mr Hetherington was standing in the dimness of the top landing, waiting for her. He led her into the front room.

Poppy gazed about her, amazed. It was a wide room with a tall bay window, furnished with heavy armchairs and a solid table covered in a green chenille cloth. There was a dark patterned carpet square on the floor, a cottage piano and two glass-fronted mahogany bookcases crammed with volumes, but what captured Poppy's attention were the walls. They were covered with framed photographs. What was even more astonishing was their subjects. Not pretty scenes of the countryside. They were all of life on the Isle of Dogs. There were women scrubbing their steps, men getting off the bus, dockers waiting to be called on, girls streaming out of Maconochie's, coal trimmers walking home covered in black dust – and lots of children, playing, minding babies, dancing to the barrel organ, selling newspapers, wading half naked in the mud, diving completely naked off moored barges, staring wide-eyed and hungry straight at the camera. Poppy quite forgot to be overawed. She went closer to look at them.

'That's my friend Elsie, holding the end of that skipping rope, and Annie and Dot about to run in. And that's Mr Turner from down our street in his lighterman's gear. Oh, and that's Body's the pawnbrokers – there's Mr Body in the doorway.' She turned to Mr Hetherington, who was watching her with a half-smile on his narrow face. 'Why have you got all them people on your walls? Where did you get 'em from?'

'I took them with my camera.'

'Coo.' Poppy had never before known anyone who owned such a luxury. 'But why do you take pictures like this?'

Mr Hetherington looked genuinely amused.

'Don't you like them?'

'Well – ' Poppy thought about it. 'They're not very pretty, are they? I mean – look at those rude boys. Why do you want pictures of boys with nothing on? And those kids waiting outside the pub. They don't look as if they've combed their hair for a week.'

'You think photographs should be pretty, do you?'

'Yes. I mean, what's the point of looking at pictures of them women at the pump? You can see that any day.'

'What sort of pictures do you think I ought to take?'

Poppy suddenly remembered who he was. She was being really cheeky, telling him what she thought. She looked down at her feet.

'I dunno. Dunno nothing about it, really. They're all very nice.'

'Come now.' For the first time, Mr Hetherington sounded cross. 'I am interested in your opinion. If I were to take a photograph of you, for instance, you would want me to make you look pretty, would you?'

"Course!' She stopped, staring at him as the meaning of what he had asked sunk in. 'Would you? Take a picture of me?'

'We'll see. First we'll find out if you really have a talent for music.'

Poppy turned her attention to what was really important. She undid the case and took out her precious saxophone.

'Over here.' Mr Hetherington brought a music stand out from behind the piano and set it up by the window. 'First, some scales.'

For the next hour or more, Poppy concentrated as she had

never done in her life before while Mr Hetherington found out just how much she knew about technique, sight reading and interpretation. He expected only to tell her once, uttered a sharp 'No!' every time she hit a wrong note and disapproved of her taste in music except when she mentioned one of the folk tunes they had learnt at school. But Poppy was used to strict teachers. Praise was rare at Dock Street School. She began to recognize the nod and barely audible 'Ah' that signalled that she had done something well. By the time Mr Hetherington said that that was enough for one day, she felt as if she had done a whole week's work. Her whole face ached, and the thumb that supported part of the weight of the instrument had yet another blister on it. She looked at him, waiting for his verdict. This was not like playing for her father, who thought that everything she did was wonderful.

He tidied the music away into a chest of drawers, except for one piece which he handed to Poppy.

'Practise this every day. I shall expect you to be note perfect by next week.'

'You mean – I can come again?'

'Of course. You have a decided aptitude. But you must be prepared to work. A dedicated musician must practise for an hour a day at the very minimum.'

'I will practise, Mr Hetherington. I promise.' Poppy had no idea how she was going to find the time or where she was going to do it, but she was quite certain that she would find a way.

'Good. Now, perhaps we might try a photograph.'

'Oh – ' Poppy had forgotten all about that. But now that he had brought it up again, it seemed like the icing on the cake. 'Will you really? I only ever had my photo took once, by this man on the seafront at Brighton. He had a monkey.'

Mr Hetherington's mouth tightened. 'You won't find any monkeys here. Come with me.'

He led the way into the side room, telling her to wait in the doorway while he lit the gas. When she went in, Poppy saw why the light was needed. The narrow window was completely covered with a black blind, shutting out all natural

37

light. Across the room were strings like washing lines, only instead of clothes, photographic negatives hung from them. Tables were lined against the longest wall, arranged with a series of basins and a sinister-looking black machine, while above them on shelves were rows of bottles like a chemist's shop. Poppy realized that this was where the strange smell came from.

'What is it?' she whispered.

'My dark room.'

'But what – what's it for?'

'This is where I develop my photographs.' He explained the process briefly. Poppy was amazed. She had never even thought to wonder how the picture got out of the camera and into a frame, let alone how it got into the camera in the first place.

'It's like magic, ain't it?'

'Not at all. It's a chemical process. But – ' For a moment his odd colourless eyes took on a dreamy look '– when the image begins to form in the tray, yes, it does seem to contain an element of magic. Perhaps we might create something magical today. You sit down here.'

He placed a stool at the end of the room opposite the blacked out window. Poppy did as she was bid and sat on it, while Mr Hetherington produced a length of blue fabric from a cupboard and tacked it to the picture rail, forming elegant drapes. Then he set a large wooden camera up on a tripod, and fussed around putting powders into a white holder.

'Now – ' He stood looking at her with his head to one side. 'Just as you are to start with, I think. Keep your hands in your lap. No, no smile.' He dived under the black cloth attached to the camera, one arm holding the powder aloft. His voice emerged, slightly muffled. 'Think of your next saxophone lesson. Are you going to be able to play that piece when you come next week?'

'Oh yes!' Poppy's face lit up with earnest fervour. There was a sudden intensely bright light, dazzling her eyes. 'What was that?'

38

'The flash. One cannot do indoor photography without it.'

More preparation, then another shot was taken. Then he told her to swivel round on the stool so that she was sitting with her back half to him.

'Good. Now, look at me over your shoulder.'

Again the flash of light.

'Was that all right? Did I look nice?'

'You were very natural.'

Poppy sighed. 'If only I'd of known you was going to take my picture, I'd of worn my best dress.'

Mr Hetherington was packing away his equipment. He had his back to Poppy, so that his voice sounded strange.

'Perhaps next time we could try something different.'

'You mean – you mean you'll take some more pictures of me?'

He shut the cupboard door and straightened up. His face was flushed.

'Oh, yes,' he said. 'I think we might take some more. As long as you prove co-operative.'

Poppy walked home on air. She could not believe her luck. She never dreamt that she would find someone to teach her to play properly. She was going to work and work at it, and prove to Mr Hetherington that she was worth all the trouble he was taking. She would listen to everything he said and do exactly as he told her. Co-operative, that's what he said she had to be. Co-operative was what he was going to get.

She wondered if he would give her one of the photographs. If only she knew where her father was, she could sent it to him, and then maybe he would remember her and Mum and he would come home. Then she would show him the sax and amaze him with how well she could play it, and he would be pleased with her and stay for ever.

39

5

1913

'Aren't you afraid she'll find out?' Elsie asked, as she and Poppy walked along the dreary street towards the Salvation Army hall.

'Yeah, a bit,' Poppy admitted.

If her gran discovered she was playing with the band, there would be hell to pay, and her mum would get it as well. But it did not stop her from going along to the practices.

'The thing is, she don't like nobody, so she don't talk to nobody. Now my mum, she loves having a gossip with the women in the street, but Gran won't give 'em the time of day, so she ain't likely to find out.'

'I hope you're right,' Elsie said.

The lessons with Mr Hetherington had been a regular feature of her life for eighteen months now. She and Elsie had both left school and were working at Maconochie's, where they found that the deadly monotony was a lot worse than that of learning things by heart or doing long pages of sums. So even more than before, the highlight of Poppy's week was her music lesson. Every Saturday afternoon, off she went to the house in Cubitt Town, and week by week her skills improved. But she never told Elsie about it. She often wished that she could, for she needed to share the experience with someone, but she was always afraid that once she started talking, she would let the business of the photographs slip out, and Mr Hetherington had impressed upon her that she must never tell anyone about that.

The girls joined the trickle of people entering the hall, boys and men mostly, all carrying instrument cases. Poppy breathed in the familiar smell of dust, damp clothing and gas.

This was always the happiest time of her week. There was the cheerful camaraderie of the other band members, the covert admiration of the older boys and young men. Although anything other than serious music making was discouraged at practices, she and Elsie always took great pains with their appearance before coming, brushing each other's hair and pinning it into grown-up styles. There wasn't a lot they could do with the navy-blue uniforms, but at least they were clean and smart. Poppy looked enviously at her friend who was growing proper woman's curves that showed, even with the military-style jacket over them. Her own body, although developing, was rail-thin, and still looked like a boy's in her uniform. She longed for a fashionable hour-glass figure, like the women in the corsetry advertisements.

There was a scraping and a coughing and a cacophany of toots and squeaks as chairs and stands were set out, players settled down, instruments were tuned up. Poppy and Elsie took their places in different rows and sorted themselves out. The band leader had been rather dubious about Poppy's saxophone at first, but after hearing her play a couple of hymn tunes faultlessly and with moving interpretation, he decided that just as the Devil must not be allowed to have all the best tunes, neither must he monopolize new and interesting instruments.

The leader tapped his baton on his music stand.

'If we could make a start, everyone? I hope you've all been practising since last week. If our performance does not improve one hundredfold we will not be up to standard for the Christmas concerts and services. We'll begin with "Once in Royal David's City". From the top –'

Christmas was always a bad time for Poppy, reminding her of another year gone and still not a word from her father. At times the memories conjured up by the carols brought tears to her eyes. He had come to hear her sing 'Away in a Manger' at school when she was six. He had taught her to play 'While Shepherds Watched' just before he left.

Poppy blew her nose and concentrated on the music.

Gradually it worked its magic on her. Her notes blended with the others to make a sweet whole. Loud and stirring, or gently poignant, she was part of the chords and the melodies. A stroke of the baton, a nod from the leader, and it was her solo piece, the first verses of 'In the Bleak Midwinter'. Poppy poured herself into the lyrical tune, drawing everything she knew out of the saxophone. All her pain at being deserted flowed into the notes. At the close of the second verse, the rest of the band began to be drawn in, until at the end they were all playing. As the sound died away at the end, they all knew they had made something good. The leader waited a few moments before breaking the silence.

'Well done. If you play them all as well as that, we'll have the unconverted flocking to us.'

There was no higher praise.

At the end of the session, Poppy came out into the winter's evening elated. The members of the band were bidding each other good night. A gangly lad with a prominent Adam's apple sidled up to her.

'You were wonderful, Poppy. You're better than any of us.'

Poppy flushed. 'Oh, get on with you.'

'You are, honest. I – er – I thought so for a long time. And I thought – are you doing anything Saturday?'

'Yes,' Poppy told him. 'I am. Sorry. See you next week.'

She and Elsie giggled about it all the way back to Elsie's house.

'I wouldn't go out with him if he paid me.'

'Blimey, no! Not him. There's one or two I wouldn't mind. D'you fancy anyone? I mean really fancy them?'

Poppy thought about it. She always liked to look her best for the practices but, in fact, she wasn't really interested in boys. They all seemed pretty stupid.

'No, not really. What about you?'

'Well – I quite like Bobby –'

'Oh, Elsie, you can't! Not him. Those spots!'

By the time they got to Elsie's house, Poppy had practically persuaded her friend out of her latest crush.

42

'I suppose you're right. He's a bit – well –'

'He's not good enough for you.'

Elsie sighed. 'You're always so sure about things. I wish I was.'

'I'm not sure about everything,' Poppy told her.

As she walked over to Cubitt Town the next Saturday, she wished she could be sure about her visits to Mr Hetherington. She knew he was a good music teacher. She would not now be one of the leading players in the band if it had not been for his tuition. And it was not just the playing; he taught her lots of other things to do with music as well. He had done a great deal for her. She supposed it was only right that she should do something in return.

As usual, he was waiting on the top landing for her as she came up the dark stairs.

'You're ten minutes late.'

'We was kept till a batch was finished.'

He tutted and sighed. 'Well, well, you're here now, I suppose. Come along.'

The session took its usual pattern, the playing of the piece she was currently working on and the perfecting of a point of technique. Then Mr Hetherington looked at the homework she had done for him, an exercise on musical arrangement.

'That's very interesting. What made you bring the violins in there?'

'I thought they made it more – more romantic. That bit needs a sort of singing, like you get with violins.'

'Romantic!' Mr Hetherington sounded disgusted. 'What does a young girl like you know of romance?'

Poppy shot him a mutinous look. Come to that, she wanted to say, what does a funny-looking little bloke like you know about it, either? But she did not dare utter it out loud. After all this time, she still did not know how he was going to react to what she said or did.

'I know how I wanted that piece to sound,' she said.

Mr Hetherington ignored that. He was shuffling through his record collection. His eyes gleamed as he found the one he

43

was looking for. He lifted the heavy lid of the gramophone and wound up the handle.

'Now this,' he said, his voice shaking with fervour, 'this is romantic. Listen!'

Through the hiss and scratch came the swell of an orchestra, soaring on notes of luscious beauty.

'Mendelssohn,' Mr Hetherington said, in tones of reverence. 'Now that is the touch of genius. Listen again.'

He played the short movement over several times, making Poppy concentrate on roles of various parts of the orchestra.

'There – hear? The clarinets, then the rest of the wood-wind –'

Poppy nodded, distinguishing the patterns within the whole. It made her little piece of arranging seem as subtle as a nursery rhyme. But it also made her want to learn more.

As always, the time went too fast. All too soon the piano lid was closed, the records put away. Mr Hetherington ushered her into the darkroom.

Poppy's heart sank. A mock pillar about five feet high stood by the blue backdrop. She knew what that meant. They were in for a classical session, with all those drapery things.

Just as she suspected, Mr Hetherington thrust a white cotton tunic into her arms.

'Get yourself into this.'

He disappeared out of the room while she changed, making haste, for she knew that he would not stay outside for long. She had worn this garment before, and knew what was expected of her. She was to take off everything and wear it over her naked body. Feeling very exposed, she slipped it on. It was nothing but two pieces of light fabric gathered together at the shoulders and held in place round the waist with a length of gold cord. Mr Hetherington said it was what used to be worn by the maidens of Ancient Greece. He had even showed her pictures of funny old black vases with drawings on them of people dressed like that. All Poppy could think was that they must have been a rude lot in Greece, for the robe was open all down each side and would have shown everything on a windy day.

'Ready?' Mr Hetherington was back.

'Yes.' Poppy twitched the lengths of fabric into place.

He handed her a narrow band of gold card, stuck round into a circle. A filet was what he called it.

'Put that on, with your hair tucked round it. You know.'

Poppy knew. She settled the band so that it came across her forehead and took the side locks of her heavy copper-coloured hair up and through the band so that they made a roll on each side of her head before falling over her shoulders and down her back. Mr Hetherington, meanwhile, was busying himself with his camera and the flash equipment.

'Now – ' He regarded her as he always did, with his head slightly to one side. 'One elbow on the top of the pillar, and the right foot across the left. Lean gracefully – gracefully! Dear me, no – not like that. What is the matter with you today? No, that's not right. Try both hands on the pillar, and your head resting on them. That's better. The face more towards me. Now the left knee forward. More – that's it. Very elegant. Very classical.'

Very elegant, very classical, with the fabric falling away, revealing the entire length of Poppy's white leg. The flashlight popped.

'I think we'll dispose of the pillar. It's not working as I envisaged. Hold this.'

Poppy obediently took the heavy pottery vase.

'Lift it to one shoulder. Good. Arch the arm. One foot to the side slightly – yes –'

Two more shots, with the vase in various positions. Poppy was beginning to feel chilled.

'What was the weather like in Greece? Cold and foggy like here? They must of been blooming parky in these things.'

'Oh no, no. It is hot, wonderfully hot. The sun shines every day.'

'Wish it was hot here. I'm getting goose pimples.'

Mr Hetherington tutted. He disliked her talking while he was composing his pictures.

'Just one more. Untie the left shoulder.'

He watched as she complied, his lips apart. The fabric fell back exposing a budding breast. Poppy stared above his head. It always gave her an uncomfortable prickling feeling inside when it got this far.

'Yes, yes – now raise the arm – hold it there –' He disappeared under the black cloth. Another flash, and then she was released.

'You can get changed now.'

He was just about to go out of the room when a question she had long wanted to ask came once more to the tip of her tongue, then was out before she could stop it.

'What do you do with all these pictures? You don't put them up with the others in your front room.'

Mr Hetherington went pink. His voice came out even higher than usual.

'That's my affair,' he said, and went out of the room.

Poppy scrambled into her clothes. It was a mystery. Why take so many pictures if he wasn't going to put them up on the walls? He must have dozens of them by now. Hundreds. Just as she fastened the last button, she heard the landlady call up the stairs.

'Oh – I'll come down,' came Mr Hetherington's voice.

Poppy went out onto the landing. She could hear the murmur of voices down by the door, one of them Mr Hetherington's. She was just going to fetch her coat and her saxophone when she noticed that the door to the back room was ajar. She had never been in that one. She assumed it was Mr Hetherington's bedroom. Gripped with curiosity, she pushed it open and looked in.

She caught her breath, almost crying out loud. For there on the walls were the photographs. A myriad of images of herself, countless pairs of her eyes staring back at her, from the first ones to those which had been taken in the last few weeks. Then there were the enlargements. She had never seen photographs so big. Over the head of the bed, there was one of her looking down while she unfastened the buttons of her blouse. On the window wall, just where it could be seen by someone lying down with their head on the pillow, one of her face looking wide-eyed with her thumb in her mouth.

Poppy felt sick. This was wrong. He shouldn't have her pictures there, not like that. She knew instinctively that it had to do with what men and women did together. She was a bit vague about the process, since none of that sort of thing went on in her house, but she had picked up enough from what others said at work to recoil from what she saw now. It was an invasion of her most secret places, something horrible and repulsive.

Through the pounding in her head, she heard footsteps on the stairs. A well-honed sense of self-preservation made her step back out of the room and pull the door shut. But she still felt dizzy and disorientated by what she had seen. When Mr Hetherington spoke to her, she hardly knew how she replied.

'Yes – ready – yes – going now –'

'I'll see you next week, then. Don't forget what I said about the timing on that piece.'

'Timing. Yes.'

He slept with her pictures all round him.

'Are you feeling poorly, Poppy?'

'No!'

She had to get away. She felt suffocated. She edged past him and ran down the stairs, her knees almost giving way beneath her. Out of the door and into the blessed ordinariness of the street.

'Oh, Dad,' she said out loud, as she started back towards home, 'Oh, Dad, help me. I don't know what to do.'

6

She did not go back to Cubitt Town the next Saturday. Instead, she took a bus up to Poplar and walked up and down Chrisp Street market, immersing herself in the noise and colour and life. She felt safe here, with all these people around her. She looked at all the stalls, fascinated by the piles of goods, the raucous voices of the traders. Then when she had seen it all, she went back and chose her few Christmas presents, a pretty cup and saucer with flowers on it for her mother, a brooch for Elsie, a handkerchief for her grandmother. She did not choose one for her father. Last year's and the year before's were still waiting, all wrapped up, for his return.

She knew now that he would not be coming back.

On Saturday evening and most of Sunday, she was busy playing in the band, and able to close her mind to what Mr Hetherington would be thinking now that she had failed to turn up. But all the same, the thought of him nagged at her. She could not help seeing those photographs in her mind's eye, pinned up all round the walls of his bedroom. She knew that she had to do something about it, but could not for the life of her think what. What she dreaded most was his coming to the house to get her. Her grandmother would go mad if she knew she was having music lessons and if Mr Hetherington demanded to know why she had not come, then she did not know what she was going to say. One thing was certain, she could not say a word about those photographs. They were too horrible to talk about.

Jane dreaded Christmas. The rest of the year, she could cope with having been deserted, but Christmas was supposed to be a family time and the thought of its approach brought on a terrible dragging depression and feeling of failure. Her mother had expected great things of her, but she had disappointed her, becoming pregnant and marrying Owen. It did not matter that she supported herself and Poppy with her sewing. It was not what her mother had planned for her.

On top of this, she was a failure as a wife. She must be, for Owen had left her. She was not pretty enough, or clever enough, to hold him.

In a brave effort to keep the depression from completely overwhelming her, she tried not to be a failure as a mother. She worried about Poppy. She was out at work now, slaving at that dreadful food factory, coming home each evening with her eyes hollow with fatigue. She did not seem to have that much fun in her life. She always went off somewhere on a Saturday afternoon. Jane did not know where, but was left with the impression that she was doing something with Elsie. And then she spent a lot of her time down the Sally Army Citadel. She was safe there, and she seemed to like it. But Jane felt there was something missing, something that she was not being told about. Poppy was very secretive and she was sure the secret was harming her in some way. Questioning her only brought more evasions, so she sought to make things better the only way she knew how. By sewing. She would make Poppy something really nice for Christmas. It was a busy time for her, since there was always lots of work in the weeks leading up to the festive season. Even on Dog Island, there were women wanting something new to wear, or at least something altered to look new. But she found time to see to her own project. If she had to sit up till midnight, she would do it. Poppy must have her present.

They decorated their room as usual, each of them trying to be cheerful for the other's sake. Poppy looked tense. There was a hunted expression in her face. Jane put an arm round her shoulders as she untangled the tired paperchains.

'You feeling all right, darling?'

''Course I am.'

There was something very final in her voice. Jane was almost put off, but she gave it one more try.

'Only – you look a bit poorly. You worried about anything?'

'No – no, nothing at all. I'm just – just tired. It's been blooming awful at work this week.'

'Poor darling.' Jane kissed her, wanting to believe the tale. It sounded plausible enough. Maconochie's was a hard place. Everyone knew that. She thought of the gift she had made. That would cheer her up.

She woke early on Christmas morning and lay still in the sagging bed, looking at her daughter. In the grey half-light, Poppy's sleeping face was relaxed and wiped clean of all worries. The carefree innocence brought a lump to Jane's throat. Such a difficult age, thirteen. Her childhood was behind her now, and all life's problems lay ahead. How she longed for some way of protecting her. As she watched, Poppy stirred. Her eyelids fluttered open. She lay staring at the ceiling for a moment, then turned her head and saw her mother smiling at her. An answering smile dawned.

' 'Morning, Mum.'

'Happy Christmas, darling.'

'Oh – I'd forgotten – Happy Christmas.'

They kissed and sat up, shivering in the penetrating chill, and pulled the top cover round their shoulders. Poppy fished out her present to her mother. Jane handed her the parcel she had wrapped. It was heavy and soft. She watched as Poppy pulled off the string and ripped open the brown paper, happy for the first time in weeks in the anticipation of Poppy's pleasure. There in the midst of the wrapping was a neatly folded garment of bottle-green wool. Poppy held it up. It was a double-breasted jacket, fitted at the waist, with long cuffs and lots of braiding.

'Oh – ' Poppy stared at it, as if hardly daring to believe that it was hers. 'For me? You made it for me?'

It was every bit as good as Jane had hoped.

'I altered it for you, yeah. Do you like it?'

'Like it – '

'There's a skirt to match and all.'

Poppy unfolded that as well. It was an A-line design with

five rows of braid round the hem. The fabric was soft and smooth, and obviously of the very best quality.

'It's beautiful, Mum. Just beautiful. Real grown up.'

'It was hardly worn. I thought, now you're nearly fourteen, you need something better than your work clothes. But I couldn't be sure if I got the size right. Try it on, then if it needs it, I can alter it again.'

Poppy slid out onto the cold lino. She put on her underclothes in double-quick time, found her one white blouse, then reached for the new outfit. It fitted almost perfectly. Sizzling with excitement, she looked at herself in the spotted mirror, bundling her hair up on top and turning from side to side in order to see herself better. Jane watched her preening herself, the lump back in her throat. Her daughter was no longer a gawky girl, but a young woman. The tight fitting waist and extra fabric round the bust gave her skinny figure the suggestion of curves. The upswept hair showed the line of her neck and made her stand properly. Fear clutched at Jane's heart. Poppy was going to be a real stunner. She had looks and charm and stubbornness. The three together could spell trouble.

Then she let her hair tumble down in untidy locks again and bounced back onto the bed, a child once more. She gave Jane a hug and a kiss.

'It's lovely, lovely, lovely.'

'The moment I saw it, I knew it'd look nice on you.'

'You're the cleverest mum in the world.'

Jane flushed. Tears pricked her eyes and ached in her throat. Before she could stop herself, the words she had not meant to say slipped out.

'I just wish your dad was here to see you. He'd be that proud.'

'Oh, Mum – ' Poppy hugged her again. 'Don't cry. One day he'll come back. And if he doesn't, I'll find him. Yeah, that's what I'll do. I'll find him, and I'll bring him back home to us.'

Jane could not answer. Life was all black and white when

you were young. How could she say that if he wanted to come back, he would have come by now? Best to say nothing. She just held her tighter.

'Tell you what – ' Poppy sat back on the bed, still holding her mother's hands. 'Will you come to the Salvation Army meeting with me? Morning or evening, it doesn't matter. Whenever we can get away from Gran. I want – I want you to see something. It'll be a surprise, a big surprise. You'll be pleased.'

Jane hesitated. She had never been inside the Salvation Army place. It would be nice. But what would her mother say? She didn't hold with Nonconformists.

As if reading her mind, Poppy said, 'Go on. She must let you go on Christmas Day.'

With a smile, Jane agreed. She gave Poppy's hand a squeeze.

'Yeah, yeah, I will. It'd be nice, all that singing and everything.'

Her weary spirits took a lift. It would be nice to be with people who had something to be happy about, and she liked singing. Most of all, she wanted to go to please Poppy.

It did not take too much effort to get away from Gran that evening. She was only too glad to get both of them out of the place for a while, since even she could not expect them to start scrubbing the house on Christmas Day.

They set off together after tea, Poppy carrying a large bag, the contents of which she refused to show to Jane. When they arrived, Poppy found her a place, then slid off, saying that she had something to do.

'Look out for me,' she said.

Jane was mystified. The citadel was crowded with families in festive mood. Those about her wished her a happy Christmas and shook her hand. She began to relax, to be drawn in to the friendliness, the joy of people celebrating.

At the front, the band were beginning to come in and take their seats. Jane tried to keep thoughts of Owen out of her head, but they kept crowding back. Then she sat up, stifling a little cry. There was Poppy, in her navy blue uniform, sitting down with the band. In her hands she carried a saxophone. Jane stared at her, transfixed. What was she doing? How had she come by it? Poppy was looking along the rows, searching for her. Their eyes met, and Poppy gave a self-conscious grin. Jane smiled back, and waved, still in a state of amazement. The little monkey! This must have been what she had been up to all these months.

Through the entire course of the evening, her eyes never left her daughter. But from the tangle of pride, fear and bewilderment, it was pride that emerged. She touched the arms of the people on either side of her.

'That's my girl, the one in the second row, with the saxophone,' she whispered.

They looked and nodded in acknowledgment.

When Poppy played her solo, she sat entranced by the beauty of the music, watching her daughter through a glistening haze as unashamed tears trickled down her cheeks. She was her father's daughter all right.

At the end of the service, Poppy came wriggling her way through the crowd to join her.

'Well, Mum, what do you think? Did you like it?'

'It was beautiful – ' She shook her head, still not quite able to take it in. 'I never would of believed it. A real chip off of the old block! But how did you learn to do it? You're so good at it. As good as what he was, I'm sure.'

'I'm not,' Poppy said. 'Not yet, anyhow. I learnt it here, at the band – and there was this teacher at school what taught me and all.'

She stopped short, flushing, as if she had not meant to let it out.

'Taught you? When?'

'On Saturday afternoons.'

'On Saturday – ' Jane was mystified, and worried. 'But, Poppy love, how did you pay for it? We ain't got that kind of money.'

Around them, the citadel was emptying. The other band

players were packing away their instruments. Everyone was cheerful, laughing and calling out Christmas greetings. The pleasure of the evening began to trickle away, leaving Poppy fearful. She bit her lip.

'What if your gran was to find out?'

'She won't, Mum. She ain't found out all this time, so she won't now.'

'But music lessons – the money –'

A new voice chimed in. 'There is no charge.'

Poppy gasped and whirled round. The colour drained from her face. Jane looked to see who it was. A man was standing beside her. He was short, shorter than Poppy, with thinning hair and a narrow face, pale despite the heat in the citadel. What impressed Jane was his stiff collar and brown suit. This was obviously somebody important, a clerk or maybe even a professional man. He addressed her in an odd, high voice.

'There is no need to worry, Mrs Powers. I teach your daughter because I believe in encouraging talent.'

Jane was flustered. She never knew how to speak to people like this. She began gabbling to cover her confusion.

'Oh, sir, that's ever so good of you. You done her proud. She was that good, weren't she? I never got such a surprise in my life as when I saw her there in that band, and when she got up and done that bit all by herself –'

But he was not really listening to her. He was looking at Poppy.

'You did not come to your lesson last Saturday.'

Poppy did not meet his eye. She shuffled her feet.

'I had to go out.'

'You mean you preferred to waste both your time and mine.'

'No, I mean I had to go out. And I ain't coming – ' She stopped and swallowed, then looked him straight in the face. 'I ain't coming back no more.'

'Poppy!' Jane was shocked. What was she doing? 'That's no way to talk to the gentleman. Not after he's been so kind and all.'

She looked from her daughter, flushed and defiant, to the teacher. His face was strangely expressionless. He almost appeared quite unaffected by Poppy's behaviour, but Jane realized with a rush of apprehension that he was very angry indeed, for when he spoke, it was with obvious control.

'I do not wish to be forced to come and enquire at your house for you.'

Poppy gave a little gasp.

Jane became voluble with fear. If he came to the door, it would all come out, the music lessons, the saxophone. Her mother had hated musicians ever since Owen courted her. The tongue-lashing they would both get hardly bore thinking about.

'Oh, sir, don't you go doing that. We wouldn't never hear the last of it. I'll see she goes. You hear that, Poppy? You mustn't go wasting the gentleman's time, not when he's been kind enough to learn you all that music. We're ever so grateful, sir, honest we are. It's her dad, you see. He plays the saxophone. Wonderful, he is. I just wish he could of been here today to hear her. He'd of been that proud –'

'No doubt.' The man was talking to Jane but looking at Poppy. 'I don't think your daughter quite appreciates what a privilege it is to be receiving musical tuition.'

'Oh, she does really, sir, I'm sure she does. She's been that interested in music, ever since she was little. Her dad, he always used to say she was a little wonder, the way she picked things up . . .'

She was so concerned with placating him that she did not see the agonized look that Poppy gave her, did not read the anguish in her eyes. Instead she gave her a little poke in the back.

'You will go next week, won't you. Poppy? She will, sir. I'll see to it. She's grateful really, sir, only you know what it is . . .'

To her intense relief, he gave a smile. A tight, frosty one, but a smile all the same.

'I'm glad to hear it,' he said. He was still looking at Poppy. 'Next Saturday, then. A merry Christmas.'

'Thank you, sir, and thank you for all you're doing for my girl. A merry Christmas to you too –'

He nodded politely to her and left, leaving Jane cut off in mid-sentence.

'Well –' she said, watching his retreating back, 'well, who'd of thought it? It's been a day of surprises today, it has, and no mistake. You could of knocked me down with a feather, you could, when I saw you sitting there with that saxophone. And then to hear as how you been having lessons. I mean, nobody round here has lessons. And he done it all for free, and all. He must think a lot of you, Poppy. Well, I mean, it ain't surprising. You got talent, there's no doubt about that. You take after your dad . . .'

It was not until they were halfway home that she ran out of exclamations and realized that Poppy was unnaturally quiet.

'You all right, lovey? You ain't saying much.'

'Yes.'

Something in her voice made Jane stop. They were far from a streetlamp, so she could not see her face at all well.

'What is it, lovey? Is it them music lessons?'

'No.'

'What, then?'

'Nothing. I'm all right, Mum. Honest. I'm just – just tired. It's been a long day.'

And as the winter weeks went by, she put down Poppy's peaky look to the weather and the long hours at Maconochie's, and her moodiness to her age. Her fear of having the music teacher come and seek Poppy out at home overcame any niggling worry she had about Poppy's odd attitude to him. Each Saturday she made sure Poppy was on time for her lesson, nagging at her to get ready and chasing her out of the house. After all, free music lessons did not grow on trees. Poppy was a very lucky girl.

7

Margaret Todd stood at the front parlour window, feather duster in hand. The parlour was her favourite room in the house, her showplace. The other rooms, even her own bedroom, were purely functional. They had squares of linoleum on the floors, the barest minimum of furniture and practically no pictures or ornaments. They were for living in. The parlour, on the other hand, was for looking at. She had furnished it piece by piece with a taste based on memories of the Big House. There were heavy hide-covered armchairs, so tightly stuffed with horsehair that they repelled any attempts at sitting on them, a large mahogany sideboard, numerous spindly sidetables in oak or black lacquer, and on the floor a rather threadbare Turkey carpet. In pride of place in the window was a depressed-looking aspidistra. Whenever she came into this room, Margaret experienced a feeling of satisfaction. This was respectability, this was what she had been working for all her life.

In theory, the room was for visitors. In practice, the only people who visited were her daughter's customers. This was a great concession on Margaret's part, but she had seen the sense of it. It was perfectly all right for Jane to work in her bedroom, but she could not do fittings there. Once a week Margaret polished all the brass and the woodwork and washed all the glass, every day she swept the carpet and dusted round. She always left the room feeling calmed and renewed. Today, however, something was occurring outside that was making her anything but calm.

She twitched back the net curtain. It was evening and people were coming home from work. On the corner by her house a group of young people were larking about. There were about eight or ten of them, lads and girls, shouting and laughing, the boys teasing, the girls giggling or answering back. Lax behaviour. She knew just what that led to. It had happened to Jane. Usually Margaret would tap on the window and chase them off, but today she saw something that stayed her hand. There in the centre of the group was her granddaughter.

Most of the group's attention seemed to be centred on Poppy, and two of the lads were vying for her favour. Margaret watched them with distaste in her heart. Scruffy louts, not an idea in their heads beyond drinking and getting their filthy hands on her granddaughter. She did not notice that Poppy was not giving in to either of them.

Anger and frustration boiled within her. It was not for this that she had forced that man to marry Jane. After all this time, all the heartbreak and disappointments, Poppy must be the one to make something of herself. Unbidden, the long-dead faces rose before her eyes, the stillborn babies with unreal waxlike features, all boys, each one called Arthur after his father. Worse, the ones that survived, lived to smile and crow at her, only to sicken and die. One reached his first birthday, had pulled himself upright and balanced, swaying on chubby legs, eyes round and amazed at his own achievement. A year and a week he lived, then fell sick of the whooping cough and died. The day after, she miscarried his brother.

Margaret glared through the window at the girl on the pavement. Of one thing she was certain, she was going to put a stop to this. She began to make plans.

A week later, she called a family meeting. The three of them sat down round the kitchen table.

'It's time for a few changes round here,' she stated. As usual, Jane looked apprehensive, Poppy defiant. She would soon wipe that expression off her face.

'I been watching you, miss, coming home with all them lot from that factory, and I'm telling you this, I don't like what I been seeing.

Poppy glared at her. 'They're my friends,' she said.

'They're not the right friends for you. Rough, they are.

Common. I never did like you working at that factory. You ought to be doing something better. You're old enough to get a decent job.'

Poppy actually brightened up and looked interested.

'I hate that place,' she said. 'They treat you like a slave there. When they're busy you got to work all the hours God sends and when they ain't they just lay you off. It ain't fair. There ought to be unions for the factory girls like what there are for the dockers and the lightermen.'

Margaret pursed her lips. That was the street talking again. They were all union mad, now that the dockers had won their victory over the employers.

'Unions are for slackers and the workshy,' she said. 'What you need to do, my girl, is to get right away from factory work.'

Poppy leaned forward.

'I'd like to work in a shop, or as a waitress. I wouldn't mind if it meant working all day Saturdays, not even if it was quite late. I wouldn't mind that at all.'

'There's no future in shop work,' Margaret told her. 'You won't never get ahead like that. No, you need something where they'll teach you a skill.'

'Like sewing,' Jane put in.

Margaret shot her a repressive look. 'We tried that once already in this family,' she said.

Jane subsided.

'You also need somewhere where they'll keep an eye on you and make sure you don't get into no trouble.'

She conveniently forgot that Jane's doomed romance with Owen was conducted under her own roof.

'So,' she said, 'what I decided was, the best thing is for you to go into service.'

'Oh, no!' Poppy cried.

Jane looked horrified. 'But that'd mean she'd have to leave home. I wouldn't never see her.'

'She'll get an afternoon off every fortnight,' Margaret said. 'It will do her the world of good. She'll be well fed and clothed, she'll be learning how to do things proper and she'll have the

59

chance to better herself and get on. A good cook or a housekeeper is a person what's respected. It's a very good job for a woman.'

'But I don't want to go into service!' Poppy wailed. 'I heard about it. You're nothing but a skivvy when you start, you're at the beck and call of everyone. They treat you like dirt. Much worse'n Maconochie's. At least now I can come home at the end of the day. If I was in service I'd be there all the time.'

That, Margaret considered, was the biggest advantage. She would be away from bad influences.

'I'd miss her something terrible,' Jane put in. She put an arm round her daughter. 'She's not fourteen yet. It's awful young to be leaving home.'

'I left home at twelve. Best thing that could of happened to me,' Margaret told her. 'Best thing for her as well. Give her backbone. Make her stand on her own two feet.'

Poppy was wearing her most mutinous expression. She sat back, her arms folded across her chest. 'I don't want to be a skivvy,' she declared.

Margaret fixed her with her sternest gaze. 'What you want and what you don't want don't come in to it, miss. I know what's best for you. It's for your own good.'

And having demolished any possible protest, she went on to the details of the plan.

'Now, I been to an employment agency and got you registered. I let them know that I knew what good service meant, and they took you on. But they want to see you before they send you off for any interviews, so you got an appointment with them Tuesday afternoon. That'll give you time to get your references. If they won't give you one at that factory, go back to school and ask the headmaster. And they'll give you one from that church of yours, I'll be bound. You spend enough time there. Then when you go, you wear something decent and respectable and you answer them polite like. None of your cheek. That way you'll get sent to the best positions. You understand?'

'Yes.' The answer sounded as if it had been dragged out of Poppy by torture.

'Now, you mind you remember that. Here's the address.' Margaret pushed a business card across the table to her. 'They'll see you at ten o'clock, so mind you're there good and early. And act civil, remember.'

Poppy took the card as if it were poisoned, looked at it and stood up. She went out of the room without another word.

'Sulky little madam,' Margaret said to her daughter. 'She'll thank me for this one day, you mark my words.'

She went to bed that night satisfied that she had done the right thing by her granddaughter.

Poppy sat on the bus, watching the drab world go by through the dirt-splashed window. Rebellion boiled in her heart. She did not want to go into service. She knew she would hate every minute of it. The only advantage, the one that had struck her the moment her grandmother had brought the subject up, was that it would mean getting away from Mr Hetherington.

She really dreaded Saturday afternoons now. The orders still came from behind the camera, he never laid so much as a finger on her, but knowing where the pictures were hung made her feel sick to the soul. He could say what he liked about Art and Classical Poses, but she came away feeling soiled. In fact she always went and washed all over the moment she got home. Many a time she had been on the point of telling her mother about it, but somehow the words would not come.

Perhaps it would be best to get right away, even if it meant being a skivvy. If only her dad were here . . . he would think of something. He wouldn't want to see her working her fingers to the bone scrubbing. He would make sure she got a job she liked.

The bus stopped opposite a Joe Lyons. She tried to peer through the steamy windows. People were having cups of coffee and plates of buns. She remembered the last time she had been in a Lyons. It had not been a little one, like this, but the big important one in Oxford Street. The Corner House. She had gone there with her mum and dad. Her parents had shared a pot of tea for two, and she had had a lemonade, and they had eaten cream slices. The puff pastry had crumbled and split as she bit it, and the cream and jam had gone all over her face. She had got in a terrible mess and her dad had laughed.

Then he had called grandly for the bill, and left tuppence under the saucer for the waitress.

'A little something for the Nippy,' he had said.

Blurrily through the window she could see a girl in her black and white uniform. Now, that would be a nice job, serving people with their teas and meals, and smiling, and taking the money, and finding tips under the saucers. People were happy when they went to a café.

The bus moved on. The conductor called out her stop. With a feeling of dread, she climbed down into the rainy morning. There it was, three doors down from the bus stop. She stood for a minute staring at the neat notice painted on the door: 'Domestic Servants' Employment Exchange.'

Domestic Servant. Slave, more like. She looked about for a clock and saw one sticking out over a jeweller's shop. A quarter to ten. Now she had to wait about until it was time for her appointment. Her stomach rumbled and she thought again of the Lyons, of warmth and friendliness and pots of tea. And then it came to her. Instead of going in to the Exchange, she could go to the Corner House and try to get a job as a waitress. She had her references with her. They might take her on, and then she would have a good job and be well away from the Island on Saturday afternoons. It seemed like the perfect solution. Except that her grandmother was expecting her to come back with a place as a housemaid.

She shifted from one foot to the other in an agony of indecision. There would be hell to pay, disobeying Gran like that. Did she dare? She thought of leaving Mum and living in some big unfriendly place where everyone ordered her about. She thought of the row there would be if she arrived home without the job she had been sent to get. She looked at the sign again. Domestic Servant. All her life, it seemed, she had been clearing up other people's dirt. She was not going to do it any longer. She walked back to the bus stop and spoke to a decent-looking woman waiting there.

'Excuse me, but can you tell me how to get to Oxford Street from here?'

It was all quite amazingly easy. They did have a vacancy at the Corner House. Her references were approved. She was given a short arithmetic test, then told to carry a tray of cups and plates and arrange them properly on a table. Poppy, remembering happy trips to cafés, set it all down neatly and correctly. She spoke up clearly, she was as civil as she knew how, she smiled at the man who interviewed her. She was given a month's trial, starting on Monday.

There was indeed hell to pay when she got home, but it was worth it.

That Saturday, Poppy walked over to Cubitt Town with feet as light as air. She would tell him that this had to be the last time. She was wearing the new green costume, with her hair pinned up. The effect was spoilt a little by her heavy patched boots, but she did not look down at them. She marched along, bouncing with confidence. She was nearly grown up, she had a job to go to, and she looked good. Independence beckoned her. A whole bright new life was just waiting to begin. Men whistled at her as she went by. She stood out amongst the ill-clad people in the drab streets. She was young and pretty. It gave her a heady feeling of power.

Mr Hetherington was waiting for her in the front room, as usual. As she breezed in and he saw the young woman that she was pretending to be, the expression on his face changed. The thin schoolmasterish smile of welcome drained away, and his cheeks and mouth became slack, as if there was no strength left in them.

'Good afternoon,' Poppy said. How small he was, and how round his shoulders were. And that lank hair was so thin on top now that the skin was showing through. How very odd that only a few weeks ago, at Christmas, she had been so afraid of him coming and upsetting things at home. Even last week, she had felt compelled to come, lest he turn up at the house and tell Gran all about the music lessons.

'What have you done to yourself?' he asked.

'Don't you like it?' Poppy twirled round, showing off. 'My mum made it for me for Christmas. Well, altered it for me. She's good at sewing. She was apprenticed to a court dressmaker once.'

He relaxed then. A trace of colour came back into his face.

'Of course, you like dressing up, don't you, Poppy? You always have liked trying new things on. I've got something new for you to wear today.'

'Oh – that's nice,' Poppy said. After all, it was going to be the last time. Best to humour him. She got the saxophone out of the case. 'I had a lot of trouble with that new piece. Couldn't get the middle bit right at all. My fingers just don't work fast enough. It comes out all dirgy and it should be *allegro*.'

'It's a question of practice.'

The lesson took its usual path. Sometimes she played alone, sometimes he accompanied her on the piano, occasionally he took the saxophone from her and demonstrated a point. Her theory exercises were marked. She had not done them well. She had scrambled through them any old how.

'I think for next week you should do these again. It's not your best work.'

Should she tell him now that she would not be coming back? Perhaps not.

'Now, let me show you what I have for you.'

Into the dark room, with its familiar smell of chemicals. Mr Hetherington handed her a frilly dress and a wide ribbon.

'You'll look very pretty in that, with your hair like it should be, hanging down with a bow in it.'

When he had gone out of the room, Poppy held it up and looked at it. This was a little girl's dress, gathered into a yoke and falling straight. It might just about go over her shoulders, but it would only come down to her knees. Poppy flung it down in disgust. She was not going to wear it, and she was not going to unpin her hair and tie a bow in it.

Mr Hetherington came back in to the room.

'Why haven't you changed?'

'I don't want to wear it.'

'What do you – ?'

'It's daft. I'm not a little girl. Why don't you take a picture of me like this, like I really am?'

She posed with her hands on her hips, sideways on, looking at him along her shoulder. She smiled the sort of smile that the girls at work used when they wanted to send the lads wild.

'No!' He stood in the doorway, shaking. His face was deathly pale. He waved a hand at her, taking in the green costume with its curving lines and nipped-in waist. 'That's not you. That's a – a travesty. Cheap, vulgar. You are young and fresh. You are untouched. You have the dew of morning still on you. There is nothing of the lies and treachery of woman about you. You are pure, you are – are girlhood personified.'

Poppy was mortally offended. She had made a real effort to look her best today, to look grown-up, and all he wanted was a kid. She thought of the messy business of the monthly curse. Then she thought of the whistles she had provoked on the way over, and of the boys and the young men who had asked her out, not to speak of the ones whom she knew would like to but did not dare ask. They would give their right arms to be seen out with her in her new outfit.

So why was Mr Hetherington making all this fuss? She looked at him, and saw a small, round-shouldered man with sweat standing out on his forehead and eyes wide with outrage. And as she looked, she knew that their positions had been reversed, that they were no longer teacher and pupil but man and woman, and it was she who held the power. It went straight to her head.

She took a deep breath, throwing out her meagre breasts, then let it out, smoothing her hands down over her hips and thighs.

'I'm not,' she said, holding him with her eyes. 'I'm not a little girl, and you know it. Look at me.'

She swayed before him, smiling, forcing him to acknowledge her woman's body. She tingled with the excitement of it.

'I'm better than all those silly old photographs. They're just pictures.'

She wanted something from him. She hardly knew what, but some word, some action, that showed she roused the right reactions in him. For a moment she thought she saw it in his face, the gleam of animal desire. She pouted and blew a little kiss, to encourage him.

His whole body contorted in revulsion. A choking cry was torn from him.

'Whore! Jezebel! How could you? How could you do this, destroy everything? Everything we did – filthy, contaminated . . .'

Poppy stared at him, horrified. She did not know what she had done.

'But – I only –'

'Out, get out!' He shrank from her, pointing at the stairs. 'Filth, dirt – get out of my sight!'

Anger swept over her. 'I'm not, I'm not filth, or dirt, or a whore. What about all them photos, eh, the ones you got in your bedroom? They ain't right, not where you got 'em. It's creepy, that's what it is. They always said you was creepy, and they was right.'

With a howl he backed away from her and plunged into the back room. Pulled as if by a string, Poppy followed him.

'Spoilt – spoilt – horrible –'

He was tearing the pictures down from the walls, ripping them up, flinging them on the floor.

Fear started in the pit of Poppy's stomach, smothering the anger, leaving her bare and defenceless in the face of madness. She spun round and made a bolt for the stairs, her boots slipping and clattering as she pelted down. The cries of despair followed her, snapping at her heels. She wrenched at the front door, pulled it open and escaped, running off down the street as if the hounds of hell were after her, running until her legs ached and her lungs felt as if they were about to burst.

She leant against a factory wall, doubled up, gasping. Never, never was she going back there again. He was mad, barking mad. Then she gave a long drawn-out moan.

'You idiot. You fool,' she cursed herself.

For she had left her father's saxophone behind.

PART TWO

The Half Moon Club

8

1917

It was past midnight and the cigarette smoke in the basement club was as thick as a pea-souper fog. Or gunsmoke over the Somme. Joe Chaplin, coughing as he tapped away at his drums, knew that it was doing his damaged lungs no good.

'Get an outside job if you can, one with plenty of seaside or country air.' That was what the doctor had said to him when he was discharged from the army. Joe had thought about it. He even made a few enquiries. There were plenty of farmers wanting labour, with all the able-bodied men away at the Front. They were even employing women. But Joe was not cut out for that sort of work. He had drifted back here to London, where he had gravitated to Archer Street as inevitably as a compass needle finding north. Then, of course, it was only a matter of time before he had got in with some old acquaintances, and found himself a place in a three-piece band whose drummer had finally been caught by the army. They had a regular booking at the Half Moon Club and on the very first evening he'd met his fate. He'd thought he had met it already, when the gas attack caught him with a defective mask. But he'd survived that, just. Survived it in order to meet her. Poppy Powers.

His eyes followed her as she moved amongst the tables, her round tray balanced on the tips of her fingers. As always, she was smiling, laughing, giving as good as she got from the customers. Joe watched as she leant over, placing full glasses on a tiny table, giving a group the impression that she was there for them alone. There were plenty of other women in the club, dubious ones picked up for the night by men out on a spree, more respectable girls making the most of the brief time

71

with their sweethearts, and, of course, the other waitresses, but for Joe there was only one. To come here each night, to be in the same room, gave meaning to Joe's life.

'Going to be a long one tonight,' Charlie the banjoist said, with the deep gloom of the confirmed pessimist. He snatched the cigarette from where he had jammed it between the strings and took a deep drag. 'They're all set to stay till dawn, this lot.'

'Give 'em a burst of "Alexander"'s and we'll take a break. We've done more than an hour and a half nonstop,' said Bob the pianist.

The trio launched into 'Alexander's Ragtime Band' and the audience joined in, singing, stamping, banging their glasses on the tables. The dancers on the minute floor jigged up and down like marionettes. There were whistles and yells of 'More!' as the last notes died. Bob stood up, waved both hands, yelled above the noise that they would be back in ten minutes. All three musicians flexed weary muscles and made thankfully for the bar.

Joe waited for Poppy to appear.

She came tripping across the clearing dance floor towards him, her tray piled high with empties.

'Rowdy lot here tonight,' he said to her. 'You all right?'

'Oh, they're fine. They're enjoying themselves.'

He could feel her hip jammed up against his as she dumped the tray on the bar.

'If there's any trouble – I saw that lot over in the corner –'

'They meant no harm. Nothing I can't handle.' She leant across to the barman. 'Two pints of mild, three whiskies, three gin-and-its and a port and lemon, please, Jimmy.'

But Joe had been watching the table in question, four army officers on leave who were getting steadily drunker as the night went on.

'I don't like the way they keep pawing you. You've only got to say –'

'Thanks, Joe. You're a sweetie. But Jimmy here'll throw 'em out if they get too much, won't you, Jim?'

The barman nodded. 'Trust me, Poppy.'

Joe felt crushed. Jim the barman was an ex-boxer, too old to be called up but still massively muscled. Of course Poppy could call on him rather than a drummer with only half his lungs working.

She was loading the full glasses onto the tray. Joe tried another tack.

'Time for one for yourself?'

She glanced over to where Mr Fairbrother, the boss, was standing by the entrance.

'Just let me take this lot over, and I will. I'm parched.'

Joe's heart soared. He watched her all the way to the table, unaware of the grins around him.

'– trying, Joe.'

'What?'

Charlie and Bob were shaking their heads at him.

'Don't give up easy, do you, boy?'

'Six months, and has she given him more than a word?'

Jim gave the bar top a wipe over. 'Ah, let him alone. He's got taste, ain't you, Joe? If I was twenty years younger I'd be fighting you for her.'

Charlie, a disillusioned man with a shrew of a wife and five children to support, was not to be put off his fun.

'No good having taste if you ain't got a chance. I mean, look at 'em in here. Officers, most of 'em, and falling over 'emselves to take her out. Got her pick, she has. What've you got to offer, eh?'

'More than a few days' leave, that's what,' Joe told him. He kept that thought in his mind as he saw a young subaltern hold Poppy's arm and talk to her earnestly, gazing up at her with a longing that Joe recognized all too well. He found he was holding his breath until he saw Poppy shake her head and disengage the man's hand.

'See?' he said in triumph to Charlie. 'She's got more sense than to fall for any bloody toff's line.'

Jimmy lined a lemonade up for her. Joe got her a bar stool. She perched on it with a sigh of relief.

'Just what I wanted.' The lemonade went down in the space of five seconds. She smacked her lips. 'Lovely. I needed that. Thanks, Joe.'

He nodded and smiled and began to say that it was his pleasure, when he was seized with a coughing fit. He doubled over, gasping, his lungs labouring to drag in air while the terrible fear of suffocation gripped him. His chest heaved, but nothing seemed to be going in. He could not even cry out, for he had no breath to do it. Then through the nightmare came a soothing voice – Poppy's – and a hand rubbing and patting him between the shoulderblades and at once, miraculously, the spasm eased until after what seemed like an age he could sit upright again. He sat panting shallowly, his eyes streaming, letting the thudding of his heart subside.

'Poor old Joe. Better now?' Her voice was full of concern. His back was warm where her hand still rested. He wanted it to stay there for ever.

'Nearly,' he croaked.

She gave him one more little pat and took her hand away. He felt bereft.

'Bloody cripple,' Charlie muttered.

Poppy sprang up, hands on hips. 'Just you say that again!' she demanded. 'Joe's in this state because he went out to fight for his country, for people like you and your kids. You ought to be grateful to him. I've not seen you make any effort to get in the army.'

'I'm too old,' Charlie growled.

'Rubbish. They're taking men older than you now. You want to watch it. Conscription'll catch up with you if you're not careful. Come on, you apologize to Joe.'

Charlie shot a look of pure malice at Joe.

'What's the matter? You sweet on him or something?'

Joe swallowed. There was a pounding in his head as he waited for her reply.

'I don't like hearing sour old men like you making fun of heroes like Joe.'

'Heroes!' Charlie's voice was heavy with sarcasm.

But Joe hardly heard him. He looked at Poppy, standing there so fierce and fiery in her defence of him, and knew the first heady notes of real hope.

Poppy walked briskly along Shaftesbury Avenue in the autumn twilight. The streetlamps were already lit and the theatres were ablaze. The pavements thronged with people all eager to forget the horrors of the war for a while and enjoy a good night out. Poppy felt part of it, the fun and fantasy of theatreland. She might be only a waitress in a drinking club, but she was doing her bit. And who knew? It might lead to better things. She held on just a little tighter to the handle of her saxophone case.

It had grieved her terribly to give up her father's beloved sax, but nothing would have induced her to go back and claim it from Mr Hetherington. So once more she had had to save up. All her tips from the Corner House went into a special fund until she had enough to buy a replacement. It was actually a better instrument than the first one, tenor as opposed to her dad's Lafleur alto, with a more mellow tone, but it never held quite the same place in her heart.

She turned down the narrow side street and stopped at a blue painted door sandwiched between an Italian grocery store and a French restaurant. The sign above her head was a painting of a half-moon with the word 'Club' underneath. Poppy knocked loudly on the door and waited. It always took a long time for them to let her in.

'Poppy!'

Round the corner came a stocky girl with a dark, intense face, and very straight eyebrows. She was carrying a banjo case.

'Mona!'

They hugged each other.

'How are you? I'm so glad you could come.'

'I've only got half an hour before I go to work.'

'We'll show those men how to really play ragtime, eh?'

'You bet.'

75

Jimmy opened the door at last and the smell of the club rushed up and folded round them – damp and sweat and smoke and alcohol. Poppy breathed it in with pleasure. It was the smell of possibilities. The two girls clattered down the steep stairs, exchanging news and gossip.

'You're early,' Mr Fairbrother said. He looked Mona up and down. 'Who's she?'

'Friend of mine. We're going to have a little jam session before the place opens up.'

The boss's face tightened. 'Who says?'

Poppy flashed him her best smile. 'Oh, come on now. You don't mind us having a quick tootle, do you? We sound as good as we look, I promise.'

She looked at him slightly sideways, using the teasing expression that she knew worked with nearly all men.

'Well – as long as you pack up when the customers start arriving.'

'Thanks, Mr Fairbrother. You're the best.'

The two girls tuned up, while the rest of the staff watched with patronizing smiles on their faces. Poppy had let drop that she played the saxophone, but had been met with only suppressed amusement. Then a few days ago she had run in to Mona, with whom she used to work at the Lyons Corner House. They both had dreams of becoming professional players.

'Pity your friend Elsie couldn't come,' Mona said, as she tightened the last string.

'Yeah. A trumpet would of made us into a proper band. But she's working overtime on the munitions. You should see the money she earns!'

'Ain't it turned her face yellow?'

'Yeah. She looks really odd. But they say it'll wear off.'

'You wouldn't get me working on them things. Not for all the tea in China. I don't want my face turned yellow or my hands blown off.'

'Me neither. But she's brave, is Elsie, in her own quiet way. And you should see how the money's made a difference to her! Her mum and dad can't tell her what to do like they used to.

She just points out who's paying the biggest slice of the housekeeping and does what she likes.'

'Good for her. You ready? What do we both know?'

' "Maple Leaf"? Can you do that?'

They swung into the tune, unsteadily at first, unaccustomed to each other's style and speed. There was a ripple of amusement round the club. The men exchanged grins as drinks were carried in, glasses were polished, tables and chairs set out. Just as they had expected, young Poppy and her fierce-looking friend were complete amateurs, just playing around. There was a spatter of applause as they finished the first number, not derisive, but indulgent.

'That was pretty blooming awful,' said Mona. 'Let's try something else.'

'No.' Poppy was seething. She was going to wipe those silly smiles off the men's faces if it was the last thing she did. They were going to really clap, from admiration. 'No, we'll get it right. Nobody's perfect first time. We'll do it both together until it flows, then we'll start arranging it.'

Mona raised her expressive dark eyebrows at this decision. 'Yes, sir!' she said with heavy sarcasm.

Poppy ignored her. She knew what she wanted.

'Ready? One, two, and –'

This time, they worked together better. They tried again, until they were both easy with it, then they started to have fun. Signalling to each other with nods and looks, they took turns to play rhythm and melody, throwing the tune back and forth to each other. Poppy felt the pressure of excitement building, the thrill and the danger. They had it, they were keeping it afloat like a child's balloon.

There was a stunned silence as they finished, then a ponderous clapping from Mr Fairbrother. He lit his first cigar of the evening and sat down at one of the tables.

'Nice little party piece, girls. What else do you do? Walk on your hands?'

'We'd have to walk on water to impress you, wouldn't we?' Poppy said.

They tried another number, but it did not work as well as the 'Maple Leaf Rag'.

'We need some rhythm. Do you know any drummers?' she asked.

Mona shook her head. 'Not girls, anyway.'

Then Poppy caught sight of Joe Chaplin standing by the bar looking at her. She had not noticed him come in.

'Hey, Joe! We need a drummer. Come and join us.'

He lit up as if a lamp had been switched on inside him. The others hooted and whistled.

Joe hunched his shoulders and came over. He stopped in front of her and held her eyes.

'I'll play with you, but on one condition,' he said, so low that Poppy could hardly catch what he said.

'Oh yeah, and what's that?'

'That you come out with me tomorrow afternoon.'

He'd asked her several times before, but she'd turned him down. Now, riding high on the excitement of making music, she forgot the reasons she'd had for saying no in the past.

'You're on. Come on –'

'You mean it?'

'Yeah, of course. I said yes, didn't I? Now come and play.'

With the drums to hold them together, they worked better. 'Fifth Avenue Rag' sparkled into life. Poppy was triumphant.

'We got it! That was the beginnings of something good. I tell you, if we keep practising, we'll soon knock spots off the lot that usually plays here.'

The first drinkers of the evening were beginning to arrive. Mona put her banjo away in its case.

'That's all very well, but the blooming Huns'll have to kill off every musician in the business before we'll get any work.'

Poppy was not to be put off.

'We'll see,' she said. 'We'll do it again, eh? And I'll try and get Elsie down here and all.'

Bob and Charlie arrived and began setting up. Poppy stowed her sax behind the drums and made to go and get her frilly apron on. She was stopped by a hand on her elbow. It was Joe.

'Don't forget. Tomorrow afternoon.'

She had almost forgotten her reckless promise. But looking at Joe's anxious face, she hadn't the heart to back out. He had a nice face. There was something about his mouth that reminded her a bit of her dad.

'Tomorrow afternoon,' she agreed, and went to get ready for the long night ahead.

9

As always, the evening started slowly. The bulk of the clientele went to the theatre or a restaurant first, then came on to the Half Moon Club. Poppy spent a lot of her time up to about ten o'clock listening to men with hollow eyes and haunted faces tell her the story of their lives. Some of them were only a year or so older than herself. She nodded and said 'Yes' and 'No' in the right places, and made sympathetic comments, though often the short years they told her about seemed to be full of laughter and sunshine. They had been brought up in a very different world to that of Dog Island. But they never told her what was really gnawing at them. That was what they were hoping to forget, trying to fill the short days of their leave with enough alcohol and nonstop entertainment to dull the knowledge that they had to go back.

One boy with baby blue eyes and a soft down of a blond moustache held her hand as he recounted stroke by stroke the Eton versus Harrow cricket match at which he had made thirty-two runs. Poppy laughed and clapped as he described a stunning boundary.

'You're a wunnerful girl,' he slurred, downing his sixth brandy. 'You make me laugh. Will you come out with me t'morrow? We could have tea at the Ritz. Go dancing. You do that? Please?'

Poppy patted his hand and gently extracted hers from his grasp.

'You're very sweet,' she said, 'but I got a young man already. He's at the Front.' It was her standard escape line. Most of them respected it. They still believed in honour.

The place was filling up now. The theatres were closing and groups coming down the stairs, laughing and chattering and singing snatches from the reviews and the musical comedies they had watched. Poppy could see other drinkers impatient to be served.

The band were taking a break when she went over to the bar with her next order. Joe was spitting feathers.

'What's that swine doing slobbering all over you? I'll smash his face in.'

Poppy was about to say 'What's it to you?' when she remembered her promise of earlier that evening.

'Oh, lay off, Joe. He's only a kid. And he's got to go back to the Front the day after tomorrow. You of all people should know what that means.'

'Yeah, well – it still don't give him the right to hold your hand.'

One of the other waitresses arrived, dumping an over-loaded tray of empties on the bar.

'Hey, Poppy, there's a crowd of Doughboys come in.'

'Americans? Where?' They'd not had any Yankees in before.

'Corner table.'

There were half a dozen of them, and they were in her section of the club. She hurried back with her order, then went on to their table.

'Welcome to the Half Moon Club,' she said. 'What can I get you?'

'You can come and sit on my knee.'

'You got some friends as cute as you? You can get them and forget the drinks.'

Poppy hardly heard them. The jumble of faces and voices blurred. There was just one clear spot, from which two dark brown eyes that looked almost black in the dim light looked back at her. Around them was a rough-hewn face surmounted by neatly parted dark hair. A firm mouth smiled at her. Then he frowned and turned to his companions.

'Hey, cut that out, you guys. This here's a respectable place and this young lady's a waitress, not a so-called hostess.'

He returned to Poppy. 'You gotta make allowances for them, miss. They've never been to England before.'

He had a dark brown voice to go with his eyes, and that fascinating accent. She had never heard it before.

'Oh, that's all right. We get them all in here.' It sounded so dull, when she wanted to say something to slay him. She did not usually have a problem with words. 'It – it's lovely to have you Yankees over here. Is it true what they say? That you're going to help us win this war?'

His eyes crinkled up at the corners when he smiled.

'We sure are, miss. All be sewn up in six months from now.'

There was a chorus of agreement from his friends. Poppy began to regain a little of her usual spark.

'That's what everyone here said when it first started. All be over by Christmas, they said.'

'But you didn't have us on your side then.'

'And that's going to make the difference?'

'You just watch us. Those Fritzes'll melt away like snow in the sunshine and before you know where you are your sweetheart'll be marching home to you.'

'That'll be difficult, seeing as I ain't got a sweetheart.'

There was a stir of sharpened interest round the table. One of the others broke in.

'Well, I say that's a shameful waste. Here's six fellows ready and willing to fill that gap.' They introduced themselves, falling over each other in an effort to impress her. All except the one she was interested in. He was sitting back watching them with an amused smile on his face.

'Now I know all your friends' names, but you ain't told me yours,' Poppy said.

He stood up and held out his hand. 'Scott Warrender, at your service.'

Scott Warrender. His name was as exotic and fascinating as his accent. What was more, it was the first time anybody had ever introduced themselves to her like that, formally. Charmed, Poppy shook his hand. His grip was firm and warm.

'And are we allowed to know who you are?'

'Poppy – Poppy Powers.'

82

'Delighted to make your acquaintance, Miss Powers.'

The atmosphere was shattered by one of the other waitresses hissing at her as she passed by. 'You better get a move on. The boss is looking murder at you.'

Scott Warrender refused to let her get into trouble because of him. He ordered for the whole table.

Back at the bar, she was intercepted by Mr Fairbrother.

'There's three more tables waiting for you. You're not here to gossip, you're here to sell drinks.'

'All right, all right. I'll get to them. But I got to keep our brave allies happy, ain't I?'

'You better think first about keeping me happy, girl.'

Poppy was not frightened. She knew she could charm more doubles out of the clientele than either of the other girls. And even if she had thought that she was in imminent danger of getting the sack, nothing would have kept her from going straight back to the Americans, or rather, to that one American.

'There we are, Lieutenant. Scotch and water. Sorry about the ice. Maybe if we get more of your lot in here the boss'll think about getting an icebox.'

'Honey, so long as you serve it, I don't care if it comes with tomato ketchup.'

Things like that had been said to her practically every night, but this time it mattered desperately that he meant it.

For the rest of the night she worked in a daze, attending to the other tables but always gravitating back to Scott. The only thing that mattered was that she should be near to him. They said nothing of any importance, joking and point-scoring for the benefit of his friends, and yet every word he spoke was like Holy Writ to her, to be treasured up and remembered.

Around them it was turning out to be a good night. People were intent on squeezing the last ounce of pleasure out of the precious minutes, the drink was flowing fast enough to satisfy even Mr Fairbrother, the band was on good form and the dance floor was overflowing. Sometime in the small hours, Scott caught Poppy's hand as she returned to him from serving another table.

'Say, are you allowed to dance with the customers?'

Poppy's heart turned a somersault. 'No, but who cares?'

'If there's trouble with your boss, I'll square it with him.' Scott stood up. 'That is, if you'd care to dance?'

In answer, she put her tray down on the table. The other Americans whistled and cheered. Scott's fingers laced with hers and they wove their way between the chairs to the floor. He swung her round to face him and took her in a close dance hold.

'I've been wanting to do this since the moment I saw you,' he said in her ear.

'Oh yeah? That's what they all say.'

'The difference is, I mean it.'

She hoped desperately that it was true.

There were far too many couples on the minute floor to be able to dance properly, so they simply held on tight to each other, shuffling in time to the music. Poppy moved within a small enchanted space, aware only of the well of excitement inside her and Scott's overwhelming physical presence, his arm around her back, his hand clasping hers, his body touching hers. There was the texture of his khaki uniform, his strong shoulder beneath her hand, his breath on her cheek. The band was playing a popular romantic song, and some of the revellers were joining in. The words and music wrapped around her: *Be always here, be always mine* – She wanted to stay for always right there, where she belonged.

She hardly heard the spatter of applause as the tune ended. Then Scott gave her a brief hug and let her go.

'I guess I better let you get back to work. But I'll be watching you, mind. I'll be watching every move you make.'

When Joe said things like that, it irritated her. From Scott, it made her feel cared for and secure.

'I'll remember,' she said.

She moved about the club in a haze of unreality, a foolish happy smile on her face. The pointed remarks of the other waitresses, the boss's anger at her breaking the rules, Joe's fury at seeing her get up and dance with one of the customers, all bounced harmlessly off the protective shell of happiness she wore about her.

It was gone three in the morning before the night began to wind down, and nearer four as the place began to empty. The band packed up, the girls collected the empties, half a dozen groups of determined drinkers ignored the warning signs and demanded refills. At Scott's table, two of his companions were asleep with their heads amongst the glasses and ashtrays, the other three were making ready to go. Suddenly afraid, Poppy went over to clear up.

'Are you going to be here much longer?' Scott asked.

Poppy looked around, assessing the situation.

'Depends how soon we get rid of this lot. Half an hour, maybe.'

Half an hour, and he would be gone.

'Can I walk you home?'

In a haze of happiness, she agreed.

The time stretched endlessly as the chairs were put up, the floor swept, the last customers helped on their way out into the street. Joe was lingering long after the other two band members had gone.

'Remember tomorrow – tomorrow afternoon?' he said to her.

'Yeah, yeah – ' she hardly heard him. She emptied the last ashtray, wiped the last table.

'I'll meet you at the Marble Arch gate off Hyde Park, at half past two. We can go for a walk, then have tea. That all right?'

'Yeah, fine.' She took her cloth and rubbish bucket back to the tiny cubbyhole that served as both washroom and cleaning cupboard.

'You won't forget, will you? Half past two.'

'No, no –'

Why didn't he just go? Scott was waiting for her outside. Her whole being was aching to be with him again. Joe hovered behind her, repeating himself. She answered at random. At last he went, seemingly satisfied.

Mr Fairbrother told them they could go. Poppy flung off her

apron, grabbed her coat and saxophone case and was up the stairs before he had even finished speaking.

The cold of the November night hit her. She stood for a moment, blinded and helpless after the heat and light of the club. The street seemed deserted. Fear's chill fingers started to curl round her heart. He was not there. Then a shadow detached itself from the darkness, took her coat from her and held it out for her to put on.

'You'll catch your death, as my ma used to say.'

She relaxed and laughed, leaning against his hands as he rested them on her shoulders.

'My mum says that and all.'

'That's one thing we got in common, then. Say, what's this you got here? A valise? You running away?'

'What? Oh – no, it's my sax.'

'Your sax? You play the saxophone?'

'That's right.'

He picked up the case, offered her his arm. Charmed, Poppy tucked her hand inside his elbow.

'You'll have to tell me which way to go. Is it far? I hope so.'

'I usually get the first workmen's tram,' Poppy told him, before she could stop herself.

'To hell with that – begging your pardon – we'll find a cab. Are you tired?'

Generally she was worn out at the end of a night spent on her feet, wanting only to crawl into bed and sleep the sleep of the dead. But tonight she could have run all the way to Scotland and back.

'No, not a bit. I'm fine.'

'You're tougher than me, then. When I was waiting tables I was washed out by the time I finished.'

'You? A waiter? But you're an officer.'

'Don't mean a thing, honey. My folks keep a hardware store in upstate Pennsylvania. I worked my way through college.'

'Oh – ' It was like a foreign language, but she did get the gist of it. 'So you're not from some posh family, then?'

'Nope. You disappointed?'

'Oh, no. You didn't think – ' She stopped short, horrified. 'You didn't think I was just after you for your money, did you? It wasn't that at all. I don't usually go out with the customers. I mean, they're very nice, some of them, and they want a bit of company while they're on leave and all that, but they all think that because you work in a club you're – you know –'

'That sort of girl?'

'Yeah.'

'And you're not?'

'No.' But oh, with him she'd be very tempted. She covered it up with a great show of virtue. 'So if that's what you were thinking, hard luck, mate.'

They were standing slightly apart. It was so dark that she could not see the expression on his face. Maybe he did just pick her up because he thought a club waitress was one step up from a street walker.

In answer, Scott took her hand and tucked it back in the crook of his arm.

'The thought never crossed my mind. I'll bet you got a ma and a pa and a whole tribe of big brothers at home looking out for you.'

'Not quite.'

'Come on, then, tell me about yourself. I'll guess you're a Londoner born and bred. What do they call it? A cockney?'

Poppy was walking on air. None of the officers in the Half Moon had ever asked her about herself. She found herself telling him about Dog Island and the lodging house and Gran and Mum, about Dad and the long-lost good times they had had, about the pawn ticket and the saxophone, about Elsie and the Salvation Army band.

At the bridge over the old entrance to the West India Dock, she stopped. Around them, the great mass of the East End was stirring into life as another working day began. Out on the crowded waters of the grey Thames, lamps glowed on the myriad ships and boats, the barges and lighters taking the first of the tide downriver. The familiar smells drifted on the damp air. Above them, the sky was just beginning to lighten. Poppy took it all in with a new heightened awareness. This was her place, and she loved it, warts and all. She indicated the low-lying expanse of the Isle of Dogs with a jerk of the head.

'I live over there. I can take myself the last bit.'

'You'll do no such thing. I said I'd walk you home.'

'No!' She could just see Gran's face if she turned up with an American officer in tow. 'My Gran – she thinks all men are evil. You know – only after one thing.'

'Why don't you introduce me? I'll convince her I'm a model citizen.'

'No, really. She wouldn't like you. She doesn't like anyone.'

'How do you get away with working in a club?'

'She doesn't know what I do. I say it's my war work.'

Scott threw back his head and laughed. 'War work! I like it. You're a case, Poppy Powers. I'd like to see you again tomorrow. What do you say? Will you take me around and show me the town?'

Poppy's heart sang. There was nothing she would rather do. They arranged the time and place, then he turned her gently to face him and kissed her on the forehead.

'Till tomorrow, Poppy.'

'Till tomorrow.'

10

The war highlighted Jane's solitary status. At first, she thought that now lots of her friends had husbands away from home, she would feel more at one with them, but it was not so. They all shared the burning worry of what was happening to their men at the Front, the joy of receiving letters home, the hope of a leave and a brief time together, whereas Jane experienced none of it. Only a nagging worry that Owen might have been called up, might even now be in France somewhere, might be lying injured. She listened sympathetically to the others, poured over battle reports with them, and when their men's regiments were mentioned, worried with them until news came. She held shocked and grief-stricken women when the dreaded telegrams arrived. She sewed mourning clothes for free. She made endless cups of tea. But still she did not quite feel that she belonged.

It would have been different if she had had a son, but a daughter working in a servicemen's canteen did not have the same sympathy value as a son at the Front.

Not that Poppy wasn't a worry. All this working at night was not good for her. She came home reeking of smoke, which did not surprise Jane, since everyone smoked like chimneys these days, but there was also a whiff of booze about her as well. She smelt as if she had been working in a pub more than a canteen.

'Do they serve drinks in this place of yours?' she asked once.

'No. Why?'

'Only I thought I could smell it on you. Not beer, more like the hard stuff. Whisky. Brandy.'

Poppy had her back to her at the time. She was hanging up her working clothes.

'Oh – lots of them have been drinking before they come in. Off back to France, you know.'

When she asked why it was that Poppy was on permanent night shift, she was told that the money was better. There was no arguing with that, but still she had a feeling of unease about Poppy's job. If she tried to dig any further, Poppy just pointed out that it was war work, and they all had to make sacrifices.

Last night, or rather this morning, she had been even later than usual getting home. Jane always woke up at about the time Poppy was due in. This morning it had been nearly time for Jane to get up by the time Poppy slid into bed. She went up to the bedroom at about eleven to get some thread, and found her wide awake and bright-eyed.

'You was late in,' she remarked. 'You all right?'

Poppy sat up. 'What time is it?'

'It's only eleven. You just stay there and have a good rest.'

'I'm not tired. I got to go out.'

Jane looked at her, frowning. 'Why? You don't never go out at this time.'

'I'm going to meet a friend.'

Something about the way she said it set alarm signals going in Jane's heart, but she did not know quite how to get at the cause. Instead she sat down on the bed and watched as Poppy riffled through her scant selection of clothes. To keep her daughter's attention, she began talking about all the other things that worried her.

'At least with this job of yours you're not around when them Zepp raids is on. You never know when they might send another one over. Wicked. All them little children killed at that school.'

'Mmm, I know. Wicked. What d'you think, Mum, this one, or this one?'

She displayed two dresses before her mother. One was a nicer colour, but the other was more fashionable, cut full and at the new short length, showing the ankles, or even the calves when it swished out. Jane nodded at it.

'That one. Suits you, that does.'

'You sure? Right. I'll go and wash.'

Jane wanted to hold her there.

'I was talking to Daisy Hodges yesterday,' she said, bringing up the first thing that came into her head. 'You know, Daisy Johnson as was. Ain't never heard her so low before. I think it's not having no kids. It's not quite so bad losing a man if you got something of his to carry him on like.'

'Yeah, I suppose so. Poor Daisy, she always used to be such fun. Gran in or out?'

'Out. Gone up the shops.'

'Good.'

She scampered out of the room and down the stairs. Jane waited for her to come back.

'That Maisie Johnson got a letter this morning, poor soul,' she said. 'Her Will's been wounded again. In hospital in some place in France, he is. That makes three in the street just in this one week. If it goes on like this, there won't be any men left.'

Poppy slid her arms into the dress.

'Don't worry, Mum. We got the Americans on our side now. It'll all be over in six months. Here, do us up down the back, will you?'

Jane obediently did up all the tiny buttons, then watched as Poppy bounced up and went to look at herself in the mirror. Then she skipped across the room and flung her arms round her mother.

'Oh, Mum, ain't everything wonderful?'

Jane knew for sure then. She hugged her daughter, then held her at arms'-length, searching the shining eyes.

'What's his name, lovey?'

Poppy blushed, and giggled. 'Oh, dear. I didn't want to worry you, but – oh, Mum, he's called Scott, Scott Warrender. He's an American and he's wonderful – you won't tell Gran, will you?'

'Of course not, dear. But – you will take care, won't you?'

'Don't worry, Mum, I'm quite all right.' She packed her black working dress into a bag and pulled on her boots. She dropped a kiss onto Jane's head. ''Bye, Mum. I don't think I'll be in for dinner or tea.'

Jane sat and listened as her footsteps clattered downstairs. The front door slammed and she was gone.

It had to happen sometime, she supposed. The strange thing was that it had taken this long. Jane had always been surprised that such a pretty girl did not seem to take much of an interest in the boys. But now – an American. No good telling her not to lose her heart, that it would all end in tears. Jane remembered what it was like to feel like that. You never listened to what anyone said by way of a warning. All she could do was wait to pick up the pieces.

When Poppy got to Trafalgar Square, Scott was there already, waiting for her. He looked so tall and handsome and distinguished there, in his uniform cap and greatcoat, that her heart nearly stood still. Of all the girls in London, he had chosen her. Then he caught sight of her and waved, and started over to meet her.

'It's good to see you again. I was half afraid you'd disappear into your Dog Island and never come back.' Scott took her by the shoulders and held her, slowly taking all of her in. He said softly, 'You look good enough to eat.'

Poppy wanted to hold him like she had on the dance floor, to feel his body close to hers. But here they were in Trafalgar Square at midday, so instead she gave a look of surprise.

'Oh, they got cannibals in Penn-whatsit, then?'

'Pennsylvania. And for all I know, they might well have up in the mountains. But I guess that wouldn't be such a great idea. I like you just as you are. How about us grabbing a bite of lunch, and then you can show me the town.'

They found a small restaurant and were shown to a table for two. It was unlike anywhere Poppy had ever been before. The cutlery, the napery, the sparkling wine glasses and the waiter could all have come out of a house in Mayfair. The rest of the clientele looked as if they definitely had. Poppy was impressed, but she would have been just as happy sitting on the kerb eating a cheese sandwich, just as long as she was with Scott.

'I told you all about me and my family. Now it's your turn.'

She sat putting food into her mouth and hardly noticing what it was as she listened to his descriptions of his home town. If the tales of nannies and boarding schools that she had heard at the club were a foreign place to her, then this was another world. Just as Scott had told her, he was no pampered rich kid. He had had to do chores before and after school, helping his father in the store while his two sisters helped their mother in the house. But it was nothing like the poverty she had been surrounded by as she grew up. When the winter came and there was deep snow on the ground for weeks, there was always a big stove throwing out heat when he came in from tobogganing with his friends, and in the summer, while children in Trinidad Street had only the filthy waters of the Thames to paddle in, he swam in the stream or went on expeditions to the mountains. It sounded an idyllic life.

Around them, the rest of the diners left and the waiters began to clear the tables. Oblivious, they sat on, until a discreet cough made them glance up. The restaurant was empty.

'Oh – ' Poppy giggled and clapped a hand over her mouth. 'We're last. I never noticed.'

'I seem to be spending my time here being swept out of places.' Scott picked up the bill, glanced at it, put down an astonishing amount of money without turning a hair and waved away the change.

'Now,' he said, as they emerged onto the pavement, 'I can't come to England without seeing Buckingham Palace. Is it far?'

'Not very,' Poppy told him.

Poppy did not let on that the palace was one of the few sights she did know how to get to. Some of her friends had hardly been off the Island in their lives. At least she had worked in the West End and theatreland and knew her way about a bit.

They walked arm in arm up The Mall. Scott was disappointed in the Palace, 'I was expecting something more like the Brothers Grimm', but impressed with the Guards. 'Now that's something more like it. A real slice of tradition.'

By the time they had wandered back through St James's Park, the afternoon was beginning to draw in.

'You know,' Scott said, as they watched the ducks scudding across the water, 'it was real frustrating last night sitting there with the band playing and not being able to dance with you.'

Poppy was visited by a flash of inspiration.

'Tea dancing! We could go tea dancing.'

'Say, that's a wonderful idea. Where can we find this tea dancing?'

A scrap of last night's conversations came back to her, from the time, a past age it seemed now, before she met Scott.

'The Ritz.'

'Poppy Powers, you got style. We'll go to the Ritz.'

It was like living in a fairytale. A motor cab whisked them to the door, there were chandeliers, marble floors, palms, obsequious waiters, the thinnest cut sandwiches Poppy had ever seen and a band in a different class altogether from the one at the Half Moon Club.

'Ain't it beautiful?' Poppy said, gazing round. 'I always wondered what these places was like.'

'You've not been here before?'

'Come off it! You seen where I come from.'

'Then it's the first time for both of us. Let's make the most of it.'

They laughed and talked and sipped tea. And they danced. Scott moved with an easy grace, leading with such assurance that Poppy found she could follow the unfamiliar steps without once falling over his feet. It was as if they had danced together every day of their lives.

Scott left her at the door of the Half Moon at seven. They had arranged that he should go back to his hotel to change and come along to the club later. Still drifting in her little bubble of happiness, Poppy went about getting the place ready for the evening, oblivious to the jibes of the rest of the staff. It was not until Joe came in that reality intruded. He marched straight over to her. Poppy gave him a happy smile.

'Hello, Joe. Ain't it a lovely day?'

He ignored her remark. 'So what happened to you?' he demanded.

She could not think what he was talking about. 'What?'

'What happened to you? I waited two hours for you this afternoon. I was worried out of my mind. I thought you'd had an accident or something. And now here you are as right as ninepence. You stood me up.'

'Oh!'

She had forgotten all about her promise to meet him. She was swept by remorse. She did not want to hurt him. In her present mood of euphoria, she wanted everyone to be as happy as she was.

'Oh, Joe, I am sorry. I – I was so tired last night. I was on my last legs, honest I was. I got home and I passed out and I didn't wake up till gone three o'clock. And of course it was much too late to go and meet you then –'

'I was there till four,' Joe said. He did not sound convinced.

'Really? Till four? But I never thought you'd wait that long, Joe. I thought you'd of gone off ages before that.'

Joe hunched his shoulders and looked away.

'Well – so long as that's really what happened –'

Poppy felt a qualm of conscience. Perhaps she should have told him the truth. But then he would have been so upset.

'Look, I got to get these ashtrays out. I'll – er – I'll talk to you later, Joe. All right?'

She busied herself with unnecessary jobs, filling up the time till Scott reappeared, and she could start living again.

The revellers at the Half Moon Club were running out of steam. Scott sat at his table, spinning out the last drink and waiting for everyone to leave. He rolled the whisky over his tongue and watched Poppy as she collected glasses from a nearby group. The taste of Scotch would always remind him of her now, of this smoky little place where they had met. He could hardly believe that it was only three nights ago. He seemed to have packed a lifetime into the short days, to have lived on a higher plane, where everything was shot through with a new depth of meaning. He never dreamt, when first he walked down the stairs of the club, that a girl with Titian hair and a dancing smile waited there to turn him inside out.

She came round by way of his table.

'How are you?'

'Lonesome.'

He laid a hand briefly on her thigh, feeling the warmth of her body beneath the thin layers of fabric. She looked down at him, her sweet lips parted, and he was seized with the desire to pull her down onto his lap, take her in his arms and kiss her.

'Won't be long now. Twenty minutes or so and this lot'll clear out,' she said, as if reading his mind.

'Can't wait, honey.'

'Be all the better for the keeping,' she said, and went off to the bar.

He followed her with his eyes. Every minute was precious now. His train left from Victoria at eight o'clock.

The band played one last, slightly flat, chord and packed it in for the night. Scott joined in with the tired applause. He did not notice the drummer get up and walk over towards him until a figure appeared at his table.

'It's you, ain't it?'

The man was tight with anger. Scott could see it in every line of his body.

'I beg your pardon?'

'I said, it's you, ain't it? You she's seeing. Poppy.'

Scott held his gaze. He wasn't in the habit of letting people intimidate him. 'So what's it to you, pal?'

'I'm not your pal. And I'll tell you what it is to me. She's my girl, that's what, so you better keep your hands off.'

Scott knew he was taller, fitter, tougher than the other man. He could take him on with one hand behind his back. But he did not want a fight, not in front of Poppy. Instead he leant back, rocking his chair onto two legs, the picture of ease.

'I think we'd better let Poppy be the one to decide what she wants.'

The drummer seemed not to hear him.

96

'You keep your hands off, d'you hear me? You better not show your face down here again or I'll –'

'Yeah? You'll what? Let's hear it.'

'I'll push your bloody face in, that's what. I'll –'

He was interrupted by the barman, who took him by the arm.

'Knock it off, Joe. You start threatening the customers and you won't never work here again. Come on, out, before you get y'self into trouble.'

The drummer was escorted, protesting, up the stairs and ejected into the night. Scott sketched a mock salute of farewell. The poor sap. He would feel the same if someone muscled in on Poppy.

He gave the man time to get going, then left the club himself, with a quick exchange of glances with Poppy to let her know he would be waiting for her outside. It was a cold clear night, with stars sparkling in a frosty sky. Scott turned up his collar and thrust his hands into his pockets. A stranger in a strange land, he felt curiously at home. Ever since he had left Birch Springs six years ago, his life had been a series of changes and adaptations. He had taken on Columbia University, New York, the bank and the jungle of Wall Street. When the United States joined the war in Europe, he was amongst the first to volunteer, and found himself pitched into the discipline of army life, then the journey to France and training and manoeuvres in Lorraine. But never since growing up had he felt so right as he did here in this sprawling, dirty old city with Poppy by his side. It was as if she was the missing piece of himself. The restless need to move on to new challenges had died. He wanted just to stay here for ever, next to her.

The door of the club opened and there she was, flushed from the heat within, bright-eyed with expectation. He drew her into his arms, feeling the pliancy of her slender body against him, and kissed her with a desperate passion, wanting to possess her, to make her part of him. When at last their lips drew apart, she laid her head on his shoulder and held him tight.

'What's the matter?' she asked.

He marvelled that she should read him so accurately. There was no point in trying to hide it.

'I'm going back today,' he admitted.

'*What?*' She went stiff in his arms, then clung to him with renewed fierceness. 'Oh, Scott, why didn't you tell me before?'

He stroked her hair, kissed the top of her head. She seemed small and infinitely vulnerable.

'I didn't want to spoil it.'

'What time?'

'Eight o'clock from Victoria.'

'That's it then. I'm not going home. I'll stay with you.'

'But honey, it's gone four o'clock.'

She said nothing, but looked up at him with a world of love in her eyes. The new possibility spread through his veins like fire. It would be easy enough to smuggle her up to his hotel bedroom.

'What's your old grandma going to say?' he said.

'I don't care. I want to be with you every last minute.'

'Oh, Poppy darling –'

They kissed again, trying with lips and tongues to hold at bay the moment of parting. Four hours, time and enough. But she was only seventeen and he had nothing to offer her. It was only a matter of time before they were sent to the Front, and then he could be dead within a week. He just couldn't do it, however much he wanted to.

'You're the best thing that ever happened to me,' he said, and reluctantly began to walk slowly in the opposite direction from the hotel.

There were other people awake in the sleeping city. Covent Garden was alive with shouts and naphtha flares and piles of brightly coloured fruit and vegetables. Scott bought a bunch of tightly curled red rosebuds. Poppy held them to her nose, for the first time fighting back tears.

A cab drivers' smoky little café offered a haven of warmth. They sat at a table sticky with sugar and scattered with cigarette ash, and drank thick sweet tea out of chipped china cups.

'Bit different from the Ritz,' Poppy said, with a visible effort at cheer.

'Yeah, I can't see this lot getting up and doing the two-step.'

It was light by the time they arrived at the Embankment. They sat on a seat with curly dolphin arms and watched the grey Thames rolling by.

'Don't you wish you could just hold on to time?' Poppy said.

'I know what you mean.'

'But it runs away. It's like – like trying to hold water.'

Scott turned her face towards him, printing every feature on his memory.

'I love you, Poppy Powers.'

'I love you, too.'

'I've never known anyone like you, you're something unique. Promise you'll write me, Poppy. It won't be so bad if I can have letters from you. I'll have something of yours to keep then.'

He wrote down the name of his regiment.

'And can I write to you?'

'Oh yes! As often as possible. But – ' she hesitated – 'it's a bit difficult. My gran – she'd take it out on my mum if she found I was getting letters from a soldier.'

He suggested sending them to the Half Moon, and she was happy. He felt he had achieved something.

'I'll be back,' he promised. 'I'll be back as soon as I get another furlough.'

The forecourt of Victoria Station was jammed with vehicles when they reached it at a quarter to eight. They left their cab in the street and pushed their way past vans and cabs and a queue of ambulances. The entrance was even worse. A vast crowd of men in khaki filled the great hall, all of them laden with kitbags and haversacks and rifles and accompanied by sweethearts and mothers and wives and children. Half of them were struggling to get onto the same train as Scott, while the other half were flooding off an incoming one and trying to make their way out. In the midst of it all the police had made a passageway for the men who had come in on a hospital train.

The white headdresses and aprons of the nurses stood out against the sea of khaki as they accompanied stretcher cases to the waiting ambulances.

Scott felt Poppy draw breath sharply beside him. He looked down to see her face had turned pale. She clutched at his arm with both hands.

'You will come back? Promise me you'll come back.'

'I will, I promise, and on my own two legs. Promise me you'll wait.'

'Till the end of the earth.'

The stream of humanity swept them towards the barriers. Somehow they managed to fight their way to the machine to buy a platform ticket, and then they were through the gate and onto the platform where the train stood waiting. The air was filled with the smell of coal smoke and steam. The carriages were already crowded, with men hanging out of every window saying their last farewells.

His arm firmly round Poppy's waist, Scott made his way up the length of the train until he saw familiar faces looking out for him. The army was claiming him back.

'Hey, come on there, Scotty, we got you a seat!'

He slung his kit on board but stayed on the platform. Oblivious to the interested audience, he kissed Poppy one last time. A porter was slamming the doors. The guard's whistle shrilled above the noise. The train gave a jerk and began to move forward.

'Get on, Scotty, you idiot!'

He made a leap for the step and climbed in, pulling the door shut behind him. Thrusting his head back out through the open window he could see Poppy amongst a throng of women, a sea of reaching hands, all running along the platform, trying in vain to keep up with the train.

'Take care,' he heard her shout. 'Oh, please take care! I love you!'

He waved until she was nothing but a blur, and then the train rounded a bend, and she was gone.

11

Darling Scott,

I hope this finds you well, as it leaves me. We are all well here although my mum says she's tired, but then she always says that.

It is getting cold here and rainy. I hope it is better weather where you are because of the mud and all that.

Everyone is much the same at the club. Yesterday we had some navy men come in. It made a change to see the blue uniforms in with all the khaki.

My dear Scott, you will think it's very funny, but I have not never written a letter before. I was never one to listen much at school. It was not that I couldn't do it. It was easy. But I was bored. What they made us do was just chanting things and lots of sums and writing about things like A Sunny Day or My Grandmother. I can spell and that, but it's not the same. I did not want you to think I was ignorant. So I went and asked this woman what lives round the corner in Trinidad Street. Her name is Mrs Ellen Turner. She was clever at school and went to the Central for a while though she had to leave because her dad was ill and they needed the money. But she said just write like I was speaking to you. Write down everything what's in your heart, she said. So now I am trying to do that.

Oh, Scott, what is in my heart is I miss you so much. I can't believe how much it hurts. It's so strange when only five days ago I did not know you was alive and now I do and it's so hard not to see you no more. When you went away on that train I waved and waved and shouted till there was nothing there, only a black dot. Then I didn't hardly know what I was doing, I was crying so much and there was women all round me all crying and all. Some lady put her arm round me and she said as I had to be brave because of the brave soldiers going off to fight and it was bad for them to see all the women crying. They liked to see us smile she said. I hope I smiled for you. I want you to think of me smiling.

Please please be careful, my darling Scott and don't get hurt and come back safe to me,

Your loving Poppy. xxxxxxxxxxxxxx

SS Toledo
November 9, 1917

My dearest girl,

I'm dashing off a few lines now while we're on the boat so that you'll get something from me as soon as possible.

I want you to know first of all that I love you very much. These past few days have been the happiest of my life. Whatever may happen in the future I shall always remember London and a girl with hair like new polished copper. You have opened a new world to me, my Poppy.

Through the rain I can see the coast of France. It's just a long dark line between the grey sky and the greyer sea. It was always one of my ambitions to come to Europe, but I would rather it was not under circumstances such as these. I've been talking to some of the British officers on the ship, and believe me, my darling, what I am going to is nothing compared to what they will have to face within a few hours. The sooner we Yankees can get in there and help them win this war, the better.

Be your sweet self when you're talking to those guys in the Half Moon Club, my darling, because they need someone to be kind to them, but keep your heart for me.

You are always in my thoughts.

Scott.

My darling Scott,

I'm sending this now so you get it for Christmas. I knitted the muffler myself. I want you to think of me every time you put it on, because I thought of you all the time I was knitting it.

Christmas is always a bit of a sad time for my mum and me because it was just before Christmas eight years ago that my dad left us. We thought he was just going to do a panto up North somewhere but he never did come back. I loved my dad. He was fun. Whenever something happens to me, I always wish he was there for me to tell him about it. I wish I could tell him about you. I know he'd of liked you. Joe at the Club (you remember Joe the drummer who tried to pick a fight with you) he says he knows someone what's heard of where my dad is. He says this man played with my dad on the Isle of Man last summer. He promised me he'd fix it for me to meet this man. I really would like to find my dad again.

Much more than that I want to see you again. That would be a real Christmas present for me. It seems such a long time now since you went away. I'm getting used to it but it's like there's this big hole inside me all the time. It's funny how when you read stories and things it sounds like love is all sweet and gentle, like all flowers and birds singing and that, but it's not like that at all. Sometimes when I'm at the club and I'm all laughing and having them on and it's suddenly like I'm standing beside myself and looking at me, and there's Poppy all larking about and there's me just aching and aching to be with you again. Does that sound strange? You'll think I'm a loony.

My friend Elsie came round yesterday after her work. Her face is still yellow but she says she don't care because she's getting lots of money. She tried to get me to come on the munitions as well, but I like it at the Half Moon. We decided we must get together and play some music again. I told her she ought to save up some of this money she's earning and buy her own trumpet. I don't know whether she will, because she's got this sweetheart what's in the army and they're going to get married on his next leave so she's saving for her bottom drawer. I'm going to be her bridesmaid at the wedding.

I got out of the way of going to church, what with always working at night and that, but now I go every Sunday evening (Salvation Army) and I always pray for you, as well as for an end to this terrible war.

Please take care and remember I love you always,

Your loving Poppy. xxxxxxxxxxxxxxxx

France
December 26, 1917

My darling Poppy,

It was real strange being away for Christmas. Every year up till now I've managed to get home to my folks. I guess quite a few of us felt homesick, though we did not let on to each other. We got together to bring a little Christmas cheer to the kids in this village. Many of them have lost their fathers in the fighting and their mothers are having a hard time bringing them up, but still the people of the village invited us into their homes and made us feel real welcome.

Today it's business as usual and all of us with the mother and father of a headache, but I have your muffler to comfort me and keep me warm. Our time together seems long ago and far away now. Once you are back here, the army takes you over, ruling your life. But one thing it cannot take over is my heart, which stays in England with you. Look after it until I can be there to hold you in my arms and kiss your sweet lips,

Ever your own Scott.

My dearest Scott,

Thank you so much for sending me that lovely photograph of you. I went out and bought a frame for it and I keep it with my special treasures. I would so love to have it by my bed so I could go to sleep looking at you and wake up to find you looking at me, but as you know I share a room with my mum, and my gran just comes in and out as she pleases. It is her house so she thinks she can go anywhere, never mind that people want to be private.

I will send you one back, as you asked me. But it's difficult. When I was younger, there was this teacher. One day I'll explain to you, when I can tell you face to face, but I can't write it. But just thinking of having my picture took brings it all back. I know you would like to have one though, because I was so very very pleased to have that one of you and to see you looking so handsome in your uniform.

This idea just come to me. I'll ask Elsie and perhaps me and her can go along together and have one each took. Her face won't look funny on account of the photo is all brown anyway.

I got some news the other day. You remember Joe at the Half Moon? He's got lots of friends, Archer Street men (that's where the musicians meet) and this bloke what's just come back from the Isle of Man said he'd seen my dad playing in a hotel there in a place called Douglas. I talked to him and it was my dad, definite. What I really wanted to do was to go right away and look, but it's a long way and expensive and anyway I can't just throw in my job, so I wrote a letter. I do hope he gets it and writes back to me. I do so want to have a dad again.

I went and sat with Mrs Turner, you know, the woman what lives round the corner. She was so worried, her husband, Harry, is in the navy, an able seaman, and his ship was hit last week and she did not know whether he was alive or dead, then while I was there the postman come and there was a letter. He is all right. His leg is hurt but that is nothing just so long as he is alive. We hugged each other and we didn't know whether we was laughing or crying. I was so happy for her because I know what I would feel like if it was you. Then her mum come over and she cried an all and her brother Jack what's on leave come in and said, 'Gawd what a performance. You lot's worse than the moving pictures.' And then we all laughed and sent the kids up for a jug of beer and toasted Harry. I really like Mrs Turner and I am so grateful to her for telling me about writing letters because now I sit here and it's almost like talking to you.

When are you coming back again my darling Scott? I miss you every minute.

All my love for ever and ever, Poppy. xxxxxxxxxxxxxxxx

Hôtel Riveau
Calais
March 20, 1918

My darling Poppy,

Words cannot express my frustration and disappointment. Here I am on the seafront at Calais overlooking the English Channel. Just twenty-two miles away across the water is Dover and a train to take me to London and you. But the wind is howling along the promenade and flinging the rain and sand and spray against the windows and the waves are as high as mountains. Nothing is moving in or out of the harbor. I went along there myself just half an hour ago to make my own enquiries and was told that the storm is not considered likely to abate for twenty-four hours and nonessential shipping will not be allowed to go until then. I can tell you, honey, I said some things that were not fit for ladies' ears.

Maybe they are wrong and I shall get a passage tomorrow, in which case I shall still have some time with you, even if it is only a day. But just in case I can't, I want you to know that if God had given me wings to fly, I would be with you today.

In the hotel we're making the best of it. There are fresh sheets and hot running water and best of all, a rest from the continual sound of guns. That is the only advantage of the storm, it blots out the sound of gunfire. I expect I shall be dragged off for a night on the town later on, but my darling girl, I shall be thinking only of you and how we should be together now.

Hoping to be with you soon,

Your faithful Scott.

Cinnamon Alley
11 May 1918

My dearest Scott,

I wanted to write you a cheerful letter, about how I have bought a clarinet and I'm learning how to play it. But, oh Scott, I'm so sad. My poor friend Elsie what has only been married two months got a telegram today. Her new husband, Ted, got killed. The poor girl she's so cut up it's terrible. And the worse of it is I don't know what to say to her because nothing is going to bring him back. He's been out there three years and never so much as a scratch and now this. It's wicked what this war is doing. My mum said once she thought it will go on until all the young men are dead and I always said rubbish, the Americans are in it now so we'll win and then it will all be over. But on a day like today I wonder if she is right.

Perhaps I shouldn't post this. You got enough to put up with, you don't want me being all down in the dumps on top of it, but, my darling darling, please keep safe. I pray for you every day,

Your loving Poppy.

France
June 3, 1918

My darling girl,

You may have heard the rumors by now or even read it in the papers, so I guess I better own up. We have been moved up to the Front. You'll understand that I am not allowed to tell you where. Now, you are not to worry too much about me, because we are all as happy as clams to be here. All this while we have been training and at times it seemed as if we were never going to get a chance to show what we can do. The French have been trying to hold this sector, but without success. It was heartbreaking on the way here. Every road south was choked with families fleeing from the enemy. There were carts and barrows loaded up with household goods and old folk and children, together with their cows and goats and fowls. While they were trying to get one way, we were pushing up with our guns and equipment, while in every ditch and under every hedge there were abandoned and blown-up artillery and vehicles and the sick and wounded. I tell you, honey, when you've seen chaos and tragedy like that, you sure know why you're there.

It's kind of quiet here now. We're all dug in and our kitchens have caught up with us at last – we were real glad to see them turn up after living on bacon and hardtack – and now we're waiting for the next move. The French are still being pushed out of the country ahead of us. I'm not saying anything against the French. They are fine people and their troops have been fighting for nearly four years now. It's no wonder they've gotten tired after all they've been through. But there's a story going around that one of their officers tried to order one of our marine battalions to retreat with them. 'Retreat hell,' the captain replied, 'We just got here.' I guess that just about sums up how we all feel.

So keep smiling, my love. You're writing to a real soldier boy now.

All my love, Scott.

My darling Scott,

Thank you so much for your postcard which I got yesterday evening. I have been so worried about you since you wrote that you were at the Front, and then the papers have been saying how bravely the Americans have been fighting so I knew that you had been in action. But it was not over yet, so I shall wait every day to hear from you again and know that you are all right. Now I know exactly what all the other women have been going through. You don't really know until it is someone you love.

Mrs Turner tells me that it is a good idea to write about all the little things you are doing because then you men can remember what it is like back home. Of course, this is not your home, but you did spend a lot of your time at the Half Moon, so I'll tell you about that. I got Elsie to come down with me the other day. I was so worried about you I had to do something, so I got her to bring her trumpet and I got hold of my friend Mona and she brought along another girl who can play the piano and we played numbers from *Choo Chin Chou* and ragtime tunes until the real band turned up and the customers started to come in. Though I say it myself, we didn't sound half bad. All we need is a drummer and we'd pass as a proper outfit with a bit of practice. But, of course, nobody would take us on, because of us being girls. We'd just get laughed at, which is not fair really when you think of what us women have been doing in this war. I wish I had played my sax for you when you was here, then I could pretend you was listening. I'm getting the hang of the clarinet, but I got a long way to go yet before I'm any good at it, and I still love my sax best. It's something about the tone. It has a voice like it can feel things. You'll think I'm daft, but when I'm playing the sax sort of says things for me, things I can't say out loud. So I'll be playing for you until I know that you are safe.

All my love and prayers,
Your Poppy. xxxxxxxxxxxxxx

Belleau Wood,
France
June 27, 1918

My Darling Poppy,

At last I have some time to write you a proper letter. We have spent all this month fighting for what was once a lovely wood, in a commanding position. The position is still important, but there is not much left of the wood. Much worse, there are great gaps in the ranks of our division. We have been shelled, machine-gunned and gassed, but here I am, filthy, hungry, dog-tired but alive, thank the Lord. I guess we all say those words pretty lightly but, honey, someone must have been watching over me because I don't know how else I come to be sitting here today with the right number of limbs. You remember Mel and Howard, my buddies at that table at the Half Moon? They won't be going home again. I last saw Charlie Matteson lying wounded before a machine-gun nest. I haven't been able to find out what happened to him but I sure hope he got back to the dressing station and is now in a field hospital. Spare some of your prayers for them, my Poppy.

I can't write you how I feel about all this. I'm not sure that I know. Grateful to be alive certainly. And I guess I have to admit it, it was the most exciting and exhilarating thing I have ever done, to come through all that and know that we have won. We have stopped the Boche at the very apex of their push towards Paris. When you look at it that way, it is a great victory. It is only when you search for the faces of your friends and find they are gone that you wonder – we all came over here knowing in our heads that war is dangerous, that men get killed and wounded, but you only know it in your heart when you see it happen.

But we have a job to do and we've sure shown the Boche that we can do it. There were times, in the lonely hours before dawn, when I doubted myself. I don't think anyone knows how they will shape up until it comes to the test. Now I am ready for anything that lies ahead. When next you write me (and make it soon, my darling) you can address the letter to Captain S. Warrender.

Yours for ever, Scott.

Cinnamon Alley
4 July 1918

My darling Scott,

Happy Fourth of July! You see, I have been finding out about America and I know this is a special day for you. I wonder where you will be spending it and if you can have a party or something. How I wish I could be there, and bring my friends. We would play all the latest tunes for you and have a party like we've never had before. Mind you, the food wouldn't be much good. They're rationing stuff here now, but they say all the nobs and the big hotels get plenty still while down here in the East End its short commons for all.

I was so sorry to hear about your friends. It seems like everyone has lost somebody close to them. When you walk about London it's like everyone that's not in a uniform is in black, or at least has a black armband. Most of the sewing my mum does these days is mourning. I'm trying to keep poor Elsie going. I saw a trumpet for sale in a second-hand shop the other day and I made her buy it. I'm not sure whether she really wanted it, in fact I don't think she did, but I'm being terrible and bossing her around, so as she won't just sit and mope which is all she really wants to do. We practise together two or three times a week. Mona is going to get a guitar so she can play that or her banjo, and I am still going to my clarinet lessons. This way we can get a lot of variety into what we are doing. Music is a wonderful way to ease your worries, even if it is only for a little while.

It seems so long since I saw you, but I remember everything we did clear as anything. I don't even need your photo. I just close my eyes and I can see you just like you was here. Please please keep yourself safe and come back to me soon,

All my love for ever,

Poppy. xxxxxxxxxxxxxxx

Belleau Wood
July 14, 1918

My darling girl,

It's amazing how much you can enjoy the smallest things. Picture us now – we have been pulled back for a few days' rest and once more we can be human beings. Some of the men, including yours truly, have been for a swim in the river. We have had a proper cooked meal. Just imagine how good it feels! We truly know how lucky we are to be alive. It's two o'clock of a sunny afternoon and I have leisure to write you a good long letter.

The countryside around here is so beautiful. Maybe one day in happier times I will show it to you. We could

Orders have just come that we have to move immediately. It seems we are to go into action again, but nobody knows where. All is confusion. Must finish. Will write later.

God bless you,

Love, Scott.

Cinnamon Alley
30 July 1918

Darling Scott,

What has happened? I know there has been a big battle. Please please write, just a postcard, anything, just let me know you are still alive. You are always so good at writing, I am so afraid something has happened to you. Please send something. I can't eat or sleep or think about anything but you. This not knowing is so terrible.

All my love for ever,

Poppy. xxxxxxxxxxxxxxxxxx

My dearest darling Scott,

I keep hoping that my letters or yours have got lost and that is why you don't write. Maybe you are hurt and can't write. If that's it then please get someone to send a postcard for you. But for the love of God, please Scott find some way to let me know you are still alive.

All my love for ever,

Poppy. xxxxxxxxxxxxxxxxx

Forest of Retz
August 5, 1918

Dear Miss Powers,

I guess you won't have been sent an official letter, so I hope you won't mind receiving this from me. You may remember I was with Scott when we all visited the Half Moon Club and had the honor to make your acquaintance.

It is my very painful duty to tell you that Scott has been posted missing. You may have read of the battle we were engaged in during the last week of July. It was a great victory, but at a huge cost. On the first day, we outran our communications and spread over a wide stretch of territory, ending up by nightfall in the positions that had been our target for the third day of the battle. Our battalion had gotten mixed up with the marines and with the French and some Moroccans. I last saw Scott at the head of a group made up of various nationalities, storming a machine-gun emplacement. If you could have seen him then, Miss Powers, you would have been real proud. He went in like a hero.

When it was all over, it took some time for us to regroup and longer for the fallen to be brought in. Scott was not amongst the dead or the wounded. I can only guess that he went so far ahead that he went right into the enemy lines.

I have known Scott since the day we both volunteered.

He is a fine man and a real good buddy and I am proud to have called him my friend. I know he believed he was fighting for the right of all men to be free from the yoke of militarism.

He did not say a whole lot about you, but I know you were real important to him. A letter from you always made his day. I hope that will be some comfort to you.

Yours very sincerely,
Joseph A. MacFarline (Captain).

12

Margaret could see that something was up. The girl was dragging herself around as if she was half dead. She knew what that look meant. She had seen it many a time when she was in service. The ones who had been flaunting themselves in front of the menservants went very quiet and liable to burst into tears at nothing. Sometimes it ended in a hurried wedding, sometimes, if the man had just been passing through with a visiting family or, worse still, one of the toffs, then it meant dismissal without a character reference. There was only one way for a girl to go then. On the streets. It was that spectre that had driven her to track down That Man when she realized that Jane had got herself into trouble.

It couldn't be happening again. Not in her family. It hardly felt like five minutes since she was worrying about Jane. Now it was Poppy. She supposed she might have expected it, with the girl working in a servicemen's canteen.

When the war started, she had hoped that Poppy would take the opportunity to make something of herself.

'You ought to go and train as a hospital nurse,' she urged. 'They're crying out for them, and it's a good thing for a woman. You'd be somebody if you was a nurse. You're quick and strong, you'd be good at it. I'll go and find out about how you start.'

But Poppy would have none of it.

'I'm sorry, Gran, but I couldn't. I know nurses do wonderful work and I'd like to be like them, but I couldn't never do it. I ain't got the stomach for it, not all that blood and that. It'd make me ill.'

Margaret argued for some time, but Poppy would not give in. She would, she insisted, throw up or faint. She just wasn't cut out for it. In the end, Margaret had to back down. She had learnt that the girl had a will just as strong as her own and was quite capable of defying her outright. Look at what had happened when she had tried to send her into service.

But this situation was different. If she was carrying, then something had to be done. Margaret was not quite sure what, but she supposed that a man could be traced through his regiment. One thing was for sure, she was letting no stone go unturned to protect her family's respectability. She tackled her granddaughter with her customary forthrightness.

'I been watching you these last two weeks. You been going round looking like you lost a shilling and found sixpence. What's the matter?'

'Nothing.'

The girl's look then should have warned her that she was on the wrong tack, but she was too set in her ways to change.

'Oh yes there is. I can tell. You're in trouble. That's it, ain't it? In trouble and he's gone back to the Front.'

Poppy rounded on her with eyes blazing.

'Trouble! That's all you care about, ain't it? Being respectable. There's men being blown to pieces and you ask me if I'm in trouble.'

Margaret had never heard such venom in her voice before. For a moment it stopped her in her tracks. Then, the habit of control came to her aid. She would not be spoken to like that in her own house, by her own flesh and blood.

'So it's true, then. And who's the father, might I ask? A good-for-nothing soldier, I suppose. I always knew it would come to this. Blood will out.'

For a moment, she thought the girl was going to go for her. Her face was contorted with fury. Instead, she stamped her foot and screamed at her.

'That's right, bring my dad into it. Blame him. He's worth a hundred of you, you dried-up old witch. You don't know what it's like to lose someone. You never loved no one in your life!'

All the heartbreak, all the years of bitterness, and it came to this. Her only grandchild turning on her.

'Losing a man is nothing, girl. Some fly-by-night soldier.

Wait till you've borne nine children and buried eight. Then you'll know what love is, and grief. No tears ever mend that.'

The girl did not seem to hear her.

'You've always hated me, just because I'm my dad's daughter,' she accused, and ran out of the room.

Margaret did not hate her. It came to her now, when the gap between them yawned too wide to bridge, that she had always loved her.

Poppy knew what missing meant. Missing meant dead.

What she had not known was that the pain of loss was real and physical and took over your body as well as your heart and mind. The days became a blur of grief, too heavy to drag herself through. But like thousands of other women she could not afford the luxury of giving herself up to it. She had a living to earn. Whisky got her to the end of each session at the Half Moon. Only long practice kept her from stumbling or dropping glasses. But by the time she got home with the dawn her slim self-control was gone. She collapsed on the bed fully clothed and howled.

Elsie knew, from the moment she saw her.

'Oh, Poppy love – ' she said, putting her arms round her, and led her off to her house, turning her two sisters out of the bedroom so that they could have something like privacy.

'If he's missing – ' she said, trying to offer some hope.

Poppy shook her head. 'That don't mean nothing. Just that they can't find the – the body – ' She swallowed, trying to hold the tears in check. 'Look at poor Mary O'Donaghue as was. Her Rory was missing after Loos. That was three years ago. He ain't never turned up. He won't, neither. He's dead. Like – ' But she couldn't quite get the name out.

The two young women held each other, sharing their grief. Nothing was going to bring their men back, but at least here was someone who understood.

'How do you bear it, Elsie? I don't know how to go on. I don't know how to live without him.'

'You just got to, lovey. You got to just go on. Ain't no other way.'

When at last the weeping subsided into dry sobs, Poppy was contrite.

'Oh, Elsie, I never knew what you was going through till now. I been horrible to you – ordering you about – and – and making you come and play – the trumpet –'

'No, no.' Her friend rocked her in her arms. 'You was right. It done me good. I'm going to do the same for you.'

'Oh, no –' Poppy recoiled in horror. 'I couldn't. I couldn't never touch the sax again.'

A wan smile touched Elsie's puffy face. 'Yes you will. I know you. You won't never give up your music. You lived for it before your Scott come along and you'll live for it again.'

Just then, Poppy found it impossible to believe her.

The days piled up, one upon another, and to her vague surprise, Poppy found that the weeks of the summer had passed and she was still functioning, even though the best part of her had died. The first shock was over, but the pain stayed with her. She simply got used to living with it. True to her word, Elsie contacted Mona, and the three of them played together twice a week before the club opened. Sometimes they were still in full swing when the customers began to arrive, and drew some half-hearted early-evening applause. Men came up and spoke to them, amazed that girls could produce such a good sound.

'Patronizing idiots,' Mona dismissed them. 'Just because we don't go out and shoot each other like they do, they think we can't do anything. If they had the sense to stop fighting, this wicked mess would be over tomorrow.'

'But they're defending us from the Germans,' Elsie protested.

Mona rounded on her. 'You don't still believe that, do you? And you a war widow too!'

'My Ted died for his King and country,' Elsie maintained. 'Ain't nothing you can say's going to change that.'

Poppy ignored them. While the regular trio unpacked their instruments and tuned up, she carried on playing sad ballads on her saxophone, pouring her feelings into the music, making it speak for her.

The club was fuller than ever, a haven for war-weary men out to forget for a few brief hours. As summer tipped into autumn, more Americans found their way there. The sight of their uniforms caught at Poppy's heart. She could scarcely form the words to ask if they had known him. But always they were from different divisions, more recently arrived in Europe. They offered themselves eagerly as substitutes and Poppy replied in kind, though inside she was breaking up. How could they sit there, wearing the same clothes, speaking with similar accents, so big and noisy and alive, when he was lying dead? Yet she could not keep away from them, returning again and again to hear their voices, to try to catch something of Scott.

It was Joe who offered her a lifeline.

'Did you ever write to your old man?' he asked her one day. 'You know, in Douglas?'

'Yes. But he didn't never write back.'

'Perhaps he moved on. Perhaps he never got it. The post does get lost sometimes, you know. Might of gone down on the boat. Plenty of them flaming submarines in the Irish Sea.'

'I suppose so.'

Thoughts of her father had been buried beneath her grief, but now she started to think about him again. Here was someone who was genuinely missing. Somewhere in the British Isles her dad was alive and performing each night in a hotel or theatre. Maybe he really wanted to come back, but felt he had left it too long. Poppy could not answer for her mother, but she still wanted him home, she still wished they were a proper family.

'You could write again.'

'Summer season's over,' Poppy pointed out.

'Yeah, but someone there might forward it to him. You never know.'

'Maybe. I suppose you're right. Perhaps I'll try again.'

'And I'm keeping my ears open for you, you know. The Archer Street men will hear of him if anyone does.'

'Yeah – thanks, Joe.'

Without noticing she did it, Poppy touched his arm,

brushing it briefly with her hand as a gesture of thanks. His face lit with pleasure.

'Anything you want me to do, Poppy, anything at all – you only got to say the word.'

'Yeah, right –' She focused on him with difficulty. He seemed to be expecting some answer from her. 'You're a pal, Joe.'

It took several false tries before she managed to start the letter. Just picking up a pad and pen brought back such sharp memories of the times when she wrote twice a week to Scott. But once she did get going, the words flowed. Six pages were covered in news about her mother, the boarding house, the Half Moon Club – and Scott. She ended by pleading with him to come home, where his family needed him more than ever, where he would be welcomed with open arms. Then she addressed the envelope and wrote 'Please forward' on the front and her own name and address on the back. As she pushed it into the letter box, she felt a little lift in her spirits.

Now that she had no personal interest in it, Poppy turned her back on news of the progress of the war. It was just a horrible black mouth, swallowing up the lives of men and ruining those of their families. So she did not at first believe it when the news filtered through to her that the end was in sight. Everyone had expected it to drag into next year and beyond.

Poppy came home in the early morning of 11 November as usual and fell into bed. The drink she had got through during the night was wearing off and she felt rather ill. Her stomach lurched queasily and her head was beginning to throb, but as long as she lay perfectly still, she was all right. Dry-eyed in the darkness, she stared up at the invisible ceiling.

She must have fallen asleep, for the next thing she knew, there were church bells ringing and ships' sirens and whistles sounding, like the New Year celebrations of days gone by, but magnified a hundredfold. Out in the street, there were people shouting and cheering.

Carefully, Poppy sat up, She could not think what was

going on. Was there an air raid, or had the Germans invaded? But that would not bring cheers. Her head swimming, she put her feet to the floor. To her relief, there was water in the bowl by the window. She splashed it over her face and felt slightly better.

The door swung open. There was her mother, looking younger and more animated than Poppy could remember her being for years.

'Oh, Poppy, Poppy, it's over! It's really over!'

'What?' Poppy stared at her, uncomprehending.

'The war, the war's over. It's peace, Armistice! It's over!'

'Oh, God,' said Poppy, and burst into tears.

There must have been many more tears shed all over the country that day, but on the whole they fell in private. Publicly, the mood was of intense relief that at last the black shadow had been lifted. In London, it escalated rapidly into a wild celebration. Work stopped, complete strangers grasped each other by the hand and clapped each other's backs, the pubs were full to overflowing.

By the time Joe got to work, roistering crowds, drunk as much on the abandoned atmosphere as on alcohol, were surging through the narrow streets of Soho. They were singing, dancing, waving Union Jacks. The French restaurant by the club had a huge tricolour draped across the window, and from out of the open door came the sound of the 'Marseillaise'. Passing revellers cheered and saluted their brave allies in victory. Caught up in the prevailing mood, Joe let himself be kissed on the cheeks, Gallic fashion, by the *patron*.

'It is a great day, a great day. You were a soldier, no? A tommy?'

'Yes,' Joe agreed.

'My sons also. They are *poilu*. My eldest, he has the wound at Verdun but still he fights on. Now they will come home, my boys. No more fighting.'

'No more fighting,' Joe echoed, and laughed. He flung an arm round the *patron*'s shoulders. 'No more guns, no more mud, no more gas.'

121

The worry that had increasingly gnawed at him had now gone. With the war dragging on and on he had wondered whether they would call him back into active service, lungs or no lungs. He ran down the steps to the club.

'Here's Joe. Here he is at last!'

Joe nodded at the other two members of the trio. 'Couldn't help being late. Couldn't get through the crowds. Bloody mad out there, it is.'

'You're telling me, mate.' Jimmy the barman agreed.

'Biggest party London's ever seen, that's what they're saying,' said one of the waitresses.

Mr Fairbrother came over. His gloomy face struck a sour note.

'Better make the best of it tonight. Might not be no more Half Moon Club after this with no soldiers to come to it.'

'Get away with you,' said Joe. 'People'll always want to have a night out on the town.'

He looked about for Poppy. Once things got back to normal, she would get over that bloody Yank. After all, it was four months now since he went missing. There she was, sitting by herself in the far corner, staring into a drink.

'Hello, Poppy. How's things?' he said.

She looked up with eyes that were dark with despair.

'What was it all for?' she asked.

The papers had told them enough times: King and Country. Poor Little Belgium. Peace for all Nations. Freedom from the jackboot of German Oppression. And when war weariness began to set in, they printed horror stories of wounded prisoners denied water, of rapes and mutilations, of babies speared on German bayonets.

Joe shrugged. 'I dunno,' he said. 'But we won.'

'Won? Yeah.' Sigh.

He put a hand over hers. She did not move. Encouraged, he gave her a kiss on the cheek.

'Look, the war's finished. That's worth celebrating, ain't it? Ain't nobody more going to get killed.'

Poppy nodded slowly. 'That's a relief, anyway.'

'Too right. So cheer up, eh? Join in the party. You only live once!'

She gave him a ghost of a smile. 'My dad used to say that.'

'Well, he was right and all. So come on, then, and join the others before we all get run off of our feet. This'll never happen again. Might as well enjoy it.'

She stood up, holding her glass.

'I'll fill that up for you,' Joe offered.

'Thanks.'

Together, they went over to the bar.

'Here's to victory,' said Jimmy.

'Victory!' they chorussed.

'And blooming good tips tonight,' added one of the waitresses.

'And so say all of us!'

It was a night such as none of them had ever known before. At first the customers rolled in and out of the club, having a drink, dancing a little, making friends with all and sundry, and passing on. They sang along with everything the trio played, humming or making up words if there were no official lyrics. People who would never normally be allowed in the Half Moon were seen sharing drinks and seats and embraces with members of the aristocracy, chorus girls, actors and MPs. Anyone in a uniform found they had more drinks than they could ever handle pressed upon them. Prostitutes and debutantes wore soldiers' hats and jackets as they jigged around the packed dance floor.

Joe tried to keep an eye on Poppy. She had her bright artificial smile on and she was scurrying to and fro, loaded down with trays of glasses. Men hugged her and kissed her and tried to pull her onto their knees. Joe's guts churned with jealousy, but she just laughed it off.

As the crazy night worn on, people stayed and it turned into the wildest party the place had ever seen. Girls danced on the tables, men climbed onto the tiny rostrum and sang with the band, couples who had been strangers only hours before openly embraced in the corners, at the tables, on the dance floor.

Just as one number was ending, Joe saw a man grab Poppy and pull her into his arms. With the skill of a circus acrobat, she managed to slide the tray onto a nearby table, only tipping some of the glasses. Without thinking, Joe leapt up and elbowed his way over to them.

'Not so fast, mate – ' he began, and raised his arm.

'A song!' Poppy cried. 'Of course I'll sing a song. Thanks, Joe.'

Joe gaped at her. His arm dropped. Somewhere, he had missed a line.

Poppy patted her admirer on the cheek. 'Got to go, sunshine. Duty calls.'

Both men looked at her. Joe began to realize what she was at. He found his voice again.

'Can't let the night go by without a song from you.' And to the drunken man, 'Sorry, mate. Got to take her away from you.'

Bemused, the man let her go. Poppy took Joe's arm, sending a hot thrill through him, and together they shoved their way back to the rostrum.

'Want to get yourself sacked?' Poppy hissed at him.

'But – you can't sing – ' Joe protested. 'Now what?'

'Course I can sing. Well enough for this lot, anyway.' She turned to Bob at the piano. 'How about "There's a Long, Long Trail"?'

'Too flaming sentimental. Have 'em all in tears.' Bob might be a sour old devil, but he was a pro. He knew how to judge an audience. 'If you must do a turn – and this is only to save Joe's bacon, mind – do "Tipperary".'

Joe could see what he was up to. It only needed a couple of bars and they would all join in. Nobody would notice whether Poppy was singing at all. And so it proved. In fact they all carried on after the band took a break and headed for the bar.

'Let me buy you a drink,' Joe said to Poppy.

She nodded. There were tears swimming in her eyes. 'Make it a double,' she said.

The abandoned atmosphere of the night was reacting on

Joe. All these couples entwined round each other. He put his arm around her. She stiffened at first, then relaxed against him.

'Oh, Joe –'

'I know,' he said, pretending an understanding he did not have. 'Bloody, ain't it? But chin up, eh? Don't spoil the party.'

She said nothing, but let him guide her to the bar, firmly clamped to his side. He kept hold of her as she downed the double he bought her, and she did not resist.

'Better?' he asked.

'A bit.'

A man beside them, sweating in his officer's uniform, bought one for each of them.

'One bright spot of the war, coming here on leave,' he said. 'Here's to you.'

'I'll drink to that,' said someone on the other side. 'Barman! Drinks for these wonderful people, and one for yourself.'

Joe raised his glass to them, and edged his arm further round Poppy's narrow body. His hand brushed the curve of her breast, soft and yielding to the touch. He felt her shiver, but still she did not protest. Instead, she downed the third drink. Tonight, he thought, tonight he would make her forget that bloody American. Tonight when everyone was frantically trying to blot out four and a half nightmare years. He could not go on waiting for her to come round any longer.

'You're the wonderful one,' he said in her ear.

'That's what they all say,' she retorted, but the sharp edge was missing from her voice. She leaned her head back against his shoulder.

'But I mean it,' Joe told her, and dared to kiss her slender neck. She felt smooth and very vulnerable, a pulse beating beneath his lips. He had never wanted her more.

'I got to get back,' she said, and tried to stand upright again.

'Not yet,' Joe begged. 'Old Fairbrother can't keep up with it tonight. He don't know who's doing what any more. Come on, live for now.'

'Live for now,' she repeated, without much understanding. Then, with a sudden access of fervour, 'Yeah, live for now. Eat, drink and be merry, for tomorrow we may be in Eastbourne!'

He guessed it was one of her absent father's sayings.

'Down with Eastbourne!' he cried. 'Another drink?'

'Yeah, another drink. Another and another and another –'

Her words were beginning to slur.

13

The bar finally ran dry at about five in the morning. By then there were people asleep with their heads on laps or on tables or indeed underneath tables, while a hard core of indefatigable souls still occupied the dance floor, just holding on to each other and swaying.

Poppy was swaying by then as well, from drink and fatigue. Oblivious to what either Mr Fairbrother or Joe might have to say, she danced with one man after another, accepted their drinks until they ran out, and sat on their knees. The faces became a blur. She smiled at them all and laughed a great deal about nothing. The bodies she was very aware of, hot beneath the khaki uniforms, pressed against hers. The one clear sensation coming through the haze of alcohol was an ever-growing need to lose herself in sweat and flesh and desire. She knew instinctively that there lay the way to forget completely. She had only to give herself up to it, to let the burning ache take over, and she would be swallowed in an oblivion too overwhelming for pain and grief.

And then she was being bundled towards the washroom at the back. The door slammed and someone was standing with his back leant against it, jamming it shut. Someone familiar.

'For Christ's sake, Poppy – '

Cold water splashed over her face. She gasped.

'You're drunk as a bloody wheelbarrow, d'you know that?'

'Stop it,' she begged feebly, and caught her breath as a second dousing hit her. 'Oh – leave me be – stop it – '

He took her by the shoulders and shook her. She felt sick. His face swam into focus, angry, glaring at her.

'D'you know what you nearly done? You nearly went off with three bloody guards officers. *Three*! How could you, Poppy?'

His anger seeped slowly into her consciousness, rousing her own.

''Snone of your business,' she said. Her mouth did not seem to be working properly.

'I'm bloody making it my business. The party's finished, Poppy. I'm taking you home.'

'Finished?' She could not comprehend it. It seemed like it was going to go on for ever, blotting out all the things she did not want to have to face.

'Yes, finished. Done. Over.'

'Over.' The word rolled round inside her befuddled head, hard, real, like a black stone. She had to climb back into the real world, to the boarding house and her grandmother and the weeks and months and years that stretched emptily ahead. Tears welled up and spilled down her face.

'I don't want it to be finished, Joe. I can't bear it. I can't go home. Not home. Anywhere, but not back there – '

His arms went round her and she sobbed great maudlin tears on his shoulder. He rocked her and patted her and gave her his crumpled handkerchief.

'It's all right, you don't have to go home. Joe'll take care of you. You don't have to go back ever again. You're safe with me – '

She did not hear the note of triumph in his voice.

Amazingly, Joe found them a cab, an old-fashioned horse-drawn growler. Poppy leaned against him in the dim interior, thinking of nothing, letting fate take over. She was cold now, after the steamy heat of the club, but Joe was warm and comforting. It was like being a little girl again, having a grown-up to make all the decisions and tell her what to do. She sighed and leaned her head on his shoulder. Everything seemed to be going round and round.

When Joe started kissing and caressing her, she let him do that too, and was vaguely surprised to find the feelings that had coursed through her at the club began to start up again. His hands ran over her small breasts, teasing and fondling, sending waves of hungry pleasure through her. She moaned, and his mouth fastened on hers, kissing and probing as if he wanted to eat her whole. Poppy submitted willingly, eager to be taken over, to submerge all chance of thought.

'Poppy, Poppy –' His breath was heaving and rasping through his chest. 'God, I want you. I've always wanted you – '

She did not want him to talk. She pulled his head down and began to kiss him. A muffled groan broke from him and he pushed her back so that she was lying on the narrow seat. Poppy's head spun. There was nothing now but the darkness, the movement of the cab and Joe's weight on her body, his mouth on hers. His hips began to grind rhythmically against her and she moved in response to meet him, creating a shaft of hot pleasure that made her gasp and cry out, and strain for more.

The cab stopped, but neither of them noticed. The cabby banged on the door.

'We're 'ere, mister.'

Joe groaned, rolled off and got painfully to his feet.

'Come on.' He helped Poppy up.

'No – ' She was only on the threshold. She wanted to stay here, to find whatever was on the far side.

'Yes, come on, it's only a moment. We'll soon be inside.'

Somehow, they managed to get out of the cab. Joe shoved the last of his money into the cabby's hand. Clinging to each other, they made it into a tall house and up what seemed like endless flights of stairs.

'Here. This is it – ' Joe was wheezing. He leaned his back on a wall, trying to catch his breath. Poppy lay against him, rubbing breasts and belly and thighs on his, feeling him hard and hot against her, arousing her to an unbearable ache of desire.

'All right – hold on – ' He scrabbled to get the key in the lock. The door swung open and they half fell into a cold room, dim and shadowed in the dawn.

Poppy found herself steered through a second door, and then she was falling, falling a vast distance and landing on her back on something soft. Joe's breathing was harsh and thick, he uttered grunts of frustration as he wrestled with his clothing. She could see him now, his face and shirt and bare legs pale in the grey light. She reached out to him, her fingers brushing his hairy thighs. He groaned and caught her hand, closing it round his erect penis. The feel of it electrified her.

'Come here,' she begged, 'here. Now –'

Then his weight was on top of her again, and his hands were running up her legs, over her belly. She strained upwards as his fingers parted her, explored her, roused her to a frenzy of need, until she was aware of nothing but a fiery gaping void inside her, desperate for fulfilment. She grasped his buttocks as he entered her, working onto him. A piercing pain tore through her and for a moment she drew back, tensing against it.

'No –' she cried, but even as the word left her lips, the need was back and she had to move with him. Her whole body was filled up now, she gasped and trembled as she climbed ever nearer to the peak she had to reach. Then he was shouting and shuddering in joy and triumph, and finally collapsed on top of her, spent and gasping.

'Oh, God. Oh, darling –'

Uncontrollable anger seized Poppy. She dug her fingernails into Joe, making him jump, then pushed onto him, taking him deeper and deeper until she was washed with a shimmering, surging release that left her dissolved into warm golden liquid.

Her head felt as large as a bus, and there was someone inside it with a sledgehammer, pounding and pounding at her brain. She groaned and tried to go to sleep again, but the pain was too insistent. She had a raging thirst, but could not even think of finding water, for her stomach was boiling in a sour turmoil. To move would be to set it off. She had to just lie there, very, very still, and wait for the horror to recede. There was someone beside her, so it could not be very late, for her mother was usually up before seven.

Then slowly she became aware of the harsh breathing. That

was wrong. And the other sounds were wrong too. The familiar background of Dog Island was changed. Fear nibbled at her. There was a strange smell too, mixed with the booze and cigarette smoke that clung from work, there was a salty odour and sweat. Male sweat. Her eyes flicked open. Grey daylight hurt her. She focused with difficulty, making the hammers in her head even worse. The ceiling was wrong, and she was facing a different way. Slowly, with infinite care, she turned her head. It was not her mother who lay beside her on the bed. It was Joe.

Panic seized her. What had happened? She tried to remember, but there was nothing. The last few hours had disappeared from her memory, as if they had never existed. Terrified, she lay trembling. What had she done? She had a sick conviction that it was something she was going to regret.

The few facts of her situation paraded before her. It was morning, or even afternoon. She had the most dreadful hangover she had ever experienced, therefore she must have drunk an awful lot last night. And instead of going home, she had come here, wherever here was, with Joe. At some point, she must have passed out. Shame began to stir in her numbed mind. She was not sure now whether she wanted to remember.

Gradually, she realized that she was cold, especially the lower half of her. She moved her hand, feeling for covers, but there were none on her. The chill skin of her exposed belly and thighs met her fingers. Searching higher, she found her skirt and petticoat hitched up over her waist. Fear lurched again within her, more strongly, building the premonition of some dreadful revelation, and beneath the agony of her head and churning of her stomach came the realization that she was bruised and chafed and sore between her legs.

Knowledge was hovering now on the edge of her consciousness. She tried to push it back. She felt too ill to face it. She just wanted to die quietly, now. But beside her on the lumpy bed Joe shifted, and a bare leg touched hers. Lifting her head very carefully, she looked at him. It was only for a split second,

131

before the weight of her throbbing skull became too much for her neck, but it was enough for her to see that he was naked between his shirt and his socks.

Her overburdened stomach rebelled. She just had time to roll over before throwing up on the floor.

'Oh God, oh no, oh God – '

She repeated it over and over, like a mantra, trying to ward off the horrible truth. But it was all coming back to her now. The Armistice. The wild celebrations. The knowledge that although thousands of men would now be coming home to their loved ones, Scott would not be amongst them. The whisky. Joe.

She had done it to get rid of the pain. To forget. But she had made it a thousand times worse. She had let Joe do to her what she had always wanted to do with Scott. Only with him it would have been for love, something wonderful, an expression of what they felt for each other. Whereas this – she had behaved like a bitch on heat. Hot shame engulfed her. She wanted to shrivel up, to die, to become nothing.

The laboured breathing beside her changed. A new need tore through her. She had to get away before Joe woke. The thought of facing him, of sharing the knowledge of what they had done, was abhorrent. She had to go, and it had to be now, however bad she was feeling. Anything was better than being found here by him.

Her head swam as she set her feet to the floor. She was still wearing her shoes. She sat looking at them. She had slept in her shoes. She had done *that* in her shoes. Tears of self-disgust trickled down her face. She was soiled, loathsome.

Somehow, she shuffled about the littered room. She found a cracked basin and a ewer with a couple of inches of water in it. She sipped a little and used the rest to wash her face. With trembling fingers, she tidied her hair as best she could and smoothed her crumpled clothing. Peering fearfully into a spotted mirror, she saw a paper-white face looking back at her with haggard cheeks and bloodshot, dark ringed eyes. It confirmed everything she now thought of herself. She found

132

her coat and bag on the floor, picked them up and made her way to the door.

It was a long way down the stairs. She had to lean against the wall and take it one step at a time, pausing every now and again for her head to stop spinning. But at last she made it to the dingy front door. She found herself in a narrow street of three-storey houses that let straight on to the pavement. Bewildered, she looked this way and that. There was no clue as to where she might be, except that it must be somewhere in London. She set off to the right, tottering along. Eventually she came to a main thoroughfare. She waited, willing her legs to keep her upright. People were giving her strange looks. A man stopped and propositioned her. She told him what to do in two simple words. Two occupied cabs went by, then, mercifully, a vacant one. She fell into it with deep gratitude. All she wanted to do now was to crawl into her own bed and never get up again.

14

There was one advantage in having a grandmother like hers. She got rid of unwanted men. Poppy, lying burrowed into her bed, heard her making short work of Joe at the door.

Half a minute later, her grandmother was in her room, looming over her bed.

'So,' she said, 'it was all a pack of lies, wasn't it?'

Poppy did not answer her.

'Servicemen's canteen, indeed! I thought that was bad enough. But a night club! Filthy den of vice. And now some good-for-nothing musician coming and asking after you. Well, he won't be coming back again.'

'Good,' Poppy said.

'And I'm not having you go back there again, either. I been far too soft on you lately. It's time you listened to me for a change.

'I'm not going to go back there,' Poppy said. Of that she was certain: she was never going back to the Half Moon Club.

This threw her grandmother for a moment. But not for more than that.

'It's about time you got up. Not good for a girl your age to be lying around in bed. You best go looking for a decent job.'

Poppy turned her back and pulled the covers over her head.

Elsie called in.

'Talk about the morning after,' she said, plumping down with a groan. 'Blimey, my poor feet! I been all over the Island and there ain't nothing. Hundreds of us munitions girls, all after jobs what ain't there. Oh well, it was good while it lasted. I got savings. Just think! Money of my own. Never would of dreamed of it before the war. We never thought about savings, did we? Just getting to the end of the week with enough for the rent was good.'

'Yeah,' Poppy agreed. She did not want to talk, not even to Elsie.

'You must of put a bob or two by? All them tips?'

'No.'

'Blimey, what you been doing with it all, then?'

'I dunno.'

Instruments, clarinet lessons. Drink. Especially drink, these last few months. It all went.

'I dunno neither. Tell you what, though, I want to keep my little nest egg. If I don't get another job, it's all going to go. I better start looking round Poplar tomorrow.' Elsie sighed. 'But I suppose there'll be hundreds of us all round there and all.'

For the first time in days, Poppy found her mind distracted by something outside of herself.

'Then don't go looking in Poplar,' she said. 'The East End ain't the whole world, y'know. Go up West.'

'West?' Elsie sounded doubtful. 'Oh, I dunno about that. I ain't been up there much.'

Poppy spoke without thinking. 'Blimey, it ain't Timbuctoo, y'know. You don't have to go on a flaming ocean liner. Just get a bus, it ain't difficult.'

'Hark at you, lying in bed like blooming Lady Muck! You're a one to talk. I don't see you getting on a bus to nowhere. You got no right to be so blooming hoity-toity with me.' Elsie stood up and gathered her things together.

Poppy gaped at her, shocked. Her friend was glaring down at her with her fists planted on her hips, clearly incensed.

'You think you're so flaming wonderful, just 'cause you got jobs off of the Island. I don't see you doing nothing now.'

Poppy swallowed. 'I can't,' she said. 'Not now. What is there left? What's the point?'

Elsie shrugged. 'You got to go on, that's the point.'

'But I can't, not without Scott. You don't –' She stopped just in time, but Elsie knew just what she was about to say.

'I don't understand? That's what you think, is it? You're the only one what's lost the love of her life? I tell you

135

something for nothing, Poppy Powers, there won't never be no one else for me. When my Ted died, it was like part of me died too.'

Poppy felt terrible. 'I'm sorry. That was a wicked thing to say, Elsie. Say you forgive me. Please. I just wasn't thinking straight.'

For a long moment they stared at each other, two girls aged into women by forces beyond their control, physically tired and emotionally exhausted. For the first time Poppy was faced fully with the knowledge that without Elsie she really would have almost nothing left. Fear lent her energy. She heaved herself out of bed and threw her arms round her friend.

'Please, Elsie. I don't deserve you, but we got to stay friends, we just got to.'

Elsie was too honest to hold out. She relented at once, hugging her back.

''Course. Takes more than a war to bust us up, don't it?' Her voice was shaking.

'A lot more.'

An hour or so later, Poppy made a decision.

'Tomorrow, we'll go up the West End and see what we can find.'

The result was jobs as chambermaids at the Savoy.

'I dunno how I'm going to get used to the hours,' Poppy grumbled as they treated themselves to tea and scones in celebration. 'It's a bit different from the Half Moon. I'll be getting up about the time I used to get home.'

'Early to bed, early to rise . . .' Elsie quoted.

'Well, it better make me healthy and wise, 'cause it ain't going to make me wealthy,' Poppy said.

'It's a lovely place though, ain't it? Beautiful. All that marble and gilding and stuff. Like a palace.'

'Yeah, I suppose so.' Poppy was just relieved to get a job. Enjoying any aspect of it was beyond her. She sighed. 'I could do with a drink. No use going in no pubs, though. We'll get taken for tarts. Have to make do with this.' She stared at the muddy tea.

'Do you good. You been drinking too much,' her friend told her.

'I know.'

'We got work, though, ain't we? I'm real pleased about that.'

Poppy did not like the job. The surroundings might be luxurious, but all it amounted to was skivvying round other people like she did at home. She missed the fun and noise and laughter of the Half Moon Club. As a waitress she was on her feet and at everyone's beck and call, but she was surrounded by people enjoying themselves and felt part of the evening's entertainment. At the hotel, she was just part of the machinery. It was only the fact that Elsie was there too that made her keep on with it. By the time she ran into Mona walking along the Strand one afternoon, early in the New Year, she was really fed up.

'Blimey, what's up with you? You look like a wet weekend, you do,' Mona said.

'So'd you if you had my job.'

'You're lucky to have one. Once all the men come back, it's off of the buses and the deliveries and the police and all that and back to the kitchen sink for us lot.'

But Poppy could only think of the men who would not be coming back. She would happily have slaved at the Savoy if Scott was returning to find her.

'Look, I'm off to watch a rehearsal. D'you fancy coming?'

'A rehearsal?'

The word cut through her depression.

'Yeah, with my dad – ' Mona nodded at the man waiting a couple of yards on, holding a violin case. There was no mistaking the relationship. Like Mona, he was short and black-haired, with a round face and thick straight eyebrows. Mona called to him. 'Poppy can come with us, can't she?'

Bert Dobson looked doubtful.

'It's Poppy, Poppy Powers,' Mona reminded him.

'Oh – ' Bert's expression cleared. 'Owen Powers's girl? That it?'

137

'Yes! Do you know him?' Excitement shot through her.

'Old Owen? Yeah. Worked with him once. Long time ago. Useful player, Owen.'

'Did you? Where was that? Do you know where he is now?'

Bert shook his head. 'No, not seen him in years. Come on, we got to get moving. I'm late already.'

As they hurried through the back streets, Poppy plied him with questions about her father.

'Can't help you much, I'm afraid, girl. Old Owen's been away for years. Not seen him in the Smoke since – oh, I don't know when. Mona said as you was wanting news of him. Funny thing, though, there was this young bloke asking after him and all. Drummer. Been in the army.'

Poppy felt queasy.

'Joe,' she said.

'What?'

Reluctantly she repeated, 'Joe. Joe Chaplin.'

'That's the one. Know him, do you?'

'Yeah.'

'Oh. Not much help, then. Tell you what, though, might be someone at the rehearsal what knows something.'

Poppy found she was shaking. Something she had not known for a long time was growing inside her. Hope.

The rehearsal was in the Toledo Picture House.

'There's good work going in the pictures,' Mona said. 'All the big places are taking on bands now. You never know, in the dark they might even let us girls in.'

Poppy drank in the atmosphere. It was like going back to the time when her dad used to whisk her off to meet his friends and show her off. The jokes, the moans, the gossip, the heavy pall of smoke, the hoots and wails of instruments being tuned up, none of it had changed. Desperate though she was to start questioning everyone there, Poppy knew she had to wait till there was a break for drinks, and then only if the practice went well.

The two girls sat themselves down in the stalls and criticized the standard of playing.

'Trombone's a bit off.'

'I could play the clarinet better than that.'

'They got to get a bit more life into that one. It's fast but it's not lively.'

Gradually, the disparate group began to sound more like an orchestra. Poppy watched and listened, learning all the while, though inside she felt like a watch was slowly being over-wound. One of these men might hold the key to her father's whereabouts. She did not care where it was. Somehow, she would get there.

The conductor kept them at it till opening time, then let them go to the pub next door for a drink. This was Poppy's chance.

Bert Dobson introduced her as 'Owen Powers's little girl'. Somebody bought her a drink. She sipped it without even noticing what it was. The men were mostly discussing the disadvantages of the cinema job. They nodded at her but carried on with their conversation. One of the younger ones came over with a hopeful smile.

'Nice to see a pretty face for once. Interested in music, are you?'

'I play the sax and the clarinet,' Poppy told him.

'Really?' he sounded disbelieving. 'Talented and pretty! It gets better and better. What did you think of today's effort?'

Poppy swallowed down her true opinion, that it was pretty mediocre, and tried to overcome her instant antipathy to any attempt at winning her over. She needed this man's knowledge of the music world.

'It's beginning to sound good.' She gave him her Half Moon smile. 'You were good. You stayed on the beat when the others were off.'

He grinned and sidled a little closer. 'It's not often I meet a girl who really knows about music. What did you say your name was?'

'Poppy. Poppy Powers. Owen Powers's daughter. D'you know him?'

He didn't, but he was sufficiently smitten to take her by the elbow and break in to the others' conversation. Several men had heard of her father, but nobody knew where he was.

'Thought he was doing the season at Bournemouth.'

'No, that was Jimmy Powers. Not related, is he?'

Poppy shook her head.

'I heard he was in Gateshead. Dead end place, that is.'

'What d'you know? You never been north of Watford. It's full of life, is Gateshead.'

'Life! What do you call life, then?'

In desperation, Poppy broke in on the disagreement. 'But is my father there, in Gateshead?'

Nobody seemed to know. Poppy eased away from them and got her escort to break her into another group. It was difficult to keep them to the point. They would keep wandering on to other musicians they had played with, and their short-comings. Then someone came up with an idea.

'Wasn't he on the Isle of Man? Some hotel in Douglas?'

'Yes, so I was told.'

'He was there. Pal of mine worked with him. Sid Evans. You know him?'

Poppy shook her head. 'But where did my dad – ?'

'All right, all right. I'm getting to it. There was a spot of trouble. Some w – ' he stopped suddenly, realising who he was talking to. 'Some – er – some mix-up over payment or contracts or something. So Owen went in a bit of a hurry, like. Now where was it Sid said he was heading for?'

Poppy waited in a dither of impatience while he racked his brains.

'Scotland. That was it. Glasgow. Got a sniff of a job in a picture house. Something like what we're doing here.'

Poppy flung her arms round him. 'Thank you, thank you. You don't know what it means to me.'

She wriggled through the crowd and got to Mona's side.

'It's wonderful. I've found him. Well, almost. He's in Glasgow, at a cinema. I don't know how to thank you. Any time you want a favour, you only got to ask.'

Mona grinned and gave her a hug. 'I'll hold you to that,' she said.

Poppy kissed her goodbye and hurried out.

In no time at all she was home and packed. It took a little longer to persuade Elsie to lend her some money, but in the end she wheedled it out of her. Just over three hours after talking to the band in the pub, she was on the train for Glasgow.

15

1919

The train pulled into Victoria Station, to the very platform where Poppy had stood and waved goodbye to him more than a year ago.

Bone-weary though he was, Scott stood up to catch a first glimpse of it. And though he knew it was totally irrational, still he felt a tug of disappointment that she was not there to welcome him. Anything could have happened. His letters could have gone astray. Even if she had received the last one, she did not know which day he was arriving, let alone by which train.

He sat down, a wry smile pulling at the corners of his mouth. If she were to fling herself into his arms, she would knock him over. He was still as feeble as a kitten.

Around him, men were heaving kitbags and suitcases down from the luggage racks, pulling on greatcoats, stubbing out cigarettes.

'This yours, mate?' A friendly seaman lifted down Scott's one tattered haversack, containing all that he had left in the world, or in the Old World, at least. He was struck once more with a longing to get away from the filth and ruin of Europe, to return to the free-wheeling openness of his homeland. But not without Poppy.

The train stopped in a hiss of steam and the returning servicemen stepped down, home at last. And this time, it was for good. They flooded towards the barriers where Londoners found families waiting for them. The echoing hall that had seen so many painful scenes of parting now saw loved ones joined. Scott limped slowly after them, glad for their happiness. His own would come soon. He hitched the haversack more firmly over his shoulder, cursing his weakness. His shattered leg, barely healed, ached abominably and would only take his weight for seconds at a time. The internal wounds still dragged at him. And the recurrent fevers that had taken him several times almost to the point of death had left him emaciated and drained of energy. Doggedly he made it to the station entrance, and hailed a cab.

'Cinnamon Alley, Isle of Dogs.' Through the long days, he had imagined saying that. Now it was happening.

'You sure, mate?' The cabby's sceptical cockney voice held music.

'Couldn't be more sure, pal.'

The man shrugged. 'Right you are.'

Scott sank back on the leather upholstery. At last, he was nearly there. He watched London slide by outside the windows, streets and sights made dear during a few days of happiness. It was refreshing just to be in a country physically untouched by war. Bombs had dropped on London, but they were nothing to the devastation of northern France or the stricken state of defeated Germany. The real damage to Britain had been done to her economy, and to her people.

The cab rounded Parliament Square and turned onto the Embankment. There was the river that flowed past Poppy's dockland home. Scott pictured their reunion, a scene he had played in his head a thousand times. She would stare at him, disbelieving for a second, then she would cry out in amazement and delight and launch herself into his arms, laughing and crying. He closed his eyes, feeling the imprint of her body, tasting her lips on his. 'Oh, Scott, oh my darling,' she would sob, holding him tight. 'You're alive, you're here. I can't believe it.' It was going to be a shock to her. If she had not got his letters, she would still be thinking he was dead.

He had not been either physically able or mentally lucid enough to write for a long while. Then a series of chances had taken him to various German hospitals, then from one prison camp to another as the war came to an end. It was only three weeks ago that he had at last been able to send word that he

143

was alive, was recovering, was coming home. In the chaos that was Germany, a letter from one more released prisoner could easily be mislaid.

Sometimes, in his nightmares, she was not pleased to see him. When his fears came to stalk him, when he considered the hundreds of men she came into contact with every night at the Half Moon, when he remembered his own words to her, encouraging her to give a smile for the others to take back to the Front with them, then he wondered if she was still true to him. Since he went missing, she might have turned to someone else for comfort.

The grey stone of the Tower loomed above him, then they were plunged from the riches of the City into the squalor of the East End, all within a matter of a few yards.

His customary confidence began to assert itself. All his life, if he set his mind on something and worked and planned towards it, he had got it. Even these last few months, when it had seemed as if it was all up for him, he had after all survived. Now he would ask her to marry him, then carry her off to the States, and give her the sort of life she deserved.

He recognized the swing bridge where he always left her to go the last part of the journey alone. Once over there, he looked out of the window with obsessive fascination. He saw nothing that could possibly hold her there. There was drabness everywhere. It was not just ugly, it was dreary with it. This truly was the wrong side of the tracks. He would take her out of all this, across the Atlantic. She would thrive in New York. She would blossom and sparkle.

The cabby had to stop to ask directions.

'Ain't never been asked to take a fare over here,' he admitted. 'You sure this is the right place?'

'Never more so,' Scott told him.

They stopped at last at a corner, and there it was. He read the sign, high on a blank brick wall: Cinnamon Alley. He knew at once which was her house, for she had described it vividly. The tallest one, with the net curtains. And yes, there was the notice in the window, 'Clean Lodgings'. He fairly jumped from the cab, hardly feeling the pain that jarred through his leg. He paid off the cabby and stood for a moment staring up at the house. Then he knocked at the door.

Footsteps plodded along a passage inside. Not hers. The door opened. An old lady stood there, dressed entirely in black, her hair scraped back in a bun and a hostile expression on her face. Scott knew just who this was.

'Yes?' The word came out like an accusation.

Scott doffed his battered cap, gave her his most charming smile.

'Good afternoon, ma'am. Is Miss Poppy Powers at home?'

'Who's asking?'

'Scott Warrender, ma'am. Captain.'

He held out his hand. She ignored it. Her sharp eyes swept up and down him, taking in his disreputable state.

'She's not here.'

Disappointment hit him like a shell. In all his reviewing of this scene, it had never occurred to him that she would be out.

'Can you tell me when she's going to be back?'

'No idea.'

'She'll be back before she goes off to work, though?'

'No.'

Scott controlled his temper with difficulty. He had to stay the right side of this old lady.

'Do you mind if I stay till she does come back? It is very important that I speak to her.'

The shrewd eyes glared back at him, uncompromising. Unexpectedly, she went into the offensive.

'You one of them Australians?'

'American, ma'am. From Pennsylvania.'

'Ha. Them.'

With two words, she dismissed the entire population of the United States as worthless. Scott tried smiling again. He'd dealt with old ladies like this before. There were plenty of them back in his home town. They worked hard all their lives and did not see that the younger generation should have it any easier than they had.

145

'I guess you have quite a job on your hands, running a lodging house like this single-handed.'

It did not work. The hostile look did not soften at all.

'Don't try to soft-soap me, young man. I know all about your sort. And it ain't no use you hanging about. She ain't here no more.'

Scott held her gaze as he took this in. She could be lying.

'Then perhaps you would do me the kindness of telling me where she is.'

'Why d'you want to know?'

If he told her the truth, it might turn her even further against him. It was difficult to tell. From what Poppy had said, they had never got on, and the old lady might be glad to get rid of her, especially if it meant her going right across the Atlantic. But on the other hand, she might prefer Poppy to marry a local boy and live where she could still try to control her life.

'I got a message to deliver.'

'You can leave it with me.'

'I beg your pardon, ma'am, but what I got to say has to be said face to face.'

She guessed. He could tell by her expression.

'Won't do you no good. You're too late. She's married.'

'*What?*' His head spun.

The old woman was stony-faced.

'I said she's married,' she repeated.

He could not take it in. Not married. Not this soon. Not his Poppy, the girl who wrote him those letters.

The grandmother was speaking again.

'You best get off of my doorstep.'

She was closing the door. Scott put out a hand to stop her.

'Who? Who's she married?'

'What's it to you?'

'I – I just got to know.'

For a moment she hesitated, running over him once more, disapproval written in the harsh lines of her face.

'Some musician bloke she met at that club.'

146

It all fitted. She had married that Joe character. Either she had gone to him on the rebound, or it had been him all along, with Scott as just a sideshow. But the result was the same: Joe had her. Swift on the heels of the pain came anger. How could she lead him on like that?

'I see.' From somewhere, he gathered some dignity. 'When you see her, wish her well from me, will you? Wish her – happy.'

He was not sure whether he meant it. He turned away hardly knowing where he was going. When he reached the corner he stopped, dazed. All these months, he had hung on to the memory of her, clawed back to life on the strength of his need to be with her again, and she had run out on him.

'Bitch,' he said out loud. 'Goddam bitch.'

He pounded his fist into the filthy brick of the building beside him. He had had it all planned out, had known just where he was going, but without Poppy the whole thing fell apart. For a few minutes he considered seeking her out, confronting her, making her pay for his anger and sense of betrayal. Then he rejected it. Why give her the satisfaction? She had pushed him out of her life. If he meant nothing to her, he was damned if he was going to let her know how much she meant to him. He looked up at the sign on the wall. Cinnamon Alley. Bending painfully, he picked up a lump of dried horse dung and pitched it at the name. Then he limped away.

He did not see the old woman dust her hands as she went into the house, did not see the satisfied look on her face.

16

The note was waiting for Joe when he got to work. He had to read it through three times before it made any sense to him, although it was short, clear and to the point.

Dear Joe,
   Can you meet me at the ABC teashop in the Strand at half past four tomorrow? There is something I want to talk about.

Poppy.

It was over three months now since Armistice night, but a day had not passed in which he did not regret what he had done. He had behaved in an unforgivable fashion. He had taken advantage of Poppy when she was at her weakest. He had got what he wanted and now he was paying the price. Or at least, he had been, up till now.

'Oi, daydream! Snap out of it.'

'What you got there that's so wonderful? A love letter?'

Joe pushed the note into his pocket. 'No, no. Nothing like that. Worst luck.'

Bob and Charlie were grinning at him.

'Bloody hell, he's blushing!'

'What's her name, Joe?'

'Is she pretty?'

'Even a cripple like him can get a pretty girl these days. They say there's two for every man. Wish I was single again,' Charlie said.

Joe ignored them. In about twenty hours' time, he would see her again.

He spotted her first. She had got there before him and was sitting staring into a cup of tea. She looked thinner than he remembered, and drawn. Her skin was white against the rich colour of her hair.

'Poppy.'

She started and looked up. There were dark circles under her eyes.

'Oh – Joe.'

Not even a trace of a smile. Not knowing what to make of it, Joe sat down.

'Can – er – can I get you something to eat?'

She shook her head. 'No, thanks.'

He ordered tea and an iced bun and looked at her across the table.

'How are you then, Poppy? I been worried sick about you. I came and called at your house, but your old gran saw me off.'

'I know.'

There was a hunched, defensive look about her. All the sparkle had gone. He wanted to reach out and take her in his arms, to protect her from whatever had hurt her.

'Poppy, I – ' he began.

But she forestalled him. 'How's things at the Half Moon, then?'

'We're as busy as ever. People want to forget. Going crazy, they are. Drinking, dancing. Old Fairbrother's even talking about getting more acts in, doing the place up a bit.'

'He must be pleased.'

'Well, you know him. Not exactly Cheerful Charlie at the best of times.'

'Yeah.'

'We – er – ' Joe hesitated. His fingers tapped a rhythm on the table top. She always used to be so open and approachable. He did not know how to deal with her when she was like this. 'We all miss you, you know. Place ain't the same without you. Why don't you come back? Old Fairbrother'd take you on again. You always could twist him round your finger when you tried.'

Poppy said nothing, avoiding his eyes.

'I wouldn't – you know – bother you, if you don't want me

to. It is that, ain't it? Why you left, I mean? Or have you got a better job somewhere else?'

'No. I'm a chambermaid at the Savoy.'

'Do you like it?'

'I hate it.'

'Then come back.'

'I can't.'

'But why? Like I said, I wouldn't – I'd leave you alone, if that's the way you want it. You don't have to be, like, embarrassed – '

'*Embarrassed?*'

She was looking at him at last. Wrong. Wrong. He had said the wrong thing and he didn't even know why. He tried desperately to retrieve the situation.

'I mean – I'll never – I'll not lay a finger on you. Come back as a friend, like. Part of the team. We had some good times, didn't we?' He wanted her back there because he still hoped to make her his girl, but he would have promised anything just at that moment.

She sighed. 'Yeah. Yeah, we did.' There was a world of sadness in her voice.

Joe leaned towards her. 'Poppy, I can't tell you how sorry I was about – you know – that night. It was just – everyone was going mad and I got carried away. I couldn't help myself. When I woke up the next morning and you were gone – I felt terrible, terrible – I didn't know what to do – ' He broke off, halted by the expression on her face. She was biting her lip, holding back tears. 'You must hate me,' he said.

Slowly, she shook her head. 'I didn't exactly say no, did I?'

'You – well – you weren't – '

'I was drunk.'

'But that don't mean that you – ' He stopped, not knowing what to say to make it better.

Poppy did not answer. Silence grew between them, an invisible barrier. Joe desperately tried phrases over in his head, but nothing sounded right. Then he had a brainwave. 'You heard anything from that dad of yours yet?'

Wrong again. If anything, she looked more miserable.

'I thought I had. I went all the way to Glasgow to look for him.'

'Glasgow? On your own?'

'Had to borrow money for the fare and all. But it weren't no use. I trailed all round everywhere, but no one had heard of him. It's like he's vanished into thin air.'

Joe started to say how sorry he was, but she did not seem to be listening. Looking into her empty cup, she said, 'My gran kicked me out last week.'

'*What*?'

'Gave me the push, told me to sling my hook.'

'But why? What? I mean – ' Joe suddenly saw a way to retrieve the situation. 'Can I help you? Do you need somewhere to stay? I'll find you somewhere.'

'I'm staying with Mona's family.'

'Ah – ' He was disappointed. 'They – er – they're all right, the Dobsons.'

'Yes, they're very kind.'

In a strange, tight voice, she asked, 'Don't you want to know why she kicked me out?'

'Well, yes. I mean, if you want to tell me.'

'I'm having a baby.'

'Oh – '

His first instinct was to run, as far and as fast as he could. The trap gaped open, home, family, responsibility, respectability, everything he had managed to avoid so far in his rootless existence. He had never looked further ahead than the next week. He did not like mapping out his life. He just let it happen.

Poppy was looking at him. There was a dangerous light in her eyes.

'Well go on, then, ask me if it's yours.'

'I – I – ' Shame tugged at him. 'I never thought it wasn't. I just – it was a bit of a shock.'

'A bit of a shock for you? It was for me and all. Just a bit.' Her sarcasm lashed at him. 'I wasn't going to tell you. I didn't want to. But Elsie made me promise to.'

154

'Well I'm – I'm glad she did, that you did.' His mind was numb. There had to be a way out. Then he looked at Poppy, the girl he had watched and wanted for so long, and through the panic came the realization that this meant he could keep her for his own. A small glow of triumph started inside, and spread through his entire body. He reached out and took her tightly bunched fists in his hands.

'We better get married right away.'

'Yes, I suppose we better.' She sounded as if she was agreeing to having all her teeth drawn. Then a bleak smile stretched her mouth. 'It'll really kill my gran, me marrying a musician.'

17

Jane hesitated at the huge entrance of the hospital. She was scared of these places. Nobody she knew ever went into hospital except to die. She felt deeply ashamed that her daughter had been forced to come here to have her baby instead of giving birth at home like all the other women in the street did. It had been Poppy's letter to her that morning, announcing the birth, that had given her the courage to defy her mother and come and see her. She approached a kindly looking middle-aged woman and asked directions.

'Maternity? Oh yes, dear – you want to go along there and up the stairs to the third floor, then turn left and it's straight on. Your daughter, is it?'

'Yeah.' Jane flushed with pleasure. 'My daughter, and my first grandchild.'

The maternity wards were full to overflowing. There had been a flush of babies this August. There were already visitors round nearly every bed. Jane could not see Poppy. She began to panic. Perhaps this was the wrong place. Then, right at the other end of the ward, she saw a young mother sitting all by herself, cradling her baby. Poppy's hair was unmistakable. She hurried down the long ward.

'Poppy? Lovey?'

Her daughter's head jerked up. She looked tired and drawn, not at all the blooming mother. Then she realized who it was and her eyes widened in amazement.

'Mum! Oh Mum, you came. You came at last!'

She held out her free arm and they hugged, both of them in tears.

'Oh Mum, I'm so glad to see you. I knew you would. I knew you wouldn't let me down.'

Jane sat back a little and smiled through her tears.

'She don't know I'm here. If she finds out, she'll give me what for, but I couldn't stay away, lovey. A girl needs her mum at a time like this.' She gazed at the baby, fast asleep in Poppy's arms. 'This him, then? My little grandson? Ah – ain't he lovely?'

Brimming with pride, Poppy handed him to her mother.

'Yeah, this is Christopher. Christopher Owen.'

Together, they crooned over the baby, wrapped up in the miracle Poppy had wrought. Then Jane gave her the present she had brought, a dozen finely worked little nightgowns with caps to match.

'I can't believe it – me a granny! Don't half make me feel old. And how about you being a mum? Do you like it?'

'Yes. No. I dunno.' Poppy sighed and sat back against the pillows. 'I love him so much. He's so sweet and soft, and when he feeds, it's – well – it's wonderful, I feel like I'm the cleverest person in the world, doing that for him. But – he's so little and helpless, and I don't know nothing about babies. Elsie, she says there's nothing to it, but she's had babies in her family, she knows about them. I feel – it's just me and him, and if anything goes wrong, I won't know what to do.'

Jane looked at her, a new worry starting up.

'What do you mean, lovey, just you and him? You did get married, didn't you? He didn't go and run out on you at the last minute?'

Poppy smiled and held out a hand, displaying her gold ring.

'Oh, yes. I got married all right. But it ain't his job, is it, looking after the baby? That's up to me, and I'm scared I won't do it right.'

'You'll be all right, lovey. It just comes to you, natural like.' Jane gave her shoulders a hug. 'Now tell me, are you happy? Is he good to you, this Joe Chaplin? Only you didn't say nothing about him before – well, before you fell for this baby.'

Poppy avoided her eyes. She picked up one of the nightgowns and smoothed out an imagined crease.

'I've known Joe for ages,' she said. 'Ever since I started working at the Half Moon. And he's a nice bloke. Thinks the world of me.'

There was something very unconvincing in her tone.

'Oh – well – that's nice,' Jane said. 'And what does he think of the baby?'

'He ain't seen him yet. The night he was born, Joe was taken bad – he got gassed in the war and he gets these bad turns when he can't breathe – so he was taken off to the Middlesex while I was in here. But he was pleased as Punch about the baby once he got used to the idea. Went out and bought lots of stuff for him. You'd like him, Mum. He – he reminds me of Dad sometimes. You know, good fun, lives for the day, that sort of thing.'

Jane sighed. 'That ain't necessarily the best sort of bloke for a husband, lovey.'

'Mum! How can you say that? We had such wonderful times when Dad was home.'

'But he ain't home now, is he?'

'He ain't dead, like what lots of them are. He might still turn up, one day.'

Jane was about to remark that pigs might fly, when she saw the pain in her daughter's face and she remembered that it was a year ago that the American soldier had been killed. She put an arm round Poppy's shoulders.

'Not like some, eh?'

Poppy nodded, biting her lip. Jane realized that things were not as straightforward as she had thought.

'You will get over it, pet. It takes time. You got to try to forget, you know.'

'I know – ' Poppy bent over the baby, laying her cheek against his soft head.

'It's the kids what matter, ain't it? They're the future. And you got me to turn to.'

'Oh, Mum –'

Poppy looked at her, her eyes swimming with tears. Jane felt the ground between them shifting. Poppy was grown up now, and a mother herself, but she needed her mum again.

'How many days ago was he born?' she asked.

'Three. Why?'

Jane nodded wisely. 'Ah, that explains it. Your milk's coming in. Everyone gets all weepy then. You'll feel all right again in a couple of days, you wait and see.'

The bell rang for the end of visiting time. Nurses marched down the ward, reclaiming their territory. Poppy and her mother kissed.

'You will come and see us when we go home, Mum? I'd like you to see our flat, and you got to meet Joe.'

It was so nice to be needed again.

''Course I will, Poppy love. It'd be lovely.'

A nurse arrived at the end of the bed, intent on rounding up the stragglers. Jane hurried off, but paused to wave from the door. Poppy waved back. She looked very small and lonely there, in her neat hospital bed. Jane resolved then and there to be the sort of grandmother that she would have wanted.

A week later, Poppy arrived home with her bag and her new son. The flat smelt musty as she opened the door. Joe was still at the Middlesex so it had been unlived in since the day Christopher was born. Feeling very isolated, Poppy laid her sleeping son in the little crib that his proud father had bought. No lying in drawers or apple boxes for Joe's son, unlike the babies in Trinidad Street.

All around her, the building was quiet. It was mid-afternoon and nobody seemed to be about. Poppy had refused to live in Joe's old rooms. Even thinking about what had happened there brought on hot waves of shame. Instead they had taken three rooms at the top of a house in Islington. Poppy had cleaned it up and given it a lick of paint, and they had bought some pieces of furniture. The effect was sparse but bright, and she had taken pleasure in creating her first home and being able to do what she liked when she liked, without her grandmother breathing down her neck. But now she would have given anything to be back in Cinnamon Alley. The baby had made her realize how important families were.

'Oh, well,' she said out loud, looking down at the little round face with its fluff of hair. 'We're our own family now, ain't we? Just you and me. And your dad, of course.'

She made herself busy, dusting, buying in food, checking the baby's things. A line of music kept going round in her head, a slow plaintive snatch of notes, and after a time words began to attach themselves. *I wonder where you can be now* – She concentrated on them, humming, trying to extend them into the start of a song.

Then the baby stirred and gave a snuffling cry. Poppy's stomach clenched in a mix of love and panic, making her breasts tingle and ache. She rushed over to look at him. His little face was turning red. His chin wobbled. A tiny clenched fist found his mouth and he sucked at it hopefully. Poppy glanced at the clock. Only five. In the hospital, babies were expected to wait until six for their feeds. Giving in to the hungry crying was supposed to spoil them and get them out of their routine. As she hesitated, Christopher lost contact with his fist. He opened his eyes and glared at her before beginning to wail in earnest.

'Oh, baby –'

The responsibility was crushing. He was all hers. She had to decide what was best for him, and provide it. If she did the wrong thing, if he became ill or did not thrive, it would be all her fault. She longed to have her mother there to offer advice.

The crying became overpowering, tearing at her fragile nerves. She bent and picked him up, rocking him to and fro. His head came round unerringly to nuzzle against her breast. Then she knew what to do. Damn the hospital and all those bossy nurses. She did what her mother said she would, and followed instinct. He was hungry, and she must feed him. It was as simple as that.

By the evening she was not so sure. Christopher was restless. He did not want any more milk, but neither did he settle down to sleep. Poppy walked about the cramped flat, keeping moving since that seemed to soothe him. Just when she was wondering whether there was something seriously wrong with him, there was a knock at the door. She fairly ran to open it. There were Elsie and Mona, carrying bottles and instrument cases.

'How's the new mum, then?' Mona asked.

Poppy burst into tears. 'You don't know how glad I am to see you!' she cried. 'He won't stop crying. I don't know what to do.'

They stepped inside. Elsie took the baby from Poppy.

'Touch of colic, I expect,' she said, and put him over her shoulder and began patting his back.

Responding to the firm touch of an experienced big sister and baby minder, Christopher obligingly belched and stopped crying. Poppy stared at them both in utter wonder.

'How did you do that? He wouldn't burp when I tried.'

'Easy. You'll soon get the hang of it.'

Mona meanwhile was clattering around in the cubbyhole that served as a kitchen. She emerged with three glasses of beer.

'Here you are,' she said, handing one to Poppy. 'Milk stout. Build you up.'

Poppy did not know whether to laugh or cry. 'You're so good to me.'

'Rubbish. We only came here for somewhere to practise. Cheers.' Mona raised her glass.

'Cheers!' Poppy responded.

'To little Christopher,' said Elsie.

All three girls drank, and wiped moustaches of foam off their lips. Poppy felt the weight lift a little from her heart.

'I've brought the guitar,' said Mona. 'All the best bands have them now instead of banjos. Come on, get out your sax, and the clarinet. We'll have a jam.'

'But what about—?' Poppy looked at Christopher, asleep now on Elsie's shoulder.

'He'll sleep right through it. Nothing disturbs them once they're off,' Elsie told her.

Poppy deferred to her superior experience. She fetched the sax.

'I been tinkering around with this song,' she said.

She played as much as she had composed. The others took it up with enthusiasm. Soon they were sorting out parts, arguing over phrasing and keys. The people in the room below banged on the ceiling. Poppy stamped on the floor. They all howled with laughter. Christopher slept blissfully through it all.

'We must do this again,' Elsie said, as she packed her trumpet into its case.

'We will. We'll do it regular,' Poppy promised.

'I tell you something, we're as good as some of my dad's friends. Better than some, in fact,' Mona said.

'Perhaps we should form a band,' Poppy suggested, just as a joke.

'Whoever heard of a girls' dance band?' said Elsie. 'You are a case, Poppy.'

The flat was very quiet after they had gone, but it no longer felt empty. She had friends and music, and tomorrow she would go to visit Joe. They did not fill the great black gap in her that was left by Scott, but they were worthy recipients of her love. And she had this wonderful baby. He was there to take all her fiercest care and devotion. She went to sleep that night with something like peace in her heart.

18

The mornings were growing chilly now that autumn was drawing on. Joe felt it in his lungs. When he lurched out into the street after a long night's playing, the contrast between the heat of the club and the cold of the air always set off a coughing fit. He refused to admit to himself that his lungs were getting progressively worse, despite the fact that today it was a good ten minutes before he was recovered sufficiently to stagger as far as Shaftesbury Avenue and wait for an early cab.

Home called him, home, bed and Poppy.

He had not had a proper home since leaving his parents' place in Ealing ten years ago. There had been a series of grim lodgings, his spell in the army, then rented rooms and flats, culminating in the one to which he had taken Poppy on Armistice night, but none of them could have been called a home. Now it was different. Not only was the flat bright and clean, but there were ironed shirts and good meals. Most of all there was a soft body to lie next to when he got into bed. Much to his surprise, Joe had found that marriage was very much to his taste.

The cab pulled up. Before going inside, Joe glanced up at the top windows of the building. Still dark. That was good. That meant the baby wasn't awake yet and he would have Poppy to himself for a while. Marriage might be wonderful, but fatherhood he had not yet come to terms with. It seemed that whenever he wanted to have some of Poppy's attention, Christopher was there competing with him. And it was always Christopher who won.

He climbed wearily up the stairs, stopping twice for a rest. By the time he reached his own flat, he was wheezing with every laboured breath.

Poppy was still asleep as he felt his way across the room and into bed. She stirred when he slid in and pressed his chilled body against her warm one, then sighed and turned over so that her back was towards him.

'Poppy?' He put an arm round her, feeling her slender curves beneath the cotton nightdress.

'Hmm?'

'You miss me, sweetheart?' He ran his hand over her. She was sweet and soft and warm, and infinitely exciting.

'Hmm.'

He took that as encouragement. She accepted his advances with resignation and though Joe convinced himself that she was enjoying it, she never again fell on him with the wild hunger of Armistice night. Sometimes he wondered whether it really had been like that, or whether it had just been his fevered imagination.

Now she rolled onto her back, letting him touch her, and returned his kisses sleepily.

'You're a lovely girl, Poppy. Lovely.'

Then a thin wail started from the crib beside the bed. Joe groaned and shifted part of his weight on top of her.

'Leave him, darling. He can wait a minute.'

But she slithered out from underneath him and sat up, pulling a shawl from over the bedhead and wrapping it round her shoulders. Deeply disappointed, Joe lay spitting curses. She leaned over to pick up the crying baby.

'All right, my darling, won't be a moment. There – there, that's what you want, ain't it? That's right –'

The ammonia smell of the baby overpowered the musky woman scent. Joe listened to her murmurings with resentment. She never talked to him like that. She never looked at him like that, either. Staring up at her in the grey half-light, Joe could see the glow of utter adoration in her eyes as she gazed down at the sucking baby.

He tried to stay awake, but before she had even shifted Christopher onto the second side, fatigue got the better of Joe and he drifted into sleep.

Years of night work had accustomed him to sleeping

through the growing light and noise of the day, even with other people in the same flat. Vaguely he heard the click of the door as Poppy went out to do the shopping and take the baby for an airing. A dream took over. He was back at the Front. Shadowy figures were all around him and in the distance artillery was booming. He was marching, marching through mud. It was black and viscous, clinging to his feet and legs, slowing him down, making every step an effort. The figures were going past him. He tried to keep up but couldn't. He tried to cry out to them to wait, but no sound came from his throat. He tried to run, but his feet were being sucked down by the mud. The others marched off into a fog of smoke and not one of them looked back. Then the smoke rolled over him. It turned from black to green and he knew it for what it was. Gas. Gas! And he hadn't got his respirator. It wrapped round him, smothered him, choked him. He was drowning, drowning . . .

'Joe! Joe, what's the matter? Oh my God –'

Arms around him, dragging, pulling.

'Come on, Joe, you must sit up.'

The green fog cleared. Air reached him. He struggled to suck it in, to defeat the terrifying clogging inside. Sweat drenched him, he could not see, or think, everything narrowed to keeping the life-giving pure air travelling through the narrow passages of his lungs.

Poppy flung up the window and leaned out, her eyes raking the street below, her heart pounding. A boy of about eleven came into view, hands in pockets, kicking a stone.

'Hi! You – boy!'

He looked up, wary. 'Me? I ain't done nothing.'

'Want to earn sixpence?'

Was it enough?

His eyes lit up. 'Yeah.'

'You know the doctor? Him down Smith Street?'

'Yeah, I know him.'

'Then go and fetch him,' Poppy ordered. 'And run!'

'Right you are, missus.'

She turned back into the room, afraid of what she might find. Joe lay where she had propped him up, his staring eyes glazed, his mouth open, his chest heaving as he struggled to breathe. The terrible whistling rasp sent a shudder right through her. She felt helpless. Then, remembering childhood fevers, she went to wring a cloth out in water and pressed it gently to his forehead, mopping the beads of sweat. The note of his breathing changed slightly, but she could not tell whether it was better or worse.

The minutes stretched out, each one an age. Why didn't the doctor come? Was that boy to be trusted? Perhaps she should have called a cab and taken him straight to hospital.

'Keep going, Joe,' she told him, her voice low and urgent. 'Keep going, just keep breathing. Don't let it beat you.'

Christopher started to whimper and she went to pick him up, drawing comfort from his warm little body. A great wave of love washed through her, warring queasily with the worry for Joe. Would the doctor never come?

It was only twenty minutes, but it felt like forever. When he did arrive, there was little he could do.

'Your husband's lungs are permanently damaged, Mrs Chaplin. What he needs is pure air, not this London smoke. And as for the job he does, I can hardly think of anything less suitable.'

'But he's a musician, a drummer. It's the only thing he can do.'

The doctor looked at her severely over the top of his gold-rimmed spectacles. 'Does he not have a pension from the army? He should have. He was invalided out, was he not?'

Poppy held his eyes. 'Could you live on what the government calls a pension? We got a baby. He's got to be brought up proper.'

The doctor gave a snort of impatience. 'Young woman, if your husband carries on working night after night in a damp basement full of smoke, your baby will soon be an orphan, and you a widow. Take my advice and move to the seaside or the country. I'm sure your husband could get some healthy outdoor work. It would be the making of him. In the meantime, he is not to get out of that bed for at least a week.'

After he had gone, Poppy sat on the end of the bed and looked at Joe. The danger was past, but his face was drawn with exhaustion. She tried to think about what she should do. Joe earned better money by far than any of the men in Trinidad Street, but they spent it as soon as it came in. What small savings they did have had been used up when he had been ill after Christopher was born, and now there was the doctor's fee to be found.

'Poppy?'

She started. She had thought he was asleep. His voice was a pitiful whisper.

'You mustn't talk, Joe. You're all right now, but you mustn't talk. You must save your breath.'

An agitated look passed over his face.

'Tell Charlie – back soon – keep job –'

The doctor's warnings were still ringing in her ears, but it was no use making Joe all worried by telling him he had to give his job up.

'Yes, yes, I'll tell him. I'll make them take on someone just to cover for you. Mona's brother Ray's free. I'm sure he'll do it for a bit, till you're better. Don't you worry about anything, Joe. You just get yourself better.'

'Tell – now –'

'I will, Joe, I promise. Now just you go to sleep.'

She waited till his eyes closed and his face relaxed. If only she was still living on Dog Island. It would all be so much easier. She could leave Christopher with her mother while she went and sorted things out. As it was, the baby was going to have to come with her. At the door, she stopped and looked at Joe. He shouldn't be left like this, but she had no alternative. Here in Islington, it was not like Trinidad Street, where everyone knew everyone else. She hardly saw her neighbours.

Just as she was leaving, her eyes fell on her saxophone case, leaning against the dresser. On impulse, she took it with her.

In the failing light of the early evening, she trailed round to

167

Mona's house to see if her brother was free to stand in for Joe for a week or so. To her relief, he was. Then she went on to the Half Moon Club.

'Poppy! Well, here's a sight for sore eyes!'

'Long time no see. How are you doing?'

'She's got the baby. Oh – ain't he lovely?'

She smiled and kissed cheeks and exclaimed back at them, wrapped round with the old warmth and comradeship.

'Why, the old place hasn't changed a bit.'

'You've not been away that long, girl.'

'It feels like it. It feels like forever.'

'To what do we owe the pleasure?' This was from Mr Fairbrother.

'It's Joe –'

Expressions of concern all round, except from Bob and Charlie.

'He's not ill again, is he?' Bob was annoyed.

'Bloody hell, he ain't what you might call reliable, is he?' Charlie said.

Poppy turned on them. 'It's all right for you two. You never went to the Front. Got away with it, you did. Sat here on your fat arses coining it in while Joe was being gassed –'

'All right, Poppy, hold on –' Jimmy the barman laid a heavy paw on her shoulder.

'No, I won't! They make me sick. If they'd seen Joe like what I have today, fighting for his life, they wouldn't go on about him being unreliable. He shouldn't be here at all. The doctor said he ought to be out in the fresh air.'

Bob was unrepentant. 'What's stopping him, then? We ain't forcing him to come here. Plenty more drummers around.'

Poppy suddenly realized she was working against herself. She had let her tongue run away with her again.

'Not as good as what he is,' she said.

There was a rumble of agreement around her.

'But what about tonight?' Mr Fairbrother asked. 'We got to have a drummer. People come here to dance as much as to drink these days.'

'Oh, that's all right,' Poppy assured him. 'I got that fixed. Ray Dobson's coming in. He'll be able to pick up Joe's part fine.'

There were reluctant noises of approval from Bob and Charlie. They knew Ray. He was an Archer Street man. He was all right.

'And – ' Poppy took a deep breath, put on her brightest, most confident smile, 'I got you a saxophonist and all.'

'We don't need a sax. Three-piece is quite enough for a little place like this,' Charlie said.

'Saxes are all the rage. All the best places got 'em,' Poppy persisted. 'It'd fill out the sound something lovely. Make it more sophisticated.'

Bob and Charlie looked unimpressed, but Mr Fairbrother was interested.

'Might be worth a try –'

Poppy looked up at him through her lashes. 'I knew you'd see it was a good idea. You know what a band should sound like.'

'Who is this bloke, anyway?' Bob asked.

'Me.'

Bob and Charlie erupted into derisive laughter.

Poppy kept her temper with great difficulty. She turned to Mr Fairbrother. He was the one who held the purse strings. If he wanted another player, he could say so and the others would have to lump it.

'Give us a trial, Mr Fairbrother. I'll do it tonight unpaid, and you can see if the customers like it. I bet you they will. After all, I'm better to look at than those two, ain't I?'

It took a lot more sweet-talking, but by the time Ray Dobson arrived, Mr Fairbrother was swayed. Christopher was tucked into an orange box behind the bar and the four of them got down to a quick rehearsal.

Poppy's fingers shook as she put the sax to her lips. She knew she had improved a lot in these last months. She and Elsie and Mona had practised regularly. But this was the real thing. If she could convince the men that she was good

169

enough, then she and Joe and Christopher would have enough to live on until Joe was back on his feet again. Bob and Charlie did not make it easy for her. They started with a difficult ragtime number. But she was familiar with everything in their repertoire, since Joe always told her what they were doing. She managed to get through it, though she felt as if she was always a fraction of a beat behind them. Ray had no difficulty. He was a pro, used to fitting in with all manner of outfits and styles of playing. He gave her a nod of approval.

'All right, ain't she?' he said to the others. 'My sister said she could play. I reckon she was right.'

Poppy flashed him a smile of gratitude. But the others remained stubbornly unimpressed. They tried another number.

'Lame,' Charlie said.

But Mr Fairbrother was watching Poppy's legs, revealed by her new shorter length dress.

'Give her a go tonight,' he decided. 'See how the customers react.'

Poppy jumped up and ran over to kiss him on the cheek.

'You're a pal, Mr Fairbrother!'

He caught her round the waist, pressing her briefly to him. His cigarette-laden breath wafted round her face. 'Yeah, and don't you forget it, girlie,' he said in her ear.

Alarm and revulsion shot through her. She swallowed it down, broke away, gave him a bright open look, as if she had not understood the remark.

'They'll like me, you'll see.'

She retreated to the tiny washroom to give Christopher a feed, then it was into action. The first customers of the night were trickling in.

She had never realized just what hard work it was. The concentration, the timing, the sheer physical effort of holding the sax and blowing through the reed. But the sense of achievement at getting it all together, the wave of triumph as the audience applauded, was intoxicating. By the time they took their first break, she was shaking with fatigue and riding as high as if she had drunk a bottle of champagne.

At the bar, she was beseiged by men wanting to buy her drinks. Intrigued by the sight of a woman playing dance music, they wanted to know more. Poppy laughed and teased and downed three lemonades on the trot. There was no need for whisky now. She had found a far more effective drug.

'They like you, girl,' Mr Fairbrother said, nodding his approval.

'Told you,' Poppy laughed.

Bob and Charlie hunched over their drinks, muttering together and giving her sour looks. Christopher woke and began to cry.

'Bloody hell,' Charlie said. 'It's like working in a bleeding nursery.'

Poppy scooped the baby up and went into the washroom. Remorse filled her. There she had been, having the time of her life, and poor little Christopher was wet and dirty and hungry.

'I'm doing this for you, baby,' she whispered to him, as he champed with greedy concentration. 'You've been such a good boy. Just go on being good and tomorrow I'll fix something up.'

And as if understanding the importance of the occasion, Christopher snuggled down into his orange box, dry and full, and slept through till the last customer staggered out of the club at four o'clock.

Bone-weary but elated, Poppy packed away the sax.

'Well?' she said to Mr Fairbrother. 'What do you think? Do I get the job?'

His hand patted her bottom, lingered.

'Yes – ' he said slowly. 'Yes, I think we might give you a week and see how it goes.'

Poppy straightened up and looked him in the eye.

'Paid? I ain't doing it for nothing. I got a baby to keep.'

His expression changed. 'Yeah, paid.'

Ignoring all the possible pitfalls, Poppy let out a cry of delight. She was a professional musician.

19

Jane looked round the flat with approval.

'It's really nice,' she said. 'So much space! You'll rattle around in it, you will, just the two of you and the baby.'

In the midst of the piled boxes and bags, Joe sat in a sagging armchair, his face pale.

'Glad you like it, Ma-in-law. Come here specially for Poppy, we have. She ain't happy away from Dog Island.'

Jane came over and patted his hand. She liked her son-in-law. Just as Poppy had said, he did remind her a little of her Owen.

'That's very thoughtful of you, that is. I knew Poppy'd be all right with a musician. And it's nice for me and all. It was a long way over to Islington. Now I'm less than ten minutes away.'

It was just around the corner from Cinnamon Alley and along the West Ferry Road, above a grocer's shop. Jane could not get over how lovely it was to have her daughter back again, and with her husband and baby as well. Now she would really have something to discuss with the other women in the street, for whom the day-to-day doings of their families formed the greater part of their conversation.

After they had drunk cups of tea and discussed Christopher's progress, Jane volunteered to help get everything sorted away. She followed Poppy into the tiny dark kitchen with the dirty cups.

'He all right?' she asked, indicating Joe with a jerk of the head. 'He don't look too good.'

Poppy shut the door, keeping her voice low so that Joe wouldn't hear.

'He ain't too good, Mum. He didn't ought to be working yet, but he was afraid if he didn't get back, the others'd find

172

another permanent drummer. But it's telling on him. He's done in by the end of the session.'

'Poor lamb. But at least it means you can stop going out all night long now.'

Poppy leaned against the cracked stone sink. She looked tired and worn. She never had been fat, and now she was really skinny. She sighed.

'I don't think I can, Mum. Now I got this job with the band, I got to keep it open. You see, I never know when Joe's going to get sick. I'm trying to put some by for if he's off work again. He didn't ought to be working down that club at all. But he don't know how to do anything else.'

'Oh lovey, and just when I thought you was getting settled and all.'

But that was life, Jane knew. Just when you thought things were all right, some problem came along.

They went into the back room to make up the bed. Jane voiced the problem that worried her the most.

'But what about little Kit? He ought to have his mum looking after him. You can't do that when you're out all night and asleep half the day.'

'I know that, Mum. I hate going and leaving him, it tears my heart in two, it really does. But I just got to keep that job open. If I leave, Bob and Charlie'll never let me back in again. They hate having me there. I get all the attention, you see. The members keep asking for encores and solos. Bob and Charlie say it's only because I'm a girl, but they know really I'm a better player than them. I know it sounds big-headed, Mum, but I am, and they hate it. They're always trying to score points off of me. Like the other night, they came in with this new piece, "Peppermint Tango". Bob, he hands it to me, all off-hand, like. "We'll have a crack at this later on," he says. And I look at it, and it's a right so-and-so. A really hard sax part. They've chosen it just to see me fail. When I try and say I need to rehearse it a bit, they say as how a pro can do anything what's given him, and if I didn't like it, I knew what I could do. Well, that really got me going. I wasn't going to let them

173

beat me. It nearly killed me, but I got to the end of that piece, and I did it well. You should have seen their faces! Specially when the audience gave me a cheer. That showed 'em. So anyway, it's not all beer and skittles down the Half Moon, by any account.'

'I can see that, dear,' Jane said. 'But if they're as bad as all that, is it really worth carrying on? When it means little Kit don't see you half the time.'

'But I'm doing it for Kit, don't you see?' Poppy told her. 'I don't want him to grow up to go and work in the docks like the boys round here. I want him to go to a nice school and stay on till he's got a proper education. I want him to get on in life. And he ain't going to do that unless there's money coming in.'

Not for the first time, Jane realized that her daughter had different standards from her. It was not just the baby, it was her home as well. The stuff they had! Amazing stuff, such as nobody even dreamt of in Cinnamon Alley. These sheets and blankets had not come second-hand and then been turned sides to middle. They had been bought brand-new. Then there was the gramophone. And as for the clothes ... She knew that Poppy had to dress up for her job, but even so, a whole wardrobe full was simply unheard of amongst her friends. If everyone she knew dressed the same way as her daughter, she would have no trouble getting business. But was it making her happy? She certainly didn't look it at the moment.

'The thing is, Mum – ' she was saying.

And then inspiration hit Jane. Of course!

'You best let me look after him, then,' she said. She surprised herself with the firmness of her tone.

'Oh, Mum – ' Poppy came round to Jane's side of the bed and flung her arms round her. 'Mum, you took the words right out of my mouth. If you could do that, it'd be such a weight off of my mind. I wouldn't be deserting him, like, if his own granny was there. But are you sure? I mean, it's a lot of extra work for you, what with your sewing and all.'

'The sewing's not what it used to be. Not with all this cheap ready-made stuff in the shops. And anyway, that's not the point. Little Kit's my grandson. I'd love to have him.'

Jane felt as if she had been given the crown jewels. It was the best thing that had happened to her in years. She was really needed again.

'You're doing what?' Margaret asked.

'I'm spending the night round Poppy and Joe's.'

Margaret stared at her daughter. She had not spent a night away from home since That Man left. It had all changed since Poppy had that baby. Jane had taken to going out when she felt like it. She even went right over to Islington to visit. And now this!

'You'll do no such thing,' she said.

Jane avoided her eyes. 'I'm sorry, Ma, but I'm going. I promised Poppy I'd look after the baby while she's at work.'

'What d'you want to do a thing like that for?' Suspicion sharpened in Margaret's mind. 'That husband of hers left her already?'

'No, he ain't.'

'What's Poppy out working nights for then?'

Jane muttered something under her breath.

'What did you say?'

Her daughter looked her straight in the face. There was something close to defiance in her expression. She took a breath.

'I said, what's it to you? You threw her out. You got no right to question what she does now.'

For once in her life, Margaret was speechless. Jane was arguing the point with her. Jane! She had come to expect it from Poppy, but Jane she could always subdue with a glance.

'So I'm going round there tonight,' Jane said, taking advantage of the silence, and scuttled out of the room before Margaret could gather her wits.

It was strange in the house that evening. Since Poppy left home, Margaret had got into the habit of getting Jane to bring her handwork down to the kitchen. They would sit one either side of the range, Jane sewing while Margaret read her daily paper, the one luxury she allowed herself. Whenever anything struck Margaret as particularly reprehensible, she would read it out to her daughter, expecting her to agree with her opinion. There was plenty in the news to excite her disapproval. It was not the same with nobody there. Margaret put down her paper only half read and fidgeted about, poking the fire and rearranging the tea towels hung over the brass rail. She did not admit it to herself, but in her heart she knew, Jane might be a poor thing and a deep disappointment as a daughter, but she missed her.

That put her in a really bad mood. The lodgers, coming down for their breakfast next morning, got the rough side of her tongue. They swallowed down their food in double-quick time and made off. Margaret cleared away and washed up, then was faced with the whole house to clean by herself. It was very quiet, without the sound of Jane treadling away at her sewing machine. When a woman came knocking on the door offering to scrub the step for tuppence, Margaret actually agreed. It was the first time she had ever employed anyone to do something for her. She stood over the unfortunate woman while she worked, pointing out bits that had not been done.

It was when she was at the door taking the bread order from the baker's boy that she noticed a group of women gathered further down the street. Idle lot, gossiping in the middle of the morning when their work could not possibly be done. Then she realized that Jane was amongst them, and that the object of their attention was a baby carriage. She stood, torn, gazing down the street. Half of her knew she should go straight inside and slam the door. Poppy had proved just as big a disappointment as Jane, and that baby was the cause of it. But the other half wanted to walk right down the street to the baby carriage, to peer inside and see this new member of her family, her flesh and blood. So she stayed immobile, unable to make the decision.

As she stood there, frozen in the doorway, Jane looked up and saw her. She said something to her friends and began walking up the street towards her, pushing the baby carriage. With the calculating part of her mind, Margaret noted that it was a very expensive one, shiny and black, and obviously bought new for the baby. Spendthrifts. She held on to the thought, letting it fill her with indignation, a defence against the assault on her emotions that was coming ever closer.

Jane stopped in front of her. There was a desperate air of conscious bravery about her.

'This is him, then,' she said, nodding at the baby. 'Your great-grandson, Kit.'

Margaret did not look under the hood. Instead she kept her eyes on her daughter. Her mouth felt very dry. A boy. A baby boy.

'Kit? What sort of a name is that?'

Her voice came out even louder and more aggressive than usual. She could not help it. Jane flinched and swallowed.

'It – it's short for Christopher.' She manoeuvred the heavy carriage round a quarter turn, so that Margaret could see right in. 'Go on, Ma, take a look at him.'

She did not want to look. She fought the inclination. But something even stronger than the need to deflect pain took hold of her and made her lower her eyes and look under the hood.

He was sitting up, holding on to the sides with chubby hands. A beautiful child, with clear rosy skin and plump round cheeks, as strong and well-grown a baby as any she had ever seen, clean and well dressed.

Two round blue eyes looked back at her with the unabashed stare of the very young. Margaret felt the world shift around her. A beautiful boy, not a poor weak little thing like all of hers, but one with a firm hold on life.

From a long way away, it seemed, her daughter's voice was speaking at her.

'. . . so forward, you wouldn't believe it! And knowing – there ain't nothing he misses. Sharp as a knife. Ain't you, Kit?'

Jane leant over the carriage, trying to distract the baby's attention, but he was fascinated by Margaret. Old and young gazed at each other, a long unbroken look. Margaret's hand crept as far as the handle of the carriage, and gripped it as if her life depended upon it. Here in the soft unmoulded features was her immortality. She wanted to reach out, to have something to love and care for, to watch over and cherish, but still the anguish of loving only to lose held her back. As if sensing her rejection, Christopher's small face suddenly reddened. His blue eyes squeezed shut and his mouth opened to let out a wail. Instinct took over. Margaret leant over and picked him up, warm and soft and vulnerable, and held him close in her arms.

'There now, what's the matter?' she asked him. 'You're all right. There's nothing to cry about. You got your great-gran to look after you.'

20

'You know what the doctor said, Joe. He said you got to get fresh air into your lungs. You got to go to the seaside.'

'I don't want to go to the bloody seaside. I hate the seaside.'

'The country, then. Get some nice country air.'

'The country's even worse. It's full of grass and cows and yokels.'

'Oh, Joe, that's just stupid. It ain't all like that. It's – it's pretty.'

'And what do you know about it, eh? Nothing. You don't know nothing outside of Dog Island. I tried it before, remember, after I come out of the army, and I hated it. That's why I come back to London and got the job at the Half Moon. I'm a Londoner, Poppy.'

Poppy sighed, but did not give up. She looked down at Joe as he rested, propped up on a pile of cushions and pillows in their bed. His face had that dreadful grey tinge to it again.

'What about Brighton?' she persisted. 'You can't say you don't like Brighton. London by the sea, Brighton is.'

'And just what would I do in Brighton?'

'Blimey, Joe, there must be hundreds of jobs going there. Piers, pierrot shows, tea dances, pictures houses, clubs –'

'Yeah, and every one of them taken by now. It's May. They're all booked for the summer season, and anything that ain't booked ain't worth taking.'

Poppy sat down on the bed and took his hand. It felt hot and dry. She resisted the temptation to point out that if he had listened to her earlier, he would have been in time to get himself hired.

'Then do something else. Sell toffee apples or deckchair tickets or something.'

Joe's eyes blazed at this blasphemy. He tried to take a deep breath to shout at her.

'I'm a musician, not –'

He got no further. His treacherous lungs closed up on him, leaving him fighting once more for breath. Poppy hung over him, holding him up, waiting for it to pass. It took a long time, and left him weak as a baby. She smoothed the damp hair back off his forehead.

'All right, you made your point. But, Joe, I'm worried about you. You can't go on like this. You won't be able to go in tonight. Please think about it. There must be some jobs still going, even if it's some back of beyond place. At least you'll be alive.'

Joe stared up at the ceiling.

'Please, Joe –'

'All right.' His voice was a whisper. 'All right. I'll think about it.'

With that Poppy had to be satisfied. It was further than she had got before. Perhaps he really was seeing some sense at last. She kissed his cheek.

'You do that. Now get some sleep.'

She went downstairs, to where Christopher was sitting strapped into a chair, banging a wooden spoon on the table. He squealed with delight as she came in. He was nine months old now, noisy and lively.

'Look at you – going to be a drummer just like your dad.'

The baby dropped the spoon on the floor and gave a cry of frustration. Poppy picked it up. Christopher threw it down again.

'Oh, we're playing this, are we? Keep Mum on the hop. I got the tea to get, young man.'

She chatted to him as she went about preparing the meal, voicing her thoughts and worries.

'I don't know what we're going to do about your dad. He's so stubborn. He'll kill himself if he carries on working at that club. But if he does get a summer season, what then? Did you and me ought to go with him to wherever, or should we stay

180

here? Lodgings are expensive in seaside places. That's why your grandpa always went off on his own. Much cheaper than dragging the family along. But your granny says we ought to all stay together. She should know. Your grandpa went off one day and he never come back . . .'

She paused, bread knife halfway down a slice. What if Joe went off and never came back? The truth was, it wouldn't hurt at all. She would miss him, but as a provider, not as a lover. That side of their relationship was something to be put up with, a duty. It wasn't so bad in the dark, but she hated it when he wanted to see her body. It stirred up all the dark memories of Mr Hetherington, making her feel used and guilty.

Now that she had Christopher, she needed a husband, and the child needed a father. She didn't want him to grow up wondering why his father had deserted them, as she had. But though she had grown quite fond of Joe, he held no lasting place in her heart. Her love was divided between Christopher, and the memory of Scott. Scott . . . with his deep dark eyes and his heartbreaking smile. She could still hear his voice, with that fascinating accent. Hardly a day went by when she did not catch sight of someone, in a street or amongst the crowd at the club, who bore some passing resemblance to him. Her heart would leap painfully, only to plummet in despair. If he had really only been missing, he would have come back for her. He was dead, but she loved him still.

A howl of protest from Christopher brought her back to reality. He had thrown the spoon down yet again, and he was hungry. Poppy gave him a crust to chew.

'There you are, my pet.' She laid her cheek against his warm head. 'At least I got you. You won't be leaving me, will you?'

It was about a week later that Joe, recovered from his latest bout of illness, came in from an afternoon out by himself. He flung his hat down on the table and stood looking defiantly at Poppy.

'Well, I done it. I hope you're happy now.'

181

'Done what, Joe?'

'Got a summer season.'

'Oh, Joe! Where?'

'Cromer.'

'Cromer? Where's that?'

'It's in Norfolk, north Norfolk. That fresh enough for you? Blooming air comes in right off the North Sea.'

Poppy slipped an arm through his and squeezed it. 'I'm sure it's the right thing to do, Joe. It'll set you up, you'll see. You'll be a new man.'

'Ha. If I don't die of boredom.'

'Oh, come on, Joe. It can't be that bad if people go there for their holidays. What's it famous for? All holiday places are famous for something.'

'Crabs.'

'Ah – still, it must be nice. What's the job? Where are you playing?'

'End of the pier show. Twice nightly and matinées.'

'Ah.'

It was a comedown, and they both knew it.

'And the pay's bloody peanuts, of course.'

'Well, Joe, I'm still sure it's the best thing to do. You can't go on like you been doing this last winter.'

'So you keep saying.'

It was not the end of the battle. Right up until he left, they were arguing over whether they should all move up to Cromer for the summer. In the end they decided that Joe should go first and see what the accommodation was like there. If he could find somewhere cheap, then Poppy and Christopher would follow.

Poppy went to see him off at Liverpool Street. It was not a cheerful occasion. She was disappointed that they weren't all off for a summer by the sea and Joe was still sulking at being sent into exile. Only Christopher was happy as he stared wide-eyed at the milling crowds and the great hissing steam engines. But after the train had pulled out, Poppy felt a curious sense of relief. He was gone. It was just her and

Christopher. When she got back to the flat, she changed a few things round. Now it was her own home. She made a cup of tea and sat playing with Christopher. It was as if a weight had lifted off her shoulders.

Joe was no letter writer. Brief postcards arrived at the flat, the first one announcing his safe arrival, then a string of complaints, about the town, the band, his landlady, the weather, the audiences. All seemed to be equally bad.

At her end, Poppy had her own problems. Her only allies at the Half Moon were Jimmy and Mr Fairbrother. Bob, Charlie and the new drummer were all equally keen to get rid of her, but the boss had his finger on the pulse of musical taste. Saxophones were in. Every club of any standing had a sax in its line-up. Banjos and pianos, on the other hand, were on their way out. They were associated with ragtime, and ragtime was of the last decade. The music of the newborn twenties was jazz. The fact that what most bands played was really nothing like jazz, but merely a syncopated dance rhythm did not matter, so long as the clientele liked the sound.

June turned into July and still Poppy managed to hold on to her job. But the weather was sticky and sultry and Christopher was teething. The thought of sleeping regular hours, breathing sea air and taking Christopher on the sand was getting more and more tempting. London was beginning to empty of its rich and carefree. Mr Fairbrother talked of closing down for a few weeks. It was not like wartime, when the place was full of officers on short leave whatever the time of year. They were back to the old system of Season and non-Season. Poppy wrote to ask Joe to find at least a double room for them. He wrote back saying his pay wouldn't keep a flea alive, let alone support the three of them, the West Ferry Road flat and a room in Cromer.

Poppy was frowning over this last communication when Elsie turned up at the flat.

'Phew, I'm tired,' she sighed, sinking into a chair and kicking off her shoes. 'My poor feet! It's a killer, that job.'

When she had got her complaints about the hotel off her chest, Elsie asked after Joe.

'Had anything from him this week?'

'Yeah.' Poppy handed her the card. 'What do you think of that?'

Elsie read it, then shrugged. 'Well, if he can't afford it, that's that. Pity. You and the little 'un could do with a holiday.'

'But the pay's not that bad, Elsie. It's dreadful compared with what he used to get at the Half Moon, but it's better than what anyone earns round here. And I got money put away.'

'You! You saved some money?'

'There's no need to look so blooming amazed. I'm getting real sensible now I got Christopher. Look at how I stopped the drinking. I ain't touched a drop of whisky in months.'

'All right, all right. Keep your hair on. So if you want to go and see him and you got the money, what's stopping you?'

Poppy did not have an answer to that.

'Sounds like you better get yourself up there, then,' Elsie told her.

Poppy laughed and gave her a hug. 'Everything always seems so simple when you're here.'

'Oh, yeah. Simple, that's me.'

'I don't mean that. I mean, you sort of pick the bones out of it. And you're right, I'm going, even if it means him and me and Christopher all sharing a single bed.'

She decided not to tell Joe what she was doing, but simply turn up. She could be off by the end of the week. But before then, another card arrived, with a Cromer postmark, but in an unfamiliar hand. It was from Joe's landlady, telling her that he had been 'taken real badly'. Poppy threw an armful of Christopher's things into a bag, packed a change of clothes for herself, took her savings from the hiding place at the back of a cupboard and set out for Liverpool Street Station.

It was a nightmare journey. The train was hot and crowded and Christopher was miserable. After what seemed like forever, they arrived at Norwich. Poppy could either get a train straightaway, or change Christopher, have a drink and wait for an hour and a half. While she was still trying to decide which was better, the Cromer train pulled out.

'That shouldn't have gone for another five minutes,' she protested to a ticket collector.

'Oh, that board be wrong, missus,' the man told her. 'You don't want to take no notice of that.'

She retreated to the ladies' cloakroom and washed a wailing Christopher in the hand basin. When the attendant tried to stop her, she got the full force of Poppy's most colourful vocabulary, backed up by a rising volume of crying from Christopher. The woman had no chance.

It was a tired and ragged-edged Poppy that finally emerged from Cromer station. She and the other passengers were immediately besieged by a troop of boys with home-made handcarts, eager to carry their luggage. Poppy thankfully dumped her bag on the nearest cart and followed the boy to Joe's lodgings.

The landlady was not the dragon she had been led to expect, but a dumpy, homely woman with a flowery apron and a broad Norfolk accent.

'So you be Mrs Chaplin. Come in, my dear. I'm rightly glad to see you. And the little one as well! You look all done in, you do.'

'What's the matter with my husband?' Poppy demanded.

'Oh, my dear, he's not at all the thing. I thought as it was just a summer cold, like. But it's gone and settled on his chest. Thass a real nasty chest he's got on him, ain't he?'

'He was gassed in the war.'

'Ah, well, that explains it. I been right worried about him, so I have.'

The fear that had dogged her from the moment she read the card now tightened its hold.

'Where is he? I want to see him.'

'Of course you do, my dear. You come right along up, and give the little mauther to me. I'll see to him.'

Poppy followed her up two flights of stairs to a room at the

185

back of the house. Through the door Poppy heard a horribly familiar sound, that of Joe's laboured breathing. Even that did not prepare her for the shock of what she found inside. Joe was lying still and flushed, his face was drawn with sweat standing out on his forehead and he looked ten years older than when she had last seen him.

'Oh, Joe –'

She dropped on her knees beside the bed and took the hand that lay on the cover. It was burning up. As she did so, Joe stirred, his head moving from side to side on the pillow.

'No good – wrong key, they got the wrong key – useless – can't play like that – can't –'

A chill settled round Poppy's heart. She smoothed damp locks of hair back off his face.

'Joe, it's me, Poppy. I've come to look after you. Everything's going to be all right now. I'll watch over you.'

As Poppy watched, horrified, he jerked upright, trying to shout at some unseen enemy. She tried to restrain him but he flung her off with surprising strength. Only a fit of coughing stopped him, reducing him to a trembling wreck. When he had finally quietened down and seemed to be asleep, Poppy crept out. Her whole body was shaking. Her knees would hardly hold her up. Slowly, she made her way downstairs to where the landlady was playing with Christopher in the kitchen.

'Has a doctor seen him?' she demanded, cutting across the woman's expressions of concern.

'He wouldn't have no doctor, my dear. Said as how a doctor had got him into this and he wasn't going to have no more to do with 'em.'

'But he's delirious! He's got to see a doctor straightaway. Never mind what he said. I'm here now and I say he's got to have one. Right now.'

Impressed into virtual silence by this outburst, the landlady scuttled out of the door to find someone to run the message. Poppy gathered a tired and bewildered Christopher into her arms and rested her head on his, fighting back tears.

'Oh, baby,' she whispered. 'What are we going to do?'

Guilt tore at her. She had insisted that he came here. If he had stayed in London as he wanted to, he would not be in this state now.

When the doctor finally arrived, he shook his head gloomily over Joe and diagnosed double pneumonia. He insisted that Joe be moved to the cottage hospital.

Poppy was terrified. People only went into hospitals to die.

'But why? I can look after him. You just tell me what needs doing and I'll do it.'

The doctor did not mince words. 'Mrs Chaplin, your husband is very seriously ill. He needs round-the-clock nursing.'

'I can do that. I'll do anything.'

'Not as well as they can in the hospital. He needs professional attention, not the ministrations of an amateur, how ever well-intentioned.'

'Oh – you mean – ?' She did not dare put it into words.

'I mean that the prognostications are not good, Mrs Chaplin. A healthy man of his age should survive pneumonia, but he is not a healthy man. Frankly, I'm surprised he's lived this long.'

Poppy sat down. She felt very cold.

'All right. Take him to hospital.'

The next forty-eight hours passed in daze of worry and fatigue. She was only allowed to see Joe during the set visiting hours, so the rest of the time she wandered about the little town with Christopher. The carefree family holiday had turned into one long wait from one visiting time to the next. At night, she lay sleepless on the bed that had been Joe's, haunted by regrets. If only she had not gone on about sea air. If only . . .

When she went to see him on the second evening, she found his bed screened off from the rest of the ward. The Sister intercepted her before she got there.

'Mrs Chaplin –'

'What's happened? He's not –?'

187

'No, he's still alive but – you must prepare yourself, Mrs Chaplin. The fever has broken, but he's not recovering as he should do.'

The Sister personally led her behind the screens. The hectic flush had gone from Joe's sunken face, leaving him ashen. He lay very still, too still for normal sleep. The note of his breathing had changed. It was slow, very slow, with a horrible bubble to it. Poppy did not need to be a doctor to know that his lungs were filled with some noxious substance.

Poppy felt for his hand where it lay neatly tucked away beneath the cover. It was no longer burning, but cold and completely limp. She held it between both of hers, trying to will some of her abundant life back into him, but no change, no flicker of recognition dawned on his face. Desperately, she began to talk, about the club, the people they both knew, Christopher, the flat – and when she had gone through all that at least three times she started on her childhood reminiscences, her father and the good times they had had, her finding the pawn ticket and earning the money for the saxophone, even about Mr Hetherington.

'And I never told anyone about that before, Joe, not even Scott. But I'm telling you, so you got to understand and wake up and start to get better again. We need you, Joe, me and Christopher –'

The other visitors had long ago been ushered out, but the compassionate Sister had let her stay. At length, she ran out of words. She sat at last in silence, listening to each painful breath.

It was just after midnight when the next breath did not come, and his overburdened lungs gave up.

21

Elsie hesitated at the street door of Poppy's flat. The newspaper cutting she carried in her handbag seemed to burn through the cracked leather. Should she show it to Poppy, or not? The question had plagued her ever since she found it this morning, when clearing out a bedroom. Poppy was so low at the moment, it could cheer her up, but on the other hand, it might make her even worse. Even though she knew her better than anybody, Elsie could not decide how her friend would react. Perhaps she had better wait and see what sort of a mood Poppy was in. She pushed open the door and went in, calling up the stairs as she did so.

'Coo-ee! Poppy! You in?'

A pause, then a flat-toned reply: 'Yeah, I'm here. Come on up, Else.'

Elsie's heart sank. By the sound of her, she was no better. At the top of the stairs, she was arrested by the sight of Poppy on her knees, packing things into cardboard boxes.

'Poppy, what on earth are you doing?'

Poppy sat back on her heels and pushed a straggling strand of hair off her face.

'What does it look like? I'm packing up.'

'But why? I thought you liked it here? Your little nest, you called this.'

'Yeah – ' Poppy sighed and looked about her. 'Yeah, I did. And I do like it but – ' She stopped, her voice strangled.

'I'll make us a nice cup of tea,' Elsie decided.

She took off her coat and went into the tiny kitchen, with Christopher toddling after her. She stopped and picked him up.

'How's my favourite little boy, then? My, you're getting big. You'll soon be too heavy for your Aunty Elsie, 'specially after a day at that horrible hotel. When are you going to say my name, eh? Aun-tie. Aun-tie.'

The little boy wriggled with pleasure and babbled at her. Out of the happy muddle of sounds came something like 'Arn-arn'. Elsie was delighted.

'You're so clever! Hey, Poppy, Kit just said "Auntie". Ain't he clever?'

Something like a genuine smile lit Poppy's weary face.

'Yeah, he's bright as a barrow-load of monkeys, that one.'

'You're so lucky to have him, you know.'

'Yeah, yeah I do know, Else. Honest I do.'

Elsie cuddled him close as she made the tea. She loved children. It was so unfair that she had not fallen for one before Ted went and got killed. It would have been something of him to cherish for ever, taking the edge off the loss.

She carried the teacups into the living-room and made Poppy sit in an easy chair to drink it.

'I brought you a present.' She delved into her handbag. Her fingers touched the newspaper cutting, but left it hidden. Now was not the right moment. She found a little glass jar and a crackling twist of paper. 'Here – cold cream. There's over half of it left in there. The waste! Fancy just leaving it behind. And there's some chocs for my little Kit. Can he have them? They're creams. She had a great big box, this woman. Heart shaped, it was, with a big pink bow on it. So pretty! I wish I could of brought that and all, but I never would of got out with it. So I just wrapped the chocs up in some of the paper.'

'Yeah, he can have them. Won't do him no harm.'

Elsie unwrapped the hoard of chocolates and offered one to Christopher, smiling as his little eyes went round at the delicious taste.

Elsie looked across at her friend. Poppy seemed a bit more relaxed now.

'So what's all this about moving, then?'

'I got to, Elsie. I can't afford to keep this place on. With what I get from waitressing, I can't manage.'

Elsie couldn't understand it.

'But you got a pension from Joe, ain't you? And he left you some money and all.'

'I know, but that pension wouldn't keep a fly alive, and I want to keep for Kit what Joe left. I feel so bad about that, Elsie. You remember how I said I thought there was something funny going on when he said he couldn't afford for Kit and me to go up to Cromer? He was only thinking of us, putting money away all those weeks. I think he knew he was – he was – you know.'

'Yeah, I know. He never was well, Poppy. I mean, ever since you first knew him he was always getting them attacks.' More than anything, Elsie wanted to keep her from blaming herself for Joe's death.

'Yeah, maybe. But I don't want it to be all for nothing, see? If I keep that money put by for Kit, it'll be, well, better –'

Elsie could see some sort of reasoning in this.

'So where are you moving to?'

Poppy did not answer for a moment. She stared down into her teacup as if she was trying to find some message of hope in the leaves.

'Back to Gran's.'

'Oh, Poppy, you never!'

She looked up fiercely, trying to justify her choice.

'Well, it makes sense, don't it? It'll be as cheap there as anywhere, and her and Mum can mind Kit for me. She's potty about Kit, my gran. It's like she's a different person when he's around. Anyway, it's stupid, having all this place just for the two of us. It's best to be with your family.'

There was no arguing with that, really. It had not seemed worth Elsie and Ted getting a place of their own when they married, what with him being in the army, and now she was widowed there was no point. She was still sharing a room with her younger sisters.

Elsie looked at Poppy, hunched over her empty teacup, defeat in every line of her body. She was struck with sudden inspiration. It wouldn't solve any problems, but it would take Poppy out of herself for a bit.

'Look,' she said, 'I'll help you finish this lot off, then you and me'll go out to the pictures. How about that? I'll treat you to fish and chips on the way home.'

'Oh, I couldn't, Elsie –'

'Yes you could. Why not? Your Mum'll come in and mind Kit. Do you good. Give me a bit of a change and all.'

She thought Poppy was going to refuse. Then she saw the hint of a smile on her friend's face.

'Can I have a saveloy and all?'

Elsie grinned. 'Yeah, and a pickled egg. And a gherkin. Anything you like.'

'All right, then. Let's go.'

The Alhambra was a grandiose name for a place that was no more than a fleapit. There were wooden benches to sit on and the building smelt of drains. But the girls were able to ignore that. For two hours, they sat entranced by a serial that left the heroine locked up in a dungeon with an unseen monster, a cowboy story, a newsreel showing strange people in far-flung parts of the Empire, and a Harold Lloyd comedy. All the while, a pianist kept up with the action, playing music to go with whatever was happening on the screen. They finally emerged, blinking, into the street with their sides aching, still bemused and half in the world of fiction.

'Oh, he is clever, that man,' Poppy said, laughing all over again at the recollection. 'The way he just stood there when that house fell down!'

'And that girl in that castle and all. That awful thing's going to come and eat her up – or worse. I'm going to have to go again next week and find out what happens.' Elsie sighed happily, replete with fantasy.

True to her word, she bought Poppy a stomach-turning selection of goodies from the chip shop. The girls walked home eating with their fingers out of newspaper-wrapped parcels. At the swing bridge over the dock entrance, they paused and leant over the rail. Elsie screwed up her greasy paper and threw it down into the water.

'That was good.'

Poppy was still chewing her way steadily through her feast.

'Do you – ?' she began, then stopped.

'Yeah, what?'

'Do you still think of Ted? I mean, like miss him?'

Elsie looked down. It was pitch black below them. Black and cold as the space inside her left by Ted.

'Yeah, all the time.'

'You never – never thought of taking up with no one else?'

'I thought of it.' Oh, she'd thought of it all right, at night in her cold bed, or when she saw women with babies on their hips. 'Thing is, I never met a bloke I fancied like I did Ted. I don't think there is anyone else for me.'

'Oh, Elsie love – ' Poppy's arm came round her. 'I'm sorry. I shouldn't of asked.'

'It's all right.' Elsie took a deep shuddering breath. Now was the time to ask. After all, Poppy had started it. 'What about you? You thought about anyone else?'

'No, I'm giving all of that up. Hoping for things. Dreams. I mean, wanting to play in a band, it's stupid. I never really had a chance. And setting myself up in that flat, that was all show and all. I'm going back where I belong now. I'm going to live with my family and work as a waitress and see my little boy's brought up proper. That's going to have to be enough, me and Kit.'

Deep inside her, Elsie knew this was wrong.

'That's – that's wicked! It's like throwing stuff away.'

'It's what you're doing. You're living with your family and doing a blooming awful job and not thinking of looking for anyone else.'

'I know, but – ' Elsie groped towards expressing what she felt. 'It's different for you. You always was different. You never let nothing stand in your way.'

'Yeah, and a fat lot of good it done me. I was stupid, that's all. Now I've grown up.'

'But you're so pretty, Poppy. Not just pretty, you got something – I dunno. People look at you when you walk down the street, and it ain't just men, it's women too. You're like that girl in the pictures, what's-her-name, the It-girl. You got It. There's sure to be somebody else for you.'

'No. Never. I wouldn't dare.'

'What d'you mean?'

'I mean, I'm like a curse or something. I'm bad for people, for men. They all go away, or die. My dad went away and never come back. Joe died. And Scott got shot or blown up or something so bad they never even found him. So I'm never going to look at no one again.'

Elsie's slow-fused temper burst into life.

'Blimey, that's just so stupid! Curse, indeed! You better snap out of that, or you'll go daft, you will. I dunno about your dad, but Joe was killed by them Germans as sure as if they shot him. It was nothing to do with you. And as for Scott, he ain't dead at all. He's alive and well in America.'

'What do you mean?' Poppy's voice was very small. She put a hand on Elsie's arm, gripping her so tight it hurt.

'Come here.' Elsie moved to stand under the streetlamp. She searched around in her handbag and found the news-paper clipping. 'I been carrying that around all day. I wasn't sure whether to give it you. Read it.'

She knew the paragraph off by heart now. It was an account of a party in some rich house in New York. It meant nothing to her, except for one name, which had jumped off the page at her.

'. . . also amongst the guests was the rising star of the East Coast Bank, Mr Scott Warrender. Mr Warrender, young, handsome and oh-so-eligible, has often been seen in the company of the beautiful Miss Francine Vanderpost. Tonight, however, it was lovely widow Mrs Georgia Hartmann who decorated his arm. Mrs Hartmann's dress . . .'

Elsie watched as Poppy scanned the piece, then re-read it twice over slowly. Her face drained of colour. She looked at Elsie, her eyes wide with shock.

'He's alive, Elsie!'

Alive and having a rare old time of it, by all accounts. But Elsie did not mention this.

'Oh, I can't believe it, and yet – ' She looked at the cutting again, her eyes feasting on his name. 'It must be true. It's here in black and white. Oh, Elsie, this makes everything different. Everything.'

'I didn't know whether I ought to of shown it you,' Elsie said.

'You were right to. So right. It's like – it's like you give me back my life again.'

In the light of the streetlamp, the two girls hugged each other, and cried.

PART FOUR

The Powers Girls

22

1921

'What a blooming awful day! My feet are killing me. Fancy a drink before we go home?'

Elsie hesitated, then agreed. 'Why not? I'm fed up of that new under-housekeeper. She's got it in for me.'

They walked along the Strand, past a man with a gramophone on a pram, playing a scratchy record of 'Keep The Home Fires Burning'. A sign scrawled with chalk on a piece of cardboard declared him to have been blinded in the war. The unbearably sentimental tune caught at Poppy's heart. She thrust her hands into her pockets and marched on, fighting the guilt. There were so many of them. She could not give to them all.

'I dunno why you keep on with it. You never liked it there,' Poppy said, determinedly keeping up the conversation.

'It's better than Maconochie's.'

'Yeah, anything's better than Maconochie's. I keep telling myself that, specially on a day like today when all the customers have been bad-tempered and I went and dropped a tray.' Poppy stopped by the lounge bar entrance of a pub. 'Here, this one'll do. They don't look at you like you're a streetwalker in here if you go in without a man. God knows, there's enough of us around these days without men. You'd think they'd realize we're not all on the game just because we like a little drink from time to time.'

They sat at a small corner table.

'You still ain't written to Scott, then?' Elsie asked.

Poppy sighed. 'No. What's the use? All I know is the name of the bank he works for, and anyway, even if a letter got to him, he wouldn't want it. If he'd still loved me, he would of come back for me after the war.'

'He might of been too ill, or injured,' Elsie said. They had been over this ground before.

'Then he could of written to me from America when he got better. He knew where to write to. But you read that bit in that paper, Elsie. Out on the town with beautiful Miss This and lovely Widow That. He's a rich man now. He ain't interested in a waitress from Dog Island.'

At first it had been an impossible wish come true, knowing that he was still alive. But then Poppy had felt betrayed. What had been the love of a lifetime for her had obviously been just a wartime fling to him. Their worlds were too far apart to bridge. Only alone at night did she allow herself to dream of some chance that would being them together again.

'Poppy! Elsie! Fancy seeing you!'

Mona was standing by their table, with a young man in tow. They greeted her with cries of delight.

'Mona – we ain't seen you in ages. Where you been? And what have you done with your hair?'

Mona grinned and patted her head with her hand. Her straight dark brown locks fell in a shining bob, framing her round face.

'D'you like it? I had it done for Christmas, in Manchester. That's where I been, up north, with him and the boys,' she nodded at the young man.

'It suits you,' Poppy said, considering. 'I like it. Aren't you brave? No one else I know has had it done.'

'Yeah, he went mad when I had it all cut off, didn't you, Ken? But he's got used to it now. Oh – you haven't met, have you? This is my brother Kenny.'

Kenny shook hands. Now that Poppy looked at him, there was a family resemblance. He was carrying a violin case.

'You a fiddle player?' she asked.

'Yeah. Got a job at the Toledo.' He glanced up at the clock above the bar. 'Got to dash, I'm on in fifteen minutes. Nice to meet you, girls. Don't work too hard, Sis.'

'All right for some, sitting on their backsides all evening,' Mona retorted.

Poppy invited her to join them. Mona pulled up a chair.

'Haven't got long, I'm selling programmes at Drury Lane. What've you two been doing this winter? How's that baby of yours, Poppy?'

They caught up with each other's news. Mona had been keeping house for the band her brother was playing in, so that they did not have to endure the rigours of landladies and boarding houses.

'We rented this house for the season instead and I went along to look after them. We had some laughs, I can tell you. They're a good bunch, the boys. Always took me along with them when they was going out. It all seems a bit flat now I'm back home again. It's all right for Kenny, he's got this cinema job. The pay! It's amazing. Ten times what I'm getting.' Mona's straight black eyebrows settled into a fierce line.

'Pay's the same all over. We get half what the men do,' Elsie said.

'Playing in a cinema orchestra's much more skilled than what waiting or programme selling is, though,' Poppy pointed out.

'Yeah, but we can all play. I'm just as good on the guitar as Kenny is on the fiddle. And you can play the trumpet, Elsie, and you're really good on the sax, Poppy.'

'And she can double on the clarinet,' Elsie added.

'So why are we all stuck in these blooming awful jobs?' Poppy asked.

'Because we're women,' Mona said.

For a few moments they all stared gloomily into their glasses. Somewhere in the back of her brain, Poppy could feel there was a solution, an answer not just to the basic unfairness of it, but to the direction of her own life. If she could just get hold of it . . . And then it burst upon her, so easy and so obvious that she laughed out loud.

'Of course! We should form a band, an all-girls band. We'd knock 'em dead!'

The other two stared at her. Elsie looked sceptical.

'Oh, I dunno, Poppy. I mean, playing a bit together's a bit different from being a real band.'

'But we could,' Poppy insisted. 'You think of that dance we went to up Poplar Saturday night –'

'Dead loss, that was,' Elsie grumbled. 'Must of been twice as many girls there as men.'

'But the band, the band was useless. We're much better than what they was, and they was getting paid for that night's work.'

'We'd need more than just us three. Sax, trumpet and guitar's a good start, but we need a piano and drums as well, at the very least. A bass and a trombone too, if we really wanted to sound like a proper jazz band.'

'But we can't play jazz – ' Elsie wailed.

''Course we can. Look at what we used to do when you and Mona came round my place, before poor Joe – well, that was jazz. Real hot numbers, we can do, as well as all the old waltz stuff. Look, Mona, your family's in the music business. You must know other girls what can play. Come to think of it, so do Elsie and I. We weren't the only girls in the Sally Army band.'

'I don't think any of them'd want to play in a dance band,' Elsie said.

'If they play with us, they got to be good,' Mona said. 'It's no use sounding like a bunch of amateurs, that won't get us nowhere, not if we're serious about this.'

'But – ' Elsie started.

Mona and Poppy looked at each other.

'I'm serious. I never been more serious in my life. Those weeks I played at the Half Moon, they were – were – I was going to say wonderful, but the others made so much trouble for me it wasn't really. But playing, that was wonderful. I'd give anything to be able to do that again.'

'Me too. I'm fed up of hanging around doing things like programme selling while my dad and my brothers get good jobs in bands. I'm with you.' Mona's eyes narrowed as she thought it through. 'We can make this work, I'm sure we can.

At first, they'll take us on for our novelty value, I'm sure they will. Even if they take us on just to laugh at us, it'll be worth it, so long as we show them we're a proper outfit and make 'em laugh on the other side of their faces.'

'Right.' A ball of excitement was growing inside Poppy. She felt alive again, more alive than she had been for months. There were choices again, and possibilities. If she could just make them happen. She turned to Elsie.

'And what about you? You're in on it, ain't you?'

'I dunno – ' Elsie looked worried. 'I'm not as brave as you. I never was.'

'It'll be fun, Elsie. God, you don't want to work at that flaming hotel for the rest of your life, do you? Come on, say you'll try it.'

'I'm not as good a player as you. I'm only ordinary.'

'Rubbish, you're good. Now say you'll join us.'

'Well –'

'Good. Wonderful.' Poppy kissed her. 'Let's have another and drink to our success.'

On top of the world, she bought another round. The girls toasted each other.

'To us! The first and best girls' band!'

'West End, here we come!'

'The Piccadilly Hotel!'

'A recording contract!'

'New York!'

It all seemed possible. Poppy could not wait to get started.

'We must start rehearsing straightaway. We got to be really spot-on before we go out looking for work. When are we all free?'

'Sundays,' Mona suggested. Then she gave a yelp and jumped up. 'My God! I was supposed to be at work half an hour ago. They'll kill me!' Grabbing her bag, she rushed out of the door.

Poppy and Elsie were left with her half-drunk gin and tonic.

'I can't believe it,' Poppy said slowly. 'I can't believe one meeting can make all that difference to me. And yet – and yet

203

it all seems so right, as if it was just waiting to happen. Don't you feel that? Like it was Fate or something?'

'No,' said Elsie. 'Not really.'

Poppy gave her arm a squeeze.

'Come on, where's that wartime spirit? You'll love it, I know you will.'

She went home with her head buzzing with questions and ideas. She sang to Christopher as she put him to bed, then got out all her old sheet music and looked it through for possible band numbers and finally lay awake half the night, planning. Line-up, numbers, rehearsal venue, costume, name, transport, dates – the problems to be solved were legion, but far from putting her off, it only increased her determination to see it through. She had something to work towards again.

Two mornings later there was a postcard for her from Mona.

> I got the sack the other day an account of being late, so we got to do it now. I think I know where I can get hold of a pianist and a drummer. Can you come to my place next Sunday afternoon and meet them? Bring Elsie and your sax. Love M.

Poppy let out a cry of joy that reverberated about the dour house, and danced round the hall with Christopher squealing with excitement in her arms.

By the time she and Christopher set out on Sunday afternoon, she was beginning to feel a bit nervous. Elsie was waiting for her at her front door, looking anxious.

'Don't worry,' Poppy told her, with more conviction than she felt. 'It's only like going to see about a new job.'

'I suppose so,' Elsie agreed, but she did not sound convinced. 'Do you think they'll be, like, professional players, these other two?'

'No idea,' Poppy said. 'I don't know no more than what you do.'

Elsie sighed. 'I hope this is going to work.'

23

'No, no, that's all wrong. Elsie, that bit comes at the end of the second verse, not now. And Phyl, the rhythm's got to be much snappier. Lots of snare. It's supposed to be an up-beat number, not a dirge.'

Poppy was exasperated. This was the band's fourth rehearsal now, and they were no better than the first day they had got together for a try-out. If anything, they were worse.

'Now, have you got that, Phyl? Elsie? Right, from the top, Marge, and keep it tripping along –'

She saw the two girls that Mona had introduced exchange glances. Little Phyllis looked apprehensive, Marjorie as if she was about to explode. Marjorie, tall and commanding with a carrying voice, was a doctor's daughter who had driven an ambulance in France during the war, while Phyllis was fluffy and gentle and seemed to tremble when anyone so much as spoke to her. Marjorie was an accomplished pianist, but obviously liked being the one to run things, whilst Phyllis had only recently taken up percussion. She had a good natural sense of rhythm, but it was going to take far more than that to bring her up to professional standard. Now, Poppy was beginning to wonder whether they were ever going to get it right.

They ran through the arrangement of 'Ain't We Got Fun?' that Poppy had scored, all playing together at first, then trumpet, saxophone and guitar each taking a small feature spot. The front parlour of the Dobsons' house was hot and stuffy. A fug of smoke from Marjorie's cigarettes hung over them. The words of the song went round and round Poppy's head. Right at this moment, fun was the last thing she was having.

'No!' Poppy's temper snapped. Phyllis had got it wrong

again. 'Listen, it should go like this – ' She hummed the tune, clicking her fingers and tapping her feet to demonstrate just what she expected from the drums. 'For God's sake, it's not that difficult, is it? We got to get the percussion right or the whole thing falls apart. If you can't do it, then say so, and we'll all pack up and go home.'

Tears welled up in Phyllis's eyes and spilled down her face. 'I'm trying my best, honest I am. I can't do no more than that!'

Marjorie sprang to her defence. 'Leave her alone, can't you? You're always picking on her. She was doing perfectly well.'

'She was not doing perfectly well. She was blooming awful, and if you can't hear that then you ain't got no ear.'

Marjorie drew herself up to her full height and glared down at Poppy, who glared back, refusing to be intimidated. She wasn't going to let this bossy woman with her posh accent tell her what to do with the band.

'She is trying her best, like we all are. The trouble with you is, you suffer from an over-inflated ego,' Marjorie yelled.

'Oh yeah, and what's that when it's at home? Trouble with you is, you use big words to hide the fact that you can't play to save your life.'

Marjorie turned her back on Poppy. She addressed Phyllis. 'Come on, Phyl. We're not staying here any longer. We've got better things to do than to stay here and be insulted by this common little idiot.'

Keeping her eyes firmly on the ground, Phyllis stood up. She looked crushed. If she hadn't been so angry, Poppy would have felt sorry for her.

'Oh for heaven's sake, you two, leave off.'

'Yeah, cool down.'

For the umpteenth time, Mona and Elsie had to intervene.

'We all need a break, Poppy. I dunno about no one else, but I'm tired,' Elsie said.

'Me and all. I'll go and make us a cup of tea,' Mona said. 'And that means you two and all, Phyl and Marjorie.'

206

But Marjorie was not easily mollified. She had hold of Phyllis's arm. 'We're going,' she stated.

Phyllis stared fixedly at her toes. 'No, please. Look – I'm sorry –'

Poppy suddenly realized what she was doing. If they left, there would be no band. She took a deep breath and made an attempt to smooth things over.

'Look – I didn't mean to upset you. I'm sorry. Elsie's right, we're tired. I'm tired, I know, and I'm bad-tempered. I been up the last three nights with Kit. He's teething.'

'That still doesn't give you the right to be insulting,' Marjorie said, but she sounded less angry.

'I know, and I said I'm sorry.' It was true about Kit. He was thoroughly miserable with his teeth and Poppy was bone-weary.

Phyllis looked up at Poppy from beneath her lashes. She laid a hand on Marjorie's arm.

'That's all right,' she whispered. 'It's all right, Marjorie. She didn't mean it. Don't let's go.'

Marjorie allowed herself to be persuaded. She plumped herself down, lit a cigarette and took a long drag. Poppy was relieved. She had invested a huge amount of hope in this band.

Mona, as usual, was contemptuous of all the over-reaction.

'You lot are such amateurs. All bands have these teething troubles, you should hear the boys sometimes. Not a good word to say about any of the bandleaders, but they know it's part of the job. They don't go marching off in a huff just because someone criticized them.'

'Amateur' was Mona's worst insult, coming as she did from a family of professional musicians.

'That's all very well, but we are women, and women should behave better,' Marjorie stated.

'But we'll be up against men, out there,' said Poppy. 'If we're at all sloppy, they'll say, "Well, what do you expect from a bunch of women?" I want the best, and I know we can do it. I have this sound in my head, the sound I want to get. Oh, I wish I could make you hear it! I'll know when we get there, and I can't accept anything less. The thing is, it's going to take a lot more hard work. I don't mind, but what about you lot?'

'We got to be professional standard, or there's no point in doing it at all,' Mona said.

'That's right,' Elsie agreed.

There was a loaded pause. Phyllis looked into her teacup, to avoid the eyes that were focused on her.

'I take your point. And yes, you are right. We do need to be licked into shape,' Marjorie conceded.

Poppy smiled. It was all right. It was going to work. She stood up, weariness forgotten.

'Right then, let's get to it. We'll do "Ain't We Got Fun" once more from the top, then I'll let you all have a treat. I'll do my new clarinet bit for "I'm Nobody's Baby", and you can all tell me how bad I am.'

There were laughs from Mona, Elsie and Marjorie. Phyllis raised a half-hearted smile and sat down at the drum set. The rehearsal was in session once more.

Mona, Elsie and Poppy sat on Elsie's front doorstep, enjoying the late summer sunshine. Christopher was grubbing around in the gutter with two of Elsie's nephews, happy and dirty, while over the road the Turner children had their gramophone, the first in the street, out on the pavement. A dozen little girls were dancing to the music, while the boys stood around miming at playing instruments. Mums looked on as they did their knitting or mending, chewing over the day's gossip.

'I like your street,' Mona said. 'It's friendly. Up our way, the kids play in the road, but the grown-ups don't sit outside like this. It ain't the done thing.'

'Think you're common if you sit on your doorstep, do they?' Poppy said.

'Oh come off it, Poppy. Don't let that stuck-up Marjorie get you going.'

'I'm not. I like her, really. But she is odd, ain't she? That first time we met her and Phyl, when she was wearing those breeches, I thought she was really strange. I mean, I know women wore them in the war, but that was to do men's jobs. But I got used to her now. She looks good with her hair bobbed, don't she? Suits her.'

She patted her own head. She had taken the plunge and had her hair cut as well. Without the weight pulling it down, it had a natural wave, and curled round her face. It was amazing how different it made her feel. She was a modern woman now. She had shed the weight of her past along with her hair. She was stepping out into the exciting new age.

Elsie was pursuing the subject of Marjorie. 'She can play too, can't she? She's really good.'

'Yeah, and she's managed to knock Phyl into shape. I thought she was going to be a dead loss, but she's not. She's kept at it and now she's a decent percussionist.'

'Marjorie's kept her at it, more like,' Elsie said.

'Well, they must get on. They share that flat,' Poppy pointed out.

Mona said nothing.

Across the road, Mr Turner came out of the house and draped an arm round his wife's shoulders. She leaned against him and together they watched the children dancing. A great wave of longing came over Poppy.

Through the ache she heard herself say, 'It's about time we tried it out.'

'What?' said Mona.

'The band. It's about time we tried it out. We been rehearsing for four months now. It's time to go out there and play to an audience.'

'Are you sure we're ready?' Elsie asked.

'No, but if we had a booking, we'd have to be.'

'We'll need a name,' Mona said.

The problem of a name had come up before, and not been solved.

'I still think we ought to be something exotic, like the Havana Five,' Elsie said.

'That's getting ever so old-fashioned. Everyone knows Hungarian bands don't come from Hungary and Brazilian bands don't come from Brazil. They're more likely to come from Whitechapel,' Mona argued.

'The Dog Island Dance Band,' Poppy giggled, 'How's that for exotic?'

'Yeah, we're really likely to get a booking with a name like that.'

'All the best bands are just called after their leaders,' Mona said.

'But we're all in this together. And besides, Poppy Chaplin and her Band don't sound right,' Poppy objected. 'Makes us sound like a comedy turn.'

'Powers don't,' Elsie said. 'If you won't have the Havana Five, then how about Poppy Powers and her Band?'

'I dunno – I still want something that takes in all of us.'

'The Powers Girls,' suggested Mona.

All three of them turned it over in their minds, repeating it to themselves, picturing it on posters, on records.

'The Powers Girls – ' Poppy said.

Her dad would be so surprised. He might even come and find out what his daughter was doing. She imagined a nightclub, like the Half Moon but bigger, plusher, a clientele of sleek young aristocrats and theatrical people. Themselves, playing for all they were worth. And there amongst the crowd, her father, listening to the music, tears in his eyes at what his little girl had achieved. At the end of the evening, he would come up to her, and they would look at each other with stunned amazement, then fall into each other's arms.

'It sounds sort of – right,' Elsie said. 'I like it.'

'What if the others don't?' Poppy said.

'There's three of us and two of them. They can like it or lump it,' Mona said. 'What are we going to wear? Men usually have white tie and tails. We got to decide on something.'

'We could have black, I suppose – ' Poppy said doubtfully.

'Look like a funeral.'

'White?'

'Think of the dirt!' said Elsie, the practical-minded.

'Red, then?' suggested Mona.

'We'd look like tarts.'

'Do we have to have all the same?' Elsie asked.

'Yes, I think we do. Mona's right, all the men wear white tie and tails. We'll have to have evening dresses made, something really stylish – ' It was going to cost a fortune. Poppy thought of her nest egg, Joe's money that she had put away for Christopher. She had meant to leave it there, safe, ready for when he needed it.

'That'll cost a bob or two,' Elsie said.

'I know, and I'm not asking you to spent out. I'll buy the dresses.'

She felt quite dizzy when she said it. Poppy Chaplin, war widow and waitress, was going to buy five evening dresses for a band that had done nothing yet but rehearse in a front parlour.

They argued for some time over this, but in the end Mona and Elsie outvoted her. They were all in this together, so they would all share the cost of starting up.

'So – we got the band, we got the name, we're going to get the dresses. All we need now is some dates,' Mona said. She looked at Poppy. 'Over to you, bandleader.'

'What?' Poppy said.

'That's your job.'

'But – I thought you said we were all in this together?'

'Getting the bookings is the leader's job. We can't all come trailing round the clubs in a bunch, now can we? We'd look like a dole queue.'

Poppy was appalled. She had not thought of the practicalities of getting work. She did not know where to start. What was worse, the others seemed to think she could do it. The responsibility was terrible. Then she squared her shoulders. If they thought she could do it, then she could. After all, she had gone out at thirteen and got herself a job as a waitress when

211

her gran had wanted her to go into service. Compared with that, persuading nightclub owners to take them on was easy.

'Right,' she said. 'Leave that to me, then.'

24

'Well, my dear, if you're not willing to – er – audition, I can't very well offer you a booking, now can I?'

'If you'd just give me and my band a chance to show you what we can do, you'd want us,' Poppy said. She could hear the familiar note of desperation tingeing her voice. This was the fourth time today she'd been propositioned. The only sort of try-out the club managers offered her was on her back.

'We sound good and we look good. Your customers will love us,' she said, giving it one last try. 'Just let me bring the girls along here early one evening, before you open, and I'll prove it to you.'

The proprietor of the club bared his teeth in a travesty of a smile. He reached out and ran a hand over Poppy's bottom.

'Sweetie, I got bands coming in here every day wanting me to hear them. Every day I turn them away. But you – you I'm willing to give a chance. If you want it, that is.'

Poppy steeled herself not to flinch away. She looked at him sideways beneath her lashes. Could she? Could she possibly? He was fifty if he was a day, fat and balding. The hand that fondled her was pudgy and damp. More than that, the long-buried fear that stemmed from Mr Hetherington rose up to haunt her. No, she definitely could not. The price was far and away too high. She drew away.

'I'm not that desperate for work, thank you very much. I'm a musician, not a tart.'

She made for the door. As she turned the handle, she made the mistake of looking back. The proprietor's oozing geniality had evaporated. Instead there was an ugly twist to his mouth.

'That's the best offer you're likely to get, you silly bitch. Who the hell d'you think you are? This is show business, not a charity.'

'You'll regret not taking us on,' Poppy flung at him, and marched off. She blundered through the basement premises, opened two wrong doors, finally found the way out and ran up the steps to the open air and safety.

Once out on the pavement, the temper that had carried her out disappeared. Now what? One thing was for sure, she could not go back and tell the others she had failed, so there was really only one thing she could do, and that was to carry on. This was the sixth day of her search for work. She had not even tried the big hotels. Those, they had decided, would come after they had established themselves. So she had started by asking in every restaurant between Soho and Chelsea. Now she was doing the rounds of the clubs. Most of them were operating illegally and tended to be hidden behind doors that you could walk straight past, since they looked as if they led to flats or offices or storerooms. Then she had to get there at the right time, between when they opened and when they started to get busy.

Poppy straightened her shoulders and settled her new cloche hat more firmly onto her head. Somewhere, someone was just dying to employ The Powers Girls.

In Shaftesbury Avenue, the lights blazed in the theatres. Poppy passed buskers playing to the queues, watched as cars and taxis drew up to drop couples in evening dress, and peered into foyers bright with chattering crowds. All of London seemed to be out enjoying itself, and after the shows, they would want to go on to a club, they would want to dance to The Powers Girls. Just around the next corner was the Half Moon Club. She had once vowed never to go back there, but a week of failure was enough to change her mind. At least they knew her there. More important still, Mr Fairbrother would not try it on with her.

The door was still the same shade of blue, but the sign had been changed, the writing in modern squared off lettering instead of the old curly style. Everything was changing. Everyone was welcoming the new age, an age of which The Powers Girls would be a part. She banged hard on the door of the club.

'Poppy!'

'Jim!' She was so pleased to see a friendly face that she kissed him.

The barman ushered her downstairs.

'Hey, everyone, look who's here – it's Poppy!'

It had been spruced up inside. The dingy paintwork was now bright blue and white, and the waitresses were busy putting checked cloths on all the tables. On the tiny dais, a band was tuning up, a five-piece, younger and smarter than Charlie's trio. But the smell was the same.

Mr Fairbrother appeared. 'Poppy, how you doing?'

Poppy flashed him her best smile.

'Very nicely, thanks, Mr Fairbrother.' She knew she looked good, despite the weary round she had done already today. The cloche hat framed her face, showing off her wide eyes and her Clara Bow mouth, and she was wearing a coat her mother had made her in the latest fashion, with a drop waist and shawl collar. She assumed an air of confidence, taking in the club with a sweeping glance. 'This is looking up a bit, ain't it? Business good?'

He saw right through her.

'Sorry, Poppy. I don't need no more help at the moment. Got three good girls.'

She put on a slightly offended air.

'Oh, I'm not looking for waitressing work. No, I was thinking more of doing you a favour.'

Not for nothing had he survived ten years of running a club. His face remained completely bland. But he could not quite suppress a glint of interest in his eyes.

'Oh yeah?'

'Yeah – er – can we sit down?'

Mr Fairbrother led the way to the nearest table, and as an afterthought, pulled out a chair for her. Poppy sat down, and shrugged out of the coat. Underneath, she had on a dress in the latest colour, eau-de-Nil, another of her mother's creations. She nodded at the band.

'When did you get rid of the other lot?'

'Oh – over a year ago. Needed a change.'

'This lot any good?'

'Customers like them.'

He wasn't giving anything away. Poppy wished they would actually play something, then she could point out their weaknesses.

'I'd of thought you'd want something a bit – well – different. I mean, all the clubs got bands these days, ain't they?'

'That's what the customers want, Poppy.'

'Yeah, but there's so many clubs now, ain't there? Opening up all over the place. You must be feeling it a bit, all this competition.'

'No. We're doing all right. Come on, Poppy, out with it. You a commercial traveller or something now? What are you selling?'

At least he was interested. He did want to know what she was leading up to. She leaned forward, holding him with her eyes.

'I'm offering you the chance to really put this place on the map, the chance to have something no other club has got.'

She waited for him to take the bait. He didn't. She soldiered on.

'You could be the first club in town to have – ' Dramatic pause. She infused her voice with breathless enthusiasm '– an all-female dance band!'

To her consternation, he threw back his head and laughed.

'Bloody hell, Poppy, you are a one! Blimey, whatever next? Who's in this band, then? You and who's army?'

Anger flooded through her. She wanted to reach out and slap him round his flabby cheeks. How dare he laugh at her? She clenched her fists in an effort at control. Only when she was sure her voice would not shake did she trust herself to speak.

'It's no joke, Mr Fairbrother. You heard me play. I was better than that lot poor Joe played with. And now I got a band together what's better than what you got here now. We got five players, and we double up to seven instruments. We can do all the latest numbers, and what's more, we look good. You'd have them all queueing up to see us.'

But Mr Fairbrother shook his head. 'You're a case, you are.' He patted her hand in a fatherly way. 'You take my advice, girl – find yourself a husband. You're a pretty girl, it shouldn't be difficult. I'd marry you myself if I could. Like a shot.'

Poppy snatched her hand away. 'Thanks, but I'd rather you let me bring my band here so you could hear what we can do.'

He stood up. 'You're a stubborn girl, Poppy. It's not a nice business this, you know. You do the sensible thing and get out before you get hurt. Look after that little kid of yours.'

Poppy pushed back the guilt. She had left Kit with her mother far too often lately. He saw more of his granny than he did of his mum. But she was doing this for him, so that he could have a chance in life. She wanted more than a job at the docks for her son. She tried one last time.

'Come on, Mr Fairbrother. At least give us a try. You'll be surprised, I promise you.'

He picked up her coat and held it out for her.

'I'll be surprised if you last five minutes. You listen to me, girl. Give it up.'

The disappointment was so severe she felt quite sick. She found herself repeating the words she had thrown at the last club owner.

'You'll regret this, Mr Fairbrother. When they're all leaving this place to come and listen to The Powers Girls, you'll wish you took us on.'

But he was not even listening. He was sorting out one of the waitresses. A scream of frustration gathered in Poppy's throat. She wanted to pick something up and throw it, break it.

'Don't take it too hard.'

She spun round. It was Jimmy, her old champion from behind the bar.

'I can't help it, Jim. Nobody will listen to us. Nobody will give us a break.' Her voice was tight.

'Breaks don't come easy, Poppy. Don't come offered to you on a plate.'

'I know that.' She realized that she had sounded self-pitying. 'I been out round everywhere trying to sell us. We're good, you know, Jim. If someone just had the brains to give us a try, they'd book us.'

'You ought to get y'selves an agent. Do the legwork for you, talk to all the managers. Pretty girl like you didn't ought to be trailing round the clubs touting for work. Gives people the wrong idea, like.'

'An agent,' she repeated. Of course. Why hadn't she thought of it before? Her Dad always relied on his agent to get him work.

''Course,' Jimmy was saying, 'you gotta pay them. But it might be worth it.'

'You're right. Oh Jimmy, you're a genius. How can I ever thank you?'

'Ah well – ' Jimmy shrugged it off. 'We saw some times, eh? During the war? It was a crying shame that Yankee bloke never come back. He was all right, he was.'

'Yes, he was.' Poppy's throat ached with unshed tears.

'Have a drink, for old times' sake?' Jimmy's voice seemed to come from far away.

She made an effort to pull herself together. 'Thanks, Jim, I will. I'll have a whisky.'

They sat and talked about old times, but Poppy only had half her mind on the conversation. An agent. They would be around daytimes, so she would have to take a day off work. She would have to go sick. They wouldn't like it. If they thought she was swinging the lead, she'd get the sack, but that was a chance she had to take. She was going to be a success as a musician, even if it did mean risking her job.

The new band was playing now. Poppy listened critically.

'They're not bad,' she said to Jim, 'but they're not wonderful. The Powers Girls'd knock spots off of them.'

Jim raised his glass. 'Here's to The Powers Girls, then.'

By three o'clock the next day, she was not so sure. If

anything, agents seemed to be more difficult to deal with than club managers. To start with, they all wanted to know what they had done already, what experience they had. If she could not give a time and place where they could come and see the band perform, they did not want to know. The only one who had shown any real interest had wanted her to show what she could do in other ways first.

In Dean Street, Poppy combed the nameplates: Import and Export, French Lessons, Suppliers to the Catering Trade, Corrective Training, Exotic Model, Appleby and Gold, Performers' Agents . . . Appleby. There had been an Appleby working for her Dad's old agent. The firm had broken up, but maybe this was the same man in a different partnership. It was well worth a try. She pushed open the door and went up the narrow stairs.

It was dark inside and smelt of spices and paraffin. Not exactly an impressive place. But perhaps that was all to the good. The big firms did not want her, but a small one with not many bands on their books might do. On the first-floor landing there were three doors, two of them unmarked and the third half-glazed, letting daylight into the dim space. On it, in black-rimmed gold letters, were the words 'Appleby and Gold, Performers' Agents'. Poppy knocked and went in.

A large desk took up at least a third of the space in the cluttered room. Behind it, an harassed-looking man was talking urgently into the telephone. He glanced at her and signalled for her to sit down, but Poppy ignored the offered chair and wandered round, looking at the photographs on the walls. Sleek-looking musicians smiled back at her, their instruments held at the ready. Five- and seven-piece bands in evening suits and tuxedos silently played against backdrops of stage curtaining. Singers gestured, their faces rapt, their mouths open for a perfect top note. Poppy imagined a picture of The Powers Girls there, dressed in their beautiful new gowns on the dais of the ballroom of a posh hotel.

'. . . can I do for you?'

She started. 'What?'

The man behind the desk had finished his telephone conversation. He was standing up and holding out his hand to her. That at least was an improvement on the others she had met.

'I said, what can I do for you? I'm Ted Appleby – how do you do?'

'Pleased to meet you. I'm Poppy Powers. Of The Powers Girls.'

She shook his hand and sat down on the chair that he nodded at. Ted Appleby came round to her side of the desk, cleared a space amongst the heaps of papers and perched on the edge. He had long thin legs in fashionably baggy trousers and a good-humoured face.

'The Powers Girls, eh? And what do you do – sing? Dance?'

'We're a band.'

'A girls' band. That's a new one on me.'

From anyone else, she would have thought that he was being patronizing. But Ted Appleby had a nice easy manner about him. She gave him her best smile, and launched into her sales talk.

'. . . you only got to come and hear us the once, and you'll know we're something special.'

'Well, I can see that you're something special, Miss Powers –' He broke off, thinking. 'We had a Powers on our books at the old place, in my old man's time. What was his name? Sax player –'

'Owen Powers?' Poppy said eagerly.

'Yes – that's it. Any relation of yours?'

'My dad. He taught me to play. Do you know what happened to him, Mr Appleby?'

He frowned, making a great show of racking his brains, then sighed.

'No, can't say as I do. Lost touch with him – oh, years ago, well before the war. How is he, the old rogue.'

Poppy's throat tightened.

'I don't know. He went away for a panto one year and never come back.'

220

'That's tough luck.' Ted Appleby looked sympathetic.

'Yeah. I wish I could find out what become of him. It's difficult, not knowing.'

'Must be. And you're following in his footsteps, are you?'

Poppy straightened up. She was here to get work for the band, not think about the past.

'That's right. When are you going to come and see us, Mr Appleby? You'll be doing yourself a favour.'

He smiled. He had a pleasant smile that creased up his face.

'I will, will I? You tell me where you're performing, Miss Powers, and maybe I'll come along. I'd like to see what a girls' band was like.'

'Well, we ain't actually got any engagements at the moment –'

'But you have had in the past?'

'Oh, yes, of course,' Poppy lied, thinking fast. 'All the usual stuff. You know, weddings, barmitzvahs, that sort of thing. But it's clubs we want, clubs, restaurants, hotels. We're a classy outfit, Mr Appleby.'

'You're a classy lady, Miss Powers.' His eye fell on her left hand. 'Married, are you?'

'Widowed.'

'Ah. I'm sorry. The war?'

'Sort of. He got pneumonia, but it was the gas really.'

'Poor bloke.'

There was a brief silence. Poppy swallowed.

'You going to take a chance on us, then? You won't lose nothing but a bit of time. Come and see us at a rehearsal.'

Ted Appleby was looking at her, a considering expression on his face.

'I think we need to discuss things first, Miss Powers. How about you coming out to dinner with me tonight, then we can talk it all over in comfort, eh? What do you think?'

The same old catch. Just a bit more subtle than the others, that was all. Do something for me and I'll do something for you. Poppy gazed at the man in front of her. He was not fat or greasy. He did not leer at her. He was not old, either. Mid-thirties at the most. Right up till when he had said that, she had liked him.

'I don't know – ' she said.

He fiddled with a few of the papers on his desk, untidying them even further.

'You never know, I might be able to find out what became of your dad. I know a lot of people in this business, and my old man still gets around a bit. We could ask about, you know, see if anyone knows anything.'

People had said that before – Joe, various members of the Dobson family – and in the end nothing had ever come of it. But still she could not resist taking it up.

'Do you really think you might find out something?'

'Can't promise. But I'm willing to have a try. For you.'

Still Poppy hesitated. Then she thought of going back and telling the rest of the girls of her failure. She took a deep breath.

'All right. I'll come out to dinner with you.'

PART FIVE

High Notes

25

1925

'And for our last number before the break, ladies and gentlemen, The Powers Girls are going to play you a Charleston – "Five Foot Two, Eyes of Blue".'

Out in the dim recesses of Angelino's nightclub, there were whistles and squeals of excitement. Young couples ran out onto the small dance floor, eager to demonstrate their prowess at the latest craze. Poppy looked along the line-up, raised her eyebrows, nodded the down beat and the band pounced into the bouncy tune. Out on the floor, elbows flailed, feet hopped, beaded skirts flashed and swung, whilst all round the club the refrain line was picked up and sung. The final notes brought a roar of applause.

The Powers Girls put down their instruments and trouped off to the bar or cloakroom. Poppy and Elsie retreated to the artistes' changing-room and flopped down on the hard chairs. Elsie lit a cigarette.

'How are we doing tonight, boss?'

'Not bad at all. New girl's all right, ain't she? She can really play that trombone.'

'Yeah. You'd never think someone so small could make so much noise.'

'I'll give her a solo spot next week. Do an arrangement for her.'

Elsie looked about her with satisfaction. 'Nice place, this. They actually think musicians are human beings.'

'Yeah, Ted did well getting this for us. And the pay's not half bad, neither.'

'I should say so.'

They both smiled, still not able to take in the amount they were now being paid.

'Do you know, I don't dare tell 'em at home I'm earning twenty-five pounds for this week's work. They'd have a fit.'

There was a knock at the door and a waiter came in with a tray and two glasses.

'Compliments of two of your admirers, ladies.'

'What are they, Tony?'

'Couple of honourables.'

'No, the drinks, you goof.'

'Oh – gin fizzes.'

'Bloody hell, I'll be playing bum notes if I have too many of them. Bring us in a bottle of lemonade, will you?'

'Right you are, Miss Powers.'

Poppy put her feet up on the dressing-table and took a swig of the drink. She realized that Elsie was giving her an old-fashioned look.

'All right, what have I done now?'

'You like giving 'em the runaround, don't you?'

'Who, waiters?'

'No, idiot, the men. The admirers, as Tony calls 'em.'

'I don't see you going out to say thank you for your drink.'

'Get away, they weren't for me. You got 'em lining up for you, Poppy. Why don't you ever go out with them?'

'I do, sometimes.'

'But never more than a couple of times, then you give 'em the push.'

Poppy shrugged and finished the gin fizz.

'I dunno. They're so stupid, most of them. You know – all fizz and no gin. Lightweight.'

Tony came in with the lemonade. 'They want to know when you're going to join them, ladies.'

'When the next set begins,' Poppy told him, then looked at Elsie. 'Unless you want to –?'

'Me? Oh no – it's you they're after.'

'They'll be disappointed,' Tony said.

Poppy winked at him. 'Take a few more bribes off 'em yet, Tone, then wheel us out.'

The waiter flounced off, annoyed at being found out.

'If you'd of played your cards right, you could of had that Lord Whatshisname last year.'

'What, and go and live in some mouldy old castle in the back of beyond? No thanks. I've got my little Kit. He's the only man I want in my life.'

'Don't you never think of the future, Poppy?'

'Not if I can help it, no. I got enough to think about with the band and Kit.'

'Well, I been thinking a lot, lately.'

Something in Elsie's tone made Poppy listen properly.

'Really. What about? Here – ' she was suddenly alarmed – 'you're not going to leave the band, are you?'

'No, no – I wouldn't never do that. But since we been doing so well and getting regular dates and earning all this money, it got me looking at things different. I mean – do you think it's going to go on like this, with us playing the posh clubs and the restaurants and everything?'

'Don't see why not. This craze for dancing just goes on and on. Look at how the Charleston's got people going. They're Charlestoning morning, noon and night.'

'Yeah – only, well I been thinking about moving.'

'Moving? You ain't never lived away from your family in your whole life.'

'I know.' Elsie looked defensive. 'But it don't mean to say I can't, does it? I wasn't thinking of going far – just out to somewhere a bit countrified. Ilford, Chigwell, that sort of way.'

'Ilford?' Poppy stared at her. She couldn't have been more surprised if her friend had said she was moving to the moon.

'It's nice there. You ought to go and see it, Poppy. There's lovely houses with front gardens and electric and bathrooms with hot water. Hot water coming out of taps, Poppy! If we really are going to go on doing as well as we are at the moment, then I could buy a pair of semi-detached and live in one and rent out the other.'

For once in her life, Poppy was speechless.

'Well. I don't know why you're so amazed. You're living in a house in Mellish Street now, just you and your mum and Kit, with a whole bedroom each to yourselves. I was thinking of gettng my sister Ivy and her old man and the kids to come with me. Do them kids good to have a bit of space and breathe some clean air.'

Poppy was still reeling with amazement when they went back for the next set. Elsie, a house owner, a landlord! It was all a long way from Body's pawn shop and the Sally Army band.

Enthusiastic applause greeted The Powers Girls as they came back onto the stage. There were twelve of them now. Mona, Marjorie and Phyl were still there, but they had been augmented by three more saxes, a proper brass section and an enlarged percussion line-up. The original five dresses that had been such a large investment had long gone. They now had a selection of costumes depending upon where they were playing. Tonight it was toning beaded numbers in purple, pink or white. Poppy looked at them with pride. It had been a long hard journey, playing the dives, travelling out to obscure places for one-night stands, never having time for a real home life, but it had been worth it. The Powers Girls were a band to be reckoned with. Angelino's was a really swanky place, full of high society.

They swung into 'Yes, Sir, That's my Baby' and the dancers poured onto the floor. Sleek young men in evening dress and pretty girls with shingled hair and flying bead necklaces and skirts right up to their knees hopped and stomped to the perky rhythm. Many of them displayed arms and shoulders still brown from a holiday in the South of France and the new cult of sunbathing.

Poppy watched them with an amused detachment, glad to be out of all that, the frenzied looking for partners. Sometimes there were bust-ups in public, right there on the dance floor.

Only last week a girl had gone up to a straying boyfriend and slapped him round the face before marching off in a huff to the cheers and whistles of other dancers. The married couples were slightly more restrained, but the swapping still went on. Poppy knew the regular faces, the society people, the stage crowd, and could follow the course of their love affairs as they danced. Round the tables cruised the hangers-on, the hopefuls, trading on looks or wit or notoriety. It was fertile ground for them. The restless rich were hungry for novelty.

As long as she kept to the up-tempo numbers, Poppy could watch it all, enjoy being part of it without actually stepping onto the merry-go-round. Some of the other band members had found the temptation too much to resist. Footloose young men and jaded older ones found something very attractive in a girl who played hot music. Several good players had succumbed and left on the arms of their admirers. Mona had married an aviator on the new London to Paris service, but had returned to the band within the year, brittle and disillusioned. Poppy had welcomed her back with open arms. The Powers Girls were not the same without their founder members. Elsie seemed happy to devote herself to her family, and Phyl and Marjorie repelled even the hint of any advance made at them. And Poppy was all right until the slow numbers started.

There had to be slow numbers. Not everyone wanted to Charleston all night long. They needed the lead up to the journey home, the promise of romance. The Powers Girls were good at the softer songs. Two of the newer members proved to have sweet voices, and now that they could use a microphone they could be clearly heard over the band. Coupled with Poppy's soulful saxophone, they could melt the hardest of hearts.

'And now for all the young lovers out there, Miss Bobby Arlington and Miss Ada Hart will sing, "What'll I Do?" '

There was a sigh of pleasure round the club. Couples melted into each other's arms. The two singers stood close together at the big microphone. Mutes were put into the trumpets. The melody flowed seductively over the audience.

There was something about the song that always caught Poppy by the throat. But just as the music affected her, so she could put her longing back into her playing. The sax poured liquid gold, an aching stream of love lost that caught at the emotions of the most brittle Bright Young Thing. The Powers Girls were on top form.

Ted Appleby was waiting by the dressing-room door as they stumbled out at four in the morning.

'That was wonderful, Poppy. Top hole. The management's cock-a-hoop.'

'Oh, good. How about squeezing a bit more out of them, then?'

'I'll see what I can do. Might well get it, the way you're playing.'

'Fine.'

'Do you need a lift home? I've got the car outside.'

'Ted you know Elsie and me always share a taxi.'

'Ah, yes.' Ted's bony shoulders sagged. 'I just thought you might like a more comfortable ride –'

Poppy almost took pity on him. She was very fond of Ted, and he had done great things for the band. But she hadn't the energy left to cope with another of his proposals.

But he did not give up easily. 'Elsie's welcome to come too.'

Elsie just happened to overhear. 'What's this? Where am I going?'

'Home, if you want. You'd like a lift in my car, wouldn't you?'

Poppy fixed her friend with a warning look, but Elsie deliberately avoided her eye.

'Oh, that'd be lovely, Ted. Thanks a million.'

Outmanoeuvred, Poppy found herself sitting beside Ted in the Austin, while Elsie yawned enormously and announced that she was so comfortable in the back that she was going to go right off to sleep. Poppy could have killed her.

'You girls were really on form tonight,' Ted said.

'People remarked on it, and that's something, as you well know.'

'Most of them still can't get over the fact that women can play just as well as men. They still look on us as a novelty act.'

It annoyed Poppy, this attitude. She wanted The Powers Girls to be taken on because they were a good band, not because they were freaks.

'It helped you at first,' Ted pointed out. 'When I got them glossy photos done of you and the girls, it was them more than anything I said about you being good musicians that got your first bookings.'

She knew very well that he was right, but this was a good basis for an argument, and kept him away from more personal conversation.

'We might just as well have been a troupe of showgirls,' she said, in her most disgruntled voice.

The exchange got them safely through the almost empty streets of the West End and into Poppy's home territory, where the world was beginning to wake up. Poppy looked at the huge bulk of Maconochie's processing works, black against the dark sky, and was suddenly aware of her own good fortune. She could still have been there, slaving away five and a half days a week for a pittance, instead of dressing up each night to do something she loved and getting paid handsomely for it.

'God, I'm just so lucky,' she said.

'You are?' Ted's voice was soft with affection.

'When I think what I might have been. I've got so much.'

Ted laid a hand on her knee. 'You would have made something of yourself whatever happened. You're a remarkable girl, Poppy.'

She shifted her leg, annoyed that he had changed her mood of reflection into something more intimate.

'No, I'm just bloody-minded, that's all.'

Ted sighed and brought the car to a halt outside Elsie's house.

'Your ancestral home, madam.'

He got out and opened the door for her. Elsie made a great show of waking up and stumbling out. Ted escorted her to the door. Poppy waved goodnight. Elsie disappeared inside.

'Do you know what she's thinking of doing?' Poppy asked, brightly chatty, as he got back into the driving seat.

'No, what?' His tone suggested that he didn't much care.

'She's going to buy up property. Elsie! She's been out round them new housing estates and she's going to buy up one of them semi-detached and live in one half and rent out the other. In Ilford!'

Her amazement easily lasted the short journey round to her home in Mellish Street.

Ted stopped the car and switched off the engine.

'You said you was lucky, Poppy. I reckon I was lucky that day you walked into my office.'

'Never know what the tide's going to bring in next, do you?' Poppy said cheerfully, and reached for the door handle.

Ted put an arm round her shoulders. 'Don't run away from me, Poppy. We never see nothing of each other these days.'

'You seen me tonight.'

'You know what I mean. Alone. Just the two of us.'

Poppy sighed. She was too tired for this. 'Ted, there ain't no two of us. I wish you'd see that.'

'There used to be.'

'No there weren't. You took advantage of me. I was new to the business and you knew I was desperate for bookings. It was that or no work.'

'No –' he thumped the steering wheel. 'It wasn't like that, I swear it. When you walked in that day – Poppy, I would have booked you if you played flat and the rest of the band all had wooden legs.'

'That's not how you played it at the time. As far as I saw it, it was go along with what you wanted or forget it. And you know that, Ted, if you're honest.'

She did not regret what she did, since it had got her what she wanted – an agent, and bookings for the band. Ted was a good agent, there was no mistaking that. He had done very well for The Powers Girls, and what was more, he was a nice bloke. Somehow, that only made it worse.

Ted changed tack. 'There's never been anyone else for me, you know. I have pretty girls through that office every day of the week, but none of them do anything for me.'

'They don't have to pass your entrance exam, then?'

'For God's sake, Poppy! Look, I'm sorry, right? Do you think I don't regret it? I got off on the wrong foot with you. I should have taken you on as a client then asked you out and gone on from there. But it doesn't change how I feel for you. You talk about Elsie moving out. You could, Poppy. You seen my place. Just think how nice it'd be for young Kit out there at Eltham. He could ride a bike around the streets safe as safe, and go and play in the park any time he wanted. He's a nice little kiddie, I really like him, and he likes me, you know he does. He'd love it, having a proper family.'

'He's got a family. He's got me and my mum and my gran.'

'But he hasn't got a father. I'd like to look after him, Poppy. And you too. I'd care for you, if only you'd let me.'

'Ted, please –'

Even if she had not still treasured the memory of Scott, she would not have been tempted. She did not want to go through all the business of being married again.

'Let's just be friends and keep it like that, eh? You're a good pal and you're a marvellous agent. Don't keep trying to spoil all that.'

She reached for the handle. His hand tightened on her shoulder.

'At least give us a kiss goodnight. Please.'

She hesitated, then relented. He sounded so sad. She leant forward and kissed him briefly on the lips, then slid out of the car. She was indoors before he had time to follow her.

Poppy shut the front door and leant against it. Another close escape. She must remember never to accept a lift with Ted again. She stood there for several minutes, just letting the events of the night subside in her mind. Then she walked up the stairs to Kit's room.

The little boy lay deeply asleep, his dark lashes long against the curve of his cheek. Washed with tenderness, she bent down and kissed the soft skin. He stirred and turned over, but did not wake. Poppy pulled the covers more snugly over him. It was just as she had said to Elsie. This was the man she wanted in her life. As long as she had Kit, that was enough.

26

'Come on, Kit darling. Where did you put your book last night? We got to go, we'll miss the tram.'

Jane stood at the bottom of the stairs, trying to hurry Christopher up without waking Poppy.

'I got it. It was under my bed. Just a minute.'

Footsteps along the landing, then the sound of Poppy's bedroom door being stealthily opened. A stage whisper.

'Bye-bye, Mum.'

'Mm? Oh – 'bye, my pet. Come and give Mum a kiss.' Poppy sounded drugged with sleep.

A happy clatter of feet down the stairs, and there he was, all shiny clean in his posh uniform. Little Owen, Jane called him to herself. It made her heart stand still sometimes, he was so like his grandfather. The same cheeky face and blue eyes, the same irresistible smile. Only the hair was different, a rather unremarkable brown where Owen's had been red.

'You shouldn't of gone and woken your mum up,' she said, without conviction.

'She likes to say goodbye to me,' Kit told her. 'Come on, Gran, we'll be late.'

Jane followed him as he trotted off down the road. He looked so out of place here, in his maroon blazer and cap, his leather satchel bouncing on his back. Boys in the street called out at him, mocking. Christopher gave back as good as he got. All the same, Jane wished that Poppy had not got this bee in her bonnet about his schooling. It was setting him apart from the other kids in the neighbourhood. No good telling Poppy that, though. Poppy went her own way.

Christopher kept up a constant chatter. ' "Weymouth, the Royal Resort". Look, Gran, it says Weymouth, where we went. That was good, wasn't it? All that sand. Mum said she was going to get Mr Appleby to get her a summer season next year. She said it's got to be somewhere good, not any old place. Weymouth was good, wasn't it? Do you think she'll go there?'

'Maybe, darling. Next summer's a long way off.'

If only Poppy would marry that nice Mr Appleby. He was just what she needed, steady and kind, and good to little Kit, and head over heels in love with her. It wasn't that she didn't admire what her daughter had achieved. But it wasn't natural, the life she led. All this working all night long and only seeing Kit between when he got in from school and when he went to bed. It was all very well, earning all this money and having a nice home and sending Kit to this posh school, but where was it getting her? What she really needed was a nice man to look after her.

'. . . music lesson?'

She realized that Kit was still talking. 'What, dear?'

'Oh, Gran, you haven't been listening. I said, do you think Mum'd let me go to Peter Horsfall's house after my music lesson?'

'I think so, dear. She likes you to play with your friends.'

'Peter Horsfall's dad has got a Morris. It's really good.'

'Mr Appleby's got a nice car and all,' Jane said, her mind still on her own train of thought.

'I told Peter Horsfall that, and he said, is Mr Appleby Mum's fancy man? I don't think he is, do you, Gran? He isn't very fancy, although he does wear those pattery jumpers.'

'No, he ain't, and you tell your friend that,' Jane said, with all the severity she could muster. 'Your Mum don't have no fancy men. She's a respectable widow.'

But somehow she had to admit that the term 'respectable widow' did not quite fit a woman who went out each night in a beaded dress to play the saxophone in a nightclub. When Poppy woke up, she would bring the subject of that nice Mr Appleby up again.

*

'Leave off, Mum. I had enough from Ted himself last night.'

Poppy sat in the front parlour, drinking a cup of tea. She was every bit as proud of her front parlour as her grandmother was of hers. The difference was, Poppy's was a room for using. There were comfortable easy chairs, a cosy carpet square, a piano for Kit's music practice, a gramophone, and the very latest wireless.

'It was him what brought you home, was it? I thought it wasn't a taxi I heard outside.'

'Yeah. That was a mistake and all, accepting a lift.'

'You ought to think serious about marrying him, you really ought to.'

'I have thought, Mum, and the answer's no. I got everything I want here. I got you and Kit and this nice house. What more should I want?'

'You're a young woman still, lovey. You could do well for yourself.'

'I am doing well for myself. You'll hear me on that wireless one of these days.'

'That's not what I meant. Don't you never think ahead?'

'Why is everyone wanting me to think ahead? You, Ted, Elsie. I'm all right.'

'But are you happy, lovey?'

'Of course I am.'

But it made her think. She was busy, she was successful, she was often frantically merry – but happy? That was another thing. She turned her mind away.

'If I was to marry Ted and take Kit and go and live with him out at Eltham, what'd you do, Mum?'

'Oh, go back and live with your gran, I suppose.'

'Wouldn't you miss Kit?'

'Of course I would, and I'd miss you and all, but you got your own life to live, lovey.'

'Well, I'm not going to marry him, so that's that.'

Her mother's words were still on her mind when she got to the club that evening. Normally, she would have confided in Elsie, but she knew just what her friend's reaction would be.

Right now, she did not need anyone else to take Ted's side. Instead, she talked to Marjorie.

'Marry Ted Appleby?' Marjorie paused in combing her severely shingled hair and turned to look her straight in the eye. 'Good God, woman, you must be mad.'

Poppy laughed, the tension suddenly eased. 'I knew I'd get a sensible answer from you.'

'That's why you asked me, I suppose.'

'Yes,' Poppy admitted. 'You don't think much of men, do you?'

'Posturing fools, the lot of them.'

'Oh, I don't know about that. Lots of them are very nice –'

Marjorie waved the comb at her. 'Rubbish. Each and every one of them will exploit and degrade you as soon as look at you. You be on your guard, Poppy. You've achieved a great deal, and you've got all of us around you. What more do you want? You've even got a child.'

'I know, but –'

'But nothing. You stay as you are, independent. This band is something to be proud of. I am. Some of these girls might be pretty empty-headed, but at least they are women. Stick with us, girl.'

Poppy was touched. Over the four years they had been together, she had grown to like Marjorie, despite her bossy manner and odd attitudes. To learn that she was proud to be part of the band meant a lot. She reached out and squeezed her arm.

'Thanks, Marjorie. You're a pal.'

Phyllis sidled up and slid an arm through Marjorie's.

'Secrets?' she asked. Her little round face looked quite sharp.

'No, not a bit. Marjorie's just telling me not to marry Ted Appleby.'

'Oh – well, I'm sure she's right.'

She looked at the two of them, Marjorie tall and regal in purple, Phyl pretty in pink. They were an odd couple, but along with Mona and Elsie they were the loyal heart of The

Powers Girls. Other players came and went, but Marjorie and Phyl stayed on.

'We're a good team, aren't we?' she said.

She thought so again that evening, as they warmed up the audience. It was a slow night, and the atmosphere took a long time to build up, but the band kept at it, and gradually the party feeling grew. A group came in, noisily engaged in some celebration. The band struck up a Charleston number and one girl danced with such verve and skill that the floor cleared around her, the audience clapping in time with the music as they watched her solo turn.

'That's Beattie Pearl, from that new show,' Mona hissed in Poppy's ear.

Poppy nodded. 'Thanks.'

At the end of the number, she called for a big hand for Miss Pearl, and the place erupted. The night was really up and hopping now.

It was as she was about to announce the last tune before the break that she noticed a strikingly beautiful blonde woman taking a seat at a table near the edge of the dance floor. She was dressed all in white with a stunning set of what could only be real diamonds clasped round her neck and wrists and dangling from her ears. She looked like the Snow Queen.

Poppy introduced a foxtrot, the couples came onto the floor. It was getting crowded now. When Poppy looked at the Snow Queen's table again, she happened to be leaning forward, so that one of the men sitting there was clearly visible. She stopped playing in mid-phrase.

Scott.

Then dancers came between them and he was no longer visible. Poppy's heart was beating so loudly it seemed to fill her head. *It couldn't have been.* She was always seeing him, in the street, in cafés, on buses. In a moment she would have a clear view again and see that the man was nothing like him. The thudding in her ears subsided just a little. She tried to pick up the thread of the music, but could only stumble through a few bars. She stared across the floor. She caught glimpses of the

Snow Queen, of another woman at the same table, of another man – but not of the one like Scott. Silently she cursed the people blocking her view, willing them to move. Behind and around her, the band carried on, bringing the tune at last to its end. The girls were bowing. Belatedly, Poppy bowed too. The audience clapped and cheered. The floor began to clear. Now, now – it was him. She was sure it was him – her head swam . . .

'Poppy, are you all right?'

Elsie was on one side of her, Mona the other, holding her up.

'Scott – ' Her mouth was dry.

'Come on.' Mona was firm and decisive. 'Take her into the dressing-room. She's not well.'

'No –'

She looked back over her shoulder as they led her away. The Snow Queen's escort was staring at her. Their eyes met and she knew, without a shadow of a doubt. It was him.

Mona plied her with a brandy while Elsie fussed round splashing her face with water and fanning her.

'I can't go on,' she said. 'I can't, not with him there. What's he doing here, in London? Why did he have to come here, to this club?'

'It's a good club, and we're a good band,' Mona said.

'I can't go on. I won't be able to play a note.'

'You got to go on. You're the leader. You're a pro. Pros don't back down just because an old flame turns up out of the blue.'

'She doesn't have to. She's had a terrible shock. You can take over,' Elsie argued.

Marjorie appeared at the door. Elsie and Mona went over and had a muttered conference. All three glanced back at Poppy. Marjorie went out and came back within a couple of minutes. More muttering, and Elsie's hands went to her face. Poppy heard her sharp exclamation of 'Oh God!' Then she came over and put her arm round Poppy's shoulders.

'You don't have to go back on,' she repeated.

A terrible feeling of doom was gathering round Poppy's heart.

'What's Marge just told you?' she demanded.

'Well – ' Elsie hesitated, her face racked with concern – 'I suppose you got to find out . . .'

'What? Find out what?'

'That woman in white, with the diamonds – she's – oh Poppy, she's Mrs Scott Warrender.'

The world swayed around her. *Mrs Scott Warrender – Mrs Scott Warrender –* She felt ice cold. From a very long way away, she was aware of the others gathered round her. Then pride and anger came to her rescue. How dare he? How dare he go off and leave her like that, then turn up with a wife?

'I'm going back out there,' she said, and her voice was clear and steady. 'Like Mona said, I'm a pro. I'm going to go in there and I'm going to hit him between the eyes with the music.'

As the band walked back to the dais, there was special applause for Poppy, as the clientele thought she had been taken ill at the end of the last set. Poppy smiled and waved and bowed, and tried not to search the pale glimmer of faces for that one particular one. But she couldn't stop herself. There he was, sitting by the Snow Queen, sitting by his wife, clapping.

She cleared her throat, then went up to the microphone, willing her voice to come out natural, her knees to hold up.

'Thank you, thank you, ladies and gentlemen. Thank you. The Powers Girls are back and I'm sure we're all going to have a simply wonderful night. We're going to start off with a special favourite of ours: "Ain't We Got Fun?" featuring Miss Elsie Booth on the trumpet.'

She stepped back and turned to the band. They were all with her, all backing her every step of the way. She felt buoyed up by their love and support. She counted them in and they swung into the perky song.

The club members got up and danced. There were smiling faces and flashing feet and an air of hectic gaiety. To anyone

241

else, it looked like a good night. Poppy's part in this number was not taxing. She could do it without thinking, so that her eyes could seek what they wanted to see. Across the room, the Snow Queen was standing up. Poppy's heart almost stopped. She couldn't bear it if he danced with her. But another man was at her elbow, someone else from their table. Scott stayed sitting down with an insignificant woman in blue. Poppy played on, mouth and fingers automatically producing the right notes in the right order, but heart and soul beside him, sitting where the blue woman was, touching his arm.

Mona leaned forward at the end of the number. 'You're doing all right. Keep it up,' she murmured.

'I'll try.'

Somehow, she got through the long hours. Part of her wanted it to be over, to be released and go and crawl into a corner and weep, part of her couldn't bear for it to end, for just to be in the same room as him was better than all those ages apart. To her relief, he danced only once, a Charleston with the woman in blue. He was good. Poppy feasted her eyes on his lean figure, his feet flying to the rhythm. In the light, she could see the detail of his face at last, and realized with a jolt that behind the set smile there was strain. The revelation started a painful excitement inside her. He must feel something, dancing to her music. She almost hoped it was pain. The number ended, and their eyes met again. He was clapping, and she knew it was for her.

The numbers piled up, one upon the other, measuring out the hours of the night. Time crept round to closing. Poppy glanced at her plan of the running order and was appalled to be reminded what she had down for the last melody – 'Always'. She could substitute something else. The girls could run through any suitable tune. But her mind was a horrible blank, she could not think of anything, anything at all. She could only go up to the microphone and announce the tender love song.

Then the worst happened. Scott got up together with the

Snow Queen and they moved as one across the floor, turning and gliding to the lilting waltz.

Poppy closed her eyes. She could not watch. The band diminished into a gentle background for her feature spot and all her pain and love and jealousy flowed into the music. The sax caressed the notes and cried, its voice hers, filled with an ache of longing, saying everything she wanted to say, reaching out to the man dancing with his wife, the man who had once been hers.

27

'Poppy? Poppy love, these come for you.'

At first, Poppy could not see her mother, just a blur of colour with a voice issuing from behind it.

'Oh – ' She tried to rouse herself. She had found it impossible to sleep when she got back from the club, what with the turmoil of emotion. She had still been wide awake when Kit left for school, and had lain there through the morning going through the events of the night over and over again. At last, exhausted both physically and emotionally, she had slipped into a troubled dream-filled sleep around midday.

'Ain't they lovely? I'll put 'em in water for you, if you want.'

Now that she could focus, she saw that 'they' were a huge bouquet of flowers – roses, lilies, stephanotis, asparagus fern –all done up with pink ribbons. Her heart gave a great painful leap of hope.

'Is there a card? There must be a card.'

'Here – ' Her mother located it and handed it to her.

Poppy took it with shaking hands, straining to decipher the copperplate handwriting.

To the lady with the saxophone.

Disappointment hit her like a physical blow. No clues at all as to the sender. It could be from anyone. Angelino's had been packed last night, and she often received gifts from admirers. And yet – it could be from him. She went up and down on a sickening seesaw. If it was from him, then what did it signify? Even if he still cared a little, he belonged to the Snow Queen. Hers or not, anything was better than ignoring each other, pretending they were strangers. He must at least have happy memories of their time together. If the flowers were from him.

'. . . then? Anyone nice?'

'What? Oh – it doesn't say.'

'Ooh, a mysterious admirer! How exciting. I'll go and find a vase. More than one vase, I reckon . . .'

For a long time Poppy sat gazing at the card, trying to fathom out its secret, but could come to no firm conclusion. She did not even know whether she really wanted it to be from Scott. The sensible part of her knew there was no future in it, the irrational part just hoped. The constant swings from one extreme to the other made her incapable of keeping still. In the end she gave up trying to rest and got washed and dressed, and went prowling around the house from one vase of hothouse flowers to another, unable to settle to anything.

'You sure you're all right to go and fetch Kit, lovey? You look ever so peaky. Didn't you sleep well last night?'

'No, not really.' It suddenly became very important to wait in, more important even than her daily journey to meet Kit and enjoy his cheerful company. 'Look – er – could you go and fetch him, Mum? Would you mind?'

'Don't be daft, it'll be a pleasure.'

'Thanks.'

It was even worse when the house was empty. Though she knew it was foolish, she delved into the bottom of her chest of drawers, scrabbling under a pile of summer blouses to find her special treasures. There they were, the souvenirs of her father, Kit's first shoes, a lock of his baby hair, his first tooth to come out, Joe's drumsticks . . . a bundle of letters, yellowing now, and a photograph. She sat back on her heels, gazing at it through tears.

'Why did you have to come back?' she demanded out loud.

She almost hated him. She had been all right up till last night. She had her life running nicely. No towering heights of happiness, maybe, but no depths of despair either. Now – now she did not know where she was. Everything was upside down.

There was a knock at the front door. Poppy gasped, her heart hammering so loudly in her chest that it hurt.

'It's nothing,' she told herself severely. 'A tradesman. Nothing.'

But her knees shook as she made her way downstairs. She had to hold tightly on to the bannister. In the hallway she stopped. Through the stained-glass panel in the door she could see a male shape, in a trilby hat. She took a long shuddering breath, and reached out to turn the knob.

On the doorstep was a tall figure in a charcoal-grey suit. Scott.

'I had to see you, Poppy. Am I welcome?'

She nodded. She could not really believe that it was him and that he was here. She took a step back, made a gesture with her hand.

'Come in.' Her voice came out as an odd croak.

Somehow, she managed to lead the way into the parlour. There she stopped in the middle of the floor and looked at him. He looked older, there was a certain hardness about his mouth, but he was still the same man, and she still loved him. The difference was, he now belonged to someone else. Anger possessed her.

'How can you?' she demanded. 'How can you just – just walk in here, after all this time?'

'I know – I know I shouldn't have come. It's asking too much of you. But when I saw you at that club last night, and found out that you were widowed, that you were free –'

'But you're not free, Scott.'

'No.' A bleakness settled on his face. 'No. I'm sorry, it was wrong of me to intrude on you like this. It's just that – seeing you there last night, so near – and then thinking of you ever since – I couldn't stay away.'

She saw it then, the longing in his eyes, and knew that it was still the same for him, that he still loved her. All anger dissolved.

'Oh Scott –'

'My sweet Poppy –'

She was in his arms, holding him for dear life, kissing him with lips that could never have enough of his. They drew apart briefly, breathless, and gazed into each other's eyes. Scott held her face between his hands.

246

'My darling girl, if you knew how often I dreamt of this moment.'

His fascinating voice. She had forgotten just how it affected her.

'I never thought I'd see you again.'

'There's not been a day gone by when I haven't thought of you.'

'I've always loved you – through everything. There's never been anyone else.'

It felt so right, holding him. This was where she belonged. They kissed again, mouths hungry from the long parting, learning again the taste and feel and contours that had for so long been only an aching memory.

'Oh, Scott, I can't believe it. I thought you'd been killed.'

'Is that what they told you? I thought I was posted missing – that's what they told my folks.'

'But missing meant dead, mostly, and I never heard from you.'

'I was in hospital behind the German lines, and then in Germany itself. I wasn't able to write, honey.'

He told without drama of the lost months of the last summer and autumn of the war, but even so, her eyes filled with tears and she hugged him tighter as she realized how close to death he had been, how much he must have suffered.

'But I wrote you from the prison camp, Poppy.'

'I never got them. I just thought you were dead.'

'Even so, you might have waited.' He pulled away, his expression hard. 'It didn't take you long, did it, to find someone else? When I came back to find you, you were already married to that drummer.'

'You came back?' Poppy stared at him. 'You came back for me? I never knew. Who did you see?'

'I went to Cinnamon Alley. All the time I was ill, I kept it in my mind. I was going to get out of there somehow, sometime, and I was going to go to Cinnamon Alley and find you. But when I finally made it, you were gone. Married.'

His voice was heavy with bitterness. They were still holding each other, but now there was a great gap between them of accusation and betrayal.

But somewhere, something did not make sense. He must have been in Germany right through to 1919.

'When?' she demanded. 'When was this?'

'Just before Christmas.'

'Just before – ? But I didn't marry Joe till March.'

There was a loaded pause while both of them considered the discrepancy.

'It was definitely just before Christmas,' Scott maintained. 'I spoke to your grandmother and she said you had left home and she didn't know where you were.'

'Oh God – that must have been when I went to Glasgow.'

'Glasgow?'

'I went to look for my father, but I never found him.'

'So – ' Scott spoke slowly, making absolutely sure he had everything right – 'you were away from home, but you weren't married?'

'That's right.'

'The old lady said you were.'

Poppy was consumed with an overwhelming anger.

'That interfering old witch! I'll never forgive her for this, never!'

United in their outrage at her grandmother's hand in parting them, they dispensed with any other recriminations. They sat together, Poppy on Scott's knee, and caught up with all that had happened to each of them since that last painful parting at Victoria Station. Between kisses, Poppy told of her brief marriage, of Kit, of Joe's death, of the formation and the rise of The Powers Girls.

Scott was full of admiration and his approval was the crown to all she had managed to achieve.

'What about you?' she asked. 'You're a rich man now, ain't you? Something in a bank?'

'Yeah, yeah, I'm on my way.'

'Tell me, then. Tell me everything. Right from the beginning.'

'That's a long story, honey.'

'I want to hear it.'

Anything to put off the moment when she had to find out about Her. The Snow Queen. His wife.

'Okay then. From the beginning.' There was a certain relief in Scott's voice. He was on safe ground talking about his career. 'When I got back to Birch Springs and wrote to my old company I found my job had been given to someone else, and that just gave me the push I needed. Put the fight back into me. I got a position with East Coast and went in there ready to take on the world. I guess I was trying to work you out of my system as well. I was real angry with you, and working full stretch and taking risks was a good way to push you to the back of my mind. Not that it worked. I kept seeing you, in the street, in elevators –'

Poppy hugged him. 'I did that and all!'

'Then about a year after I joined the bank, I got a call to go up and see the vice president and I thought, it's either promotion or I'm out on my ear –'

Walking into the vice president's suite that morning, Scott decided that this was where he was heading. The polished secretary in the outer office, the huge corner room with its panoramic view of Lower Manhattan, the power. The vice president himself seemed rather an insignificant figure compared with all this glory, a small bald-headed man with a disarmingly quiet voice. A gruelling half-hour's interview taught Scott not to judge by appearances. Mr Vanderpost knew every last thing that was going on in his particular area of the organization, and then some. Scott found himself being offered the chance to head up a department of his own, working on a new project. Not only that, but the vice president offered some advice – to get out there and meet the people who counted, starting with a cocktail party that his wife was giving that very evening.

'I tell you, my feet didn't touch the ground when I walked out of there. That was the start of it all.'

Something in his voice sent a sick shiver of foreboding through Poppy. She knew what he was going to say next.

'That was when I met Francine.'

Of course. The girl mentioned in the newspaper cutting. Miss Francine Vanderpost.

'You married the boss's daughter,' she said.

'Poppy, honey, it wasn't quite like that.'

'No, you didn't only marry her to get in with her dad. She's beautiful as well.'

The words came out before she could stop them. She couldn't help it. This Francine had everything – money, looks and the man Poppy loved.

'I did not marry her to get in with her dad, as you put it.' There was a dangerous edge to Scott's voice.

Close to tears now, Poppy blundered on. 'Oh, so it was a love match, was it?'

Scott sighed. 'I'm condemning myself in your eyes whatever I say, aren't I? But you got to remember, honey, that you were married to your Joe. I couldn't have you. And yes, she was – is – very beautiful. Like – like spun glass. I admit that I wanted her. She was also very charming and very much in demand. I was flattered when I realized that she found me attractive.'

'And?' Poppy prompted. She had to know the whole story now, however much it hurt.

'And we started seeing a whole lot of each other.'

He had realized from the start that Francine was volatile and spoilt, but she was so lively and amusing with him that he let himself be dazzled. Until the day they had a row over a trivial incident. Francine flounced off and Scott decided to let her stew in it. Four days later he found himself summoned to the vice president's office.

It was the first time Scott had seen Mr Vanderpost less than in total command of the situation. He was clearly embarrassed at being embroiled in an emotional situation. His daughter, he told Scott, had locked herself in her room and was refusing to eat. He was afraid for her health. She had always been highly strung, but since she had met Scott, she had seemed a great deal more stable. Scott was a good influence on her. He did not say so in so many words, but in fact he was issuing both a threat and a plea – Scott must get in touch with Francine at once.

'It was a difficult moment,' Scott said. 'I was worried for Francine, I didn't want her to do herself any harm, but I could see that if I gave in then, I'd be at the mercy of her and her father for ever more. So I told Vanderpost that she knew my number and she had only to call me. Then I took off for the weekend to visit some friends upstate. But when I got back –'

When he got back, having wondered all weekend whether she was all right and whether he had made the right decision, there she was, a pathetic bundle in a white fur coat, curled up in the doorway of his apartment. She clung to him, begging forgiveness, promising undying devotion. He ended up making love to her, and the following morning asked her to marry him.

'I see,' Poppy said.

'No, you don't see. She's not like you. She could hardly be more different from you. I think that was part of the attraction. I couldn't have married anyone who was just a – a shadow of what you are.'

Poppy struggled to understand.

'I suppose – Joe was nothing like you. What I liked about him was he reminded me a bit of my dad, but you don't. You're not like my dad at all. Oh, it's all –'

She broke off, for she heard the clatter of feet on the front steps and the rattle of the front door opening.

'Mum! I'm home!'

Poppy jumped up, flushing. She straightened her dress, glanced at Scott, who stood up as well. 'I – er – I'm in here, darling.'

Kit erupted into the room, then stopped short, staring at Scott.

251

'So this is your son? He's a fine young man.'

'Yes – ' Poppy glowed with pride. 'Kit, darling, this is – a – a very old friend of mine, Mr Warrender. Come and say "How do you do" nicely.'

Scott held out a hand to the boy. 'Hi there, Kit. Pleased to meet you.'

Kit solemnly shook his hand, saying to Poppy, 'He doesn't look very old. Why does he talk funny?'

'Kit!' Poppy was annoyed. It was very important that her son should make a good impression. 'Don't be so rude.'

But Scott laughed. 'I thought you Londoners sounded real strange when I first heard you. I'm from the United States, Kit. We all talk like this.'

Kit looked impressed. 'We've got the United States on the map at school. It's underneath Canada.'

'Well, that sure puts us in our place, don't it?' Scott said.

Another, slower step in through the door. Poppy swallowed. This was going to be more difficult. Her mother came into the room and stopped dead, frozen in the act of taking off her hat. Her eyes went from Poppy to Scott and back again. Covering her confusion with a brazen show of indifference, Poppy made the introductions.

Scott shook Jane's hand. 'Honoured to make your acquaintance, ma'am.'

Jane looked flustered. 'Likewise, I'm sure.'

Scott tried to talk to her, to draw her out, but she was uneasy.

'I'll – I'll – er, go and make us a cup of tea. Would you like a cup of tea Mr – er – Mr Warrender?'

'Please, call me Scott. But I don't have the time for a cup of tea right now. I have to leave in a minute.'

Poppy could hardly contain her disappointment. To have him return, only to be snatched away again. And she couldn't even talk now, not with Kit still staring at Scott with fascination and her mother hovering in the doorway. She thought quickly.

'Look, Mum, I'd love a cup of tea. And Kit, would you go and help your granny, please?'

To her relief, Jane took the hint. She took Kit by the hand with unusual firmness.

'Yes, come along, lovey. Come and light the gas for us.'

Poppy and Scott stood frozen while the voices retreated down the hallway. Then they came together again, drawn as if by magnets.

'Do you have to go?'

'I do. But I must see you again. Where can we meet?'

The difficulties of their situation suddenly reared up in front of her. His wife must not find out. She ought to refuse to meet him again. She ought to put him right out of her head and heart. But she couldn't.

'Oh, God, I don't know.'

'Do you mind if I come here again?'

That did not seem right, either. It was her home and she was a free woman, but somehow she did not want him here when her mother and Kit were around.

'It's not – ' she could not explain how she felt.

'Please, honey. I can't just let you go again. I know I'm asking a lot, but I got to see you. I need you.'

'I know, I know. I want to see you.'

She racked her brains. It was not like ordinary courting. They could not go for a simple drink together, in case they were seen. She could maybe borrow a flat, but that made it all so horrible. It degraded their love.

'I can't think –'

'Listen, don't worry about it, I'll fix something. Can I ring you somewhere?'

If only she had had a telephone installed. She did not want to have to rely on his leaving messages with friends. Then the solution came to her.

'At the club. We're there for the next two weeks.'

'Right.'

He drew her into a passionate kiss that sent her senses spinning.

'I love you, Poppy Powers.'
'I love you too.'

28

The suite at the Mayfair Hotel was mercifully empty when Scott arrived back. He poured himself a whisky and sank into one of the green satin armchairs, closing his eyes. Poppy . . . he had told himself he could get along without her. He had managed to all this time. He was an envied man, successful, rich, married to one of the most beautiful women in New York, but just seeing Poppy last night up on that stage had shot his carefully constructed defences all to pieces. He was left with just one definite idea, one urgent need – to speak to her again.

And now that he had seen her, he knew just what he had lost. If he had not taken that old harridan of a grandmother at her word the day he came back from France, if he had just stuck around a few days . . . He indulged in a dream of what might have been. Poppy would have loved New York. Together they would have made a great team. He could see them hand in hand, hitting the town. From Broadway to Harlem to skating in Central Park, she would have taken to it with that open enthusiasm of hers. And he – he would have been happy.

The door of the suite rattled and he started guiltily, as if caught in some sinful act. Francine. The familiar feeling of weariness dragged at him. What sort of mood would she be in? Whatever it was – high, piqued, bored, jealous, furious or any of the variations and combinations – he did not feel ready to cope with her right now.

'Oh Scotty, honey, here you are! I've had such a wonderful afternoon – you can't imagine.'

She waltzed in and perched on the arm of his chair, enveloping him in a cloud of expensive perfume.

'Nina took me to this wonderful beauty parlour. I didn't

think the British had that sort of thing. They're so behind the times. But Nina knows this place and this clever girl gave me a complete make-over. Don't you think I look beautiful?'

She jumped up and twirled in front of him, stopping to pose like a film star photograph.

'You always look beautiful, Francie.'

Immediately the words left his lips, he realized he had made the wrong response. Her lovely mouth drooped into a pout.

'You're not *looking* at me, Scott. You never never do. You just look through me. I've been completely transformed, I've been through agony, you just don't know what I've endured at the hands of that woman, all for you, so I can look nice for you, and you don't even notice!'

Scott made an effort. If he did not stop this, there would be sulks and silences and pointed remarks all evening.

'Of course I notice, darling. Your hair's a new style – much nicer than the old one, and – er – your eyebrows are a lovely shape, and your lips are a real pretty colour and what's that beautiful fragrance? That's new, isn't it? It's just right for you.'

To his relief, she gave a smile of satisfaction.

'You're dead right, it is new. This wonderful clever man mixed it just especially for me. He was just fascinating! He took a drop of this and a drop of that, and sniffed it, and shook his head, and tried something else.'

'He sure did a good job. It smells divine,' Scott said dutifully. It had probably cost a fortune, but he didn't care, just so long as it kept Francine sweet.

She rattled on about the rest of her afternoon. Scott had to admire each of her improvements extravagantly. He directed his eyes to the right places, but all the while he saw Poppy. He listened to what Francine was saying, but it was Poppy's words that ran round his head.

'. . . mean you didn't like it how it was before? Are you saying I looked ugly?'

A dangerous note in Francine's voice dragged him back to the present.

'No, no, honey. You never look ugly. Never.'

'I don't believe you've been listening to a word I've been saying. You've been sitting there nodding your head and agreeing with me, and all the while you've been miles away.'

There were times when her perception brought him up short. Most of the time, she was so obsessed with herself that she did not notice his preoccupations, but just occasionally she would put her finger right on him.

Her blue eyes cooled to ice chips, her whole face sharpened.

'Who is she, then? Who are you thinking about when you should be thinking about me? Is it Marcia? You danced with her last night when you wouldn't dance with me. Dammit, I am your *wife*! Why didn't you dance with me?'

'I did dance with you, Francie.'

'Once! But you got up and did the Charleston with Marcia. What's she got that I haven't?'

'Nothing, nothing at all. I just danced with her to be polite. We were taking her and George out, after all.'

This sort of argument could go on forever, he well knew. The way out was to distract her, if possible.

'Where do you want to go tonight? We ought to go somewhere real lit up, so they can all see how lovely you're looking.'

'Nina's got tickets for a show – what's it called? *Frasquita*.'

Scott took a gamble. 'I heard that was a bore. Real slow moving. Not like *No, No, Nanette* or even *Rose Marie*.'

Francine tossed her newly styled head. 'Well, I think you're the bore. We seen both of them on Broadway, and everyone knows they're never as good when they come to London – ' She went on at some length, with Scott throwing in the odd remark every now and again to annoy her. Now she was safely sidetracked from searching for someone to be jealous of. In the end, she gave what she considered a knock-out blow.

'Well we're going, whether you like it or not, and you better look like you're enjoying it, because Nina got the tickets from a friend of hers who's in it. And we're going to dinner with her and Ned after, so you better get yourself ready real quick. You know I hate being kept waiting.'

She flounced off to the bathroom, thus making it difficult for him to get ready. Scott retreated to the bedroom and sat on the vast pink-frilled bed. Theatre and dinner should keep them going till midnight, but then what? If he thought the moves out beforehand, he could probably manipulate the party into going back to Angelino's. He could then sit and look at Poppy all night long. Just to be near her again would be wonderful. But it was not fair to Poppy to parade his wife in front of her again. He was going to have to wait until he could fix something up.

The evening seemed to go on for ever. Just as he had said to Francine, the show was a bore, but it left him free to think his own thoughts. The dinner was more difficult. They were just a foursome and he was expected to play his part in the conversation. When at last the meal was over, talk turned to what they should do next. They could stay at the restaurant which, like all good establishments, had a floor and a dance band, or they could go on to a nightclub. Various places were suggested. A need to talk about Poppy, however obscurely, led him to throw his contribution in.

'There used to be this little place I went to in the war, the Half Moon. I don't know whether it's still there –'

Francine jumped in: 'Oh Scott, we don't want to hear about your old wartime memories. It's all so boring.'

'I think they closed it down a while back. It was raided by the police,' her friend Nina put in. She gave Scott a smile by way of compensation. 'Someone I know used to go there a lot. He loved it. He was there when the police came. I never knew it had been going all that time. When was it that you went there?'

'October 1917. It was a real dive, but there was something about it.' He relived those few intense days in his mind.

The discussion went on around him, until a name jolted him back to the present.

'. . . Angelino's. You'd like that, it's very amusing. They've got a ladies' dance band playing there at the moment. The Powers Girls. They're good, too.'

'We went there last night, didn't we, Scott? With George and Marcia. Scott was a real bore. You're being a real bore tonight too, Scott. It's like you're on a different planet to the rest of us.'

'All men are bores. Ned's the most dreadful bore. He's going off to play golf tomorrow afternoon and leaving me all alone. Golf! I think I shall go and spend a lot of money. Why don't you come along, Francie?'

Scott held his breath.

'Yeah, that might be fun. Scott hates shopping, don't you, Scott?'

'Why not come and play golf, old man?' his host offered.

'No – er – that's real kind of you, but I got some business to see to,' Scott said quickly.

'Business! We're supposed to be on vacation, you know.'

They pressed him for a while but he held out. Elated now, he sneaked off to find a telephone. When he got through to Angelino's, he was told that Miss Powers was on stage, so he left a message for her to wait in at home for him tomorrow. Now all he had to do was to get through the hours in between.

When he woke the next morning, Francine was still fast asleep. He slid carefully out of bed and looked down at her to check that she hadn't stirred. Devoid of make-up, she looked dangerously fragile. This vacation was supposed to be a leisurely tour, an opportunity for her to slow down. She spent her time in New York rushing from party to first night to private viewing, with bouts of concentrated shopping in between, and it had been telling on her. The doctor had forecast another breakdown if she did not take a rest. The country bored her and the sun made her ill, so Europe was suggested. Somewhat to Scott's surprise, she took up the idea, deciding that it would be a good chance to see friends who had married into the English aristocracy.

To make it a real break, it had been decided that their little daughter, Amy, should stay behind. Francine, the doctor

259

insisted, needed to leave all her problems and responsibilities behind her. It was Scott's view that any problems Francine had were entirely of her own making, and she certainly did not let Amy be a burden or cramp her style. The child's upbringing was left almost entirely to the Spanish-American nanny who had been engaged before the baby was even born. It was Scott who went into the nursery each evening to play with the little girl before she was packed off to bed. However, Francine liked to maintain the fiction that being a devoted mother was wearing her down, and Scott did see that trailing the child round England might not be a good idea.

Now that they were here, of course, Francine was living just as fast as she did at home. She seemed unable to stay still, driven ever onwards by a feverish need for admiration and entertainment. The body beneath the satin cover was rail-thin, and there were dark smudges under her eyes, livid against her white skin. Guilt caught at Scott. If she was to find out about what he was about to do, it could push her right over the edge. But he could no more forget Poppy than cut off his right hand.

He padded out of the bedroom and located the telephone directory in the lounge. Ten minutes and three calls later, he tucked a closely written piece of paper into his wallet and ordered coffee and the *Wall Street Journal*. Even the arrival of these did not wake Francine, so he got dressed, left a note to say he had gone out to clear his head, and went downstairs to hail a cab.

That afternoon, Poppy was waiting for him. He saw her at the window as his hired Bentley drew up, saw her face light up. She was at the door to greet him, flinging her arms round him in joy.

'I was so glad to get your message last night. I was afraid you would disappear again.'

He kissed her warm lips, revelling in her passionate response.

'Honey, I've been living for this moment. Now we're together, don't lets waste a second of it. Fetch your coat and hat – we're going for a drive.'

'In your posh car? Oh, lovely! I'll be with you in two ticks.'
She was too, much to his surprise.

'I've never known a woman get ready so fast.'

'Oh, I'm just like the morning milk, I am.'

'How's that?'

'Pasteurised before you see it.'

'Past –?' Then he gave a shout of laughter and hugged her, all the tension of the day dispelled. 'I love you, Poppy Powers.'

They drove out to Kent, since Scott had been told that it was pretty there. It was a perfect afternoon, crisp and bright, the bare winter branches etched black against a pale blue sky. They passed orchards and oast houses and villages grouped round willow-hung ponds. They stopped the car and climbed to the top of a hill. They had tea and home-made scones in a tiny shop with doors so low that Scott had to bend his head to get through. They never stopped talking except to kiss. The afternoon was a perfect jewel, unconnected with the chain of everyday life. Scott could not recall ever having been so happy and carefree.

Her head resting on his shoulder, Poppy sighed. 'If only we could just go on like this for ever.'

But the short winter's afternoon was already drawing in. Under the trees evening was gathering. They were following the road signs for London. Scott stopped the car in a layby overlooking a steep valley. Now for the difficult part. He had easily put it out of his head all afternoon, but there was no getting away with it. He gripped the steering wheel.

'Poppy, there's something I have to say to you.'

'Oh.' All the life and laughter had died in her voice. 'I don't think I want to hear it, thank you.'

He did not want to say it, but he had to.

'I want you to know that I love you just as much as I did back in '17. More, if anything. But – things aren't the same now. I can't leave Francine. She needs me.'

'I need you.'

He could not bear to look at her. 'I know, and I need you, but it's different. Francine – she's so volatile. I don't know

261

what would happen to her if I wasn't there. She's already had one breakdown, soon after Amy was born. She's a responsibility, like having another child to care for. She needs someone stable in her life. I can't just ditch her.'

A long silence welled up to accuse him. He tried to fill it by repeating what he had already said, trying to justify himself. In the end he ran out of words.

A tight little voice beside him said, 'I see.'

'It's not that I don't want to be with you, Poppy. I do, more than anything in the world, but it just can't be.'

'Right. Well, that's that then, ain't it?'

He leaned his head on his hands. Suddenly, all the arrangements he had made that morning seemed tawdry.

'Hell, Poppy, I'm sorry.'

'So am I.'

'It's my fault. I've been totally selfish. I should never have come round to see you yesterday, I should never have taken you out today. It was such a shock, seeing you there on the stage at Angelino's. It made me realize just how much was missing from my life. I just couldn't resist it, Poppy, I had to see you again. Now I've only made everything much worse.'

Her hand touched the back of his neck, making his overwrought nerves jump, then stroked him gently, tenderly.

'I'm glad you did. It would of been awful, seeing you there and never knowing – I'd still be thinking you'd gone off and forgotten me.'

He took her in his arms and she sobbed on his shoulder, making him feel a total hound. Then they drove back to town in silence, while the key he had carried in his pocket all afternoon burnt against his flesh.

They pulled up outside the house in Mellish Street. Poppy gathered up her gloves and bag.

'Well, I suppose this is it,' she said, with a horrible false normality.

'Poppy, wait, please –'

Almost of its own accord, it seemed, the key appeared in his

262

hand. He put it on top of the dashboard. The words tumbled out.

'You're really going to hate me now. I fixed this up this morning. I hired this apartment for you – us. For a month. It seemed like the best way, somewhere private, but you won't want it now, I'm sure. Only – won't you just take it, please?'

For a long while she just stared at the key with its brown address tag. Scott was on the point of snatching it up and putting it back in his pocket, of apologizing for even having thought of the idea, when her hand stretched slowly out to pick it up.

'You will see me again?' he asked.

'I don't know. I'm going to have to think about it.'

She let herself out of the car and in to her house. He was left staring at the street door.

29

Long practice got Poppy through the evening. Most of the band, and certainly the clientele, noticed nothing amiss. She had her introductions off by heart, and they played nothing that they had not done fifty times before. It was not a classic night, but as long as nothing went seriously wrong, and the band kept up a steady rhythm for dancing, everyone was content.

The original band members saw the difference in her though. At the first break, Elsie tried to speak to Poppy, but Poppy felt she could not confide in even her oldest friend.

The hours dragged by, with Poppy churning the decision round and round in her mind as she played the bright melodies and smiled. Most of all she dreaded being called to the telephone. If he were to ring her now, she did not know what she would say to him. But he did not. He was giving her time to make her own mind up. She was grateful for that.

At last the final tune was over and the revellers were making their way home. Elsie and Poppy got into their taxi. Poppy leaned her head back against the leather seat, glad of the comparative quiet. She let out a great sigh. From her corner of the cab, Elsie made an attempt at cheering her up.

'Maybe they'll get divorced. Everybody does, these days.'

'I don't think so.'

She lay awake, still thinking, still coming to no firm conclusion as she became more and more tired. Kit came to say goodbye before going off to school. She held him tight. She still had him, thank God, and of one thing she was certain, she must do nothing that might hurt her son.

But for herself? She veered back and forth. She was not going to go to this horrible flat, like a kept woman. She was not going to have anything more to do with him. There was no future in it, only heartbreak. It would be wrong. And yet – and yet – everybody these days had affairs. To have just a part of him, for a little while, was so very much better than nothing. And he did love her. What they had was something far greater than a smutty affair. They would be hurting nobody, so where was the harm in it?

In the end, it was not a case of making her mind up in any logical manner. She simply could not stay away. The next afternoon she put the key in her handbag, asked her mother to pick up Kit, and hailed a taxi. As she gave the driver the address, all the turmoil subsided. This was the only possible thing she could do.

Scott had chosen well. The taxi drew up outside an anonymous modern block in a street off the Clerkenwell Road. Close enough for both of them to travel to, yet a world apart from where either of them was living. She paid off the cab and ran up the stairs with her feet hardly touching the ground, happy, eager, longing to be with him. This was it, this was what she wanted, it was going to be wonderful. As she found the right door, her footsteps faltered. Supposing he wasn't there? Supposing he hadn't been able to get away? She wouldn't be able to bear it, not after all this soul searching. Her fingers trembling, she fitted the key in the lock.

'Poppy!'

She had scarcely opened the door before he was there, dispelling all her fears, sweeping her into his arms, kissing her as if their very lives depended on it.

He held her face between his hands, taking in every feature. 'I was so afraid you wouldn't come.'

'I had to. I couldn't stay away,' Poppy confessed.

'My darling girl. I don't deserve you. But don't stand here, come inside. Tell me what you think of this place. I was beginning to hate it, but now I think I might grow to love it.'

His arm round her waist, he led her into a small living-room. Everything about it was neat and totally impersonal. A stiff three-piece suite, a table and chairs, pictureless beige walls. But the gas fire made it beautifully warm, and on the table was a great basket of flowers.

'Oh – ' Poppy went over to them, bending over to drink in their scent. 'How lovely.'

'Not as lovely as my Poppy.'

He took off her coat and hat, laid them on a chair, kissed her again. The quiet, the remoteness of this place, a strange island in the middle of the huge noisy city, wrapped itself around her. There was a faint sound of traffic through the windows, and a hissing from the fire. They were cut off from real life, the only two people who counted in the whole of London. It was so good just to be there with him, feeling him close to her, tasting his hungry lips. When they broke apart, breathless, she found he was looking into her eyes.

'I was here all yesterday afternoon. When you didn't come, I thought I had ruined it for ever.'

'No, I don't think you could ever really do that.'

Now that she was here, she was not sure how to play it, what came next. She was glad when Scott led her over to the settee and sat in the corner, drawing her onto his knee. She kicked off her shoes and curled up with a sigh of happiness, her arms round his neck. He ran a hand over her body, sending prickles of fire through her.

'You're very tense.'

'I'm – nervous,' she admitted, feeling foolish.

'Listen, honey, you don't have to do anything you don't want to. I'd be happy just walking through a park with you and holding your hand.'

'You would?'

'I would. Look, we can go sit in the armchairs on either side of the fire if you like, and talk about the weather.'

She laughed and nestled her head under his chin. 'No thanks. I like it here.'

He caressed her again, a smooth insistent touch that released all the pent-up anxiety within her, made her unwind and unfold until her whole body glowed with sheer pleasure.

'You're a wonderful girl, Poppy.'

So many times it had been said to her before, in so many different circumstances, but from his lips it sounded new-minted.

'You're the only one who ever counted, with me,' she told him.

He was stroking her breasts and belly and thighs now, rousing a rapidly growing need. She pulled his head down to kiss him with fierce hunger, devouring him with lips and tongue. He undid the buttons of her blouse and slid his hand inside, then kissed all the way down her neck until he reached her breast, nuzzling and sucking at the nipple. She moaned and moved against him, conscious only of an overwhelming need to be lost in him, to be one with him.

'Come with me, baby.' He stood up, lifted her up in his arms, carried her through into the bedroom. Breathless, desperate, they shed their clothes, helping each other, until they knelt, naked, facing each other, each taking in the beauty of the other. Poppy stared at his hard muscled body, loving him, wanting him, and was proud of her own soft curves under his hot gaze. She wanted to give all of herself to him. And then they were together, rolling back on the bed, turning over and over, giving and receiving pleasure in a mounting mutual need, reaching together for the ultimate fulfilment.

Poppy clung to him, shaking, as she drifted slowly down. Scott shifted slightly, looked down at her, wiped away the tears that trickled down her face with his fingers.

'What's wrong, honey?'

'Nothing. Nothing's wrong – it was wonderful – ' Sobs shuddered through her. 'I just – I've never known anything like that before.'

'Me neither. Nothing so – complete.'

He kissed her eyes. She gave a feeble smile.

'Now I know what all the fuss is about.'

'You didn't before?'

'No.'

'Ah – that's good, I'm glad, that makes me like the first. We can make it even better, I'm sure.'

'Better than that?'

'Better than that. I'll prove it to you.'

It was the start of a wonderful, magical time, a time of intensity, when everything was defined in sharp lines of black and white. Poppy realized that she had been living up till now in a grey half-world of small pleasures and shallow feelings, that contentment had nothing at all to do with happiness.

Her life revolved round the bare little flat. Everything else was subordinated to the need to be there with Scott. Occasionally, their signalling system failed, and she spent long hours waiting in vain, but it was all worth it when he did arrive. He always brought some sort of treat – champagne, smoked salmon, flowers, out of season fruit. Poppy reciprocated with jellied eels and pork pies. They had picnics in bed, they bought a gramophone and danced, they spent long hours just talking.

Poppy at last told the story of Mr Hetherington and Scott was shocked, his face tight with anger.

'The bastard. Men like him should be shot. To do that to you, a little kid –'

'He never touched me,' Poppy pointed out, wanting to be fair.

'But he took away your innocence. That's vile enough.'

His disgust swept away any lingering feelings of guilt. Mr Hetherington was exorcised from her mind.

'But it's all right now that I've told you. The memory won't touch me any more.'

'I'm glad, baby. I want you to be happy.'

Just as Scott promised, their lovemaking grew better with each meeting, as they got to know each other's bodies and what gave the greatest pleasure. Every time Poppy thought that surely nothing could surpass what they had just experienced, she was proved gloriously wrong.

One afternoon, when the rain was pouring down outside, they lay entwined on the floor in the living-room, letting the sweat dry on their sated bodies. Poppy was drowsy with the heat of the fire, the hypnotic drumming of the raindrops. Scott smoothed a damp strand of hair off her forehead.

'It's so good that I can do anything with you and not worry that I'm doing you some harm. Not like –'

He broke off. Poppy was suddenly painfully awake, jealousy searing her.

'Not like your wife, eh?'

'There's no comparison, honey.'

All this while, she had managed to keep the thought of this other woman firmly at bay. But now she seemed to be so very much present that she was almost in the room with them. Poppy felt physically sick. She spoke without thinking.

'Oh yeah, she's the delicate little flower and I'm your bit of rough trade.'

'That's not what I meant, and you know it.'

There was a note of careful patience in his voice that she missed.

'That's what it sounded like.'

She could not bear the thought of him being with his wife, sleeping all night long beside her. His wife had all the rights to his time, his loyalty, his protection. All Poppy had were a few snatched hours. Soon he would be going back to New York, to his daughter, his home, his job, to the real part of his life, and all she would be left with would be memories. Misery swamped her.

'Listen, honey –'

'I don't want to listen! None of it means anything.'

She was appalled by how swiftly the mood had changed. A moment ago they had been so happy.

Scott sighed. 'I don't expect this sort of thing from you.'

'What do you mean, *this sort of thing*? You take it from her all the time, do you?'

'Yes, I do. Cheap emotionalism. Scene-making. Playing games. I thought you were above all that.'

Now she had really done it. She had set him against her. Poppy wanted to curl up and die.

'I'm sorry I'm such a disappointment,' she said. She supposed that was the wrong thing to say too. She seemed to have completely lost control of the situation. She became very aware of the fact that she was sitting naked on a living-room floor in the middle of the afternoon. She felt suddenly very exposed. She got up and put on a dressing-robe and sat in one of the armchairs, curled into a defensive ball. Tears gathered in her throat in a painful lump, but she fought to stop them. She must not cry. What was it he had said? Cheap emotionalism.

'I've gone and spoilt everything,' she said.

'Oh, Poppy – ' Scott came and sat on the arm of the chair. 'You haven't spoilt everything and you're not a disappointment. Far from it. You're everything I dreamt of and more. I shouldn't have brought – her – into it. I'm sorry. The last thing I want to do is to hurt you.'

'I know – ' She couldn't stop the tears now. 'It's just – soon you'll be gone and I don't know how I'm going to bear it.'

'I don't know how I'm going to bear it, either.'

Poppy said nothing. She did not dare. She would not be able to help pointing out that it was within his power to make a future for the two of them.

'We don't have to think about it yet. We've got another week,' Scott said. 'We'll make it the best of all. Every moment.'

Another week. The band's contract with Angelino's had finished and they had a break until starting at a restaurant, with only a country house party to play at on the Saturday. Scott managed to get some hours to be with Poppy every day, but still the time went by too quickly. The days were overhung with the knowledge of their coming parting. Poppy had the feeling that she was riding perilously on the crest of a wave, and any minute she was going to go crashing down to drown in the green water.

On the Friday afternoon, they met for the last time in the little flat that had become their haven. Scott was due to go and visit some friends of Francine's, then they were departing for Paris and Rome before returning to New York for Christmas. The reality that they had held at bay for so long had caught up with them. Their lovemaking that day had an edge of

270

desperation to it. Poppy could not enjoy it fully. She was too miserable.

The moment she had been dreading arrived. Scott produced a small jeweller's box from his jacket pocket.

'Something to remember me by.'

'I won't forget,' Poppy said, her voice tight with unshed tears. She took the box. Inside was a gold brooch in the shape of a saxophone, set with diamonds.

'Oh – ' She turned it so that it caught the light. 'It's lovely. And so right. I shall wear it always.'

'Let me pin it on to you.' Scott took it from her and fastened it to her dress. He kissed her gently on the lips. 'I shall never hear a saxophone without thinking of you, and these times we had here.'

There must be something she could say or do, anything – scream, faint, fling herself down the stairwell – anything just to hold on to him, to make him change his mind.

'There's something I want to ask of you,' he said.

Poppy's hopes soared. He was going to suggest that they ran away together. She would go, right now, without question, taking only what she stood up in.

'Anything.' Her heart was thudding painfully.

'Will you write me?'

The disappointment was so severe that for a moment she could not think straight.

'I –'

'It would be something to look forward to. Like the letters you sent me in France. They were a lifeline.'

But this time it would not be the same. She would write to him about her family, about the band, about the venues they played at, but what about him? If he told her of New York night life, she would know that his wife had been with him when he visited the places he described, and he would say nothing about his home life, for that would be forbidden territory. Even if he said he loved her, it would have a false ring to it, for he did not love her enough to be with her.

'No.'

'Poppy! Whyever not?'

'Because things were different then. Being apart because of a war isn't the same as being apart because of – someone. I don't want to be just one tiny part of your life. It's all or nothing.'

'Oh God, Poppy, I wish it could be all. I truly do –'

They shared one last, despairing kiss, then Poppy broke free.

'If ever it can be all, then you can write to me,' she said, and turned away. Without saying goodbye, she ran out of the flat and down into the street, and did not stop running until she hailed a taxi. Then she broke down and wept.

30

'I've not seen nothing of your Poppy for weeks,' Margaret complained.

'She's – er – she's very busy at the moment,' Jane said.

'You're looking shifty. It's no use lying to me. There's something up, ain't there? What's she been up to?'

'I don't know,' Jane sighed. 'I wish I did. She don't say nothing to me.'

They sat in the back room of the house in Cinnamon Alley. There were soft touches now to the spotlessly clean room – a rug on the floor between the two chairs, a pretty vase and a photograph of Kit in a tortoiseshell frame – and in the corner a wireless stood, solid and silent. All were presents from Poppy.

Margaret knew just where to put the finger of blame. 'I been wondering about her for the last couple of weeks. It's a man, ain't it? She's taken up with somebody.'

Jane looked unhappy. 'I really don't know, Mum. Not for sure. There was someone – but it was only the once. What I can't make out is why she's being so close about it.'

Margaret's satisfaction with bring proved right was tempered by fear. She had wanted Poppy to better herself, and she had. She had money and a good position, if you could call being a bandleader a good position. So any men who did come courting were not the rough lot from hereabouts. But if Poppy were to marry, she'd go away, and take Kit with her. That was the dark terror that dogged Margaret.

'What was he like, the one you saw?' she asked.

'Oh, very nice. A real gentleman. The same –' Jane stopped short.

Margaret regarded her with the darkest suspicion. 'The same what?'

'Well – I suppose it don't do no harm. It was during the war she first knew him. Then about a month ago he turned up again.'

'And this is the one she's been seeing?'

'That's just it, Mum. I don't know. She introduced me to him, and he was ever so polite. "Please call me Scott", he said. That's his name, Scott Warrender –'

'Scott Warrender? What sort of a name is that?'

'He's American, Mum. They all have funny names.'

Deep in the recesses of her mind, a memory stirred. A shabby soldier with a strange accent at her door, asking for Poppy. Polite, oh yes, but a threat, a threat to her carefully conceived plans. Besides, he had not been good enough for her granddaughter. To start with, he didn't look as if he would last to the end of the month. She had to protect Poppy from making a mistake in her life, so she sent him packing.

'What did he look like?' she asked.

'Oh – very nice, tall, dark – very nice-looking – lovely suit – and you should of seen the car he had outside! A Bentley, Kit said it was.'

It was worse than she had thought.

'Why don't you ask her about him, if you're worried?'

'I tried, Mum, but she won't say nothing. She's been in a very funny state ever since he arrived.'

'She's your daughter – make her tell you.'

'She's a grown woman, Mum. She's twenty-five years old and a widow.'

'Your daughter's still your daughter, however old she is. I've always looked out for you, now haven't I?'

'Yes, Mum. Look, I got to go and get Kit. I'll miss the tram if I stay here much longer.'

This was new to Margaret.

'Get him? I thought Poppy got him in the afternoon.'

'Well, yes, but she's out today.'

'She ought to be ashamed of herself, making you make that journey in all this rain. Stair rods, it is, out there.'

'I don't mind, Mum. Honest.'

'You let her take advantage of you, my girl. You ought to stand up to her a bit. Always was headstrong.'

Jane went off, her umbrella up against the downpour. Margaret was left feeling profoundly disturbed. She made herself a cup of tea, but that did not help, so she took refuge in work. Poppy had tried to make her give up taking in lodgers, offering to pay the rent on the house for her, pointing out that it was not like the old days, that people did not have to go on working till they dropped, not now they had the old age pension. But the lodginghouse had been her life for so long, Margaret could not imagine it empty, with no one to cook and clean for, no one to bully.

When Jane and Poppy left to move to the house in Mellish Street, she was forced to employ a woman from down the street to come in and do the heavy work. She resented the extra expense, but it did leave her energy to rule her kingdom the way she always had. Jane called in on her every other day or so, Poppy a couple of times a week, and best of all, her darling Kit would come bursting in after school or at weekends, full of everything he had been doing. That was the highlight of her life, seeing him, listening to his chatter, watching how strong and healthy and bright he was growing. But now there was this American. Poppy marrying and going off to live out in one of those new estates would be bad enough. Poppy going to live in America was unthinkable, if she took Kit with her. If Margaret couldn't see Kit any more, there would be very little to live for.

This dreadful prospect was still gnawing at her late in the afternoon when the front door banged open, sending a cold draught racing through the house. For a joyful moment, she thought it was Kit. But then a voice hailed her from the hall – Poppy, in a state, by the sound of it.

'Gran! Gran – '

She dried her hands. There was a hysterical note in her granddaughter's voice. She was going to need dealing with firmly.

'Come through,' she called. 'I'm out the back.'

Poppy had a wild look to her. Her face was blotched and puffy from crying, but it was not grief that blazed in her eyes, it was fury. She fixed Margaret with a look that pinned her to the spot.

'You! You ruined my life!'

Margaret swallowed. There was something about the girl, something not quite rational, that frightened even her.

'Now then,' she said, as calmly as she could. 'That's no way to talk to your grandmother. You sit down and I'll make you a nice cup of tea.'

'Tea! I'd rather have poison! You got something to answer for, you have. You spoilt my chance of happiness. Why can't you keep out of other people's lives, eh? Why do you have to come snooping in and changing things behind people's backs? You made my mum's life a misery, and then you ruined mine. I'll never forgive you!'

She marched up to Margaret and glowered down at her. For the first time in her life, Margaret felt afraid of her own flesh and blood. She could feel the waves of anger and hatred flowing out from Poppy. She became very aware of her own age and weakness. If she did not hold her granddaughter back with words, she would crumple up.

'You're beside yourself,' she said. 'Now calm down. Stop shouting like that. Sit down and tell me what this is all about.'

She sat down herself, as her knees were shaking, but Poppy paced about the little room, flinging her arms out.

'You think you can rule all of us – Mum, Kit, me – but you can't. We got our own lives, we got a right to choose for ourselves. But you don't like that, do you? You like to have everyone do what you want. You chased my dad away. It's no wonder he made off, he couldn't stand the thought of coming back here, and I'm not surprised. You got rid of him and made my mum unhappy, and you got rid of the only man I ever loved and made both of us unhappy – '

So that was it. It was the same American. Margaret felt on slightly safer ground now. At least she knew what it was all about.

276

'He weren't good enough for you,' she stated. Of that she was quite sure.

'Not good enough? Who are you to judge that, eh? You see him once and you get rid of him, just like that. Did you find out anything about him, anything at all? Did you know that he was decorated for bravery, or that he'd been badly wounded, or that he'd been in prison camp? No! You just looked at him and sent him away with a lie – '

Margaret had to stop this. It was almost beginning to make her feel that she might have made a mistake.

'A lie, did you say?' she asked.

'Yes, a lie. You told him I was married. I was nothing of the sort, not then. I'd gone up to Scotland to look for my dad.'

Margaret kept her nerve. She had long ago calculated back nine months from Kit's birth, one of a great rash of babies that August. Victory babies, some people called them. But then some people would say anything.

'After the Armistice, that was, weren't it?'

That brought the girl up short. For a brief moment she looked confused. Then the truculence was back.

'So what if it was?'

'So it was hardly a lie. You'd already fallen for Kit then. What were you planning to do? Cuckoo it on him, this American?' She had righteous indignation on her side now. 'Talk about me ruining your life. Seems like I saved you from a very nasty situation. Dreadful thing to do to a man, that is. Wicked.'

Poppy was staring at her as the meaning of the words seeped into her head. The colour drained from her face.

'There, that's made you think, ain't it?' Margaret said. She was back in control. It was going to be all right.

Poppy's mouth opened and shut. She reached out and held on to the back of the chair with a hand that trembled.

Her voice was small and strangled now. 'That still didn't give you the right to send him away. I'll never forgive you for that. Never.' She turned and stumbled out, leaving the doors open behind her.

Margaret got up slowly, went to close the front door. Already Poppy had disappeared, swallowed up by the torrential rain. The triumph at coming out on top of the confrontation swiftly evaporated, leaving only a terrible cold fear. Supposing she stopped Kit from coming to see her?

Poppy was glad to have to go to work on Saturday night. She knew that if she stayed at home, she was in danger of drinking herself into a stupor. As it was, she had a couple to get herself moving, and set out with Elsie in a taxi to meet the charabanc she had booked to take the band out to the gig. Of course, it was no use trying to hide her emotional state from her friend. Elsie knew from the moment she saw her. She tried to offer comfort.

'Tell me about it, lovey. Get it off of your chest.'

'I can't. Not now. Not tonight. If I start, I'll end up crying and I won't be able to stop, and then what use will I be?'

'You don't have to come with us. We can manage without you, you know.'

'I do know. But I want to come. It'll help me hold myself together. So just talk to me, Elsie. Tell about what you been doing. What about this house of yours?'

Elsie looked dubious but took her at her word, much to Poppy's relief.

'I'm signing the documents Monday. Me! I'm going to own a house! Two houses. You'll have to come out and see them, Poppy. They're nearly finished now. Brand-new. Ain't no one else lived in them at all. They'll be all clean and fresh, not like Dog Island. It must be better, mustn't it, living out there? I mean, it stands to reason. It's like country still. All trees and grass and that – '

Elsie had hardly got into her stride by the time they got to the Embankment and picked up the charabanc and the rest of the band. Checking that everyone was there and had everything they needed kept Poppy's mind employed for a while, and then after they got started, there were complaints to deal with and reminders to give. Some band members, like Phyl

278

and Margie, did not like doing private parties. They found the behaviour of the upper classes at play obnoxious. Some of the younger girls needed to have the rules laid down. No more than two drinks. No going off with men during the breaks. If they wanted to accept dates, that was up to them, but this evening they were working. Some of them looked annoyed, or said 'Yes, miss,' to her cheekily, as if she were a schoolmarm.

'Yes, well I mean it,' Poppy said. 'I once had two girls disappear halfway through a night at one of these parties and they never came back. We had to carry on without them. That's not professional, that ain't. And what's more, I don't want this band to get the reputation for being a pick-up outfit.'

You can talk, she said to herself, as she sank down in the seat beside Elsie. One bunch of flowers from a man who sees you at a nightclub and you're his. The raw pain of it gripped her, making her catch her breath. In desperation she turned to her friend.

'Tell me about what these houses are like inside, Elsie.'

'Do you really want me to?'

'Yes, I do. I want to know everything. Perhaps I'll buy one myself.'

'Oh, that'd be lovely, Poppy! I do wish you would. There's lots going still on the estate. Kit'd love it out there, he really would. And your mum. If she could see them kitchens! She'd think it was dreamland. They got these heaters over the sink. Geysers, they're called. You turn on the tap and woomph! the gas comes on, and then hot water comes right out of the tap, just like that! It's amazing – '

Eventually the charabanc turned off the main road and into a twisting lane, then in between two matching lodge cottages and up a long gravelled driveway, to stop in front of an imposing house. The curtains were mostly undrawn and lights blazed from the windows. As the girls stepped down from the charabanc, they could see liveried servants hurrying to and fro.

'Blimey. What a place,' one of the younger members of the band said.

'They're only people living in it, and pretty degraded specimens at that,' Marjorie told her.

Poppy went to the door, but before she could knock, it flew open to reveal a woman dressed in diaphanous Eastern trousers, a veil and two gold discs held up by a length of gold ribbon.

'You're the band? Thank God! Johnny's so useless. He couldn't remember whether he'd booked you.'

A middle-aged man with a highly disapproving expression on his face appeared. 'Shall I show them round to the tradesmen's entrance, my lady?'

'Good God no, Saunders. This is a highly prestigious band, not the butcher's van. Bring your people in here, Miss Powers, and Saunders will show you where you can leave your things, then he'll take you to the ballroom.'

It gradually became obvious to Poppy that this was a theme party. There were potted palms in every corner, a tented ceiling to the ballroom, heaps of cushions where there should have been chairs, and little brass tables with hookahs on them. The house guests, as they drifted in, were all dressed as bedouins, corsairs, slave girls or belly dancers.

'What do you think it is – Lawrence of Arabia?' Mona asked.

'Sheiks,' Elsie guessed.

'Shakes?'

'Yeah, like Rudolph Valentino. You know.'

'If they'd of told us, we could of hired something to blend in,' Phyllis grumbled.

Poppy did not care. What did clothes matter when Scott was with his horrible wife at some horrible friends of hers?

The evening was much like many others they had played at. Some of the guests were already drunk when they arrived. Those who were not proceeded to get so as quickly as possible. All were in high spirits. They shrieked at each other in their nerve-jangling accents, and did not seem to care what was played so long as the band kept up a seamless stream of foxtrots and tangos with a good sprinkling of Charlestons.

The fancy dress seemed to have been a good excuse for most of the women to wear as little as possible. The men were openly drooling over them.

'It's disgusting,' Marjorie said, when they took their first break. 'I'm used to seeing them necking all over the place, but there's a couple copulating in the conservatory. Quite openly! I felt like throwing a bucket of water over them.'

At any other time, Poppy would have found it funny. Now it just made her depressed. She broke her own rule and had her third large whisky of the evening. What did it matter? These people wouldn't notice if they played the same tune all night.

It was some time after eleven that she noticed yet another couple coming in to the ballroom, a desert prince in a long white robe with a red headdress, accompanied by a blonde slave girl in silver and blue. The music faded around her, the multicoloured crowd blurred. Across the room, the prince stopped still and stared back at her, and she knew that fate had played a last trick on them. It was Scott.

PART SIX

Bright Young Things

31

'He should never have come. Bloody men! How inconsiderate can you get? To turn up here like this with his wife in tow. It's terrible.'

Marjorie voiced everyone's thoughts. They were all united in their outrage.

'I don't think he knew,' Poppy protested. 'I don't remember telling him where we were playing tonight. It wasn't deliberate, I'm sure. He wouldn't do that to me.'

The girls were sceptical. It was nice to know that they were all with her, but it did not ease the pain of knowing that out there in the ballroom, Scott was with his wife. She touched the saxophone brooch pinned to her shoulder.

'We got to go back on,' she said.

There was a flurry of hugs and kisses and reassuring words from the band, and they all trouped back into the sweaty atmosphere of the tented room.

A few couples were still dancing to a gramophone, but many had drifted away to other parts of the house, whilst others were reclining on the heaps of cushions, drinking and talking and flirting. Scott and the Snow Queen were nowhere to be seen.

'Let's get this lot moving,' Poppy said grimly, and announced a really fast number. She watched with satisfaction as the drunks fell over their feet and got in the way of the still sober, who became annoyed. That had sorted them out. A man of about her own age came up with a request.

'Would you play "Birth of the Blues"? I heard you do it at Angelino's. Your solo was utterly brilliant.'

She was in the middle of her solo piece when she saw Scott come in again. This time she managed to keep going. She

285

closed her eyes and tried to think only of the music. Pain and anger flowed into the notes.

When she stepped back to blend in with the rest of the band, she saw that Scott was leaning against a pillar at the side of the room, his face pale, staring at her. The Snow Queen came up to him, spoke to him, and then the pair of them took to the dance floor. Poppy felt physically sick. At the end of the number, the Snow Queen stayed hanging on Scott's arm, making up to him as another couple talked to them.

The man who had made the request appeared in front of her, clapping loudly.

'That was amazing! Too, too brilliant! You must be one of the best in London. Can I get you a drink?'

'Thanks.' Poppy found her voice, though it came out oddly. 'I'll have a whisky.'

Mona was at her shoulder. 'You're doing fine, girl. Keep it up. I'll announce the next one.'

The young man came up with her drink, and she knocked it back in two gulps while Mona introduced the next number. Then they were away again, this time with the singers doing a spot.

Couples came and went from the ballroom, changed partners, paired off with other people, but Scott and the Snow Queen stayed together, never missing a dance. Poppy saw other men coming to ask her to dance, but always she refused. They were like a honeymoon couple.

Just before the next break, she saw Scott get away at last and come towards her. Her knees turned to string. A great howling cry was building up inside her, ready to burst.

'Hi! Great playing. Can I make a request?'

He was acting, playing a game for his wife's sake. Frozen-faced, Poppy nodded.

'Can you do "Always"?'

'No.'

Absolutely not. If she played that, she would crack up.

'Look, Poppy –' He leaned forward, speaking urgently. 'This is just awful – I had no idea. If I'd have known it was you playing here tonight, I would have done anything rather than come.'

'Yes.'

There wasn't a great deal else she felt she could say, without letting go and getting hysterical.

'Say you forgive me, Poppy.'

'Yes.'

She supposed that she did. She obviously did not sound very convincing, as Scott still looked distressed.

'I got to go – '

Tenderness overcame the anger. On impulse, she said, 'Take care. God bless.'

For a moment she thought he was going to take those last two steps forward, to kiss her, but he didn't. She recognized the longing in his eyes, but he did not give in to it.

'God bless you, Poppy.'

He turned and went back into the crowd, back to the Snow Queen.

Mona took it upon herself to announce the next number. Poppy had no idea what it was they were supposed to be playing. She mimed, rather badly. Then, thankfully, she realized that the band were putting down their instruments ready for the break. Somebody was talking to her.

'. . . supper?'

It was the young man who had asked her to play 'Birth of the Blues'.

Elsie took her arm. 'Come along, lovey. Let's get away from this lot for a while.'

But Poppy did not want the gushing sympathy of the band. They meant well, they all wanted to help her, but she could not cope with them at the moment. Better by far to be with somebody who knew nothing about her.

'Thanks,' she said to the young man.

She vaguely heard Elsie's protest as she walked off on his arm.

It was a good thing that he chattered on without needing encouragement, because she only heard about one word in ten of what he said. In fact, it was not until he found a seat for her in what he claimed was the garden room, and disappeared to return with two laden plates and a bottle, that she realized that it was now supper time. She looked at the food with horror.

'Oh – I couldn't eat a thing – '

'Really? Not while you're performing, eh? You will drink, though, I hope? That mean old horse Sibby only puts out rubbish for parties, so I've been down on a raid to the cellars and found us something decent. Nice bottle of Dom Pérignon.'

He produced glasses from his pockets and uncorked the champagne.

'Whizzo! There we are. Here's to the most beautiful saxophonist in town.'

'Cheers,' Poppy responded automatically.

She took a couple of gulps. It fizzed merrily down her throat. The last time she had drunk champagne, she had been in bed with Scott. To stop herself from howling, she finished the glass.

'That's what I like to see,' her escort said, and refilled it.

He proceeded to talk about the party, the hostess, the guests, a stream of slanderous gossip which she would have found highly amusing normally. All she was required to do was to nod and say 'yes' and 'no' and 'really?' occasionally, while he worked his way through both plates of food. He was an ideal companion, distracting her from dwelling exclusively on her plight, whilst being totally undemanding. The champagne mixed with the whisky she had already drunk, blurring her senses. By the time she was escorted back to the palm-fringed enclosure at the end of the ballroom, she was far too drunk to notice the sour looks from one or two of the younger girls, who saw her breaking the rules she had laid down earlier that evening.

Elsie took her arm and spoke in her ear. 'You just busk through it, pet. We'll take over.'

'But – '

'Don't worry about a thing. We got it all under control.'

The night dragged on, mercifully dulled by the amount of alcohol she had taken on board. Her supper escort appeared at regular intervals to bring her drinks and tell her how wonderful she was. Sometime in the small hours of the morning, Scott and the Snow Queen left. She did not see them go, she just realized after a while that they were no longer there. The house with its hoards of screaming, crooning, dancing revellers became insubstantial. There was just a black void, gaping, ready for her to fall in to.

'What can I get you, old thing? More champagne? Whisky?'

'Whisky.'

'Sod that,' Marjorie's voice cut in, at her most serjeant-majorish. 'You get her a large soda water. And absolutely nothing else in it, mind, or I'll have something to say about it.'

Large maudlin tears started in Poppy's eyes. 'Margie, I want another drink – '

'You'll have no such thing. Act like a bloody pro, for God's sake.'

The words reacted on her as no others could have done. She could no longer play a decent note, but at least she gathered the wit to pretend.

The ordeal came to an end at around five in the morning. The girls thankfully packed up their instruments and went to claim cups of coffee. Poppy's admirer produced one for her, strong and black.

'Drink up, old thing. Make you feel better.'

It made her feel a lot worse. She just managed to get to an open window before throwing up.

For a long time she lay draped over the windowsill, too ill to move, thankful for the cold winter air on her face. She was still there when Elsie found her.

'Poppy – '

'Go away. I want to die.'

Mona's voice floated over. 'For crying out loud, Elsie, it's no good asking her. She's pissed as a bloody newt.'

Vaguely in the background, she heard voices conferring, anxious, annoyed, exasperated.

' – broken down – '

' – God-forsaken hole – '

' – till morning, and then it's Sunday – '

Something of the sense of it filtered through to her. She managed to stand upright, hanging on to a curtain. Several of the band members, some of them already in their outdoor clothes, huddled in a group.

A man appeared. 'What's the problem, ladies?'

Poppy looked at him. Her eyes were not focusing. 'Who are you?' she asked.

'I'm Roddy, sweetheart. Roddy Ffitch. Remember?'

She did recall something. He was certainly familiar.

'Our chara's gone and broken down,' Elsie told him. 'The driver can't get it started at all. We're stranded.'

'Oh, if that's all – ' He turned to Poppy. 'I've got my jalopy here. Get you home in two shakes of a lamb's tail.'

Poppy was overwhelmingly grateful. She just wanted to get into her bed and pass out.

'Oh yes, please.'

'Oh no.' Elsie put an arm round her and talked urgently in her ear. 'Don't be a fool, Poppy. You know what happened last time you did this. You ended up marrying Joe.' She glared at Roddy Ffitch. 'I'm sorry, but she doesn't accept lifts with strange men.'

'But I'm not at all strange, old thing. I'm utterly utterly trustworthy. Look – I'm happy to take as many of you as the old bus will hold. Three or four, at least. Have you all back in Town in an hour.'

'There are rather more than three or four of us,' Mona pointed out.

'Leave it to me! Roddy will fix it. Now you ladies all stay right here and I will see what I can rustle up.'

Poppy rather lost track of events after that. Sometime later, she was helped into her coat, then ushered into a car. With a splattering of gravel, they started off on what seemed like an endless journey.

She almost wished it would really go on for ever. Her stomach felt slightly better now, and while she was travelling she did not have to make any decisions or face any problems. But all too soon they were riding through the suburbs. Someone was dropped off. Then they were speeding on into the East End. Somewhere behind her head, Elsie seemed to be giving instructions.

'Here we are, old thing. Home at last! Let me help you out.'

With Roddy's arm round her waist, she staggered up to the front door.

'Now then, are you sure you'll be all right? Is there someone at home to look after you – get you to bed and all that?'

Miraculously, her mother appeared. At last, at long last, Poppy was able to sink down and sleep the sleep of the dead.

32

The Powers Girls packed up for the night and started to leave for their various homes. It had been another private party, in a Mayfair mansion this time. Poppy slipped out quickly, avoiding Elsie. She did not want to go home yet. She needed to think.

It was bitingly cold outside after the sweaty heat of the party. Poppy turned up her coat collar and marched along the street, trying to make sense of the last few weeks. Whichever way she looked at it, Scott was never going to be hers. And now there was Roddy Ffitch, charming and amusing and free – and flatteringly in love with her. What was she going to do about him? She had no idea.

She sighed and turned the corner into a street of small art galleries and exclusive shops. Thinking was no use, it just made her more confused. To distract herself, she looked in the tastefully arranged windows, at gorgeous hats, carved and gilded antique furniture, oil paintings ... then she stopped short, her heart pounding in her chest. She was no longer an experienced woman, a mother and widow, standing in a Mayfair street, but a young girl, terrified by the workings of a warped mind. She could even smell the pervasive odour of developing chemicals, catching at her throat. There in the middle of the gallery window was a photograph of herself as a child, her thumb in her mouth, her wide eyes wistfully gazing.

She felt sick. There were others – her looking over her shoulder, her with her long hair falling forward as she unbuttoned her blouse, the Grecian ones with the pillars and the urn.

'Why –?' she gasped out loud. 'Why – how –?'

On a discreet green card at the side of the display, in gold lettering, she found an explanation of sorts: *Arnold Hetherington – the unsung genius of the East End. An Exhibition of Photographs*.

Utterly appalled, she read it three times. Exhibition! She was the subject of an exhibition. Those horrible, sick photographs that she had endured sittings for in order to learn to play, were here, on display for all the world to see. People were going to look at those pictures, they were going to buy them and hang them on their walls. Men with minds as strange as Mr Hetherington's might take them home and slaver over them in private. She doubled up, retching over the pavement, heaving until there was nothing left in her stomach.

She wanted to run as she had done that day to escape from Mr Hetherington, but this time she did not know where to run to. Going home meant returning to Dog Island where the memories of those early days were around her all the time. Then it came to her.

'Roddy,' she said out loud.

He knew nothing of the details of her early life. He would take her in, shelter her from the staring eyes. She hurried along the road heading for his rooms. By some miracle, a lone taxi appeared. She sat hunched up on the back seat as it bore her through the empty streets.

Roddy answered the door at the fifth ring. He was wearing a red paisley dressing-gown and his hair was flopping into his eyes. When he realized who it was, his face lit up.

'Poppy, darling! This is an unexpected pleasure. Come in, do.'

Poppy fell into his arms and wept.

'Hold me,' she sobbed. 'Just hold me.'

Roddy led her inside and sat on the sofa with her for a long time, until she subsided into shuddering silence. Then he poured her a whisky.

'There,' he said. 'Better now, old thing?'

She nodded. She did feel better, in a way. She felt completely empty, as if all emotion had drained away.

Roddy got a glass for himself and sat down beside her again, putting an arm round her shoulders.

'Well now,' he said. 'Here you are in my little den in the dark hours before dawn. How about you and me getting married?'

Safety. Poppy could think of nothing better.

'All right,' she said.

When Jane was told the news, she was stunned.

'But you've only known him a month!' she protested.

'Long enough to know you love somebody,' Poppy said.

She had that stubborn set to her face. Jane knew very well that there was no moving her when she looked like that, but all the same, she had to try. Her daughter's whole happiness was at stake.

'But Poppy, love, are you really sure? I mean, what do you know about him?'

'He's sweet and kind and generous and he adores me. That's enough, ain't it? More than you can say for a lot of men.'

'That's all very fine, I'm sure –' Jane was confused. This was the trouble when she tried reasoning with Poppy. The girl had all the answers, and yet Jane knew in her heart that she was wrong.

'But he ain't one of us, now is he? I mean – he's one of the nobs, his dad's a lord or something.'

'Oh, Mum – that sort of thing don't matter so much these days. And anyway, it ain't as if he's ever going to get the title – he's got two older brothers and they're both married with kids of their own.'

'But he's still, like, aristocracy, ain't he? I mean, for a start, he don't do nothing, does he? He don't even look after a stately home or whatever it is what lords do. He just goes around enjoying himself.'

'Well, they're all like that, ain't they? It's just the way they live. They all got private incomes. They don't have to work for a living. Look at it this way, Mum, if it weren't for people like them, the Bright Young Things, people like me'd be out of a job.'

Jane sighed. 'But are you sure, lovey?'

'Of course I am. I wouldn't say I'd marry him if I wasn't, now would I?'

It was unanswerable, but Jane was still not convinced. She was quite sure that if it hadn't been for that American coming back again after all these years, Poppy would never have fallen for this Roddy Ffitch, but she did not dare mention that. And after all, what was the point in waiting? She had spent her life waiting for Owen, seen her youth go by, and for what? Perhaps Poppy should snatch at this chance. After all, she had wanted her to get married. If only it was to that nice Mr Appleby. He would have taken good care of Poppy and little Kit. But this Ffitch man – he was what her mother would call a fly-by-night. It worried her terribly.

Poppy pushed her plate away. 'I'm sorry, Mum. I can't manage any more of this. I got to go and get ready. Roddy's picking me up at half past two, and we'll go and fetch Kit.'

'What does Kit think about all this? He ain't said much to me, except about the car. He loves the car.'

'Oh, Kit likes him. He thinks he's funny.'

'But does he know he's going to have a step-dad?'

'Not yet. I'll tell him when it's the right moment.'

It was not until Poppy had gone off that the other aspect of the situation struck Jane. What was going to happen to her? Poppy would go off and live in some place up West, she supposed. And, of course, Poppy would take Kit with her. Jane couldn't afford to keep this house on all by herself, and in any case she didn't want to live alone. The only possible solution did not take long to present itself. She would go back to her mother's, in Cinnamon Alley. At least there she would be needed. Her mum might not admit it, but she was getting on now. She could do with some help about the place. But it was a dismal prospect. Here she was important, she held the family together. Poppy might pay for everything, but she, Jane, was in charge of the household. If she went back to her mum's, she would just be the daughter of the house again.

Worst of all, there would be no Kit. A bleak chill caught at her heart. She had been so happy here, in this house. She had been wanted and needed and loved. She had had a purpose in life. And now it was all going to change. It wouldn't be quite so bad if she thought Poppy was making a wise choice, but as it was, the whole situation filled her with foreboding.

'But Poppy, are you sure?' Elsie said.

'Oh, for God's sake, Elsie! Why does everyone keep saying this? *Are you sure, Poppy? Isn't it a bit sudden?* Yes, I am sure. I love him and he loves me. Ain't that good enough any more?'

The two of them were making last-minute adjustments to their makeup in the cloakroom of the Petite Fleur restaurant.

'No, it ain't, and you know why not.'

'No I don't. Why did you marry your Ted? Because you loved him. You never regretted it, did you?'

'I never had time to regret it,' Elsie said.

She stared at the face in the mirror. Whatever would Ted have said if he could see her now? Arms bare, hair bobbed, face painted. He'd of had a fit. The old-fashioned sort, her Ted had been. Things had changed so much since those days. She was swept by a sense of loss.

'Oh, Elsie –' Poppy put an arm round her shoulders. 'I'm sorry. That was so tactless of me. I could bite my tongue out.'

'It's all right. I'm fine, really. It's just – sometimes it still hurts. I'll never really get over losing him.' She pulled herself back to the problem in hand. 'That's just it, Poppy. You do flaming well know why you're marrying this Roddy bloke. It's because of your Scott.'

'He's not my Scott, he's Hers.'

'Yeah well – that is why, ain't it? Because he's Hers.'

'No it ain't! It's got nothing to do with it. I'm marrying Roddy because I love him.'

'So you keep saying.'

'What's that supposed to mean? Why don't you like him, eh? He's mad about me, he's wonderful to me, he's even keen for me to carry on with the band after we're married. There can't be many men would let their wives go on working, especially a job like this, with all the odd hours we work.'

Mona came bursting in, face flushed. 'Sorry I'm so late. Got held up.'

She hung up her coat, adjusted the shoulder straps of her dress, scrabbled in her bag for a comb. Then she noticed the faces of the other two.

'Oh – am I butting in on something?'

'Not at all.' Here was an ally. Elsie was glad to draw her into the argument. Perhaps Poppy might listen to Mona. 'I'm trying to make Poppy see she's only going for Roddy on the rebound.'

'Yeah, well, that's obvious, ain't it? Plain as a pikestaff.'

Poppy rammed the top onto her lipstick, shoved it into her bag and shut it with a snap.

'Fine friends you are! I don't care what you say. I'm going to marry Roddy and that's that. Why can't you just be happy for me?' She slammed out of the room.

Elsie looked at Mona. They both pulled grim faces.

'She's making a big mistake,' Mona said.

Much later, when the last customer had gone home or on to a nightclub, the waiters pushed two tables together and the girls in the band sat down to finish off whatever was left on the menu. This was the nicest part of working at the Petite Fleur. It made such a lovely ending to the night, sitting round the table and chatting as they ate, relaxing after the strain of performing. Talk inevitably turned to Poppy's forthcoming marriage. Not everybody saw it as Elsie did. Some of the younger girls thought it wonderfully romantic. They were quite starry-eyed about it.

'Where's the wedding going to be, Poppy? Westminster Abbey?'

'Or St Margaret's? All the posh weddings are at St Margaret's.'

'No, no, they'll have it at a little church in the country, you know, at the gates of the big house – isn't that so, Poppy?'

For the first time, Elsie noticed that her friend looked slightly apologetic.

'We're having it at Caxton Hall, actually.'

'Caxton Hall?' They were all astonished. 'The registry office?'

'But that's hardly a proper wedding at all,' one of the sax players protested.

'It's legal. And anyway, we don't want a great big fuss.'

'Are you wearing white?'

'No, of course not. I'm widow, ain't I? I'm going to have a new outfit made special. And a fur coat. Roddy's buying me a fur coat as a wedding present.'

That met with almost universal approval.

'And are all his family going to be there?' The trombonist was an avid gossip column reader. Nothing pleased her better than to recognize someone she had read about.

'Well – er – I don't think so. They can't come.'

'What, none of them?'

'Do you mean can't, or won't?' Marjorie asked.

'Oh, they've all got very good reasons for not coming. Prior engagements, that sort of thing –'

'Rubbish. They've refused to come, haven't they? What's the matter, don't they think you're good enough for their boy?'

'I really don't know. Anyway, I don't care. We don't need them, they'd only get in the way and spoil the fun. I want all of you to come. You're the ones who count.'

'Just try and keep us away,' said Mona, speaking for them all. 'Where's the reception going to be?'

A very slight pause.

'Well – er – Roddy's fixing that up. It's a surprise, you know. He's very good at fixing things. He knows so many people –'

'You can't keep it a surprise for too long, Poppy. You won't know what to put on the invitations,' Phyllis pointed out.

'Oh, I'm sure he'll let me know in good time. It'll all fall into place, you'll see. Just keep the date free in your diaries, that's the main thing.'

The whole conversation left Elsie with a sense of unease. It was supposed to be wildly romantic, rushing into this wedding because they couldn't wait to get married, not worrying about fiddling little details, but somehow she felt that there was something profoundly wrong somewhere.

'Poppy, my old china –' Johnny Flowers, restaurateur extraordinary and owner of the Petite Fleur, descended on them. In the company of the band, he dropped the French accent he had acquired while working as a waiter and later as a restaurant manager in Paris, and reverted to his native cockney.

'Listen, my favourite saxophonist. I want to offer you a little wedding present. Let me do the reception for you here, in the Petite Fleur.'

There was a moment's stunned silence, followed by a gasp of astonishment and Poppy's cry of joy. She flung her arms round him.

'Johnny, you don't mean it – you do mean it! Oh – that's utterly wonderful of you. How can I possibly thank you?'

She kissed him loudly on the cheek. They all clapped and whistled.

Marjorie leaned sideways and muttered in Elsie's ear, 'He's not doing it for free. He never does anything without a purpose. That's how he's got to be so successful.'

'Darling, you don't need to thank me. I'm doing this because I like you. Little ray of sunshine round here, you are. Besides, the publicity will be blooming amazing. Can't you see the headlines? *Youngest Son of Viscount Weds Bandleader.* You will be titbit of the week.'

Such devastating openness was irresistible. Poppy laughed and kissed him again. She turned a flushed, excited face to the girls.

'There – didn't I say it would all fall into place? Now that we know, I can invite you properly.' She made a wide gesture, encompassing the restaurant and the band with her arms. 'You are all invited to celebrate the marriage of me and Roddy, here, at the Petite Fleur, on the seventh of February.'

Along with all the others, Elsie clapped and cheered. But still a leaden weight of doubt hung on her heart.

33

Poppy padded round the flat. It still gave her a faint sense of surprise that she should be living here. She had to suppress the feeling that it was somebody else's home and she was just borrowing it. It wasn't just the address, or that fact that there was a shiny entrance hall and lifts to all the floors, or even the modern all-electric fittings, more miraculous even than in Elsie's new house. Perhaps it was because she had had no hand in the decoration.

'Darling, Mitzi will see to the interiors,' Roddy had said. 'You have such a lot on your hands, managing the band. Just leave everything to her – you'll be astounded, I promise you. She is just too, too talented. An artist. I'm sure she is about to become *the* decorator.'

So she did as he advised, and she certainly was astounded. The flat was done up in the very latest of fashion. The walls and the carpeted floors were all in the palest of colours, lemon, cream, eau-de-Nil. The furniture was low and insubstantial, chrome and glass tables, leather and chrome sofas. The lighting was from fan-shaped wall fitments that spread a diffused glow over the rooms. Poppy had never seen anything like it outside of the covers of a magazine. The very first thing that popped into her head was the thought of what her gran would say about it – it was all going to show the dirt something terrible.

Now, having lived in the place for a month or so, she realized that dirt was not the problem here that it was on Dog Island. The air itself was cleaner, even the people were cleaner. What little dirt did find its way in was cleared away by the cleaning lady. It was a different world.

She went into the kitchen, filled the electric kettle and plugged it in. The convenience of it charmed her. It was like being in a play house. Not that she used the kitchen for very much. She and Roddy seemed to have nearly all of their meals out.

They went to cocktail parties every evening, and drank amazing concoctions and ate pretty but insubstantial canapes. Roddy's friends were curious about her. She could just imagine them waving their cigarettes and shrieking to each other above the noise of the gramophone. 'A cockney saxophone player, my dear. Just too, too delicious!' But they were kind enough in a patronizing way, talking to her, asking her about herself. Sometimes they asked her to play for them, but she always refused, telling them to come and listen to the band later that evening. When the parties began to wind down, Poppy would go off to work, and much later Roddy would join her for the delicious after-hours supper at the Petite Fleur. Sometimes, if Roddy woke up in time, they would go out to lunch somewhere. It was one long round of fun.

Today, however, Roddy was still asleep at two in the afternoon and Poppy was feeling slightly jaded. She took two aspirins, made a cup of tea and went to sit in the lounge. On one of the low tables was a copy of the *Tatler*. She flicked the pages over, and experienced once again the thrill of seeing herself on its pages. She had featured in several magazine and picture paper articles in the past, but never in a society rag. There was a lovely photo of her and Roddy together, and another of the guests at the reception at the Petite Fleur. Johnny had got his publicity all right.

'Darling –' Roddy's voice, faintly querulous, from the bedroom.

'Coming, darling.'

She put down both magazine and teacup and padded in to see him. He was lying in the rumpled sheets, pale and tousled, an overgrown little boy. He lifted a hand towards her, then let it drop as if there was no strength left in his arms. Poppy bent over and kissed him.

'How are you, my pet?'

A groan. 'I've got the mother and father of a hangover. Be an absolute angel and fix me some hair of the dog.'

'An Alka-Seltzer would be better,' Poppy argued.

He groaned again. 'Disgusting stuff. Makes me sick. What I need is a brandy. A big one.'

Poppy went and did as he asked. One thing they did have plenty of in the house was drink.

He struggled half upright and took the glass from her, then took large sips, putting his head back and letting it roll down his throat. Slowly a look of relief flowed over his face.

'That's better. You're a real little Florence Nightingale.' He held out the glass. 'Just a little drop more, and I shall be tickety-boo.'

There was no doubt about it, he did look distinctly better once the second dose of brandy was inside him. His charming blue eyes in his chubby boyish face smiled at her, then travelled over her body. He reached out and pulled her down on top of him.

'Come and kiss the patient, Nurse Nightingale. He needs lots of love and attention.'

She giggled and returned his brandy-flavoured kisses. He slid a hand inside her satin robe.

'Mmm – beautiful beautiful Poppy. You're so thin. I love your thinness. I want it all –'

There were no towering heights of passion, no dizzying explosions. It was all over very quickly. But she was loved, she was needed, and he was all her very own, legally, to keep. And that was what she wanted. If her body felt slightly disappointed afterwards, she endeavoured to ignore it. She was safe now, she was owned.

Roddy gave a sigh of pleasure and patted her bottom.

'Better get up, I suppose. People to see, things to do.'

He heaved himself out of bed and went into the palatial black and white bathroom.

Half an hour later, he was gone. He went out with a cheery wave of the hand and a blown kiss for Poppy, looking as if he had never even sniffed a drink the night before. Poppy had yet to find out just what it was that he did when he went off like this. 'I fix things,' he explained airily, when she asked. Further than that, he did not detail.

It was Kit who noticed, a few days later, that the car was missing.

'Where's the Bugatti?' he asked Roddy. 'It's gone, but you're here.'

'Oh, old Buster Bligh is back in the country again, so I've given it back to his loving care,' Roddy explained.

'Wasn't it yours, then?' Poppy asked.

'Darling, don't tell me you only married me for the car. I shall go and shoot myself –'

'Of course not, idiot, it's just –'

It was just that she had assumed it was his. It was a silly thing, but somehow it mattered.

'Now, if I were to buy a car, I would buy something British.'

'I love the Bugatti. I want it back,' Kit wailed.

'Kit –'

Poppy tried to catch him in her arms, but he ran off to his room.

Roddy looked irritated. 'Really, darling, you must do something about a school for him. He's a nice little sprog on the whole, but he's around far too much.'

Poppy couldn't think what he was on about.

'But I have done something about a school. He started at the new one when we got married.'

'A day school.' Roddy was dismissive.

'But – what sort of school were you thinking about?'

'Well, a proper prep school, of course.'

'You mean boarding?'

'Of course, boarding.'

Poppy went cold. 'But he's still a baby. He's not seven years old yet.'

'I went off to school at seven. We can get him in to my old place, if you like.'

'Oh, no.' Poppy was quite certain. 'I'm not sending him away. It's cruel. I don't know how people can do it.'

Roddy just laughed. 'Cruel? It's good for them. Character building, makes them stand on their own two feet and that sort of thing.'

'He can stand on his own two feet,' Poppy said.

Growing up on the Isle of Dogs was enough to make any child self-reliant. Perhaps he could manage to fit in to this prep school of Roddy's, but she could not bear to send him away.

'Really, darling, it would be the best thing for him. Everyone sends their children away to school.'

'Maybe your sort of people do. P'raps they don't like their children. After all, they don't see much of them, do they? But it's different where I come from.'

'Oh, for heaven's sake!' Roddy threw up his hands. 'It's really not terribly amusing, darling, this harping on about your origins.'

Something in his tone of voice goaded her beyond endurance.

'Look, I'm proud of my origins, as you call it. At least where I come from, we all work for a living, we don't just swan around doing nothing all day long!' She glared at him, seething.

He laughed. 'Work! What a perfectly dreadful idea. I leave that all to you, my sweet. You're so much better at it than I am.' He ambled across the room and into the hall, taking his hat and coat off the stand. 'Now I really must be off to swan around and do nothing. Toodle-oo!'

With a cheery wave he was gone.

For a moment, Poppy just stood there, looking at the door. Then she wrenched it open and ran after him onto the landing. He was running lightly down the stairs. She took in a lungful of air.

'That's right, run away! Don't stay and fight like a man. You knew you was losing, so you went. You're good for bloody nothing, you are –'

He paused and looked up at her, his boyish face slightly pained. His voice came floating up the stairwell.

'Really, darling. You're not in the East End now, don't you know?'

Poppy slumped over the bannister rails, appalled at what she had said, how she must have sounded. Then she gripped them and leaned over, calling after his retreating footsteps.

'Roddy – Roddy, come back. I didn't mean it –'

But he was gone.

Slowly, she turned, to see Kit's small figure framed in the doorway. His face was white and his eyes looked enormous.

'Mum?'

'Oh, Kit –' She swept him into her arms and held him fiercely to her, but his hot little body was stiff and resistant.

'I don't like him. I don't like it here. When are we going back home to Granny?'

Poppy was stunned. She had not realized that he did not understand the situation properly. She drew him inside and sat down with him on the sofa.

'Kit, lovey, this is our home now. This is where we live. I know it's very different from where we was before, but it's nice, ain't it?'

'No.'

'Why not, pet? Why don't you like it?'

'I want my Granny. And I don't like him.'

This was terrible. Kit was unhappy. She was hurting the person she loved most in the world. She tried to see a way through it.

'We'll go and see Granny tomorrow, pet, I promise. And Roddy's nice really. I thought you liked him? You always used to be so pleased when he came with me to pick you up from school.'

'I don't like it when you shout at him.'

'Well, I don't like it either – but you mustn't get worried, darling. It don't mean nothing. Roddy and I love each other really, and you'll get to love him too, you'll see. After all, it's nice to have a dad, ain't it?'

Kit still looked unconvinced. 'He's not my real dad.'

'No, darling. Your real dad died and went to heaven. But

306

Roddy's your step-dad. We're married. That's why we're living here now. When people get married they want to stay together forever.'

'Oh –' His face creased in thought. 'Is that why you shouted at him?'

She smiled. With a child's logic, he had got to the point. They were married, so they shouted at each other. She felt suddenly better. All married couples had rows.

'Yeah, that's right. It's just your mum getting all worked up about nothing.'

Kit scuffed at the carpet with the toe of his shoe. Poppy could see that something was still worrying him.

'What is it, darling? What's the matter? Come on, out with it. I can't make it better if I don't know, can I?'

He shook his head. Poppy waited. The silence hung heavy on her heart.

'I don't want to go away to boarding school,' he burst out.

'Oh, so that's it.' She had lost sight of the reason for the argument. She hugged him close. 'Kit, darling, I promise I will never never send you away. Not to boarding school or anywhere else.'

He gave a great sigh of relief. 'When's tea?'

Poppy wished her worries could be solved so easily. Roddy did not reappear that evening. She left Kit in the charge of the cleaning lady's sister, as usual, and took a taxi to the Petite Fleur. Roddy did not turn up for the late-night supper.

'Where's the dashing bridegroom, then? You newlyweds had a tiff? Johnny asked, with devastating accuracy.

'Course not,' Poppy lied. 'He had to go and see someone.'

Johnny grinned, totally unconvinced. 'Never mind, girl. I got some *estouffade de boeuf* left over.'

'What's that when it's at home?'

In great detail, he described the beef, the bacon, the wine, the mushrooms, the garlic . . . Poppy was not really listening. She was wondering just where Roddy had got to.

Johnny had stopped speaking.

'Beef stew, in other words,' she said.

'Beef stew? Poppy, taste it. Close your eyes, let the flavours fill your mouth! Then tell me that it's beef stew. God Almighty! I know you was brung up on Dog Island, but you ought to learn to appreciate the good things in life.'

That was the second time that day she had had her upbringing flung in her face. Poppy ate and tried to appreciate, but the food tasted of leather. She made her excuses and went home early.

Roddy was not there.

In the still of the small hours, the flat felt horribly empty, even though Kit and his minder were asleep there. Poppy slid into the cold bed and felt small and alone in its vast space. She did not sleep.

He did not appear the next morning. Poppy spent a miserable day trying to work out some new arrangements for the band and failing to get anywhere. By four o'clock, when Kit came in from school, there was still no sign of him nor any telephone message. Poppy swung from unhappy to defiant.

'Come along,' she said to Kit, 'we're going out for tea today. We'll go and have cream cakes at Claridge's.'

They had just reached the street door when a magnificent car drew up at the kerb. It was a long-nosed open-top tourer with blue bodywork, sweeping mudguards, four headlamps and on top of the radiator, an elegant silver mascot in the shape of a flying stork. At the wheel, grinning with unconcealed delight, was Roddy. He jumped out.

'What do you think of her, eh? Not a bad little old bus, is she?'

Poppy looked from him to the car and back again.

'It's not yours, is it?'

Kit was at the front, looking at the name on the bonnet.

'His – pan – spaniel?'

'Hispano-Suiza. Beautiful, isn't she? As beautiful as my darling Poppy.' Roddy put his arms round her and gazed into her eyes. 'I'm grovelling, darling. Abject apologies and all that. I was an utter hound yesterday. Can you ever forgive me?'

He looked so soulful that it was very difficult not to give in to him at once. Poppy made a last ditch effort.

'But where was you last night?'

'Coming up with the readies, old thing. Hate it, but one can't live one's entire life on credit, unfortunately. And as you so rightly pointed out, I have no visible means of support –'

'I wish you'd forget I said that,' Poppy interrupted.

'Forgotten! Quite gone, I assure you. But anyway, it's all hunky-dory now, and here we are, a lovely lovely car for my Poppy to ride in. Aren't you going to jump in? You too, Kit, old bean. Let's go for a spin.'

Slightly dazed, Poppy got in. The Hispano-Suiza was as luxurious inside as it was impressive on the outside. In her relief and happiness at having Roddy back, she let all the questions that crowded her mind fly out of the window. What did it matter that she did not know where he had gone to, where the money came from to buy this ridiculously extravagant machine? Roddy was rich, and the rich were different. One day, she might come to understand them. In the meantime, the man who loved her was driving her through the streets of London, and all who saw them pass turned their heads in envy.

34

'I say, old thing, see to these beastly things for me, will you?'

Roddy waved a hand at a pile of brown manilla envelopes.

'Well I —'

'You're an absolute angel. I adore you.' He took her face in his hands and kissed her. He tasted of gin slings. 'I don't know what I used to do without you, d'you know that?'

'I sometimes wonder as well,' Poppy told him. He seemed to have no idea what real life was about. And now, for once, he was up and about before ten in the morning.

'What's got you up at this hour?' she asked.

'This jolly old strike. Who'd have thought it, eh? The great unwashed have actually done it. They've risen up against us. Revolution, in England's green and pleasant land!'

Poppy thought that the only surprising thing was that it hadn't happened before. She could remember the dockers' strikes of 1911 and 1912. She had grown up with children who went to school with no shoes on their feet, known families who lived for weeks at a time on nothing but bread and thrice-brewed tea. And all that before they sent their menfolk off to fight for King and country. Now things were hardly better for some. There was widespread unemployment in the land fit for heroes. All the strikers were asking for was a fairer deal, a chance to support their families.

'You better watch it, then,' she said lightly. 'You'll be first against the wall, you will. Bloated capitalist!'

'Capitalist, me? Darling, I haven't a penny to my name. Now, be a good girl and kiss me bye-bye. I'm off to volunteer my services. Do you think they'll let me drive a train? I've always wanted to do that, ever since I was a little boy.'

He was still a little boy now, Poppy reflected, as he rushed off into the warm May sunshine. She turned to the pile of bills he had left. Electricity, telephone, rates, wine merchant, tailor, hatter, garage . . . the list went on and on. Mixed in amongst it all was an unopened bank statement on their joint account. She drew it out and studied it. She was new to all this banking business, to the joys of a chequebook. Up till the time she married Roddy, she had dealt only in cash. But she was learning fast. The only money inwards seemed to be what she had earned from club and restaurant bookings and the record contract they had recently signed. The money outwards, on the other hand, was mostly what Roddy had spent. It was certainly true what he had said just now in jest. He hadn't a penny to his name. The allowance that she had fondly imagined would be forthcoming from his family was non-existent. When she had mentioned it, he had laughed.

'The jolly old family? Oh, they disowned me years ago. A proper genuine black sheep, I am. My name isn't mentioned aloud in the family pile for fear it will give the Old Man a heart attack.'

Quite what he had done to deserve this, she could not discover. Roddy was adept at changing the subject when he chose to.

Poppy picked up a pencil and began totting up the amounts on the unpaid bills. The total brought her out in a sweat. The only way she could think of to settle all that was to get a six months' contract at a top hotel. She sorted through them again, putting them into piles of things that had to be paid and those that could wait, then wrote out cheques for the rent and the utilities. After some thought, she wrote others for a proportion of the outstanding amounts to tradesmen in order to keep them sweet, but felt terribly guilty about it. They were trying to run honest businesses, after all. She sealed them all up and left them for the daily woman to post. What were they going to live on now? The only answer possible was credit. She wondered if it was any use tackling Roddy about it when he came in, but decided against it. He would just brush it aside as irrelevant. Instead she picked up the phone and got on to Ted Appleby. He was going to have to get the band some extra work.

Just as she expected, Roddy did not appear for the rest of the day. She guessed that he would go out and make a night of it after the novelty of real work, so she put Kit to bed, let in the babysitter, and went off to try and find a cab.

The club they were playing at, the Blue Diamond, was hopping that night. The barman invented a series of new cocktails – Bus Conductor's Bell, Special Constable, Train Whistle – and everyone was exchanging strike stories. The whole thing, from what Poppy could make out, was a terrific lark.

Marjorie was disgusted. 'I suppose that husband of yours is strike breaking?' she asked.

'Well – yes – he went off this morning. I ain't seen him since.'

'You should shoot him, Poppy. It's people like him who will turn this strike into a long-drawn-out war.'

'What I say won't have no effect on him,' Poppy said. 'One word from me and he does exactly what he wants.'

She said it as a joke. It was only later that she realized that it was only too true. It was an unsettling thought.

To her utter astonishment, Roddy was home and in bed when she arrived back. She undressed as quietly as she could and slid in beside him. He stirred and turned over, wrapping an arm round her, and she cuddled up to him, safe and secure. Any doubts she had harboured earlier in the evening flew straight out of the window. She was all right. She had a man of her own.

More astonishing still, she was woken by Roddy bringing her a cup of tea.

'Here we are, my angel, a cup of the best – what is it? Flowery?'

'Rosie,' Poppy laughed, pulling herself up and settling the pillows behind her back. 'Rosie Lee.'

'Oh yes, of course. Rosie Lee, tea. Got to remember that now I'm a working man. Poppy darling, you can't think what fun it all is. I met up with some friends – Bunny Chalmers, you know Bunny, and Tommy Meredith, all that crowd – and

312

they said, "Roddy, you can drive a car, can't you? Come along with us and drive a bus." '

'A bus?' Poppy simply could not imagine him doing anything so responsible.

Roddy pretended offence. 'There's no need to look so amazed, darling. I can drive anything. And it was such a lark!'

He went on at length about his day's adventures, then bent over and kissed her.

'Must dash, angel. Duty calls! Should have been at the depot ages ago, but not to worry. People are so glad to see a bus at all, they'll welcome us with open arms whatever time we arrive. Oh –' He paused at the bedroom door – 'there's a cocktail party at Bunny's this evening, don't forget. Toodle-pip!'

He was quite irresistible. Poppy sipped her tea and tried to think her way through this strike business. Her natural sympathies were all on the side of the strikers, but somehow she could not blame Roddy for going out with his bus. He had no idea what life was really like for most people. And how could she deny him his fun when he was enjoying himself so much?

A trip over to see her mother and grandmother that afternoon made her realize that this was not going to be like the strikes before the war. Troops were already in the docks unloading and lorries were being escorted through the picket lines by armoured cars. Her gran was scathing about the whole thing.

'Bunch of fools, thinking they can take on the government. Causing all this bother because of their nonsense. They get decent hardworking folk a bad name.'

Her mother looked frightened. 'There's soldiers in the streets, Poppy. They say there might be a revolution, like in Russia. What'll happen to us all then?'

'You'll be all right, Mum. You're one of the workers.' Poppy tried to put her mind at rest. 'I been right through town from up our end, through the City and down here, and there ain't no fighting. There don't even seem to be no bad feeling,

313

neither. Everyone thinks it's all a bit of a lark. There's young men like my Roddy driving trams and undergrounds, and the debs who dance at the club are running canteens and delivering newspapers in their cars, and all the offices and shops and teashops and that seem to be open, so it's not a very general strike. Loads of people are still working.'

'So they ought to,' said Gran.

Jane sighed. 'I hope you're right, dear. The war was bad enough. We don't want no revolution as well.'

At the cocktail party that evening, the talk was all of the strike and what people were doing to 'do their bit'. Poppy found that it was assumed that she should be on their side, that of the strike breakers. What, they wanted to know, was she doing? Poppy told them that she was keeping the nightlife going, and that was good for morale. They were all delighted at this, and promised to come along and listen to her later at the Blue Diamond.

When she got to the club, she found that Marjorie had quite the opposite expectations of her.

'We've been helping out at the offices of the *British Worker* all day long,' she said, as she got on their stage makeup. 'Phyl's been on the switchboard. She's really good, she picked it up in no time at all. And I've been doing anything that needed doing. I've made tea, read proofs and folded papers. The atmosphere there, Poppy! You have to be there to appreciate it. This is the great turning point for the working men and women of this country. If we can hold out now, we will break the power of the exploiting classes for ever. Imagine that! A fairer land for all of us to live in!'

Poppy did not want to say anything that might throw doubt on her enthusiasm any more than she had wanted to spoil Roddy's fun. Not, she realized, that anything she might say would alter the attitude of either of them one iota.

'Sounds really exciting, Marge,' she said.

'That lot out there,' Marjorie said, indicating the club's clientele with a contemptuous jerk of the head, 'will be dancing to a different tune by the end of the month. They'll

314

have to earn their bread by honest toil. They won't be dancing the night away every night in clubs.'

Poppy had to reply to that. 'So what will we do to earn a crust, then, Marge? I can always go back to being a waitress. What are you trained for?'

'We shall entertain the workers,' Marjorie told her.

'Well, that's all right then. I don't really fancy being a waitress again.'

They went out to a club packed with excited people. Poppy was almost reminded of the war, in that there was an 'all in it together' atmosphere. But it was an excitement without the edge of tragedy. It was all a party, an imperial thrash, a monumental beat-up, and they were going to enjoy every moment of it. Seldom had they been so easy to entertain.

Roddy turned up with the heroes of the bus depot, and did a marvellously flashy tango with a girl wearing ruby earrings who had been making tea for them all day in the canteen. They ended up drinking coffee and brandy at the Mayfair home of Pips the Conductor's family, swopping stories that became more and more far-fetched as night turned into day. At half past six the gallant bus crews decided it was not much use going to bed and they might just as well turn up early and help get the public to work in their offices and factories. Poppy, feeling more than a little left out of it, kissed Roddy goodbye and went back to the flat. Unlike them, she had responsibilities. Seeing Kit came before playing at buses.

It was all over far too soon. Within days, the glorious revolution fizzled out. Poppy had to comfort a desperately disappointed Marjorie and coax her to carry on playing to the hated oppressing classes as they celebrated victory at the Blue Diamond. What was more worrying, Roddy did not come home.

He had hardly been home at all during the strike, what with driving and parties, so she expected him to pass out and sleep the clock round. But the day after the strike was called off, he still did not appear. The Hispano-Suiza was not in the garage.

Poppy started telephoning round his friends. There were rumours of various parties. Lots of people had either seen him or heard of his being somewhere, but nobody seemed to know exactly where he was at that moment. Two days later, he was still missing. Poppy was frantic.

'He's just disappeared into thin air,' she told Elsie. 'I don't know what to do. I've even telephoned all the hospitals and been to the police, but they don't know anything. It's terrible. There must be a jinx on me or something. Dreadful things always happen to the men in my life.'

'That's rubbish,' Elsie told her. 'He's at some party somewhere, like as not, and he's forgotten to phone you.'

Poppy shook her head. 'No, he wouldn't do that. Not for this long. He'd contact me if he could. I've got this horrible feeling he's in trouble.'

Then early the following afternoon Poppy got a phone call.

'Poppy? Sibby here. Would you be a sweetie and come and collect your husband? I'm trying to clear up before mine comes back and he is rather making the place look untidy.'

'What? Who?' Poppy could not place the name, though it sounded familiar.

'Sibby. Sibby Melhurst.'

Understanding burst upon Poppy. How could she have been so dense? Lady Sybil Melhurst had been the hostess at the party where she had met Roddy. And where she had last seen Scott. Right now, there was a distinctly sharp edge to her voice.

'Would you come along straightaway? I really can't be expected to cope with him.'

It was not a request. It was an order.

'I will. Right away,' Poppy told her.

The journey from Paddington seemed to take forever. All the way, Poppy kept turning the few words of the telephone conversation over in her mind. What had Lady Sybil meant by not being expected to cope with him? When she finally reached the branch line station, there was only one ancient cab waiting. Poppy marched in front of the regal-looking lady

316

in tweeds who was about to hire it, opened the door and jumped in. The name of the house she was going to was enough to convince the driver that she was not to be argued with.

The first sight of the place brought memories flooding back. Poppy stood at the front door and shook. She would never forget that dreadful night.

'Yes?'

The very same butler opened the door, with the very same expression of disdain on his face. Poppy stared him down.

'Mrs Ffitch. I am expected.'

If anything, the man's face became more haughty.

'Oh, yes. Please follow me. Lady Melhurst left orders. She is too busy to see you at present.'

She was led upstairs and along a corridor to a pretty green and white bedroom. Sprawled on the bed, and looking almost as white as the paintwork, was Roddy.

'Darling – what's happened?'

Poppy was so shocked at his appearance that the events of the night she met him were almost pushed out of her head. She had never seen him looking so ill. She placed a hand on his forehead and found that he was ice cold.

'I suspect that sir has been over indulging,' the butler pronounced.

Poppy rounded on him, furious. 'Oh yeah? And he's the first one what ever done that in this house, is he?' she hissed.

The man said nothing.

'Don't think I don't know what goes on here. And her ladyship's on hot bricks wanting all the evidence moved, ain't she? So don't just stand there, go and tell someone to get our car round the front. It's the Hispano-Suiza. Then get someone else up here to help me get him downstairs. And look sharp about it.'

Visibly shaken, the butler left.

Behind her on the bed, Roddy groaned faintly. Poppy sat down beside him. His eyes flickered open.

'Poppy?'

His voice was a croak.

'It's all right, my darling. I've come to fetch you home. We'll soon have you as right as rain again.'

'Can't move.'

Poppy stroked his face.

'You'll have to move. Your wonderful friend Lady Sibby wants you out. You're an embarrassment to her. But don't worry, you'll be better off at home. I can look after you proper there.'

It was a nightmare journey home. She lost her way three times and had to stop twice for Roddy to be sick. When they finally got back home, she got him into bed and managed to make him drink some water.

'Now, see if you can get some sleep,' she said.

He clutched at her hand with surprising strength. He seemed to be afraid.

'Don't go away.'

'Of course I won't. I'll be right here.'

'Don't let them get me.'

'Nobody's going to get you.'

It was only later, when he had fallen into an uneasy sleep and she was hanging up his clothes, that she found something odd in his jacket pocket. A twist of paper containing some white powder, and a slim silver tube. She stood looking at them, a chill dread spiralling slowly through her.

'So that's why you're so ill. It's not just a hangover,' she said out loud.

She went and threw them away. But the feeling of fear stayed with her.

35

Poppy knew almost as soon as it happened, but she did not say anything about it for a long time. She had so hoped that when it happened again she would be joyful, that it would be welcomed, but as it was, the uppermost feeling in her heart was of anger. How on earth was she to be expected to cope? She had enough responsibilities. She finally told Roddy about it in June.

'You feeling strong?' she asked, as he wandered from his bed and into the living room at midday.

'Not yet, why?'

'I got something important to tell you.'

'Wait a mo.'

He fixed himself his first drink of the day, gulped it down, poured another then collapsed into an armchair.

'Fire away, old thing. So long as it's not money. I don't feel up to talking money.'

Poppy looked at him with exasperated affection. His silk dressing-gown was flopping open top and bottom to reveal his tanned chest and thin legs. He had been spending most afternoons sunbathing and was beginning to go a nice colour. Only last week he had been talking of going to the South of France, and had been genuinely surprised when Poppy pointed out that she could not come as the band was booked until the end of July. He certainly did not look ready for the news she had to tell him.

'It's not money,' she said. 'At least – not directly. It's – I'm – you're going to be a father.'

For a long moment, Roddy gaped at her. She almost thought that he had not heard her. Then he took a swallow of his drink. Poppy felt a tug of apprehension. She never knew just how he was going to react nowadays. Lately, he had been going through periods of suffering from mood swings, quite unlike the old even-tempered Roddy she had married.

He stood up and launched himself across the room at her.

'Darling! How wonderful! A baby – a son and heir. You clever old thing.'

He dropped onto the sofa beside her and hugged her. Poppy was so glad that she burst into tears.

'I say – what's all this? You should be happy.'

Poppy tried to explain between sobs. 'I am – happy – I thought you wouldn't be.'

'Me, not want a little chip off the old block? How could you think that? I'm delighted, old thing. Best news I've had since you agreed to marry me.'

Poppy had not seen him so animated so early in the day since the strike. He was lit up, his mind racing, bursting with plans. Schools, nursing homes, names, godparents, all had to be just right for his son. He ran over half a dozen alternatives for each, rejecting most as not good enough.

'It may be a girl,' Poppy reminded him. She wanted a girl. It would be lovely to have a daughter. She would make sure that she was everything as a mother that her own mother and grandmother had failed to be.

'A girl –' This possibility obviously had not occurred to Roddy. 'Well, that would be delightful. I'd like a little girl. She must look just like you, just as pretty, and when she's grown up everyone will say how they can't tell the two of you apart.'

Poppy laughed. Some of her earlier fears were beginning to dissolve. So long as Roddy was pleased about the baby, they would be able to work something out.

'Now, which doctor did you see, and when are you going next?' he asked. 'We don't want any old quack. Harley Street or nothing.'

'I haven't seen no doctor. What do I want a doctor for? I'm not ill, I'm having a baby.'

Roddy was horrified.

'But you have to see a doctor, darling. Everyone does. I'm sure they do.'

320

'Only if something goes wrong at the birth. I never saw one at all for Kit, even though I had him in hospital. A midwife delivered him. He just went on growing until it was time for him to be born, and then he came out. What could a doctor have done about that?'

'Well, I don't know, but my wife and my child are going to have the best advice there is.'

To prove his serious intent, he was fiercely protective of her for the rest of the day, treating her as if she were made of the rarest bone china. He was intensely proud of his achievement, insisting on telling everyone at the party they went to that evening about the forthcoming happy event and asking all and sundry about doctors and nursing homes. Poppy, more sensitive than he was to people's reactions, saw eyes glazing over with boredom. Babies were not fashionable. They got in the way of the fun.

When the time came for Poppy to leave for work, he was most concerned.

'Are you sure you'll be all right, old thing? It's not too much for you, performing all night? Shouldn't you be resting or something?'

'I'm no different from what I was yesterday, and I managed then all right,' Poppy pointed out. 'It hardly shows at all yet, and these modern fashions are wonderful. Nobody'll notice for ages.'

'All the same, I think I'll come along and keep an eye on you,' Roddy said. 'We don't want you overdoing things.'

Poppy felt wonderfully cared for. It was going to be all right. Roddy was going to take his new role seriously.

Now, of course, she had to tell the band about it. There were mixed reactions from them. The younger, newer girls thought it utterly sweet and were very excited. Rather like Roddy, they immediately started asking about names and making their own suggestions. The other four original members were less ecstatic.

'Well, I'm pleased if you are, Poppy love,' Elsie said.

'How's the proud father taking it?' Mona asked.

'Oh, he's delighted. Like a dog with two tails.'

'Just about as bloody useful as a dog when it comes to providing for the kid,' said Marjorie.

The others spoke up in Roddy's defence, but so half-heartedly that Poppy could see that they really agreed with Marjorie.

'You never did like him, none of you!' she flared. 'Well, for your information, he's being real good to me over this baby. He's going to be a lovely dad. You'll all have to eat your words, you will!'

She swallowed down tears, not wanting to ruin her stage makeup, but she felt like running away and having a good cry. It seemed as if all her friends were against her. She played badly that evening, and that made it worse.

She tried to draw strength from seeing Roddy's face in the crowd. And there he was, at one of the front tables, watching her every move, listening to every note. She was reassured.

It was sometime in the early hours of the morning that Phyllis sidled up to her and slid an arm round her waist.

'Don't you take no notice of what them others said,' she advised. 'They're only jealous. I think you're so lucky. I'd love to have a little baby, I really would. Something of my very own to love and care for. Sometimes I wake up in the night and I just long and long to have one, all little and soft and sweet.'

'Oh Phyl –' Poppy hugged her, close to tears yet again, but this time for her friend and her situation. 'It ain't too late, you know. If you want one that bad –'

But Phyllis shook her head. 'No, I couldn't. I couldn't go through all that – you know, with a man. Not even for a baby. I ain't made that way.'

It made Poppy feel sad for the rest of the night.

Roddy's good intentions lasted all that week. Every night he came to the club with Poppy, fussed over her in the intervals and drove her back home in the dark before dawn. He made an appointment with the most fashionable Harley Street doctor and escorted Poppy there himself. Then he utterly astounded her with a burst of practicality.

'Expensive business, this breeding. Never thought about it before, but we're going to need a lot more of the old readies. Have to see what I can do about it.'

Poppy's hopes soared. 'I would so like to be able to give up work and look after the baby,' she said. 'I never could with poor Kit. I know my Mum was lovely with him, but it tore my heart out to have to go and leave him with her.'

'Work? Dr Trevison-Smythe would have a fit. And what's more, I won't hear of it. No, the moment you think it's the least bit too much for you, you must give it up.'

'Well, as long as there'll be enough coming in –'

Roddy gave her a kiss. 'Just leave it to me, old thing. Roddy will fix it. You're not to worry about a thing.'

He was good at fixing lifts, arranging parties, trading favours. Poppy wanted to believe he was good at fixing a secure future for their child. She let herself be convinced.

'You're wonderful,' she said.

'But of course. Now, I may have to leave you for a while. A week, maybe. Shall you be able to manage? You must telephone me if there's any problems, anything at all.'

'Well, yes, of course I can. But where are you going?'

'Ah – now that'd be telling.'

More than that she could not get out of him. Nor did he leave the promised telephone number. An inspection of his wardrobe after he left revealed that all his country clothes had gone with him. He returned only three days later, in a temper. Poppy had never seen him angry before. She soon found out the cause.

'So much for blood ties!'

He dumped his case in the middle of the hall and made straight for the drinks cabinet. Poppy waited until two double gins had gone down before venturing a question.

'What do you mean, blood ties?'

'Family, that's what. Nearest and dearest. Now, wouldn't you think that they would be delighted to know that there's going to be another little branch to the jolly old family tree? Wouldn't you think that they'd welcome me back into the fold with open arms now that I'm a reformed character and a family man?'

'Well – yes,' said Poppy, since that seemed to be the answer expected of her. Something about his anger made her fearful.

'So would I. That was why I went. Quite ready to eat humble pie, I was, and tell them I'd been a naughty boy and I'd seen the error of my ways and all that. But would they listen to me? Not a word!'

Poppy made sympathetic noises and stroked his head. He shied away like a nervous horse.

'Do you know what they suggested? The only offer they were willing to make? They said they would pull strings to get me a post in the colonies! I ask you – can you see me being a District Commissioner in the middle of the African jungle?'

Poppy had to admit that she could not.

It gradually dawned on her that the sole reason Roddy had tried to heal the breach with his family was in order to secure the allowance that she had once assumed he must receive. Not just a bachelor's allowance, but enough for a family to live on in the style that Roddy was accustomed to. He had three more large drinks, changed, and went out, still fuming. Poppy did not see him again for two days.

Even the modern straight-up-and-down fashions could not hide Poppy's condition for long. At the end of August, Ted Appleby took her to one side.

'Er – now look here, Poppy, you and I have known each other for long enough to be straight and not take offence, now haven't we?'

Poppy pasted on a bright smile.

'God, Ted, that sounds serious. What of I been and gone and done?'

'Nothing, Pops, it's just – well, it's this baby. I mean, it just won't do. You can't go leading a band when you're – um – expecting. It makes people uncomfortable.'

'You mean they don't like to be reminded of the consequences of what they all want to be doing with the people they're dancing with?'

'Well, yeah. In fact that's just it, in a nutshell. It sort of puts them off.'

Poppy had known it would come to this. She had just hoped she would be able to hold out a bit longer.

'I see.'

There were Kit's school fees to be paid for the new term, not to speak of all the new uniform he needed. And that was nothing to the bills that Roddy was running up.

As if reading her mind, Ted reasoned that as leader of the band, she must feel that she was entitled to take out a salary, even when she wasn't actually performing.

'After all, girl, you're the one who does all the arrangements and directs all the rehearsals. You can still do all that. And I'll nose around and get you some session work with the record companies. And another thing – you've written some nice songs over the years. Why don't you try to come up with some more, and I'll see what I can do about selling them? You'll be all right, girl, you'll see. Trust old Ted.'

She did trust him, which was more than she could say for Roddy. He did not seem to be able to function now unless he had at least half a bottle of spirits inside him, and when that failed to give him a lift, he snorted cocaine. Poppy had a horrible suspicion that the only money he did bring in to the household came from dealing in the stuff. Twice she had tried to confront him with her suspicions, but as usual he had put her off with evasions and gone out, which served only to confirm what she thought.

To a woman, the band refrained from saying 'I told you so'. For that Poppy was hugely grateful, but it did not solve the problems that seemed to be piling up on her. As autumn turned into winter and the baby inside her grew larger and made its presence known by kicking its hard little heels up under her ribs, Poppy lay awake each night worrying about what was to become of them all. Sooner or later, the growing list of creditors was going to refuse to be put off any longer, and then what would happen? Roddy's solution was to jump into the car and take off for the continent, but she could not lead a gypsy life with a child of seven and a newborn baby to care for. She did not know what to do. She tried to take Ted's advice and write songs, but somehow now that she was pregnant, she found it tremendously difficult. It was as if the energy needed to make a new human being drained all of her creative powers. She could only produce one work of art at a time.

In the early hours of the first of December, Poppy was woken from an uneasy sleep by a dragging pain in her back. She was alone and cold in the wide bed, so she pulled some pillows from Roddy's side and tried to arrange them to make herself more comfortable. She lay and worried, going over in her mind the many people to whom they owed money and trying to decide what to do about them. As usual she came to no reassuring conclusion. Then the pain came again, and this time she knew what it was. She rubbed the lumpy form pushing against her swollen belly.

'Oh, baby, you're not supposed to be coming for another two weeks yet,' she told it, but it was not listening to her.

The problems with money suddenly seemed trivial. There were real decisions to be made. Roddy had booked her in with one of the most expensive maternity homes in London. They couldn't afford the fees, but then they couldn't afford anything else, and yet Roddy went on cheerfully extending their credit. She decided that she would go there and to hell with it. They couldn't very well send the baby back after it was born.

She already had the baby's first layette packed, but had not got her own things together. She got up and lumbered around finding nightdresses and bedjackets and toiletries, and tried to make up her mind what to do about Kit. She had had it all planned that she would take him down to her grandmother's a couple of days before the baby was due. Now it was not so simple. She did not want to have to bundle him into a cab all by himself in the middle of the night and send him right across London. By now, the pains were extending round into her abdomen. She timed the gaps between them. Twenty minutes. She would go with him to Dog Island. There would still be plenty of time to get to the maternity home. She reached for the telephone, thanking God that she had had the sense to pay the bills for that.

Kit was wildly excited. Getting up in the middle of the night and being told he was going on a taxi ride to Great-grandma's house was a huge adventure. Poppy chivvied him into getting dressed and choosing some toys to take with him while she packed a bag for him. Outside, the cabbie hooted his horn. Poppy pulled on a coat, picked up her case and called to Kit. At the door, she hesitated. What would Roddy do if he came home to an empty flat? Part of her was tempted to let him realize just what it was like not to know where someone had gone to. Then she relented. She plodded back in, picked up the topmost of the pile of bills, turned it over and scrawled 'Have gone to give birth to your child' on the back. Then she placed it where he was sure to see it – on top of the drinks cabinet. Satisfied, she shut the front door behind her.

'Where are we? Where are we now, Mummy?'

Kit bounced up and down on the seat and peered out into the darkness.

'Is that the Thames? Look – it's the Thames, there's a bridge.'

Poppy braced herself against another contraction. They were definitely getting stronger. It had not been like this when Kit was born. She had a feeling that this one was going to be a much shorter labour. She leaned forward and knocked on the glass.

'Can't you go any faster?' she asked the cabbie.

'What's the matter, missus? Baby on the way?' He thought it was a huge joke.

'Yes,' Poppy snapped. 'And if you don't get a move on, it's going to be born on the floor of your cab.'

'Blimey, why didn't you tell me that? I thought you was doing a moonlight.'

The man sounded appalled. The cab accelerated, rounded the Tower of London and bounced over the cobbled streets of the East End. Never had Poppy been so glad to see the swing bridge onto the Island. Kit shrieked as he recognized their old street, and then his Great-grandma's house on the corner of Cinnamon Alley.

'Here it is! Stop!'

Poppy sat perfectly still, waiting for another contraction to subside, then very carefully got out of the cab and walked up to the door just as her Gran opened it.

The old lady had her brown dressing-gown clutched about her, the same one that she had worn since Poppy was a child. Her sparse hair was bundled into a net. She looked very much older than the last time Poppy had seen her. But her voice was just the same.

'Lord help us, girl, what are you doing on my doorstep at this time of the morning?'

Poppy tried to explain that she wanted to leave Kit there while she went to the maternity home. But as she spoke, she felt something give inside her and a warm trickle of water ran down her legs. Her grandmother looked at her and at the telltale puddle. She spoke to Kit.

'You get yourself inside, young man, and go and rouse your granny. Tell her to make up a bed in the spare room.'

Then she looked back at Poppy. Her tone softened.

'As for you, you ain't going nowhere. You'll stay here where you ought to be, with your family, and have my next great-grandchild where I can take care of it proper.'

Three hours later, bruised, torn, aching, but triumphant, Poppy sat up in the narrow bed in a room stuffy from an unaccustomed fire, and gazed at the crumpled features of her new daughter. A pair of fierce blue eyes stared back at her, as if demanding why she had been forced out into this strange world. Poppy bent and kissed the damp wisp of fluff on the palpitating scalp. The baby was beautiful, a strong healthy infant with rosy skin and rounded limbs. Out of the mess that her life had become, she had achieved something that was perfect.

Her mother and grandmother stood and admired the baby while the street's midwife busied herself clearing up the mess.

'Four generations,' said Jane, with awe in her voice. 'Four generations of us women in this one room.'

'What are you going to call her?' Margaret wanted to know.

'Belinda.' She had decided on that a long time ago. But now it seemed important to add to it. 'Belinda Margaret Jane,' she said.

Her grandmother beamed. 'Quite right too,' she said.

36

'Poppy, you don't have to come back yet. The girls are doing fine.'

Ted Appleby was doing his best to sound convincing. He might even have convinced Poppy if she had not been to listen to the band playing the night before.

'Ted, they are not doing fine. You know it and I know it.'

'They were okay.'

'Okay's not good enough. Lots of bands are okay. If that's all we can do, we're going to slip backwards. I want us to go up, not down. I want to play the big hotels. I want to get a spot on the BBC. The way they were playing last night, you won't even get us into second-rate nightclubs.' She could tell by Ted's expression that he agreed with her. 'I am right, ain't I?'

'Well – I've heard better. But, Poppy, it doesn't mean that you have to go back on stage yet. Go in there and give them hell by all means. Rehearse them till they drop, but you shouldn't be up all night performing. It's not a month yet since the baby was born. You should be resting.'

'What do you know about it, for God's sake? You're not a woman. You're not even married.'

Poppy spoke without thinking, goaded by the fact that the last thing she really wanted to do was to leave her darling Belinda and go back to work. She was not prepared for Ted's reaction. He was usually so easy-going that she could say anything to him. Now he was glaring into her face, his eyes hot with bitterness.

'No, and why not? Because you wouldn't marry me, that's why. You go off and get hitched to that sponging bastard Ffitch instead. And that's why you got to go out and perform again, ain't it? That's why you can't afford to let the band slip. You got him round your neck like a millstone. You got his debts to pay. I know, I'm not stupid. He's living off you. You just gave birth to his baby and you got to go out and support him. It's disgusting.'

She had not realized that he still cared so much. She had been so tied up with her own problems, with the need for money and the demands of the new baby, that she had not noticed how Ted was feeling.

As if reading her mind, he said, 'Yes, I do still love you. I know I'm just good old Ted to you, but I'm the only one who really looks out for you.'

It was too much. She couldn't take responsibility for his feelings as well. And yet she couldn't help feeling guilty.

'I know, Ted, and I appreciate it, honest I do. I don't know what I'd of done without you all this time. I just wish – you shouldn't keep carrying a torch for me, you know. You ought to get yourself someone nice, who'd love you like what you deserve. Someone like Elsie. You're both of you such nice people and you're both lonely.'

Ted sighed and turned away. 'It doesn't work like that, Poppy. Elsie's a real pearl, but she isn't you.'

It was such a tangle, so many people all in love with the wrong one, all getting hurt. She couldn't cope. She just had to concentrate on the practical side of life. Like getting enough money to stave off the creditors.

'Ted, I know you got my best interests at heart, but I got to work New Year's Eve. You got us booked for the Petite Fleur and I can't let Johnny down. I got to make sure it's a brilliant night.'

It took a bit more arguing, but Poppy had made her mind up. When it came to actually leaving for work on New Year's Eve, though, it was rather different. Belinda was crotchety, refusing to settle. Poppy felt dreadful.

'She knows. She knows I'm going to go out and leave her.'

'She'll be all right, lovey. Don't you worry. I'll soon get her off to sleep. The little pet.'

Her mother had come right across London by bus and tram to look after the baby and Kit. All Roddy's fine words about nannies had come to nothing. There was not enough room in the flat for a nanny, even if they could afford the wages and the keep. Besides, it was bad enough leaving her tiny daughter with her mother, let alone some stranger. Roddy had made a few protesting noises about having his mother-in-law about the place, but could not be bothered to put his foot down. He simply solved the problem the same way he solved all of them. He went out. Poppy could not even remember where it was he had said he was going, if he had told her at all. She assumed he would turn up at the Petite Fleur later on, since he liked the food there.

'Oh Mum, she's so little and so sweet. I can't bear it. She's sure to miss me.'

There was a movement in the doorway. She looked up and saw Kit standing there in his pyjamas, clutching his teddy bear. His lower lip was trembling. She held out her arms to him.

'Kit, darling. I shall miss you too. You know I hate going out and leaving you.'

The boy came running into the room, but it was his grandmother whom he flung himself at.

'It's all right,' he said, his voice muffled in her bosom. 'It's all right when Granny's here.'

Jane rocked him, avoiding Poppy's eye. Poppy was glad that Kit was happy with his gran, but terribly hurt that he had not come to her. She was a failure all round. She kissed Kit on the head, but he only nestled closer to his grandmother. She bent to kiss Belinda, and the baby's little face creased up as she gathered breath to start crying. Poppy felt as if she was being pulled to pieces. She snatched up her bag and the cases containing her sax and her clarinet.

'Goodbye, darlings. Be good. I love you all.'

Only her mother replied, telling her not to worry.

She worried all the way to the restaurant.

The band caught the full force of her turmoil of emotions. She let rip with a lecture that left them in no doubt that their leader was back. Only the best was going to be good enough tonight, or Poppy was going to know the reason why. Anyone who couldn't pull their weight was going to find themselves out of a job. She then went through every number with them, making them write her comments and instructions on the scores. Every point she made was to be adhered to, or else. The Powers Girls had to be first rate. Even Marjorie was silenced.

When Johnny put his head round the door to say hello, he found a very subdued group of women putting the final touches to their stage makeup.

'Bloody hell, what's up with you lot? This is a celebration tonight, not a bloody funeral. Cheer up, for God's sake. You'll frighten the customers away.'

Poppy looked at them all. He was right. They were here to entertain. She forced brightness into her voice, pinned a smile on her face.

'How about a few glasses of bubbly to get us going, Johnny? Start the old party spirit, y'know? Oh, and girls – I forgot to tell you. Ted thinks he can get us a spot on the wireless. So go out there and give it all you got – there might be a talent spotter from the BBC watching us!'

It was a total lie, but it had the desired effect. When The Powers Girls lined up on the cramped dais, they exuded enough sparkle to put the crown jewels in the shade.

As long as they were performing, Poppy could think of nothing else. She put everything she had into getting it right, into drawing the very best out of the band. The restaurant was packed, and the diners were all in a party mood. They played quietly at first, providing background music as people ate. A few wilder spirits got up and danced between courses, to be applauded like a floorshow by the other diners. Poppy was satisfied. The band were pulling together better than she could have hoped for when she had last heard them play. When they took their first break at eleven o'clock, though, her mind went straight back to wondering what might be happening at home. Her breasts ached unbearably from the milk that Belinda should have had.

Poppy hugged herself, holding back the tears. 'I should of brung her along, like I done with Kit when he was tiny. What's she going to do when she wakes up for her feed and finds it ain't me there? What if she don't take to the bottle? That formula stuff ain't the same as mother's milk.'

'She'll be fine,' Elsie told her. 'Your mum knows what she's doing. And you can feed her in the morning. She won't be going without.'

'I hope you're right,' Poppy said.

As the Petite Fleur's wonderful food was eaten or toyed with or put aside, the evening began to hot up. By the time midnight approached, the floor was full. All over the restaurant, people were looking at their watches. Johnny signalled to Poppy.

'Now!' cried a score of voices.

The band launched into the sentimental strains of 'Auld Lang Syne'. People joined hands and sang. Poppy found she could hardly play for the lump in her throat. *Should old acquaintance be forgot and never called to mind* . . . There was one who would never be forgot, but did he remember? Or was he celebrating the New Year with the Snow Queen, with never a passing thought for her?

All around the restaurant, people were kissing and wishing each other a Happy New Year. Poppy felt an arm round her waist. Elsie kissed her cheek.

'Happy 1927, Poppy. Hope it's a good one for you.'

Poppy kissed her back. 'And to you, Elsie. The very best. I hope it brings you someone to love you. You deserve it.'

Whatever 1927 brought, it couldn't be worse than 1926. She couldn't make that many disastrous mistakes again. She looked round at the band, and counted them in to the first number of the New Year – 'Bye-Bye, Blackbird'.

It was way beyond the usual hour before the last carousing customer left the Petite Fleur. Some had gone soon after midnight, to nightclubs or private parties, but many wanted to stay on, drinking from Johnny's well-stocked bar and dancing to the inspired music of The Powers Girls. It was only when the very last group had gone and the waiters were clearing the tables that Poppy realized that Roddy had not showed up. She felt only relief. She did not want to see him tonight.

'I better get back,' she said to Elsie, as they packed up their instruments.

'No, stay. They'll all be fast asleep at home. You'll only go and disturb them all if you let yourself in now. Stay and have a meal, it'll do you good.'

Poppy let herself be persuaded. She finally got back just as Belinda was snuffling into wakefulness. She crept past her mother and Kit as they lay sound asleep and picked up the baby. She was warm and soft and gave off a distinct whiff of ammonia. Poppy held her to her body. Even the smell was good. She tiptoed into her bedroom, kicked off her shoes, pulled her beaded and embroidered dress off, dropped it over a chair and settled herself against the pillows in the wide bed. She put the hungry baby to her breast, wincing as the eager gums clamped on to her rock hard nipples, groaning in relief as the sucking eased the pressure. For half an hour she was content, almost happy. There was just her and her baby alone in the dark night, and nothing else mattered in the world. She fell asleep sitting up, with Belinda warm against her stomach.

She did not worry particularly when Roddy did not turn up the next day. She supposed that he was at some party that had carried on into the first day of the New Year. What concerned her far more was the flood of bills that fell onto the mat, all demanding instant payment. She shoved them all inside the bureau and shut the lid. She could not face them, not right now. There were just too many. Maybe tomorrow she would feel stronger.

But the next day brought more bills and a visit from a pair of toughs.

'Mrs Roderick Ffitch?'

They both had cropped heads and badly fitting suits. Poppy knew instantly why they were there at her front door.

'No,' she said, and tried to shut it in their faces.

They were far too strong for her. They barged their way into the hall with frightening ease. Poppy's heart beat fast, but she tried to keep her voice level. She had met plenty of this type back home.

'You got no right. Get the hell out of my home.'

The one who had spoken before gave an unpleasant smile. 'Naughty, naughty. Swearing! That's not the way to behave, now is it?'

Poppy faced them squarely. 'Cut the sauce. Who sent you?'

'Now, that's more sensible. We don't want no trouble, do we, Vince?'

The other one gave a silent shake of the head.

'You just pay us what you owe, and we'll leave. It's as easy as that.'

'I'm not paying you nothing. I'm not stupid. Show me who you are.'

The spokesman produced a dog-eared card from his breast pocket. Poppy looked at it. It was just as she feared. Debt collectors.

'I still don't know who you bought the debts off of. You could say anything.'

The man sighed in a theatrical manner.

'Been through this before, have we? Proper hard little nut, ain't we?'

Poppy ignored the insult. 'I'm not giving away nothing to the likes of you without proof.'

'I don't think you got much choice, darling. You see, me and my mate here don't like being asked for proof and all that sort of thing. Makes us cross. And when we get cross, we just take whatever takes our fancy.' He pushed past her into the lounge, where he began picking objects up and putting them down.

'You leave that alone! You take one thing from here, one thing, and I'll call the police.'

'Oh, I don't think you want to do that, darling. Not with what your old man's got piled up against him. He owes all

336

over town, now don't he? Once they get to know that we paid you a visit, they'll all want their share. You won't be able to fob them off with a bob or two and a sob story no more. They'll be sending in more blokes like us. And believe me, darling, we're pussy cats compared with some.'

Poppy swallowed. 'I ain't got no money in the house.'

'That don't matter. I bet you got some nice sparklers. We can start with that ring you got on your hand there.'

'No!' Poppy put her hands behind her back.

The men laughed.

From the room across the hall there came a hiccuping cry. Poppy froze. The men stopped short. The cry escalated rapidly into a high wail. The spokesman's face stretched into a travesty of a smile.

'Ah. Your baby, is it?'

Poppy nodded. A terrible fear gripped her.

The man did not have to make any more threats. He merely held out his hand.

'Let's have it, then. And all the money you got in the place.'

Poppy pulled her engagement ring off her finger and thrust it at him, then she ran into the bedroom and snatched up her purse, shaking out its contents onto the bed. She gathered it all up and gave that to him as well.

'That's more like it. It's easy when you get started, ain't it? We'll be back tomorrow, and we'll expect more. A lot more. A couple of grand at least. You make sure you got it when we arrive.'

The door slammed behind them.

'Bastards!' Poppy screamed.

From the nursery, Belinda's cry wobbled with angry hunger.

'All right, all right!' Poppy rushed in to pick her up. Her little face was scarlet. With trembling fingers, Poppy pulled at the buttons of her blouse. She got them undone at last and sat down on the floor to put the wailing baby to her breast, but for once it did not have a calming effect on her. Her mind went round and round, trying to think of ways of raising money at short notice. She knew that their credit had run out all over town. She could only fall back on the generosity of friends, and even they were not going to be happy lending when in effect it was to Roddy.

She changed Belinda, then wandered around the flat with the baby on her shoulder, trying to formulate a plan of action. But she could see no way out.

The telephone rang just as she was passing it, making her jump and catch her breath. She stood looking at it, her heart beating fast, irrationally afraid of picking it up, expecting to hear a man's voice on the other end, demanding money with menaces. Perhaps it would stop. But it went on ringing and ringing, ordering her to lift the receiver. In the end, she was unable to refuse. When she heard a woman's voice at the other end, she cried out in relief, not hearing what was being said to her.

'– Poppy? Poppy? Do you hear me? Why don't you answer?'

'W – what?'

A strange croak issued from her throat.

'Poppy!' The person on the other end was shrieking, a hysterical edge to her voice. 'Poppy, did you hear what I said?'

'I – no, no I didn't. I'm sorry. Who – who is it?'

'Sibby, for mercy's sake. Sybil Melhurst. Will you *listen*? You have to come down here at once. At once, do you hear me? If it got out that it happened here – oh my God!'

There was a clatter, as if the phone had been dropped at the other end. Lady Sybil's voice still came clearly over the wire, but from a distance.

'Saunders, the police are outside. What are they doing here? Get rid of them. I don't care what you say, just get rid of them. Tell them to come back tomorrow, anything, but don't let them into the house.'

Another clatter, and Poppy's ear was assaulted by a piercing order.

'Poppy? Are you still there? I want you down here immediately.'

Poppy managed to find her voice at last. 'But why?' she demanded. 'What's happened?'

'Haven't you been listening to anything I've been saying? It's Roddy. I think he's taken an overdose. He's dead.'

37

'You going to be all right, pet?' Jane asked.

The last terrible weeks had left their mark on Poppy. Her white face was tight with strain and marred by great dark smudges under the eyes.

Poppy nodded. 'Yes.'

Jane was not convinced. Poppy had managed to keep going in public, coping with the police, the inquest and worst of all, the press. She had managed to a certain extent to hold together in front of Kit, who was frightened and confused by all the drama around him. But Jane had heard her at night, when she was able at last to let go, and she was afraid that her daughter was getting to the point where she could not cope with much more. Now there was the funeral to face.

'You been wonderful, you know, lovey. I don't know how you been able to keep going, really I don't, and all so soon after having a baby and all. I don't know how you done it. They all think so in the street and all. They're proud of you.'

This was a slight exaggeration. Most of the inhabitants of Trinidad Street were flattered by the notoriety brought on them by the return of one of their own, and sorry for her in her distress. But there were some who thought she had got what she deserved, trying to prove she was better than the people she had been born amongst.

'Oh – that's nice.' Poppy's voice was flat and expressionless.

'I still think it's wicked, his people not having nothing to do with the funeral.'

This was a sore point with Jane. She could not understand how anyone could so totally cut off their son. Her own opinion of her late son-in-law was pretty low, after the way he had died and the mess he had left Poppy in. But the attitude of his parents shocked her. Even if they disapproved of him in life, they should come forward to do something for him in death. Jane expected better of the upper classes.

'It's all this publicity. They can't stand it,' Poppy said.

'Then they ought to give you something on the quiet, like, for the arrangements. Like what that Lady Sybil did.'

'Don't talk to me about her.' Poppy's voice suddenly came alive with venom. 'I wish I could of afforded to throw her blood money back in her face. I really choked on that, I did. It really grieves me to have to use it. I just hope she feels as bad about it as I do. She bloody well ought to. It was all her fault. Everything. I wouldn't never have met Roddy if I hadn't been playing at her place that night and she hadn't invited Scott. And Roddy wouldn't never have started using cocaine if it wasn't for her. And he wouldn't never of died if he hadn't of gone to her New Year party. I've a good mind to tell the press she gave me money. That'd teach her.'

'Oh, Poppy, you promised not to.'

'What's a promise to someone like that? She don't deserve to get away with it. Let that husband of hers see what she's like. She ruined my life for me. It's like being caught in a nightmare.'

Jane put her arms round her. Poppy's thin body was stiff and resistant.

'You'll wake up one day, lovey, and it'll all be in the past. And you got us, you know. Your gran, she might sound hard, but she loves you really. And you got your children. And you know you always got me.'

'Oh, Mum –' Poppy clasped her tight and then let her go. 'Don't you sometimes wish you could stop being a grown-up? That someone'd come and take it all off of your shoulders?'

'I know, darling, but at least you have had a life of your own.'

Poppy looked at her. 'What?'

'You had a life of your own. You've had two husbands, and two children, you had homes of your own, and on top of that you got that band together and got famous. You done it yourself.'

'Yeah, and look where it got me. Two dead husbands and up to my eyes in debt.'

'But you're young, Poppy. You're only twenty-six. You got lots more chances.'

Whereas she was forty-four. She had had one chance, when she met Owen, she had taken it and it had fallen apart in her hands. It was far too late now to hope for anything else.

The funeral cortege drew up at the door of the lodging house on the corner of Cinnamon Alley. Two press photographers waited in the street to catch Poppy as she got into the car behind the hearse. The small procession moved off at walking pace, Poppy, Jane and Margaret in the first car, Ted Appleby and the original band members in the second. At Elsie's suggestion, they were taking Roddy out to Ilford to be buried. Jane had thought it a good idea at first. It had seemed nicer, laying him to rest somewhere clean and countrified. Now, crawling through the crowded streets of the East End, she began to wonder. It was just dragging the whole thing out. She reached for Poppy's cold hands, and took them in her own.

A small congregation of mourners and a rather larger crowd of hangers-on and the curious had gathered at the chapel in the cemetery. Jane was horrified when people started pushing forward to catch a glimpse of Poppy. It had been bad enough when it happened at the inquest. To invade a funeral like this was dreadful.

'They're wicked, gawking at you like that. Why can't they leave you alone?' she cried.

Margaret was in total agreement. 'Don't give them the pleasure. Pull that veil right over your face,' she advised.

Jane was relieved when Ted Appleby took charge. You needed a man at a time like this. With him one side of Poppy and Jane the other, they managed to shield her from the worst of the stares of the crowd and the invasive lenses of the photographers.

Once inside the chapel, she thought it might be better. But the service was dreadful, conducted by a minister who made little effort to hide his disapproval of the way Roddy had lived and died. He spoke of God's forgiveness, but Jane could tell that he thought Roddy did not deserve to be let off. She was disgusted. Whatever you might think of someone when they were alive, you shouldn't speak ill of them when they were dead, and especially at the funeral, in front of the widow. She kept stealing glances at Poppy. Beneath the black veil, her daughter's white face looked frozen.

By the time they came out again, a policeman had arrived to control the crowd. Jane caught her mother's eye and saw her own disgust mirrored there.

'A policeman, at a burial. It's shameful,' Margaret muttered.

A thin rain was falling over the cemetery, turning everything to shades of grey. Jane could feel water seeping through her shoes as she stood through the committal. She shifted, and as she did so, happened to glance across between the bowed heads around the grave. A middle-aged man was standing by one of the young trees a few plots away. He was dressed in black and standing with his hat in his hands as if he were one of the mourners, and yet he was keeping apart. Jane felt breathless, as if someone had just caught her in the solar plexus. She stared at the man's head, at the distinctive hair, thinning and greying, but definitely still with a touch of red to it.

'Owen,' she mouthed wordlessly. 'Owen.'

It was him. She knew it without a doubt. She knew the set of his shoulders, the way he stood. The people around her faded, the words of the minister dulled into nothing. Owen was really there, not ten yards away from her. She wanted to go to him, to hear him speak, but her legs had no strength, she was paralysed. So she stood, oblivious to what was going on around her, gazing at him.

And then it seemed that it was over at last. People were beginning to move. The number of bodies between her and Owen thinned, till at last there was nothing but a stretch of soaking grass and a row of recent graves and the man she was still married to. Still she stood there, unable to move, willing him to come over.

'Mum?' Poppy was at her elbow. 'Mum? You all right?'

Vaguely she thought that it was her who should be saying that to Poppy. It was Poppy who needed looking out for today. She ran a dry tongue round drier lips.

'Poppy,' she croaked. 'Poppy, it's your dad.'

'What? What do you mean?'

'Your dad. There. Look.'

He was looking at her at last. He was smiling an uncertain smile.

'Where? Who? It is! It is, it's my dad. It really is my dad. Oh –'

Nothing held Poppy back. She stumbled across the wet turf and fell into his open arms. Jane saw her back heaving with great sobs, saw Owen comfort her. The ability to move came back to her. Slowly, she walked towards them. Owen looked at her over Poppy's shaking shoulders.

'Hello Janey,' he said. 'You haven't changed a bit.'

PART SEVEN

Speakeasy

38

1928

'Mum, can you lay on something a bit extra tonight? I thought I'd ask Ted round for a bite.'

''Course I can, lovey. What a nice idea. I'm sure Ted would like a nice family meal, him living all by himself. You ought to have him round more often.'

'Now then, Mum. We been through this hundreds of times, and I'm not going to change my mind. In fact, the reason why I'm inviting him round here is I want to talk business and I don't want him taking me out to a restaurant. It only makes for problems on the way home. With you lot all here, he'll have to behave himself.'

'More's the pity, if you ask me.'

Poppy sighed. It seemed as if she had been having variations on this conversation for years now. Perhaps she should write a piece of music around it, a different instrument for herself, her mother and Ted, with Ted cajoling, her mother nagging, herself always refusing. There would be lyrical parts and dramatic parts, in fact it could grow into a full orchestral piece, with several movements.

'Look, Mum, don't let's go on about it, eh? I just want to talk to Ted about the way the band's going. I'm finished with men. I'm not good at picking them and I'm not good for them and the whole thing's been an utter disaster. I've got Kit and Belinda, and you and Dad and this house and the band. That's quite enough. So let's drop this Ted business, right?'

Reluctantly, her mother gave in and talked about food instead. Poppy nodded in approval of the proposed Lancashire hotpot and gooseberry pie.

'Ted'll love that. Good home cooking. Are they goose-berries from Elsie's?'

'Yeah, lovely juicy ones, they are. I wish I could get your Dad interested in the garden.'

'Dad?' Poppy laughed. 'You must be joking. I can't see Dad with a spade in his hand.'

In fact, she couldn't see her Dad with anything more taxing than a glass and a cigarette in his hand. He didn't even play an instrument seriously any more. He liked to play around with Poppy's ideas for songs, making suggestions for arrangements and occasionally helping with the scoring, but the day-to-day slog of a professional musician was far too much for him to contemplate.

Poppy and her mother accidentally caught each other's eyes and looked quickly away. They both knew he was everything that Gran had always accused him of, but neither of them was going to admit it.

There had been terrible rows after Owen turned up. Margaret had refused to have him over her threshold, threatened never to speak to Jane again if she took him back, accused him of only appearing now because he thought Poppy was a rich widow. Poppy held on to her dream with single-minded strength. Her dad was back. She was deaf to the logical part of her brain that saw through his all-too-plausible explanations of what had happened during the missing years. She needed to believe in him, so she did. Jane was washed from side to side, but in the end let herself be persuaded by her husband's protestations of love and regret. She never had been able to resist his silver tongue.

Now Jane looked out of the kitchen window to where the July sun burned down on the neat garden with its newly grown rectangle of grass, its young flower borders and its crazy-paved path leading to a shed and sapling apple trees. With her back to Poppy, she asked:

'You don't mind, do you? I mean –'

She stopped, unable to put it into words. Poppy knew just what she meant. She could see clearly now that the terrible stress of Roddy's death was behind her. Her Gran had been exactly right. Her father had come back to live off her. She was supporting herself, her parents and her children. The only member of the family who stayed fiercely independent was Margaret, who still kept the lodging house in North Millwall, refusing to make the move out to the suburbs.

"Course I don't mind, Mum. After all, if Dad and Ted hadn't put the screws on the Ffitches, I would still of been paying off Roddy's debts. We wouldn't be living here now, in this nice house.'

She would never have thought, at the time of the funeral that she would have been so content living out here a few roads away from Elsie. But much to her own amazement, she found suburban life rather pleasant. It was nice after a long night's work in a smoky club or restaurant to come back to the deep quiet of Macey Drive, and to wake at midday to the sound of birdsong. Kit had settled into yet another school and was doing well. The ups and downs of his young life seemed to have had no adverse effect on him. In fact they had made him into a cheerful and self-reliant boy, proud of his famous mother.

There was a thump and a howl from the smallest bedroom.

'That little monkey! She's climbed out of her cot again.'

Poppy ran upstairs two at a time. Belinda was sitting on the floor, looking put out.

'Belinda Bun! What have you been up to, as if I didn't know? We'll have to put you in a cage.'

She picked up the little girl, who crowed and bounced in her arms, warm from her afternoon nap. Poppy cuddled her, rubbing her cheek against the coppery baby curls. Belinda was the one gem that had come out of her brief time with Roddy. Of one thing she was determined, her daughter was going to have a secure and happy childhood. Nothing, Poppy decided, was going to be allowed to spoil the secure little world she had created these past eighteen months. And by nothing, she mostly meant no man. No more love affairs.

After the mad round of parties that had been her life with

Roddy, the gentle pattern of family life was soothing. If she had been living in Macey Drive as an ordinary wife and mother, she might have found it chronically boring, but as it was, it formed a pleasant contrast to her working life.

Just as she expected, Ted was delighted to be invited to dinner. He arrived early, as Poppy was chasing Kit off to bed, and presented her with a bouquet of roses. She shoved them into a vase and showed him into the front room, asking her father to find him a drink while she went to see to Kit. She closed her eyes to Ted's disappointed expression.

As she expected, Jane's Lancashire hotpot and gooseberry pie were a great success. Ted patted his stomach as the meal ended.

'Good English home cooking. Can't beat it. Lovely stuff, Mrs P.'

Jane flushed and smiled. 'Glad you like it, I'm sure.'

Talk was all of the music business, of the latest shows and gossip and hit songs.

'Our Poppy's working on a new one, ain't you, Pops?' Owen said.

'Oh yeah? What's it like, Poppy? A hot one?'

'No, it's a sweet number.'

'It's a real tear-jerker. They'll love it,' Owen predicted.

'That's one of the things I want to talk to you about,' Poppy said, jumping in to avoid any discussion of what had inspired the lyrics. 'We need a new record contract. The terms we got from HMV last time were blooming awful. The Powers Girls are a real name now. They ought to be begging us to record for them, not the other way round. Just think how good we'll look on the covers, before people even listen to the music. And of course, if we could get a spot on the wireless, we'd be made.'

'Poppy, you know what the BBC is like. I'm working on it, I promise, but Reith doesn't like popular music at the best of times, and popular music played by women is anathema to him,' Ted said.

'A-what-ema?'

'He can't stand it. But you're right about HMV. And as it

so happens, I was talking to someone from Columbia the other day, and they're very interested in you. You get this new number of yours worked out and rehearsed, and I'll see to it that he comes along and listens. Then we'll let them come to us.'

'And what about the sheet music?'

'Poppy, I do know what I'm doing, you know. There will be a sheet music deal. And a piano roll, with a bit of luck. I take it you have got something for the B side?'

Owen broke in, eager to play a part in the conversation. 'You should hear it! Smashing little number, "Tap Your Toes". You can do a good black bottom to it. We been working on it, ain't we, Pops? Sounds lovely with the new line-up. I thought we ought to make more of the brass, so we wrote in a bit special –'

He carried on for some time, waving his cigarette to emphasize the points he was making, until an outsider might have thought that he was the moving force behind the composing and arranging side of the band. Poppy let him talk. Jane slid out and made tea.

Ted finally managed to break in to Owen's flow.

'So how's the new line-up shaping, Poppy?'

'They're going to be good. They're not quite right yet, but they're getting there.'

This was the latest development of The Powers Girls. Poppy had taken on new players, expanding the band to produce a much fuller sound. They were large enough now to play the big dance halls and the ballrooms of the West End hotels.

'When can I come and hear them?'

'Any time you like.'

'Right. I'll be there tomorrow.'

'So what about fixtures, Ted? I've taken a gamble, I've taken on all these new girls. We're too big for the average restaurant. How about a really good residency at a hotel?'

'Yes, that's what we're waiting for,' Owen chimed in.

Ted sat back with the expression of a man who has all the aces. 'Now, that was what I wanted to say to you.'

'Yes? You got us something?' Poppy leaned forward, fixing her eyes on him. 'Come on, out with it.'

Jane came in with the tea tray.

'Ah, the cup that cheers! Lovely, Mrs P.'

'Well?' Poppy demanded. 'Are you going to tell us, or do we all have to die of old age first?'

In answer, Ted reached into his breast pocket and produced a business card. He handed it to Poppy.

'The Cadogan! You got us a contract with the Cadogan?'

'Not quite, but I'm all but there. Just need to fine tune the arrangements.'

'How much?' Owen wanted to know.

'Five hundred a week for the band, plus fifty for Poppy.'

'*Fifty*? Fifty pounds a week?' Poppy was elated.

'Ambrose is getting £10,000 a year at the Mayfair,' Owen pointed out.

'Ambrose is Ambrose. He's the best-paid bandleader in the world,' Ted said.

'He's got a spot on the wireless,' Poppy said.

'For God's sake!' Ted was rattled. 'One step at a time, Poppy. You got your new line-up. You'll have a three-month run at the Cadogan. I'll get you a record contract. Then see what comes of it. We'll get you into the BBC yet.'

'Thanks, Ted,' she smiled at him, smoothing his ruffled feathers. 'It's wonderful news, really it is. You wait and see, I'll make the Cadogan the most fashionable hotel in London.'

'Fifty pounds a week.' Jane was still stunned by the figures that were being bandied about. 'Him next door, he's got a good job with a bank, and he don't earn that. I know that because She let it drop only the other day that He's got a rise. I think she was trying to impress me.'

Ted sat back in his seat, satisfied with the effect he had made. He offered Owen a cigarette and they talked of the new contract, of the numbers the band would play and the dresses they would need.

It was some time later that Ted came up with his second proposal.

'You know, you don't have to be based in London,' he said.

'You do if you want to make a name. That's where all the money is,' Poppy said.

'In this country, yes. But what about when they go travelling?'

'What do you mean?'

'The liners. The transatlantic run. Those ships are floating hotels. They have dining rooms like stately homes, they have sprung dance floors, they even have swimming pools on board. Travelling on one of them is like one big party on the water. And what's more they have an international clientele. You get on the *Berengaria* or the *Aquitania* or any one of those that goes across to New York, and you could make your name in the States.'

The happy warmth of the occasion drained from Poppy. She looked at the faces around her, pink with heat and food, content and smiling at the course the evening was taking, and instead of being at one with them, she felt set apart, as if watching them through a pane of glass.

'What's the matter, lovey?' her mother's voice came to her across a great distance. 'You look like you seen a ghost.'

'It's the heat,' Owen said. 'It's stuffy in here. I'll open the French windows.'

Ted's face took on a resigned look, and Poppy knew that he understood her reaction.

He sighed. 'You wouldn't have to land there, you know. You needn't set foot in the place. Just play on board the ship.'

But Poppy shook her head. 'No,' she said. 'Not New York. Not anywhere near it.'

'It'd be wonderful for your career.'

'I don't care. I'm a Londoner. I'll stick with what I know. It's not done me badly this far.'

'You're being stupid.'

'I don't care. I'm not going to New York, and that's that.'

Jane got up with a clatter, announced that she was going to make some more tea and left the room. Owen stayed out in the garden, smoking. Poppy said nothing. Ted leaned across the table and took Poppy's hand.

'I'm sorry,' he said, breaking the awkward silence. 'I rather hoped it was all in the past by now.'

'It isn't. I don't think it ever will be.'

'There's no future in it, you know.'

Tears stung at Poppy's eyes. 'You think I don't know that?' she said.

If he was going to leave the Snow Queen, he would have done it when he was in London that time. Of course there was no future in it. That was why she had married Roddy. She knew that now. But she was not going to make that mistake again.

'Look, Ted, just drop it, will you? I don't want to talk about it.'

'I've ruined the evening now.'

'No, you haven't ruined the evening.' She made a great effort to smile, to put warmth back into her voice. 'It's been a lovely evening. One to remember. Our break into the hotels!'

When her mother came back with the teapot Poppy raised a cup in a mock toast.

'To The Powers Girls!' she said.

'The Powers Girls!' the others echoed.

'May they never play flat,' said Owen.

The evening ended with laughter.

39

'Poppy, I wish you would just consider it. You'd enjoy it on a liner, I guarantee you. They're marvellous things, floating palaces, and you'd have really appreciative audiences. Everyone's out to have a good time.'

'I told you, Ted, I don't want to.'

'Cunard are dying to book you, Poppy. They've asked me several times, and every time the offer has been bigger. The Powers Girls would be the top band, playing the first-class ballroom.'

'I don't care. I don't want to go to New York.'

'You're being selfish. The rest of the band would love to do it.'

Poppy and Ted sat in the bar of the Cadogan Hotel, discussing the future of the band. Their contract at the hotel was coming to an end, and though the management wanted to renew it, Ted was always eager to help the band scale ever greater heights.

Over the question of a job on the transatlantic run, however, Poppy was adamant. She would rather scrub floors. When she got up to get ready for her evening's work, they were both feeling thoroughly irritated with each other.

'I don't think I'll stay this evening,' Ted told her.

'Suit yourself.'

'I'll be in touch.'

'Okay.'

Most of the others were already in the artistes' dressing-room when Poppy arrived. She made an effort to be cheerful and not take out her annoyance on them, but it was hard. Some of the new, younger members of the band were giggling together over their latest boyfriends. It made her feel old. They would stay with The Powers Girls for a while, but their first loyalty was not to the band. It was merely a small part of the lives that spread out before them, full of exciting possibilities. Poppy sat putting on her makeup with fierce concentration. Elsie, sharing a mirror with her, came straight to the point.

'What's up with you, then? Cat got your tongue?'

'No.'

'So what is it? Come on, something's bothering you.'

'Oh – it's just the new lot. They don't really care about the band at all.'

'They're all right. They're just kids.'

'I'm sure we weren't like that at their age.'

'There was a war on when we was their age, remember? We all had to grow up quick.'

'I suppose so. But I'm glad I still got all our originals here. I'd feel really lonely otherwise.'

She looked along the line to where Phyl and Marjorie were getting ready. Then she realized that Mona had not yet arrived.

'Bloody hell! Now Mona's not here. Have we had a message?'

Elsie was just pointing out Mona's absolute reliability when Mona herself came in.

'Sorry I'm late, Poppy, I been round my mum and dad's. Our Kenny's just got back from the States.'

Poppy sighed. There seemed to be some kind of conspiracy this evening to keep mentioning that country.

'He's coming round to pick me up after the gig, then we're going on to a club. Why don't you come, Poppy? Why don't we all go? Have a night on the town.'

'Oh – I don't know,' Poppy said. 'I want to get back to the family.'

'For God's sake!' Mona slapped on makeup at top speed. 'Don't be so bloody middle-aged. Come out for once and let your hair down. You know you like our Kenny.'

It was true. She always found Ken Dobson good company, and a fund of gossip about the music business. Besides, a

356

niggling something almost like a vain hope wanted to hear anything about what might be going on on the other side of the Atlantic.

'All right, I will,' she decided.

It was the old firm that piled into a taxi with Kenny and went to a drinking club that Marjorie had heard of. They all settled in to a good session of talking shop. Just as Poppy had expected, Kenny had plenty to say about how English bands were doing in New York. She listened to accounts of the hotels and speakeasies there, of the ways in which people got round Prohibition, of the wonderful times to be had in Harlem. It sounded like a musician's paradise.

'If you think people are wild here, you should see them over there. The whole place is crazy,' Kenny said. 'They're living like there's no tomorrow. Drink! I ain't never seen nothing like it. And changing partners like a Paul Jones –'

He launched into a juicy tale about a bandleader's divorce case. Poppy felt her attention slipping. Unsuccessful marriages were not her favourite subject.

'. . . but then, like I said, they're all at it. Papers are full of them. What was the name of that chap you was sweet on, Poppy?'

'What?'

'That Yank? The one you thought was dead but wasn't. It was Warrender, wasn't it?'

Poppy felt breathless. 'Yes,' she said, carefully.

'I thought so. I thought I recognized it. He had his name in all of 'em, him and the ex-wife and the kiddie – ow! Bloody hell, Mona!'

He stopped short as his sister kicked him in the ankle. Mona glared at him, furious.

'Ain't you got any sense at all?' she hissed at him, and then turned to Poppy.

'I'm really sorry, Pops, honest I am. I never knew nothing about it. It's just as much a surprise to me.'

Poppy was almost afraid to move, as if the bubble of hope might burst at a touch. She held Kenny's eyes.

'We are talking about the same person?' she said slowly. 'Scott Warrender?'

'Yeah, that's it. Big in finance. Wife's called Fran — something. Francesca?'

'Francine.'

'Francine. That's the one. Society girl. Run off with an actor.'

'And they're divorced?'

'Not yet. Going through it. There's a big hoo-ha over the kiddie.'

Poppy looked round at her friends, at the expressions ranging from Mona's excitement to Marjorie's foreboding.

'Oh, God,' she whispered. 'He's free. He's really free.'

'Don't go doing anything hasty,' Marjorie advised.

'Hasty! Bloody hell, she's known him since she was seventeen,' Elsie said.

'We all do stupid things at seventeen. It doesn't mean to say that we have to go on making it worse.'

'True love —' sighed Phyl.

'Rubbish.'

'It ain't rubbish,' Mona weighed in. 'God knows, I'm no romantic, but anyone can see that this one's the real thing. She's suffered enough for it over the years.'

'All the more reason not to go rushing off now.'

'All the more reason to do just that. If she doesn't get a move on, they'll both go and marry somebody else again —'

'Stop it, stop it, stop it!' Poppy put her hands over her ears and shouted. 'I can't think! It's all too much!'

Her friends were shocked into silence.

She needed to get away, to think it all out somewhere quiet.

'I'm going home,' she decided.

She hardly heard the babble of apologies and sympathy and support. She got a taxi back to the Cadogan, found her car and began the drive out to the suburbs. The revelations of the evening raced round her head in disconnected phrases. Somehow, she managed to arrive in front of the garage of the house in Macey Drive. She switched off the engine and sat for a long time behind the wheel, trying to see her way through the web of ties and emotions. In the end, she knew there was only one thing she could do. She let herself in to the house, rang Ted's number and told him to book the band with Cunard on the run to New York.

When she put the phone down, she found that her mother was standing on the bottom stair, her face full of concern.

'What was all that about, lovey?'

Poppy gave a brief and garbled explanation. Her mother looked even more worried.

'Come into the kitchen, lovey. I'll make us both a nice cup of tea.'

Light-headed now with the seesaw of events, Poppy followed her. Jane put the teapot and cups on the table between them.

'Poppy, love –' Jane began, then stopped. She rubbed her hands over her face. 'Poppy, are you sure you're doing the right thing? I mean – it's a long time now since you last seen him. People change. You have this idea about what they're like, and – well, sometimes it's not right. What you got in your head is only, well, a dream. Not the real person at all.'

She was right, of course. If anyone should know about that, her mother did. The faces of all the men who had let her down floated before Poppy's eyes. Joe. Roddy. Her father. And lingering like a dark shadow, touching her nerve endings with a shudder, Mr Hetherington. But though she wavered for a moment, she was not to be put off.

'I know what you mean, Mum, but I got to go. I got to give it one more try. I'll regret it all my life if I don't.'

From the moment she saw the *Berengaria*, on a blustery March day in Southampton dock, Elsie was enchanted. It was love at first sight. From her three tall funnels to the fancy gold scroll work on her stern, the liner was a beauty. Elsie was charged with a sense of excitement that she had not felt in years. This was adventure. On a ship like this, anything could happen. She clutched at Poppy's arm.

359

'Ain't she just beautiful?' she breathed.

Poppy shrugged. She was looking pinched and worried.

'If you say so.'

She was no better when they had been shown through a bewildering maze of passages to their cabin deep in the bowels of the great ship. While Elsie opened doors and looked in lockers and exclaimed over the clever design, Poppy sat on her bunk with her head in her hands.

'This whole thing's stupid. I should of just waited until I heard from him. He could of contacted me through Ted if he wanted to. Now I'm stuck on this horrible ship for weeks and weeks.'

'For God's sake, Poppy, buck up! This ain't like you.'

Elsie sat down beside her and hugged her. She hated to see her so gloomy when there was so much to enjoy.

'It'll turn out fine, Pops. I know it! I feel it in my bones. God knows, you deserve a break. Now look, leave all this.' She nodded at the trunks and suitcases piled into the limited floorspace. 'We'll sort it all out later. Let's go and explore, eh? Find our way around a bit before the passengers come on board. Come on, it'll do you good.'

Reluctantly, Poppy agreed.

The ship was a floating wonderland. The first-class smoking-room looked like something out of an ancestral castle, with its oak panelling and tooled leather frieze, the dining saloon was three decks high with a doomed roof, the swimming pool was designed like the Roman baths at Pompeii. The two friends looked into the Turkish baths, the gymnasium, the Imperial suite. They got lost countless times and had to ask the way of cabin crew busy making sure everything was prepared for the next voyage. Everywhere there was fancy scroll work, painted ceilings, classical pillars, banks of flowers and plants.

'Ain't it incredible?' Elsie kept saying, as each new wonder was discovered.

'Amazing,' Poppy had to agree.

'She can carry three thousand passengers and a thousand

crew, without being the least bit crowded,' Elsie told her. She had read all the brochures.

By the time they made it back to their little cabin, she was happily bewildered. This, she was sure, was going to be the trip of a lifetime.

The band were engaged to play at the tea dances and in the first-class ballroom every night, where the atmosphere was that of one long party. On top of this there were the private parties in the staterooms, where trios or small combos from the band would be booked to play. There was something about being at sea that seemed to strip away people's inhibitions. The pleasure was fast and furious. If the girls in the band had accepted every drink that was pressed upon them, they would have lived the entire voyage in an alcoholic haze. They certainly never had to buy one for themselves. Neither was there any lack of admirers, from the crew as well as the passengers. Even Elsie, who considered herself past all that sort of thing, found men eager to take her to parties, to go swimming with her, to walk her round the decks.

But most of all, she liked to be up on deck by herself with the wind on her face, just watching the ocean rolling grey-green and vast till it blended in with the sky. It gave her an odd sense of belonging.

Her only unhappiness was that Poppy did not share her feelings.

'I ought never have come,' she would repeat a dozen times a day. 'I don't know how to contact him. He won't be working at that bank no more, not now he's divorced from Her. Her father was his boss. And even if I did find him, how do I know he still feels the same way about me? I can't go running after him like this. What'll he think of me?'

'He'll think you love him, which is no more than the truth,' Elsie told her.

'But does he still love me? He could of got in touch with me, you know. I know I've moved, but he could of written to Ted. He could of come over to London. Why should I have to go to him?'

'Perhaps he thinks the same. That you don't want him no more. He might think you got someone else. He don't know about Roddy, remember. Anything could of happened since you last saw him.'

'I ought never have come. It's a disaster.'

Elsie could see that something had to be done. She went up to consult the men in the radio room. She wanted to send a message to someone in New York, she explained. She did not know where he lived or where he worked, but she knew he was something to do with money and shares and that sort of thing.

The radio officer smiled at her.

'An old beau?' he asked.

'No, a friend's –' She stopped and laughed. 'That's what everyone says, isn't it? "I'm doing it for a friend." But it's true. I'm trying to get them together again.'

'Ah – playing cupid.' The officer was interested. He put his mind to the problem.

'Do you think he might work on the Stock Exchange?'

'I suppose so.'

'Could you ask your friend?'

'Oh no! She'd have kittens if she knew what I was up to.'

'Well, we could try sending a cable there. If his name is known it might be forwarded on.'

Elsie was pleased with this. It was well worth a try. Together they drafted the wording: POWERS GIRLS ARRIVING NY BERENGARIA THURSDAY. ELSIE.

'I got to put my name on it. My friend'd really slay me if she thought he'd think she was running after him,' Elsie explained.

'Of course. Very wise.'

He was a nice man, she decided. His eyes crinkled up at the corners when he smiled, and he had a pleasant voice.

'You'll let me know if there's reply?'

'Right away. It'll be our secret.'

She then spent the next few hours worrying over whether she had done the right thing. The ship was approaching the coast of America when the radio officer sought her out to give

362

her the reply. She was too stunned by its contents to notice that he looked rather disappointed. She rushed off down below to work on Poppy.

'I'm giving you an hour's notice. You got to be up on deck to see us come in to New York harbour.'

Poppy shrugged. 'You go, Elsie. I'm tired. I saw Southampton, and it wasn't much.'

'I'm not talking about Southampton, you idiot, I'm talking about New York! The Statue of Liberty. The skyscrapers. You can't stay down here and miss it all. It's one of the wonders of the world.'

It took some doing, but in the end she succeeded. She and Poppy squeezed themselves into a place at the rails of the lower promenade deck as the ship steamed into the great natural harbour, and to Elsie's satisfaction, Poppy was roused out of her diffidence. Together they gazed at the sinister collection of buildings on Ellis Island, at the amazing size of the famous statue on Liberty Island, at the fantastic collection of towers crowded onto Lower Manhattan.

'It's so big!' they kept repeating to each other.

Ahead of them now they could see the piers, see the crowds of people waiting. Elsie glanced at Poppy. She was looking at the gleaming buildings with a world of longing in her eyes.

'He's out there somewhere,' she murmured.

Elsie threaded her arm through her friend's. 'That's right,' she agreed.

The *Berengaria* eased nearer and nearer to the quayside. The blur of the crowd was beginning to separate into individual people. Arms began to wave, names were shouted. Elsie scanned the eager faces tipped up to gaze at the towering sides of the liner. So many people, so many hats and suits and overcoats, so many bright buttonholes. The ropes were thrown and caught and tied, the ship nudged gently alongside, the engines stopped. People who had identified each other were shouting greetings from ship to shore, lifting up babies, blowing kisses. Still Elsie searched the faces. It was impossible. There were too many. Desperation was beginning to grip her.

Then she let out a yell and clutched at Poppy, shaking her in her excitement.

'There! Look, look – there – see!'

She pointed, then waved wildly, to receive an equally joyous wave in reply.

'What? Where?' Poppy had gone quite white.

'*Look*!'

There was a gasp beside her as Poppy saw who she was supposed to be looking at.

'Scott?' she said, in a very small voice, as if not daring to believe her eyes.

And then she was jumping up and down, waving and yelling, with tears rolling down her face.

'Scott! Scott! Oh Elsie, it is, it's Scott. He's here, he's come to meet us!'

The gangways were down, the first passengers were walking ashore. Scott shouldered his way to the front of the crowd. Elsie held tightly onto Poppy. She was almost afraid her friend might jump straight over the side and into his arms. He was directly beneath them now, twenty feet down on the pier. Elsie thought he looked a lot older than when she had last seen him. Poppy was laughing and crying all at the same time, repeating his name over and over. Scott cupped his hands to his mouth and shouted up to her.

'I love you!'

'I love you too!' Poppy cried, but the words were strangled with sobs.

It did not matter. Elsie could tell by his smile that he understood.

40

Manhattan was an extraordinary place – bigger, faster, brighter, noisier than anything Poppy had imagined. She stared at it through the windows of Scott's automobile as he took her on a whirlwind tour, not quite believing that she was really there.

'All these years, I've wanted to show you all this,' he said. 'I used to plan trips, thinking about what you'd like to see. And now you're here.' He took his eyes off the road to look at her, putting a hand on her knee. 'You are here, aren't you? You're not just another daydream?'

'I think so – I'm not sure – perhaps I'm still on the boat, in my cabin, refusing to come up on deck and see us come in to New York harbour.'

'Now,' Scott said, 'just take a look at this – Broadway! We must take in a show while you're here. Just choose whichever one you want.'

He drove slowly past the theatres, pointing out the shows, naming the stars, commenting on the ones he had seen. Poppy looked this way and that, and made what she hoped were the right noises, but she could not take it all in. A terrible worry was weighing on her mind, the one that had been with her all across the Atlantic, now made ten times worse by actually being with Scott again. In the end, she could not contain it any longer. She cut through Scott's running commentary.

'It is true, isn't it? You did divorce her? You are free?'

Scott did not answer immediately. He drew in to the side of the road and stopped. In the half-minute or so that it took, Poppy had time enough for every one of her worst fears to be revived. She was aware of his arm along the back of her seat, of the fact that he had turned to face her, but she could not bear to look at him. She clasped her hands tight in her lap. It was going to be like that day out in Kent all over again, when he stopped the car and admitted that there was no real future for them.

'Honey, I'm sorry –'

Poppy stared at her hands. She did not want to hear any more. She wanted to get out of the car now and run away, but she seemed to have lost the ability to move.

' – I've been running on like a radio commentator. Avoiding the issue, I guess. The truth is, I don't know where we stand. I know how I want it to be, but it seems a hell of a lot to expect after all these years, and what you've been through.'

'You never answered my question,' Poppy said. She hardly recognized her own voice. It sounded cold and distant. She had to have an answer before she could listen to anything else.

'But of course it's true, honey. All those years I was fool enough to act as a prop to Francine, thinking she was too fragile to look after herself, and then she goes and proves me wrong by flitting off and taking herself to Hollywood. She's already dumped the guy she went with. Last I heard, she was trying to get into the movies.'

Poppy did not care in the least about what Francine might be doing. She had gone, that was all she wanted to know. Gone out of his life. The relief made her feel light-headed.

'And you're really free,' she said, just for the pleasure of having it repeated.

'Free as a bird. Look – do you want to see any more of the town?'

'Not really,' Poppy admitted.

'Then let's go someplace and talk.'

They talked late into the evening, as they ate a dinner of which neither of them noticed a mouthful. Both their former relationships were gone over in detail. After hearing all about Roddy, Scott was even more puzzled as to why she had married him in the first place. Poppy sighed. He could be very dense sometimes.

'Why do you think? The same reason that I married Joe. Because I couldn't have you. Oh, I thought I loved him at the time. Perhaps I did. He loved me, and he made me feel wanted. I desperately needed someone to belong to me.'

'Well, I guess that makes sense of a sort. All the same, I was jealous as hell when I read you'd married this Roddy guy. I bought all the English magazines after that, trying to get word of you, so I found out later that he'd died, and in suspicious circumstances.'

'But if you knew I was widowed, why didn't you get in touch with me after Francine left? That was last summer, wasn't it? Months ago?'

All that time wasted. It didn't matter so much now that she was here, now that everything was open between them, but still she wanted to know.

Scott took her hands across the table.

'I wanted to rush straight across the Atlantic and snatch you up before you went and got married again, but I couldn't, not if I wanted to keep my little Amy. I had a hell of a time of it while it was all going on. The tabloids really got their teeth into us. If I wanted to get custody of Amy, I had to be pure as the driven snow. Any hint of any interest in another woman on my part, and they would have been on to it, and then my chances of getting Amy would have been all shot to pieces. The courts don't often find in favour of the father, but since Francine had gone off and left Amy as well as me, and I was seen to be leading an exemplary life since she went, she was judged to be an unfit mother and I was allowed to keep Amy. But it was a close thing.'

Poppy could understand this only too well.

'I'm so glad you got her. I know how you feel. After Roddy died, my dad and Ted went and saw the Ffitches to try and get some money out of them to pay Roddy's debts, and at first they said it was my bad influence that sent him off the rails and they'd only pay up if I gave up Belinda. How could they even think for a moment that I would do a thing like that? But Dad and Ted threatened them with telling the papers and in the end they backed down and paid up. But I felt terrified for weeks afterwards. I couldn't let Lindy out of my sight.'

'What's she like, your Lindy? Does she look like you?'

'Oh, she's so beautiful, Scott. And that forward! I got a picture –'

It was late evening before they finally ran out of words, and sat with legs touching beneath the table and hands clasped on top, gazing at each other.

'We could go dancing, if you want,' Scott said.

Poppy thought of all those hundreds of nights, playing for other people to dance, and how she had wished she was out there on the floor in his arms. But not now, not tonight. There would be plenty of other nights. At last they had the luxury of time.

'No,' she said.

He looked into her eyes, trying to read her meaning.

'There's my apartment, if you don't think I'm pushing you –?'

'I can't wait to see it.'

Scott kissed her hands. 'You don't know how good it is to be with somebody who doesn't fool around playing games.'

'We never had time for that, did we? You were always about to go.'

'This time it's you who's about to go. We've only got until the boat sails.'

'But I'll be back –' she smiled at him, teasing. 'Maybe.'

Despite the long talk and the clearing of the ground, Poppy still felt nervous as Scott unlocked the door of his apartment. Supposing she couldn't do it right? Supposing he was disappointed with her? It was such a long time since they made love for the last time in that little flat off the Clerkenwell Road. She chattered in a low voice, not wanting to disturb Amy and her nanny, AnnaMaria, looking around at the airy rooms with their spare modern furniture and white walls and bright cubist paintings.

Scott put his arms round her and silenced her with a long kiss. All the fear dissolved. It was going to be all right. Here was where she belonged. She nestled against his strong body, responding eagerly to his lips.

'I love you, Poppy Powers.'

Poppy took a long, shuddering breath.

'I love you too.' She pressed closer to him, delighted in the feel of him against her, conscious of a consuming need growing within her. 'I'd almost forgotten how good it was to hold you,' she whispered.

He ran his hands over her, sending shivers of need through her.

'I've never forgotten the feel of you. There's not a day gone by when I haven't thought of you.'

He led her into the bedroom, and they undressed each other, kissing and touching, rediscovering, until at last they stood naked and glowing with desire. Scott cupped her small breasts in his hands and kissed them.

'I've got older since – since last time,' Poppy said.

'You're more beautiful than ever.'

He kissed and fondled, making her groan with delight, then knelt, making a trail of kisses down her belly, lower and lower, until she cried out, on fire for his touch. She lay back on the bed, opening out to him, shuddering with a pleasure and need that was almost too much to bear.

'Come here,' she whispered. 'I want to feel all of you.'

They rolled over and over on the bed, drowning in a delight of the senses, in the touch and taste and smell and look of each other, rising on a swelling tide of passion. Poppy wrapped her legs round him and he plunged into her, taking her higher and higher, until at last they dissolved into an engulfing wave of mutual pleasure.

They clung together, rocked with the intensity of the moment. A great pool of suppressed emotion welled up in Poppy and spilled over. She lay sobbing with the joy of release while Scott held her to him.

'Never leave me, Poppy. Stay here always.'

'Always,' she promised.

She calmed in his loving arms, wanted and fulfilled, and they slept for a while wrapped together. They woke to explore each other more gently and leisurely, setting the pattern for the night, relearning how best to give pleasure, rising to new peaks of enjoyment.

When morning sent its grey light into the room, Poppy was feeling happy and secure. She was a woman loved and in love. She lay with her head on Scott's chest and discussed the immediate future.

'How many trips did you say you were booked for?' Scott asked.

'Six, initially. Returns, that is.'

'Right. I'll tie things up here while you're away this time, then I'll take a berth on the ship and come over with you. We can sail back and forth across the Atlantic together.'

Poppy laughed helplessly. It was all so wonderful, she felt drunk with the glory of it.

'You're mad! I'll be working every evening.'

'I'm mad about you, baby. And I'm not going to let you slip through my fingers this time. I'm not even sure if I can trust you to go to England and back this time without marrying someone behind my back.'

The trip back across to England passed in a haze. Poppy's mind and body were totally preoccupied with thoughts of Scott. The others carried her along, covering mistakes and prompting her when she forgot names and introductions. Mona grumbled that she was worse when she was happy than when she was suffering, and Marjorie hinted darkly that it would all end in tears, but they were happy for her. The brief time at home was occupied with the children, in hearing about what Kit had been up to in her absence and reassuring a confused Belinda that she was going to come back again. Leaving them was the one blot on her joy at getting back to the *Berengaria* again and setting sail for New York. This time there were no doubts and regrets. She was going to be with the love of her life.

Back in New York, Scott was at the pier to meet her. They went straight back to his apartment. Poppy was introduced to Amy, and to her relief found her almost as appealing as her own children. They then shocked AnnaMaria by going to bed the moment Amy did.

The next evening, Scott insisted that they should go to Harlem.

'You can't come to New York without hearing some real jazz.'

'What do you mean, "real jazz"? I hear it all the time. I play it.'

Scott shook his head.

'Honey, I love you very much and I truly admire what you do, but what you play is not jazz. You wait till tonight. You won't know what's hit you.'

Poppy doubted it. She had heard the best bands in England, she had heard visiting bands from America, black and white, she had been to see Florence Mills in *Blackbirds* five times. But she was more than happy to go with him for a night on the town, so she put on her gold dress with the bands of red and gold sequins that clashed gloriously with her hair, and they took a cab to Harlem.

'Where are we going?' she asked. 'The Cotton Club?' She had heard of that one.

'No, that's too full of socialites. To hear the real stuff you got to go where the neighbourhood people go. They know music when they hear it. We'll try Tillie's Chicken Shack or Mexico's, or maybe Pod's & Jerry's. Tillie's does the best food. You just got to try the fried chicken and sweet potato pie. Pod's & Jerry's is where you'll hear real stride piano, and Mexico's has the wind players. Mind you, even Mexico's is too high class for the real raw stuff. To hear that, you got to go to a rent party, where all the new talent cuts its teeth. But I guess the likes of you and me won't get invited to one of them.'

'Why not?'

Scott laughed. 'Wrong colour, baby. They keep the best for themselves. It's all prettied up for us white folks.'

Poppy was still not convinced, but she was curious to see and hear for herself. They got out at Mexico's.

They were greeted by waiters and clientele as they went in.

Scott introduced Poppy all round, proudly naming her as the leader of a famous English dance band. She found herself bombarded with questions from people wanting to know about the scene on her side of the water, and was happy to talk about it, but when conversation turned to local talent, she had to admit her ignorance. She had not even heard of most of the names they mentioned. Her new friends gave knowing grins.

'You gotta real big treat coming up tonight, baby. They's some real hot cats comes to this joint.'

And as the night warmed up, she began to see what they meant. The band was like nothing she had ever heard before. The players pulsed with a life that made The Powers Girls seem like a bunch of convent schoolgirls. She listened open-mouthed, fingers and feet tapping in time with the rhythm, and when she and Scott got up to dance, she found she was moving with an energy and abandon she had never known before, fuelled by the heat of the music. The cabaret came on, a line of long-legged chorus girls in satin and feathers, moving in breathtaking unison, followed by a singer whose smoky voice ran up and down the nerves of the spine and spoke to the soul. Poppy was hooked.

Scott reached out to put an arm round her bare shoulders, caressing the turn of her neck.

'Enjoying it?'

She looked at him with eyes brimming with love and happiness. 'It's just wonderful.'

The place was still jumping at four in the morning, when musicians began to come in from dates at clubs and speak-easies all over the town. Poppy was wide awake, this was her time. She picked up a change in the atmosphere. A lot of the people who had come for the dancing and the cabaret had gone home. Those who stayed were there for the music. The band changed its style. They were not sticking to the tempo for dancing now, but picking up the melody lines and playing around with them, varying the rhythm, the feel, the order, throwing the spot from one to another so that each player could show his stuff. It was Poppy's first brush with the art of improvization. She experimented a lot at home while she was working out new arrangements for the band, but it was all carefully written down and kept to a dance tempo. Pushing music to the limits like this was electrifying.

The leader peered through the heavy smoke to a table at the side of the room.

'Hey, Lester, you out there, man? Come and blow that horn.'

A man got up and waved a hand in agreement. Amidst shouts and whistles he ambled over to the stand, carrying a saxophone.

'That's Lester Young,' Scott said. 'Now the fun starts.'

A muttered exchange with the leader, then the band started in on 'Hard-Hearted Hannah', conventional enough at first, but then Lester Young started to show what he was made of. The tune was squeezed, stretched, embroidered on. Fans all over the room shouted their appreciation at each new turn. It was a mind-bending ten minutes of virtuoso playing, ending in a storm of applause.

There was a stir in one corner of the shadowy room, and a young man stood up, self-consciously clutching a sax.

'Eddy! Come on, Eddy – play it, man.'

Scott explained the situation to Poppy. 'This looks like the new boy in town. You can't just slide in to the scene in New York. Sooner or later the challenge will go out, and if you don't take it up, it shows you're scared you can't take the heat. The word must have gone out to young Eddy here, and now the other boys are fixing to cut him down. This should be good.'

The newcomer squared his shoulders and strutted up to the stand, putting on a show of confidence. The stage lighting glistened on his sleeked back, fashionably straightened hair, glinted off his sax. He flexed his long fingers and put his lips to the reed. He launched into a fast hot number, notes rippling at steam train speed, racing up and down the scales, slowing to blur into a raucous shout. The listeners yelled encouragement, spurring him on to greater efforts. Poppy could scarcely breathe, feeling for him in this ordeal. He was good, anyone could hear that, but he was not as good as Lester Young, and when Lester himself joined in, it became obvious.

'Not yet, anyway,' Scott agreed. 'Give him another two or three years and he could be up there with the best, if he can stand the pace.'

A man who had recently arrived at the next table leaned over to talk to Scott.

'Hey, is it true your lady can play the sax?'

'True as I sit here.'

In the shadows beneath the tables, Poppy could see the dark shape of an instrument case between his feet. Another musician come to cut it, probably one of the names she had failed to recognize earlier in the evening. Scott went on at length about The Powers Girls. Poppy could see plain scepticism in the face of the other man. He spoke directly to her.

'How about you getting up and blowing us a number?'

'Oh, no,' Poppy was horrified. 'This is way out of my league.'

'Come on, Poppy. You can do it,' Scott said.

'I ain't got my sax with me.'

The man gave her a considering look. 'What do you play, alto?'

'Tenor.'

He reached down and opened the instrument case.

'You can play mine.'

Poppy was conscious of a high honour. But still she did not want to get up and make a fool of herself in this company. Scott, however, was not going to let her refuse.

'Hell, Poppy, this is Don Byas we're talking to. Don Byas is offering to lend you his sax. You can't refuse that.'

Poppy could do just that. What she had heard that night had proved Scott more than right. What she played was dance music. She was not a jazz musician.

Other people became aware of the situation. Poppy found herself cornered. They were all clearly amused at the thought of a woman, and a white woman at that, having any idea of how to play the sax. In the end, it was give in or leave, and she had no intention of leaving.

'All right, all right. I'll do it.'

She took the offered saxophone and ran up and down some scales, getting used to the feel of it. It was a nice instrument, with a beautiful mellow tone.

'Sounds good,' she commented.

She glanced at Scott, who was looking at her with love and pride in his face, and it came to her just what she was going to play. Something just for him. The thought gave her the confidence to walk up to the stand with the shouts and whistles of the audience in her ears.

Once up there with the band, she felt a bit better. With the lights on her, she could not see the people out there on the floor. But they were still there, and they knew what they were listening to.

The leader raised expressive eyebrows. 'What's it to be, sister?'

' "Can't Help Loving That Man Of Mine".'

He nodded and passed the word on to the band. Poppy closed her eyes and concentrated, letting the first bars pass while she got into the mood. Then she joined in, taking the lead, pouring her heart and soul into the music. She almost forgot the critical ears out there listening. This one was for Scott. All those years she had played her loss, her love, her loneliness, and he had not been there to hear her. Now at last he was here with her, and she put everything she had into her playing, letting the sax say all that she felt for him. A stillness fell over the club as the audience caught the emotion, felt its sincerity. She drew out the last long note. There was a moment's silence, then a burst of genuine appreciation. She had caught their hearts.

Poppy bowed and stepped down off the stand, dizzy with the emotional effort. She wove her way back to the table, where Scott swept her into his arms.

'I knew you could do it! Isn't she just wonderful? What a performance!'

Don Byas took the sax from her shaking fingers. He was looking at her in amazement. 'Sister, you sure can play this thing,' he said.

Poppy was floating. She had the man she loved. She had the approval of fellow musicians. It was all too good to be true.

41

'But what are they all doing?' Poppy asked mystified.

The scene below her on the trading floor of the Stock Exchange appeared to be one of chaos. Dozens of men in shirtsleeves were running about, waving, shouting, flourishing pieces of paper. On a huge board covering the length of a wall more men were constantly putting up numbers, taking them down and replacing them. The noise was like feeding time at the zoo, the atmosphere frantic. Poppy could not make out what was going on.

'They're making money. Lots of money,' Scott told her. He was gazing at the activity with the same expression of sharp excitement that gripped many of the faces below. 'Look at it, Poppy. Listen to it. Smell it. That's a human greenhouse down there. They're growing money.'

'But how?'

'They're trading, like you'd trade anything – corn, fish, potatoes. People want to buy and people want to sell, and they're all out to get the best price they can.'

'But – potatoes and that are *things*. If I want to buy potatoes, I go to the shops and I pay my money and I go home and make chips. All they get here is a piece of paper that says you own so many shares.'

Scott took a bill out of his fold and gave it to her.

'What's this?'

She looked at it. 'It's a hundred-dollar note – bill.'

'And what's it worth?'

She shrugged. 'A hundred dollars, I suppose.'

'No it's not. It's just a piece of paper, practically worthless. You can only go out and buy a hundred dollars' worth of goods with it because we all agree it's worth that much. It's the same with these shares. The companies they're issued by might not be worth the sum total of their shares if all the shareholders wanted to sell back at the same time, but because we all think we can sell for more, we go on buying. It's confidence, you see. Confidence and margins.'

'What are margins?'

'That is the wonderful system by which you buy a hundred thousand dollars worth of shares for a one thousand dollar down payment and a loan from the broker.'

'A loan of ninety-nine thousand?' Poppy was incredulous. 'But – how on earth do you pay back that amount?'

'You don't. In theory you pay it back when you sell, but in practice you just go on and buy up the next lot.'

Poppy tried to take all of this in. 'So everyone's using money they haven't got, and making more out of it?'

'That's just about the way of it, yes.'

It all seemed too easy. There was a flaw in this somewhere, something very worrying. Poppy frowned.

'That's all very well as long as you sell for more. But what happens if the price goes down?'

'It doesn't. That's the beauty of it. There are ripples, rumours. I've had my fingers burnt a few times when I've gone for the big risk stuff, but I've always managed to recover.'

'The prices just go up and up all the time?'

'Yes, it's what's called a bull market. You can't lose. Everyone's doing it, clerks, messenger boys, hat-check girls, they all have a flutter on the exchange.'

Poppy supposed he knew what he was doing. He was certainly master of the game. The rate at which he lived here made Roddy's extravagances look like economies. The difference was that Scott paid as he went. There were no piles of dunning letters and unpaid accounts lying unopened around his apartment. All the same, the system by which he made all these riches still worried her. It went against all her childhood conditioning.

'What if it doesn't keep going up?' she asked. 'It can't go on for ever, surely?'

378

'Sometimes I do wonder – ' Scott was still watching the action. His eyes roved over the numbers on the giant board, focused on a new price being put up. 'American Agricultural Chemicals – see? Up three-quarters. I bought a block of them yesterday. It's like a giant carousel, Poppy, and it's going faster all the time. I can't jump off now, while it's turning.'

Poppy was sure her grandmother would disapprove strongly. 'Neither a borrower nor a lender be' was one of her favourite sayings. But then she had been doing things of which her grandmother disapproved all her life, and here she was now in New York, going out each night wearing five-hundred-dollar dresses and drinking bootlegged French champagne as if it was lemonade, while her gran was still on Dog Island and still working hard every day of her life at the age of sixty-nine.

'If it's as good a gold mine as you say, maybe I should have a go,' she said.

To her surprise, Scott was not happy about this.

'Just because everyone's doing it, it doesn't mean to say it's a good idea for all of them,' he said. 'I know what I'm doing, I've been in and around this game since just after the war. You stick to what you're good at, sweetheart. You wouldn't put a sax in my hands and push me into the line-up of The Powers Girls, now would you?'

Poppy laughed. 'I'd like to see you in one of our dresses.'

The spring and summer of 1929 had passed in a happy whirlwind of travelling back and forth across the Atlantic. In between Scott's keeping his investments going and Poppy's engagements with the band, they had met each other's families and gone for a holiday in fashionable Florida. Now, at the insistence of the entire band, The Powers Girls were back on board the *Berengaria*. Numerous shipboard romances had sprung up, some to die almost as quickly as they were born. But to Poppy's delight, the most prosperous was that of Elsie and the chief radio officer. Their engagement had been announced on the last trip, setting off a great wave of celebrations, and they were planning to marry in the spring.

379

'I'm so happy for Elsie,' Poppy said, as she and Scott sat over smoked salmon salad.

'She's a great girl. I'll always be grateful to her for sending me that cable. She brought us together again.'

'And we brought them together, in a way. She might not have got to know Bob so soon if she hadn't gone to send the cable. He thought she was sending it on her own behalf, you know. She said it was for a friend, but he didn't believe her. He thought she was trying to contact an old flame and he was disappointed. He was delighted when he found out on the return voyage that she really had been doing it for me. She deserves some happiness, does Elsie.'

Scott took her left hand and turned it so that the diamond and emerald ring on her third finger caught the light.

'Not long now,' he said.

'I can hardly wait. My mum's in a terrible state about it all.'

When and where the wedding should take place had been the subject of long and sometimes heated discussion. They had swung from a quick quiet ceremony in New York with just a couple of witnesses, to a knees-up on Dog Island, to a romantic sealing of the knot on board the *Berengaria*, but in the end they had settled on a wedding from Poppy's home in Ilford. At last, at the third attempt, she had her father there to give her away, and she was not going to miss the opportunity. The only disappointment was that once again it was not going to be a church ceremony, as Scott was divorced, but in all other respects it was going to be the wedding of the year, with a huge number of guests and a full-scale dance afterwards, so that the maximum number of people could share with them their happiness in finally coming together. It was all planned for mid-November.

'You sure you won't miss Elsie and the girls from the band too much?'

'I shall miss them terribly, but not half as much as I've missed you over the years. I still can't quite believe I shall have you to myself all the time.'

'We'll go away on our honeymoon and never come back.'

'I wish you'd tell me where we're going. I don't know what to pack.'

'I told you before – all you need is your bathing costume, and possibly not even that. You'll love it, I promise you.'

Poppy gave a happy sigh. The mystery over the honeymoon destination was all part of the fun. She was sure that if Scott said it was going to be wonderful, then he was more than right. Everything had fallen into place with an ease that she would have never have believed possible a year ago. The children all liked each other and their prospective step-parents, the future parents-in-law were charmed by their offspring's choices, even Poppy's gran had grudgingly admitted that Scott was better than the last two. A couple of bands in New York were already beginning to make approaches to Poppy to make guest appearances after she made her home there. Just occasionally, a superstitious doubt surfaced in Poppy's mind. It couldn't all go on like this. Her luck just wasn't that good. But she pushed it down with the thought that she had had her share of bad times in the past, and now things had turned her way. From now on, everything was going to be fine.

The *Berengaria* made her stately way to and fro across the Atlantic with The Powers Girls presiding in the first-class ballroom. They had a whole new repertoire of the latest numbers and could play anything the dancers cared to request – 'Ain't Misbehavin' ', 'Singin' in the Rain', 'Without a Song' – they knew them all. Tycoons, show business personalities and minor royalty sailing on the great ship all remarked on the vivacious quality of the band. Poppy's happiness inspired all the players to new heights. The Commodore of the Cunard Line, Sir Arthur Rostrom, personally complimented Poppy on the standard of the band. He had, he admitted, been sceptical about a ladies' band playing on board the fleet's flagship, but now he was entirely won over. Poppy found out his favourite number and played it whenever he put in an appearance.

She had started reading the financial columns with as much interest as a born New Yorker in an attempt to understand just how it was that Scott made his living, and it was during the September sailing that she began to notice that the prices were not going up and up all the time, that rather they seemed to be drifting down. She made her way along to where an enterprising young man named Michael J. Meecham had recently set up a stockbroker's office on board the ship.

'I've been watching the key blue chips and they've all fallen since the third of the month,' she said, proud of her mastery of the jargon.

Like many another man sailing on the *Berengaria*, Michael Meecham was rather taken with Poppy. He was more than ready to take time out to talk stock prices with her, even though she did not hold any shares herself.

'There's nothing to worry about at all,' he assured her. 'It's just a technical adjustment. The market had got a mite overheated, but you don't want to go listening to Babson or any of his followers. It'll all pick up again by Christmas.'

Scott took much the same attitude when they met again in New York.

'I guess it had to happen some time. It's a safety valve. Some of the dead wood will get cleared out of the way and then we'll all be on the up again. In the meantime, you can still make money on a bear market, if you know what you're doing.'

Poppy accepted his word for it. He was the expert. Her mind was too full of wedding preparations to let mere points on the stock market get her down. As the ship pulled away from the pier, she and Scott held each end of a pink paper streamer and waved and blew kisses.

'Next time!' Scott mouthed at her, as the streamer broke.

'Next time!' Poppy mimed back. 'I love you!'

There was just one more round trip to make. The *Berengaria* was returning at the end of October, and when she sailed out from the Chelsea piers at the beginning of November, both Scott and Poppy would be on board, en route for their wedding. Poppy leaned on the rail and watched till first Scott, then the pier, were too far away to be distinguished. Elsie came and joined her, and together they gazed at the dramatic Manhattan skyline until even the skyscrapers were dwarfed by distance.

'To think I never wanted to do this,' Poppy said. 'All that time, I held out against coming to New York.'

'Just think what we would have missed,' Elsie agreed. She took a deep breath. 'Smell that sea! Don't you just love it? And the smell of ship as well. You can keep New York, it's this liner I love. I just knew, the moment I stepped on board that it was going to be wonderful.'

Poppy threaded her arm through her friend's and they huddled together against the autumn chill coming off the ocean.

'Ain't we lucky?'

'Ain't we just?'

The *Berengaria* set sail for New York via Cherbourg in the third week of October 1929. The Saturday and Sunday were the usual carefree shipboard days. Passengers ate the magnificent meals, worked them off in the gymnasium or the swimming pool, strolled the decks, went to parties, played bridge, danced and flirted. It was just like any other voyage. Only Michael Meecham was worried. He received some alarming cables during the weekend from his contacts in New York. Brokers were sending out margin calls by the thousand.

During Monday the twenty-first, news started to spread through the first-class passengers of heavy selling on Wall Street. Meecham's small office was packed. Those who could not get in waited outside on the deck for news. By the end of the day word came in that six million shares had been sold on the Stock Exchange. The tickers were running up to two hours behind. Tuesday was just as bad. Wednesday was worse. Eight million went on Wednesday and the *New York Times* Index dropped twenty points. In the ballroom, The Powers Girls played cheery numbers like 'Keep Your Sunny Side Up' but it did little to shift the air of impending doom. Poppy tried telling herself that Scott would be all right. He had his finger on the pulse, he knew what he was doing. She just wished the ship would go faster and get them to New York so that she could be by his side in this crisis.

By Thursday, shareholders on board the ship, like those on shore, were desperate to get out while they could. In the afternoon, news came in that a consortium of the biggest and most prestigious bankers had got together to halt the stampede. Opinion on the ship wavered. Some were convinced, others still clamoured to sell. By the end of the day 12.8 million shares had changed hands, and the name 'Black Thursday' was already being bandied about.

It was a haggard-looking Scott who met Poppy at the Chelsea Piers. Poppy ran to embrace him.

'My poor darling! You look awful. Has it been terrible?'

'It's been a nightmare,' Scott said, and kissed her hard.

Poppy responded eagerly. She smiled up at him, a world of love in her eyes.

'As long as we're together, that's all that matters,' she said.

'You're a gem, Poppy,' he said, but the bleak expression in his face did not soften.

Sitting beside him in the automobile, Poppy hardly noticed his silence. She was full of her own news, of the children and wedding plans and the dramatic events of the voyage over. She chattered on, happy to share all the things she had been saving up to tell him. In a few days they would be together. For propriety's sake they had agreed that Scott should stay at a hotel for the few days between their arriving back in England and getting married.

'We'll eat in tonight, if you don't mind,' Scott said, when they arrived at the apartment.

'Of course not.'

She played for a while with Amy, then watched with pleasure as Scott helped put her to bed. It always gave her a warm feeling to see the two of them together. When the little girl was safely tucked up, they made their way back to the drawing-room. Poppy wrapped her arms round Scott, running her hands down his back and over his buttocks, thrilling to the feel of him. This was the moment she had been waiting for.

To her consternation, he hardly responded. He held her shoulders and backed off, his face sombre.

'We got to talk, Poppy.'

Hurt and rejected, she tried to ignore the signals. 'We can talk later. I've been waiting for this for three weeks.'

'No, I got to let you know what the position is first.'

The seriousness of his voice got through to her, cutting short a suggestive remark about positions.

'All right,' she said.

The maid served them an exquisite meal, which neither of them tasted. As one scarcely touched course succeeded the next, Scott talked and Poppy listened and the tale of the momentous week unfolded. Poppy's surface understanding of finance was left far behind as he described the details of the dealings and desperate measures taken on the Stock Exchange, but the gist of it was clear – Scott's affairs were on the brink of disaster.

'But can't you do anything? Pull out?' she asked.

'That's what everyone's trying to do. That's what caused the slide.'

She just could not believe it. She had seen people on the ship white and shaken and talking of ruin, but she had assumed that they had invested foolishly. They were not like Scott.

'I don't understand – how can it all just fall down like this? I mean – how can you be rich one day and poor the next. Either you've got money or you haven't, surely?'

Scott ran his hands wearily over his face.

'It's not as straightforward as that, honey. Remember that day I took you to the Exchange?'

'Yes.'

'Remember the hundred-dollar bill?'

'You said it was really just a piece of paper. It was only worth a hundred dollars because we all agreed it was.'

'Right. Well, this past week everyone's had doubts about what their shares were really worth. And once the doubts set in, the value tumbled like a card castle. It was only ever paper.'

Poppy floundered, trying to grasp at any sign of hope.

'But you said you could still make money from a – a bear market.'

'So I did, honey. Up till last week. But what's happening now isn't just a bear market, it's a crash.'

'What about the bankers?' Poppy asked. 'They calmed it down when they stepped in on Thursday.'

'Only for a while. It will be all hell let loose again when the exchange opens on Monday.'

'Won't they step in again?'

'They won't be able to, sweetheart. Rumour has it they went in with a hundred million dollars. Not even the big boys will be able to raise money like that twice in a fortnight. If things go on like they have, they'll be wiped out as well. And me with them.'

Poppy got up and walked round the table. She put her arms round him and pulled his head against her breast, kissing his hair.

'Just as long as we're together, darling, that's all that matters.'

Scott drew her down onto his knee.

'You're one in a million.'

'I'm not. I just love you, that's all.'

She kissed him and this time he responded with hunger.

'Come on,' Poppy whispered. 'Let's go to bed.'

They made love with a fierce desperation, Poppy doing everything she could to make him forget his troubles and lose himself in her. Thrusting and biting and rolling over, they finally erupted into a climax of animal energy and lay panting, clinging to each other, limbs entwined. Scott fell asleep, the sweat drying on his naked body, but Poppy lay awake and as the satisfaction of her senses gradually evaporated a nagging anxiety crept in. What if this crisis on the money market changed the way they felt for each other? She studied Scott's face in the soft light from the one lamp they had left on. He was relaxed in sleep, but still there were harsh lines running from his nose to the corners of his mouth, lines that she was sure had not been so marked last time they had been together. Gently she pulled the covers over them both. Nothing, she vowed, was going to tear them apart now. Not after she had waited so long.

Scott's prognostications turned out to be only too true – there was no stopping the landslide fall of the market. On Monday the index fell forty-nine points. By the end of Tuesday a record 16.4 million shares had been traded. Rumours of men jumping from windows proved to be true in several cases.

Scott came home and slumped into a chair.

'That's it, then,' he said, in a strangely dead voice. 'I'm cleaned out.'

Poppy put a drink into his hand and sat on the arm of the chair, stroking his head. For once, she did not know quite what to say. It was no use telling him that it was not the end of the world when to him it so obviously was. She almost pointed out that they were not destitute as she still had money, but instinct stopped her. Now was not the moment.

He roused himself to play with Amy and put her to bed, but Poppy could see that it was an effort. He did not even try to eat. She had to do something, had to make him see that things were not as black as he thought.

'Let's go out,' she said. 'Let's see a show, then go on to Harlem. Forget it for a while!'

'On what, might I ask? You need money for a night out.'

'I've got money,' Poppy said. The moment the words were out of her mouth, she knew she had said the wrong thing.

'No!' He jumped up, sending his chair crashing to the floor. He was shaking. 'I'm not taking your money. Jesus, who do you think I am? A leech like the last two you married? I'll not do it, do you hear? I'll not take a red cent of what's yours.'

'All right, all right.' Poppy tried to stay calm. 'I'm sorry. But look, you haven't lost everything. You've still got all this – ' she gestured at the expensive apartment with its

387

luxurious fittings and the white walls adorned with cubist paintings.

'Mortgaged. And as for the paintings, they soon won't be worth a pinch of salt. Don't you see?' Scott began to pace about the room. 'It won't stop at this. There will be a domino effect. Companies will go bust, people will be thrown out of work, real estate will go down. Who's going to buy a painting when they can't afford food?'

'It can't be that bad,' Poppy protested. 'You're exhausted. You've been under a terrible strain. It'll all look better in a day or so.'

'Better! It will look worse, if anything. It's a disaster. Not just for me, but for the whole country. The economy will collapse.'

Poppy still could not understand how all this could stem from people losing money that did not exist in the first place. The whole situation seemed totally crazy. She fell back on what she was sure of, what she knew to be true.

'We still got each other, Scott. After we're married, we can think what we're going to do. There must be something. Maybe you could get a job in England. There's lots of things you could turn your hand to, I'm sure, and I still got – ' she bit the rest off, but it was too late, for he could guess that she was going to say that she still had the band.

'No.'

He stopped at the far end of the room with his back to her. He appeared to be studying the painting that hung there, a wonderful burst of fragmented dancing figures in bright reds, yellows and oranges that contrasted painfully with the mood within the room. Poppy knew that she did not want to hear what he was about to say.

'I'm not going to let you do it, Poppy. Not a third time.'

'I don't know what you mean.'

But she did. She was just putting off the moment of admitting it.

'I'm not going to be a dependent. You've done it twice, supporting men who couldn't look after themselves, leaving

388

the children to go and work all hours with the band, trying to
pay off debts they've run up.'

'Joe never ran up debts, and he couldn't help being ill. He
was gassed,' Poppy said, just in order to argue about
something other than the main issue.

'But he still left you up to your neck in it. It's taken you a
long time to get where you are, Poppy. You deserve your
success. I'm not going to drag you down.'

'Drag me down? I've never heard such a bloody stupid
thing in my life!'

A burning anger came to her rescue. She was not going to
lose everything she had waited for, not now. She marched to
Scott's side and caught hold of his arm.

'Maybe you got problems at the moment, but we can sort
them out together. It's ridiculous, all this talk about you being
dependent. You'd soon find something.'

'Not what you deserve,' Scott stated.

'Deserve? Who gets what they deserve, for God's sake?
Look, I been poor, I'm not afraid of it. I was dirt poor as a kid
so I can cope with not being rich like you was last week. That's
nothing. What do you think I am, a spoilt bitch like your
Francine?'

'Of course not! But it's because you were poor as a kid that I
don't want to be living off you now. Can't you see that? I'm
saying this for your own good.'

'I know what's best for me, thanks very much!'

'No you don't. Not when it comes to picking husbands.
You're a born loser. Only this time I'm pulling out before you
get the chance to make another mistake.'

'No, no, you can't do this to me!' Poppy flung herself at him,
trying to break down his resolve. She tried tears, pleas, insults,
seduction, but he was unyielding. He loved her too much to let
her sacrifice herself on a bankrupt. The wedding was off.

42

1932

The pink marble ballroom of the Carleton Hotel was packed
with guests. The light from the chandeliers sparkled on the
jewels of the women, glinted from the polished hair of the men.
The air was heavy with perfume and still quivering with
carefully disguised excitement. The dancers were not really
concentrating. The Prince of Wales had just left and everyone
was either discussing him or pointedly talking about something else to show that they bumped into him every day of the
week.

Up on the stage, The Powers Girls were trotting through the
last number before the break. As always, they looked
stunning. Their peach silk gowns were made in the new
elegant fashion, long and slim, the bias-cut skirts flaring out
slightly from the knee to the ankle. Along with the soft,
romantic dresses, their style of playing had changed, becoming smoother and more sophisticated. The day of the flapper
had passed, and in her place was the mature woman.

Poppy looked along the line-up with pride. They were top-
rate, her band. From Phyl and Marjorie to the newest
eighteen-year-old, they knew their job perfectly. There were
some very promising players amongst the younger girls. Far
from having to search around for talent, she now had a
waiting list of girls wanting to join the band and could pick
and choose from amongst them. Thanks to Ted's astute
managing, they were paid just as much as an equivalent male
band. The Powers Girls did not come cheap. After all, she was
rumoured to be the Prince of Wales's favourite bandleader.

The number came to an end. Poppy bowed and spoke into
the big black microphone.

'Thank you, thank you very much, ladies and gentlemen. The Powers Girls are going to take a short break now, but we shall be back soon and at ten o'clock we shall be broadcasting live on the BBC, when we shall be playing our latest record release, "I Still Remember You".'

Poppy moved amongst the players as they chatted in the artistes' changing-rooms. Making the most of the limited time, the girls were smoking, drinking, making adjustments to dresses and makeup, but most of all, gossiping. The younger ones were in a state of high excitement over the royal visit, the old hands took it all in their stride. Poppy spoke to nearly everyone, asking after boyfriends, remarking on good playing, promising solo spots to those whom she thought were ready for it. She finally sat down by Marge and Phyl and kicked her shoes off, flexing her feet.

'You all right?' Phyllis asked. 'You look tired.'

'Yeah, yeah, I'm fine.'

Poppy took a long swig of the lemonade she had ordered. She never drank on duty these days, and especially not when there was a broadcast coming up. Any slip she made then would be heard not just by the people in the ballroom, but by the thousands listening in all over the country.

'Something's on your mind,' Phyl insisted.

'Spit it out,' Marjorie commanded.

Poppy hesitated to confide in them. Now that Mona had, like Elsie, married for a second time, Phyl and Marjorie were the only ones left of the original line-up. They had been with her through all her ups and downs, knew everything about her. The thing was, she knew just what their reaction would be if she were to tell them what was bothering her.

'Kids all right?'

'Oh, yes, they're fine. It's just –'

She couldn't really put her finger on it herself. It was just a feeling, a fear of her own weakness.

'Ted was round our place for tea this evening,' she said.

'You've not gone and said you'll marry him?' Phyllis gasped.

'Oh, no! Not that –'

'Pity. Best thing you could do,' Marjorie commented.

Poppy stared at her, stunned. It was the last thing she expected to hear from Marjorie.

'He's a decent bloke, Ted is, and he's been devoted to you from the start,' said Marge. 'Oh, I know what you're thinking. You think I'm dead against marriage, but I'm not. I was against your marrying Roddy because I could see him for what he was.'

Phyllis nodded in agreement.

Poppy was lost for words. She just sat there listening as Marge went on.

'But it's different with Ted. He's all right. He'd treat you well. You ought to get him while the going's good.'

'But – I don't love him. I'm still in love with Scott. I always have been.'

She touched the gold and diamond saxophone brooch that she still wore pinned to her dress every evening.

'A romantic dream, my dear. I've nothing against your Scott, but let's face it, he isn't here, is he? And Ted's always here. In the end, it's things like loyalty that count.'

She and Phyl looked at each other, and smiled.

It confirmed everything Poppy had been brooding over. Ted was always there, and one day, perhaps when she was low, or worried about something, or just feeling that time was catching up with her, she had a suspicion that she would give in and accept him.

'Everyone's on at me to say yes,' she said.

'Everyone's right. We know what's good for you far more than you do. You're a rotten judge of character. Didn't we all warn you against that Roddy?'

'Yes, you did,' Poppy admitted.

'And weren't we right?'

'Yes, you were.'

'There – I rest my case, m'lud.'

'I'll think about it,' Poppy promised.

At the end of the evening, The Powers Girls went their

separate ways. It had been a good night. The broadcast had gone well. The management, delighted at the frequency of royal visits, had complimented Poppy on the band's playing. On the surface, everything was fine. But Poppy could not see her way forward.

She unlocked the door of her new Austin and started on the journey home. The atmosphere in the hotel ballroom had been hot and sweaty, so she wound the windows down to let in the summer air. Moonlight silvered the streets of Mayfair. It was a perfect night.

The Season was in full swing, with balls and parties going on in the elegant streets and squares. She passed houses with light and music streaming from their windows, queues of expensive cars outside them waiting to pick up or put down revellers. Poppy regarded them with interest but no envy. She had more than enough in the way of material things – a nice new house, a car, holidays, plenty of clothes. Her children wanted for nothing. It was only when she caught sight of a pair of debs getting out of a car and running, laughing, across the red-carpeted pavement to a party that she felt a twinge of something between sadness and nostalgia. To be young like that again, to have all of life in front of her with no mistakes to regret, now that would be wonderful. And yet – she knew that if she were to go back, she would do it all over again.

As she drove, the question that had been plaguing her of late would not go away: *What was she going to do with the rest of her life?* Her Gran had asked just the same thing only a couple of days ago when she went down to Cinnamon Alley to visit her.

'You're not getting any younger,' she had pointed out with her usual lack of soft soap. 'How old are you now? Thirty?'

'Thirty-two,' Poppy had admitted.

'There you are then. You're no spring chicken no more. You ought to get yourself married again while you still got the chance. Take that Ted Appleby. He's steady.'

Steady was just about the highest recommendation that her gran could give of a man. When she spoke of her long-dead Arthur, it was to say that he was steady.

'But I don't want to marry again, Gran. I got all I need,' Poppy pointed out.

It was true, up to a point. She had fame, fortune and success. The band had achieved everything she dreamt of. Managements were falling over themselves to book The Powers Girls, they had their regular spot on the BBC, their records sold in thousands. And her family was healthy and happy. Kit and Belinda were doing well at school. Kit had won a scholarship to the local grammar school. Lindy was the star of her ballet class.

It was only as she came to consider her parents that the glow faded. There was no doubt about it, her father was what her grandmother had always accused him of being – a waster. Charming, yes, but quite content to live on his daughter's income and be looked after by his wife and never lift a finger to help either of them. She had finally come to terms with this now, accepting him for what he was, but it made her sad that her mother felt the need to apologize for him at regular intervals.

'What you going to do when you get to forty?' her gran said. 'You won't look so good up on them stages when your looks begin to go.'

Poppy worried about that at times herself. It was all right for men to be ageing bandleaders. They looked distinguished with grey hair and lines. But women were supposed to be young and beautiful.

'My Scott will come back before then,' she said.

Gran looked at her with scepticism. 'You heard from him, then?'

Poppy had to admit that she hadn't. She had not heard from him since the day she last saw him two and a half years ago. He had refused to write to her, saying that she must consider herself free. She had insisted that she would wait for him forever if need be. They had parted in tears, without reaching a compromise.

'Don't do to let your life slip away from you, girl,' her gran said.

'You always done what you thought best. You won't do the sensible thing and come and live with us now,' Poppy said.

'I'm old. I've lived here in this house most of my life and I ain't moving now. But you still got a lot of years ahead of you. You ought to think what you're going to do with them.'

'I do think, I think all the time,' Poppy said.

And here she was, still thinking now as she drove out of the old part of London and into the new suburbs. The trouble was, she didn't seem to be coming to any decision.

Poppy turned into a cul-de-sac and stopped the car in the gravelled driveway of a neat detached house with shingle-hung gables and stained glass fanlights. Home. She switched off the engine and sat looking at it. Her little castle, with her family safely asleep inside. So long as she still had them, she was all right. She let herself in at the front door.

'Poppy – ?'

She looked up, startled. Her mother was standing at the top of the stairs.

'Mum?'

Jane was looking terrible. Her face was haggard, her eyes red and puffy.

'Mum, what is it? What's happened?'

'Oh, Poppy love, I'm so glad you're back.'

She ran up the stairs to meet her. They clasped each other, and Jane burst into tears. A sharp fear tore through Poppy.

'What is it? Tell me, Mum. Is it the children?'

'No, no – ' Jane sniffed and took a shuddering breath. 'No it's not them. They're all right. Oh, Poppy, it's your gran. She – she's dead.'

43

'She's got to have a cracking good send-off,' Poppy said, for the hundredth time.

'The best,' her mum agreed. 'Everything she would of wanted.'

It was difficult to believe that her gran had really gone. All her life, through the various ups and downs, Gran had been there, unchanging, ruling over the house in Cinnamon Alley. Everything was still in its place there, down to the dishcloth carefully washed out and hung over the edge of the sink to dry. But the heart had gone out of the place. Already, after only two days, a thin film of dust had settled. Poppy rushed about with polish and duster, keeping it at bay. Her gran would hate to have people run a finger over her chairs at her own funeral and find dirt lurking.

'I don't care what Dad says, she's not having one of them motor hearses. She'd of wanted horses, I know she would. Horses with plumes, and mutes in black crepe. The lot.'

'That's right, lovey. She always did like things to be done proper.'

Both women looked about the kitchen of the lodging house, remembering the tyrant who insisted on decent behaviour at table from rough working men, and got it. Poppy avoided her mother's eyes. Neither of them wanted to be reminded of the less happy memories. It wasn't right to speak ill of the dead.

All the same, Poppy couldn't help thinking of all the battles she had fought with her gran. Every room in the house brought back a painful echo of a rebellious young girl and an unbending woman. She tried to push them out of her head. She shouldn't be thinking like this. She led the way back into the front parlour.

Margaret lay in a splendid mahogany coffin in the centre of

the room that had been her pride and joy. Poppy and Jane sat on the straight-backed chairs that had been placed on either side of the casket, staring at the shine on the highly polished wood. So many hours Poppy had spent shining things up to Gran's exacting standards.

'She always meant well,' she said.

'Oh, yeah,' Jane agreed. 'She done it all for us, you know. She wanted us to have a better life than what she done.' Her face crumpled and tears trickled down her cheeks. 'I was a terrible disappointment to her. She sacrificed everything for me, and I let her down.'

'Oh, Mum – ' Poppy went to put her arms round her. 'You couldn't help it. You just fell in love. Ain't nothing wicked in that.'

It was just that Gran had never understood. She had not understood Poppy either, and her unassailable love for Scott, holding out for all these years against someone as eminently steady and suitable as Ted Appleby.

'She was disappointed in me and all.'

'Oh, no, Poppy – ' Jane took a sobbing breath and shook her head vehemently. 'She was proud of you, you know. Proud of what you done. Every time you was on the wireless, she stayed up special to listen in.'

This was news to Poppy. Her gran had never breathed a word of it to her.

'She never said. Not once.'

'Oh, well, that was her way, weren't it? She wouldn't of wanted you to get a swollen head. She never believed in spoiling.'

This was such a massive understatement that Poppy could not restrain a wry smile.

'No, you're right there, Mum.'

The two women held on to each other, seeking comfort not only for grief but for guilt. Though a truce had long been called in the battle with Margaret, neither of them felt they had loved her enough.

The day of the funeral was close and sultry. Poppy lay

awake on the lumpy horsehair mattress in the room in which she had given birth to Belinda, and listened to the familiar sounds of the Isle of Dogs getting ready for work, so different from the quiet of the suburbs. It was as if the years had rolled back and she was a girl again. She wished that it was so, that her grandmother's sharp tongue and the boredom of the classroom were all she had to care about.

It was no use lying in bed and torturing herself. Her gran would never have approved of that. The answer was to get up and get going. If her gran was to have the send-off she had vowed for her, then she must get to work.

She was not alone. By the time she had taken her mother a cup of tea, there was a tap at the door and a woman from round the corner in Trinidad Street appeared. She stood in the hallway, a clean floral apron over her drab dress.

'You need a hand, deary?'

Poppy accepted the offer with thanks. Soon there was a small army of women in the house, scrubbing, polishing, cutting up bread and ham, setting out plates and cups and cutlery. Poppy was touched beyond measure. Her gran had never been close to her neighbours, but here they were, gathering round in time of sadness to give Jane and Poppy their strength. Jane sobbed her gratitude.

'I dunno how to thank you.'

One of the women patted her shoulder.

'Bear up, deary. Times like this you need your friends, don't you? You was always one of us. You altered that mourning dress for me when my Bert died at Ypres and you didn't never ask a penny for it. You don't forget things like that.'

By ten o'clock the lodging house was spotless enough even for Margaret's high standards. The food and drink that Poppy had ordered had been delivered and was set out on the big deal table in the kitchen. The women drifted off home to change into clothes taken especially out of pawn for the occasion. Poppy and Jane put on the outfits that Poppy had bought at Selfridges. Somehow, she had not been able to shop for her grandmother's funeral at Harrods. She would have felt the old lady's disapproval at such criminal expense.

Her father arrived with the children. Belinda was bewildered by the whole occasion, asking questions in a high clear voice and demanding answers when those around her felt unable to reply. Kit was withdrawn, hiding his emotion behind a morose glare. Poppy put her arms round his resistant body.

'Your great-gran's in a better place now, darling. Just try to remember that. Her arthritis and her bad chest won't be troubling her now, and she'll still be looking down on you.'

But nothing Poppy could say could make it any better for him.

Owen flitted around trying to encourage everyone to make a start on the drinks. 'Just to give us a bit of strength to see us through.' Poppy had a terrible suspicion that he was not in the least bit sad. On the contrary, he was triumphant. He had outlived the enemy. She almost found herself hating him.

Floral tributes were delivered from people in the street, wreaths and small bunches of flowers from those caught in the Depression who could ill afford shoes for their children. Poppy shed tears over each one.

Elsie came with Bob, her husband, and a large contingent of her family. Poppy hugged her, smiling for the first time that day at the feel of her swollen belly. Elsie's second child was due in the autumn.

'Thank God for babies,' Poppy said. 'Makes you realize what it's all about, don't it?'

After that there was a rush of arrivals – Marjorie and Phyllis, Mona and her husband and some of the Dobsons, Ted Appleby. The wreaths made a blaze of summer brightness in the small front parlour, filling the air with fragrance. The guests stood about talking amongst themselves in low voices. Poppy was suddenly aware that nearly everyone was in pairs, partners sticking together for support on this difficult occasion. Despite having all her family about her, she felt terribly alone.

The funeral procession drew up at the door. Margaret was carried out to a hearse that was as correct as she might have wished for, from the plumes on the horses' glossy heads to the gold lines on the black-painted wheels. What seemed like a small mountain of floral tributes were arranged around her coffin. Men in top hats and crepe walked in front. Poppy, Jane, Owen and the children climbed into the carriage behind, and a line of friends in cars followed after. As they crawled through the streets, people stood still to show their respect to the dead, and men bared their heads.

The Church of St Luke's was well filled with people from Trinidad Street, the smell of camphor from Sunday best clothes overpowering the scent of flowers. Margaret had not been a regular church-goer, but Poppy knew that she would have wanted to be buried within the Church of England. She never had approved of Nonconformists, or Poppy's affiliation to the Salvation Army. The service brought back painful memories of Joe's and Roddy's funerals. She tried to join in with the hymns, but her voice died in her throat. Instead she mouthed the words. Beside her, Belinda clung to her hand while Kit stood fiercely stiff, his voice wavering from adult to child as he sang.

At last it was over, and it was into the carriages again for the interment. Poppy was sweating. Her black dress clung to her. Her hat was cutting in to her forehead. Belinda complained of being thirsty, Kit snapped at her to shut up. As they stood at the graveside in the sooty cemetery, Poppy longed for a strong arm to lean on, a shoulder to cry on. It came to her that now she was the real head of the family. It was no use looking to her parents. They depended on her. Now Poppy was the only real grown-up in the family. The burden was entirely hers.

The woman who had come from Cambridgeshire as a bride with such high hopes was laid to rest in the crowded soil of East London. Her family placed flowers on her remains and walked away, their duty done. Now there was just the funeral tea to be got through.

'She would of approved of this,' Jane said, for at least the twentieth time that day.

They both surveyed the loaded table. It could not have been more different from the food at the Petite Fleur or the parties that she used to go to with Roddy.

'I don't know about all this beer, though,' Jane said.

Poppy knew very well. Margaret had not been a teetotaller, but she had definitely disapproved of drunkeness. But it was no use offering the men tea. There was tea for those who wanted it, but the whole funeral would be rated a very poor affair if there was nothing stronger to drink. So she had got in a barrel from the Rum Puncheon at the corner.

She indicated the population of Trinidad Street with a jerk of the head.

'Some of them have been out of work for three years, Mum. The rest have been on short time. It's my way of giving them a decent feed-up and as much as they like to drink. They was always so good to me when I was a kid. I been lucky, I got plenty now, so why not share it about a bit?'

Jane gave her a hug.

'You're a good girl, Poppy love. You always look after your own.'

Poppy nodded. It was true, but who was there to look after her? She was there for everyone else, handing out emotional and financial support, but there were times when she didn't want to be the strong one. It would be so wonderful to have someone by her side, someone to watch over her. But not just anyone. It could only be Scott.

The guests were flocking in, still sombre and well behaved at this point, respectful of the woman they had just laid to rest. Owen headed straight for the beer barrel and appointed himself barman. The men shuffled over to his side of the small kitchen. Jane handed out cups of tea to the women. Poppy cut pork pies into generous wedges and pressed platefuls of food in to the hands of the mothers, urging them to go out and give them to the children playing in the street outside.

Poppy's hand was wrung and her shoulders squeezed as

each person took care to come and make some remark about her grandmother.

'She was a good woman.'

'A real hard worker.'

'Never a speck of dirt in the house.'

'Loved them kids of yours, 'specially the boy.'

'Street'll be empty, like, now she's gone from Cinnamon Alley.'

Poppy thanked them, and smiled, and asked after their families, and had the pleasure of compliments in return.

'You got no side to you, girl. Still one of us, ain't you?'

But despite what they said, she couldn't come back here now. She had moved on.

The thundery heat was becoming unbearable. All the doors and windows were thrown open, but it did nothing to lower the temperature or stir the fug of close-packed sweating bodies. Gradually, people began to move out onto the street, taking their cups and plates and glasses with them. Poppy whisked away empty dishes and put out more food from the larder.

'You all right, Pops?'

It was Elsie, large in her black maternity smock.

'Yeah, yeah, I'm all right. I got to be, ain't I? What about you? You'll get swollen ankles if you're not careful.'

'I could do with a sit down,' Elsie admitted. 'Come out and sit on a step with me, like what we used to.'

She was about to refuse, but then she saw Ted bearing down on her, and knew with a terrible certainty that she must escape before she went and did something she might regret.

'All right,' she agreed. 'Good idea.'

She picked up a glass of beer and the two of them shoved their way out into the street and found an unoccupied step. Poppy held Elsie's elbow as she lowered herself and finally subsided with a grunt of relief. Then Elsie put an arm round her shoulders.

'You don't have to be brave, you know. Go on and have a good cry, if you want.'

Poppy shook her head. If she started, she would never be able to stop.

'Tell me about you. You and Bob, and the little 'un, and this new one.'

So she sat listening to Elsie, watching the guests talking and the children playing. Kit and Belinda, after a wary start, had joined in with the kids from the street. The boys were playing cricket, the girls were crouching in the gutter with five stones, practically all of them still clutching sandwiches or slices of cake.

She became aware that Elsie had asked her a question.

'What? Sorry, I wasn't listening.'

'I said, have you got your sax with you?'

'Well – yes, I have. It's in the car. Why?'

'Why d'you think? Get it out and play it.'

'What, now?' Poppy was scandalized. 'It's my gran's funeral, for God's sake.'

'So? Do it for her. Play something she'd of liked. Look –' she gripped Poppy's knee. 'I know you, it's all building up inside of you. You need to play it all out. Go and get your sax, it'll be good for you.'

Poppy gave her a kiss on the cheek and stood up. Elsie was right. What she really wanted was Scott, but since she couldn't have him, then playing the sax would help. She went to fetch it.

A knot of curious children formed the moment they saw her open the black case. The beautiful golden instrument drew sounds of admiration.

'You going to play it, missus?'

'Don't be daft. She can't play that.'

' 'Course she can. She plays on the wireless. My mum said.'

'Blimey.'

Poppy put the sax to her lips and ran up and down a couple of scales. That alone had a comforting effect. She was at her best making music.

The notes attracted the attention of the adults. Conversations lapsed as people looked in the direction the sounds came from, trying to see what was going on.

For the life of her, Poppy could not think of a tune to play for her grandmother. She could not think of any she had ever expressed a liking for, not even a hymn. So she played some that everyone could sing along with – 'When the Red, Red Robin', 'Margie', and one of her favourites, 'Bye-Bye, Blackbird'.

People linked arms and swayed. They sang or hummed along. Easy tears of sentiment glistened in several pairs of eyes. Poppy warmed to her role. This was better than the Carleton Hotel. These people really appreciated her playing for them. Though a different world, it almost reminded her of that first night at Mexico's. Like the inhabitants of the East End, the people of Harlem lived hard lives and knew how to enjoy themselves.

Mexico's . . . where she had gone with Scott, two people in love, looking forward to being together for the rest of their lives. Where she had got up and played for him, put all her heart into a tune that would always be his. The longing was almost unbearable. She closed her eyes, and she was back in that club once more, on the stage with the legendary Don Byas's sax in her hands and the spotlight hot on her face. She put the reed to her lips, and began to play 'Can't Stop Loving That Man of Mine'. She played it for Scott.

Nobody noticed the cab drawing up at the end of the street. They were all too entranced by the golden river of notes flowing from the saxophone. Neither did they notice the stranger in the lightweight suit who got out and walked towards the funeral party, his eyes on the woman who was making the music.

The last notes died away, drifting into the heavy summer air. The audience clapped. Poppy reluctantly came back to the present. It was not Mexico's, but Cinnamon Alley. The faces around her were white, their clothes drab. For a moment she was confused. Her eyes were drawn beyond the group around her to a tall figure in a wide-brimmed trilby hat standing at the edge of the crowd. She found herself looking into the eyes of the man she loved.

404

'*Scott?*'

Her lips moved but no sound came out. It was not true. She was seeing things.

He smiled. 'Sister, you sure can play that thing.'

It was him, his voice, that fascinating accent.

'Scott!'

Without taking her eyes from his face, she lifted off the sax and someone took it from her hands. The crowd became a blur, unreal. With a cry of joy, she started forward. Her body was light, her feet did not seem to touch the ground. The world contracted to just her and Scott, and the diminishing distance between them. She flung herself at him, and he caught her in his arms, strong and safe, and he was real and solid, his heart beating against hers.

'Poppy, my love. My precious girl.'

He held her as if he would never let her go, held her so tight that the breath was almost squeezed from her body. She clung to him in return, revelling in the feel of him, the scent of him, the quick rise and fall of his breathing.

He released her just a little and looked down into her face.

'I always meant to come back to Cinnamon Alley to fetch you. I thought about it all the time I was in Germany. Now at last I've done it.'

His expression darkened as he brought her left hand between them and examined it. Relief flooded through him at the sight of her bare fingers.

'You're still free?'

'You know there was never anyone but you. Not really.'

'The same for me, sweetheart. No one but you.'

Their lips met then in a consuming kiss that swept away the years of loneliness and longing.

When at last they drew apart a little, Poppy reached up to caress the lines of his face with her fingers. He had grown thinner in the intervening years, and there was a sprinkling of grey hairs at his temples, but to her he was more attractive than ever.

'I said I would wait for you,' she reminded him.

'I told you not to, but I hoped you would. It was that that pushed me on.'

'You've made it, then?'

He looked prosperous, but she knew how sensitive he was about these things. She was glad he had found her here, back in Cinnamon Alley, rather than in a place like the Carleton.

'I'm on my way. And it's due to you. I thought about you and the band, and how people want to be entertained, however poor they are. So I went into radios. I'm a partner in a manufacturers, we sell all over the States.'

'That's wonderful, darling!' Poppy didn't care about the money, but it mattered to him that he was not poor. If he could provide for her in the way he thought right, then he would not go away again. 'I'm so proud of you. I knew you would do it. I believed in you completely.'

Scott kissed her forehead, her eyes, her lips.

'You're a wonderful woman, Poppy Powers. I love you.'

'I love you, too. I always have. Right from that night at the Half Moon.'

They kissed again, revelling in the taste and feel of each other's lips and mouths, very aware of bodies tight with need and separated by only thin layers of clothing. Poppy took a shuddering breath.

'You're not going to go away again, are you? Promise me?'

'Just so long as you promise the same. For ever.'

'For ever,' Poppy agreed.

The Isle of Dogs at the turn of the century was a close-knit community. Here in Trinidad Street, the lives and loves of the four families tangle and interweave . . .

When Tom Johnson, a union leader at the docks is sacked and set upon, his daughter Ellen has to leave school and her dreams of an office job. But she can still dream of Harry Turner . . .

But Harry, a young lighterman struggling to keep his battered family together, is bewitched by silver-tongued beauty Siobhan O'Donoghue. And Siobhan, ambitious for greater things, will use any weapon to repay the people of Trinidad Street for her disappointment.

And Gerry Billingham, if he doesn't go a deal too far in pursuit of a retail empire, will be there to pick up the pieces . . .

Through good times and bad, from the coronation of Edward VII to the dock strike, some will find what they are looking for – and Ellen and Harry realise too late what they have lost.

A SILVER LINING
Catrin Collier

Alma Moore's lover, Ronnie Ronconi, has gone to Italy with his bride Maud. Alma is left alone to face whisperings and innuendo in an upright Welsh community fiercely critical of 'fallen women'.

Life isn't much easier for Bethan Powell who returns home without her husband, bringing the child who has shattered their marriage.

Two women, forced to confront society and their own emotions, and only one man, Charlie Rashenko, a Russian refugee haunted by his past, is prepared to help them.

A Silver Lining is a superb follow up to the bestselling *One Blue Moon*.

THE SINS OF EDEN
Iris Gower

EDEN LAMB is handsome, rich and selfish – and women could not resist him.

ROGGEN LAMB, his sister, lives with Eden in the big house. Headstrong and intelligent, she has socialist leanings and a mind of her own.

NIA POWELL is the daughter of a defrocked clergyman. She is talented and lucky in business, but not in the business of love . . .

KRISTINA PRESDEY has loved Eden for as long as she could remember – and is bullied into marrying someone else.

Three women whose lives tangle inextricably with Eden and, as the Second World War disrupts and darkens their hometown of Swansea, the consequence are shattering.

Author of *Morgan's Woman* and *Black Gold*, Iris Gower has written yet another rich and compelling story which is impossible to put down.

'Iris Gower is a novelist who is not afraid to look life, with its pleasure and pain, in the face'
MARIE JOSEPH

WOUNDS OF WAR
Margaret Thomson-Davis

The war changed Joe Thornton so violently that Jenny is now afraid of her husband . . . Widowed by it, vain, silly, Hazel is adrift in the world, the props alcohol and her strong-minded daughter, Rowan . . . And Amelia's private war with her mother-in-law is still going on . . .

Their children have their own battles to fight: the civil rights movement for Rowan; Ban the Bomb for Harry Donovan and the Thorntons. And for all of them, there is the family battlefield.

But with the help of charismatic Rebecca, the three women find their painful way through friendship and new loves to their own kind of peace.

DON'T MISS

Rag Woman, Rich Woman
'Stirring sagas of family life, generously spiced with sex, tragedy, humour . . . and excitement'
EVENING TIMES

Daughters and Mothers
'Marvellously rich novel of life in post-war Scotland'
WESTERN MAIL, CARDIFF

JESSIE GRAY
Emma Blair

She turned her back on Glasgow – but could she turn her back on love?

The first time she laid eyes on Tommy McBride was in July 1947, when they were still at school. Before she knew anything about heartbreak or pain.

Then, she was the sheltered, dreamy minister's daughter, determined to take a bite out of life. And he was the fighter from the wrong side of the tracks hell-bent on proving himself in the world. They had nothing in common, they had separate destinies.

But in 1947 the world was about to move into new decades of turbulence and change – and it was only the fighters and the dreamers who would make it theirs.

CRIME FICTION AVAILABLE IN ARROW

☐ Trinidad Street	Patricia Burns	£4.99
☐ Jessie Gray	Emma Blair	£3.99
☐ This Side of Heaven	Emma Blair	£4.99
☐ Hearts of Gold	Catrin Collier	£4.99
☐ One Blue Moon	Catrin Collier	£4.99
☐ A Silver Lining	Catrin Collier	£4.99
☐ The Sins of Eden	Iris Gower	£5.99
☐ A Better World Than This	Marie Joseph	£4.99
☐ The Clogger's Child	Marie Joseph	£3.99
☐ Footsteps in the Park	Marie Joseph	£3.99
☐ The Gemini Girls	Marie Joseph	£4.99
☐ Leaf in the Wind	Marie Joseph	£4.99
☐ The Listening Silence	Marie Joseph	£3.99
☐ Maggie Craig	Marie Joseph	£4.99
☐ Polly Pilgrim	Marie Joseph	£3.99
☐ Since He Went Away	Marie Joseph	£4.99
☐ The Travelling Man	Marie Joseph	£3.99
☐ When Love Was Like That and Other Stories	Marie Joseph	£3.99
☐ Dickie	Sheelagh Kelly	£5.99
☐ Erin's Child	Sheelagh Kelly	£5.99
☐ For My Brother's Sins	Sheelagh Kelly	£4.99
☐ Jorvik	Sheelagh Kelly	£5.99
☐ A Long Way From Heaven	Sheelagh Kelly	£5.99
☐ My Father, My Son	Sheelagh Kelly	£4.99
☐ Two Silver Crosses	Beryl Kingston	£4.99
☐ Maggie's Boy	Beryl Kingston	£4.99
☐ Neither Angels or Demons	Pamela Pope	£4.99
☐ A Collar of Jewels	Pamela Pope	£4.99
☐ A Sense of Belonging	Margaret Thomson-Davis	£4.99
☐ Daughters and Mothers	Margaret Thomson-Davis	£4.99
☐ Rag Woman, Rich Woman	Margaret Thomson-Davis	£4.99
☐ A Woman of Property	Margaret Thomson-Davis	£4.99
☐ Wounds of War	Margaret Thomson-Davis	£4.99
☐ Hold Me Forever	Margaret Thomson-Davis	£4.99
☐ Remember Me	Sheila Walsh	£4.99
☐ Until Tomorrow	Sheila Walsh	£4.99

ARROW BOOKS, BOOKSERVICE BY POST, PO BOX 29, DOUGLAS, ISLE OF MAN, BRITISH ISLES

NAME ....

ADDRESS ....

....

....

Please enclose a cheque or postal order made out to Arrow Books Ltd, for the amount due and allow for the following for postage and packing.

U.K. CUSTOMERS: Please allow 75p per book to a maximum of £7.50

B.F.P.O. & EIRE: Please allow 75p per book to a maximum of £7.50

OVERSEAS CUSTOMERS: please allow £1.00 per book.

Whilst every effort is made to keep prices low it is sometimes necessary to increase cover prices at short notice. Arrow Books reserve the right to show new retail prices on covers which may differ from those previously advertised in the text or elsewhere.